ATLANTIS *Splitting*

I0561362

Highest Light Series #2

ATLANTIS
Splitting

Jean Brannon

Absolute Love Publishing
Atlantis Splitting

Published by Absolute Love Publishing
USA

Illustration by Katerina Dotneboya

ISBN-13: 979-8-9855746-3-0
United States of America

By Jean Brannon

Atlantis Writhing
Atlantis Splitting

Dedication

For my dad, Jennings Brannon, who helped me believe I could change the world. And for Matthew Scott Heldwein, who is helping me do just that.

Praise for The Highest Light Series

"*Atlantis Splitting* is a balm for the soul. It embodies the imaginative heart of the author, yet is a grounding and centering guidebook on moving through a dark night of the soul and rediscovering our divinity and the power of the heart. Like the characters in the novel, this book reminds us to keep moving – our story is still being written."
- **Meg Ming, The Intuitive Guide for Healers**

"A captivating journey rich with visual splendor and anticipation woven into every page. *Atlantis Writhing* induces seeded memories to awaken the potential not only to heal on very deep levels, but to incite a return to natural harmony and inherent wholeness. As you're swept away in an incredible romance, you'll cultivate understanding and love for the sacred relationship with yourself and discover how true love versus mission may not be so different. Book 1 in Jean Brannon's Highest Light Trilogy will leave you yearning for more."
- **Tania Marie, Author, Artist, and Reiki Master Teacher**

"Journey with cosmic energy beings as they face the challenges of fighting for what they believe. Witness a romantic love affair filled with pure selflessness. Beautifully done."
- **Ashley Ebba, Tantric priestess, yoga teacher, and model**

ONE

He moved like death, as one with the dark. Under a cherry moon, Alaric's unformed form slipped through scarlet shadows toward the palace that for a thousand years had been his prison.

When he at last hovered above the familiar rubble and ashlar walls, he faltered. Triggered by traumatic memories, he had to will himself to stillness, to the undetectable, untraceable state of non-duality. Thus cloaked in No-Mind, he seeped through the castle's foundation and into the dungeon beneath three towering stories. As he wafted along the castle's dank underbelly, he sensed Elysia's soul. Even here, in its surgically induced weakness, her essence proved a potent elixir. He dropped beneath his breath to escape the seductive images just a fraction of her had evoked. Once he'd anchored again in No-Mind, he floated along one of the lower level's narrow sandstone passageways. Then he breached an oak door bound with chains and a heavy padlock.

Beyond the barred entrance sprawled a cavernous chamber. Sycamore beams buttressed its curved ceiling. From caged sconces, candlelight licked the gloom. Rows of tables bearing crystals as well as dusty leather-bound books secured the room's perimeter. In the center loomed a dark crystal ball balanced upon a three-legged pedestal. Each of the stand's iron legs had been forged in the image of a three-headed dog. Surrounding the sphere sat three iron chairs fashioned like thrones.

On the far side of the dungeon, an enclosure originally built to punish wayward servants caught Alaric's eye. Behind rusting bars stood an ash bench. Upon its weathered top rested six test tubes. Five of the tubes glowed with an iridescent beauty, each one a unique hue. The sixth one sat empty, he realized, because it had held Quenna's essence. Until her transition, that is, when her soul once again claimed its wholeness.

Yet a cage wasn't the only thing imprisoning the essences. Black mats surrounded the cell. Curled upon each cushioned pad lay a giant three-headed dog, a violent hybrid known as a Cerberus. Slowly, ever so carefully, Alaric approached the creatures, allowing his energy to merge and settle so it created no vibrational shift that would alert these guards. Like smoke from a candle, he drifted closer. Only one of the dogs was awake, as it appeared perhaps the beasts took turns keeping watch. And two of the heads of this Cerberus looked to be asleep, so he felt Highest Light had provided a perfect opportunity.

With a surgeon's precision, Alaric began to funnel into his energetic field the essences held within the tubes – while simultaneously channeling back in an identical-looking substance spun from Source. He flowed the funneling and channeling evenly, so as not to induce an electromagnetic disturbance and reveal his presence.

One by one he gathered each soul fragment, siphoning and pouring in the crypt-like quiet, until only one tube remained. Then he heard footsteps outside the door, as he felt an all-too-familiar energy approach. One he'd know anywhere. One that repulsed him, and yet despite his best efforts to avoid her, here she was. There was the click of a key turning, the rattling of chains, and then Linasia thrust open the door just as he began collecting the last Ahlaielian essence.

In every possible way, Linasia was a vain and voluptuous woman. Tall and buxom, with full lips and rounded hips, she sauntered into the chamber in a negligee matching the blue of her eyes. Grasping a mirrored case lying among the crystals, she fussed with her white-blonde bangs and ponytail teasing the small of her back. Alaric knew it mattered not it was the middle of the night, and she thought she was alone. Never had he seen her without her carefully tended mask. Even here in the dungeon, once she finished with her hair, she pulled a lipstick tube from the case. Gazing into the mirror, she retraced red lips until they shone. She kept puckering and pouting as she perfected her handiwork. Alaric watched without emotion as he continued to draw and replace the final essence.

Throwing the makeup back into the pouch, she flung the satchel aside and plopped upon a chair. Placing her hands on either side of the crystal, she tapped it with tapered nails. As the sphere filled with smoke, Linasia sat back, shutting her eyes.

"I've heard your request for an audience, Lorelei," she called out in her raspy voice. Alaric breathed himself even deeper into his energy field at the mention of Lorelei. It had been a few thousand years since he last saw or even thought of her. But the sphere clearly was emitting her essence. He recalled her wrath, all those millennia ago, when he'd first met Elysia – and Lorelei's deadly jealousy. "Tell me. What's so urgent you need to wake me? What news have you of Poseidia?"

"The hour grows late." A softly feminine voice emanated from the misty crystal. "And Gadeirus grows madder – in every sense of the word – by the minute."

"Yes," Linasia whispered, a frown creasing her pale forehead. "I'm fed up with his drunken derangement. But we still need him until we have enough political clout to replace him, which I'm working on."

"I understand," Lorelei replied. "And, yet this whole affair with Elysia has deteriorated matters considerably in the last two days."

"That eternal bitch," Linasia muttered. "If Gadeirus could just have his way with her a few times and get it out of his system, we'd all be better off." Alaric forced himself to sink back beneath his breath, knowing he could not give way to rage or else he risked exposure – no matter what was said.

"I'm afraid, in his state of mind, a liaison may only feed his obsession," Lorelei observed. "What I'd like to suggest is another plan. An immediate course of action."

"I'm listening."

"If we kill her, she'll no longer be a factor we have to consider."

"What did you have in mind?" Linasia settled deeper into her seat.

"A boating incident," Lorelei replied, as Alaric prayed for the strength and wisdom to take appropriate action. "As we speak, she's piloting Alaric's craft back to the dock. He was spotted disappearing from the boat's bow earlier, so we're as of yet unaware of his whereabouts. But it presents the perfect opportunity at least to make her vanish. I have sea nymphs and a couple of Poseidia's best warlocks on standby. They can conjure weather and magic potent enough to make it look like she drowned. Say the word, and she will be dead within minutes."

In that moment, Alaric knew he could no longer remain invisible. He wouldn't be able to reach Elysia in time to save her from this latest evil. And so, as he'd always done before when it came to her, he did what he had to do. Wrapping the essences in a protective web, he projected them out of the castle – while simultaneously materializing in front of the Great Central Sun's gatekeeper.

"Linasia?" Lorelei's voice sounded suspicious. "Did you hear what I said?"

"Yes." Linasia's eyes widened at the sight of him as the dogs awoke, ready to attack. She raised a hand, and their teeth-bared snarling softened to growls. They circled him, hackles raised, their snake-like tails swishing malevolently. "The dogs are startled is all, but I heard every word." She leered at him. Reaching behind her, she removed a beaded hair clasp. As her tresses tumbled down, her eyes implored his. "I'm considering it," she murmured, and Alaric unbuttoned his shirt. As it fell from his fingertips, Linasia smiled. "I believe we should hold off. At least for the time being."

"*Why*?!" Lorelei's exasperation revealed she'd never anticipated dissent. "This is such an incredible opportunity! A *gift*!"

"A gift laced with arsenic, my friend." Linasia swaggered toward

Alaric, tossing the clasp beside the sphere. As she raked her claws across his chest, he closed his eyes, descending into himself. From that deep silence, he asked his heart once again to ice over. And Elysia to forgive what he was about to do.

"But –"

"No one wants to be rid of Elysia more than I do," Linasia hissed in a tone made all the more convincing because it revealed her true feelings. "Trust me. But she's crucial to you being able to get your hands on Alaric. If you lose her, you've already lost him. And you just told me you have no idea where he is, didn't you?"

"Yes, but –"

"All right then. Don't start getting all impulsive on me. I've got enough of that with Gadeirus." Ambling over to a nearby table, she picked up a large gold band. Sauntering behind Alaric, she feathered her fingers down one of his arms. His eyes remained closed, as energetically he continued to withdraw.

"So, you want me to leave her alone then?"

"For now," Linasia purred. Opening the band, she snapped it shut over Alaric's wrist. His eyes flashed open, their cold fury barely contained as he assessed the gold and crystal cuff, with its copper inlays, silver wires, and green flashing light.

"I suppose I have nothing further to report at this time," Lorelei sniffed.

"Message me when you do," Linasia ordered, and the crystal blackened. She made a dispersing gesture, and the dogs retreated to their beds, though their flaming eyes continued to study Alaric with interest. Turning to face him, she began laughing. "Well, well. What have we here? A shape-shifter caught off guard?"

"Hello, Linasia."

"Oh, come now." She grinned triumphantly. "Don't look so glum. You're really lucky I don't like being observed during my transmissions. That's why I use smoky quartz. If that had been a traditional crystal ball, she would have seen you."

"Clearly, I'm fortune's child," he whispered.

"That body belongs to no child, lover."

"And what of this trinket?" He turned his head toward the wristband as she kissed his chiseled cheek, her painted lips smearing his skin.

"What of it?" She guided his mouth to hers. "It's a gift. From Gadeirus' best witch. I just received it, so your timing couldn't be better. Makes quite the charm bracelet, don't you think?" She giggled against his lips. "Just a little enchantment is all. Some magic to ensure you won't be leaving any time soon."

"What do you mean by that?" He took her by the wrists and held her away from him.

"Just what I said." She smiled seductively. "It short-circuits your ability to teleport and mind-message. Among other things."

"What other things?" He gazed behind her eyes, his voice smooth as silk, and again she laughed.

"You know – things shape-shifters do," she cooed, and Alaric found he had to breathe himself deeper so he didn't lose himself in wrath. "Telepathy. Teleportation. Mind-messaging. The usual suspects."

"I see."

"Do you?" She cocked her head, an amused look on her face. "Do you see that once again your fate is in my hands?"

"I see that you are eager as always to strike a deal." He kept staring at her. "What do you want from me now?"

"The same thing I've always wanted, lover." She pulled free of his grasp and caressed his rippled abdomen. "I want your lips on mine, on my body. I want you pleasuring me like I am *her*."

"I can only give what I have," he replied, as she pushed him into one of the chairs.

"You know, Gadeirus had one of his best seers tracking you." Hiking up her negligee, she climbed onto his lap. "How the king described you with Elysia made me desire you more than ever."

"Linasia –"

"So, you asked me about a deal?"

"Yes."

"And what is it you want?" Smiling up at him, she stroked his sable and gold locks.

"Is it not obvious?" He peered steadily into her eyes, beyond them.

"When it comes to her, you are pathetically obvious," she countered. "But you're in a very weak position to be bargaining."

"Humor me."

"All right." She traced her index finger along his jaw. "I know you came here for the essences."

"Yes."

"Even if I gave them to you, what good would it do?" She shrugged. "I told you that cuff binds you here with me. So, you can't leave with them."

"But *you* can," he urged, his eyes glowing mostly gold in the dungeon's dim light. Ever so gently, he combed his fingers through her hair. "Take them to the Great Central Sun gateway and give them to one of your messengers." His voice was smooth and soft as he began to kiss her neck. "Someone like Jack. You know you can trust him to deliver the essences in secret to Jonastus, who will know what to do with them."

"You make a convincing argument," she sighed, as his lips nuzzled her ear. "I could perhaps be persuaded to go in the morning. After I've been pleasured to my satisfaction."

"There's no time for that now," he whispered. "The Ahlaielians are rapidly deteriorating. Quenna has already made her transition. So, there is an urgency here." Slowly, deeply he kissed her, and she moaned against his mouth. "You understand urgency, do you not?"

"Yes," she gasped, as he parted her lips with his.

"And so, will you do this for me?" He held her away from him, just far enough so he could stare into her eyes. "Do we have our deal?"

"Yes," she replied dreamily. Again, his mouth found hers. "Oh, yes."

"Then you will leave shortly?"

"*Yes!*" She cried out when his lips once more brushed her neck. "On the condition you will pleasure me fully as soon as I return."

"I've always kept my end of the bargain, have I not?"

"You have at that. And then some." She looked him up and down before lifting herself from his lap. Then she strolled toward the door, hips swaying beneath her filmy gown. As she placed her hand on the iron handle, she turned toward him. For a long moment, she pondered his expressionless face. "You're welcome to come with me and watch as I change into something less comfortable."

"You don't need the distraction." He smiled, and she giggled as she tugged the door open. It creaked when she slipped through before slamming shut, sending tremors across the dungeon. And then Alaric was alone with the dogs, in a tomb's deep silence. They watched him curiously, tilting their multiple heads as he collapsed, trembling, into one of the chairs. For a moment, he rested his head in his hands. His breath came in hitches. He told himself to breathe, just breathe, as his eyes misted over. Then, in one sudden movement, he was on his feet, sweeping his shirt from the floor. Shaking his head, he buttoned and tucked the shirt. By the time he'd rolled its sleeves to his elbows, his breathing had stilled, and his eyes held no emotion. Turning to the dogs, he glowered at the pack leader, which was the largest one seated front and center. The Cerberus growled, but as Alaric continued to gaze at his three sets of eyes, growling gave way to whimpering, and then the dog quieted. He looked attentively at Alaric.

"*Agatah,*" he murmured, in the Old Tongue, and the dog came to him. "*Namna,*" he whispered. Obediently, the dog lay at his feet. "*Ativa sadhu,*" he added, which meant "very good," and the dog relaxed. He reached down and petted the Cerberus' three heads, each of which slithered with writhing serpents. In all his long years, Alaric had never been more grateful for his snake lineage.

As he waited for Linasia, he studied the gold cuff, feeling into its oppressive energy. He breathed himself into a state of alert readiness, preparing for this one remaining window of opportunity, a final hopeful glimmer. Nothing so far had gone according to plan, and it appeared he wouldn't be able to contact Elysia as he'd promised, either. But he couldn't think of her now, as this last chance at redemption demanded his complete attention. He simply had to get it right this time, as the only path left to their happily ever after opened before him. And no matter how steep or narrow or rocky or long the journey, he had no choice but to pick himself up and keep moving forward. Yet first he would have to clear the way. With all his focus and intention, he coiled himself. And prepared to strike.

TWO

Beneath the sky's cherry moon, just above Zacktronymus' pock-marked complexion, hovered a sphere. Its pearly glow pulsed, its heartbeat slow and steady, as two sets of boots approached. Two pairs of eyes studied the orb, as two frowns formed.

"I was hoping against hope," Tyrius muttered at last, kicking the sand. "But they're right where he said they would be if he got into trouble."

"Yes." Jon's beryl blue gaze softened. "He had to reveal himself because they were ready to kill Mother."

"*What*?!" Tyrius clasped his receding hairline. "Are they okay?"

"For now," Jon murmured. "Something is blocking most of Father's energy, though. Something ... unnatural."

"I know what we promised him." Tyrius' black gaze bored through Jon. "But –"

"We must abide, Tyrius." Jon's serenity held steely conviction. "We must see our plan through."

"But we can't just *leave* him!" Tyrius paced impatience into the sand beside the throbbing orb.

"We're not abandoning him," Jon replied, his voice as soothing as his adopted father's. Gently, he touched Tyrius' shoulders, halting him in the dust. "As we speak, Alaric is working to resolve his ... situation. If he ultimately needs our help, we will of course provide it. But we all agreed the first priority was securing these essences."

"Yes," Tyrius sighed. "Yes, of course. Forgive me. My passions and impulses run deep."

"I understand." Jon's cherub-like smile lit his face as his hands floated to his sides. "And there is nothing to forgive. You're only looking to help in any way possible."

"Indeed, I am." Tyrius scanned their surroundings. Scattered shrubs and brownish grassy clumps dotted the high desert plain. The barest breeze uprooted a tumbleweed, blowing its shriveled remains across the flatlands, which stretched to the horizon. "Tell me, Jon. Is it safe for you to be psychically tuned in the way you are?"

"It is." A strengthening wind blew dark curls from Jon's forehead, and in the rosy moonlight, Tyrius thought his friend resembled an angel more than ever. "I'm firmly anchored in Highest Light and observing through my mind's eye's carefully coded lens. I am undetectable, and through that No-Mind vibration, so are you."

"What do your visionary eyes see? Does our purpose remain secret?"

"Yes. For the moment. Linasia has not sounded an alarm. Not yet, anyway."

"So we must be swift." Tyrius eyed the pulsating sphere. "Although I don't feel right leaving him here."

"Neither do I."

"Jon, are you sure –"

"Yes."

"But –"

"Tyrius, it's Mother who concerns me."

"Elysia? I thought Alaric's action spared her?"

"He thwarted the Dark Heart's assassination attempt," Jon replied. "But Gadeirus' seers have been watching. And his scientists waiting, in this most uneasy calm before the storm. Tonight's palace dinner should prove to be the deluge, when the heavens part and Lesser Light forces rain down their full fury. Upon Mother and all of her friends as well."

"We must warn them! We have to –"

"But we cannot." Jon's certainty kept stifling Tyrius' resistance. "Any contact will be intercepted. Even a coded message. Hundreds of psychic eyes and ears are turned upon them."

"Lords with swords!" Tyrius scratched day-old stubble. "Are we just expected to leave them then, wet and shivering, as lightning strikes and thunder rages?"

"The essences must come first."

"But how can we –"

"Because we must." Sliding a burlap bag from his pack, Jon knelt by the luminescent orb. Carefully, he cupped the energy sphere and secured it in the bag. "I can monitor both my parents without being detected. And I intend on doing so. If either situation begins to deteriorate, we will adjust our plans. But right now, we need to get to Alpha Centauri. The sooner, the better."

"Yes." Tyrius peered at Jon, pure determination hardening his jaw. "Time to fly."

And so, they hastened across the hundred yards separating them and a waiting craft – Tyrius' own *Black Sprite*. The tiny ship's hull looked dull and dark like cast iron. No lights illuminated her slim shape. As they approached, a doorway parted and they boarded the entrance ramp. The opening sealed seamlessly behind them as they settled into cockpit seats. Jon nestled his pack inside a covered stowage area, while Tyrius flipped switches and pounded the virtual keyboard to the left of the craft's controls. Engines whirred to life, and then all was again still as the *Black Sprite* began her vertical ascent.

"Just like when we landed, we'll be flying blind for a bit," Tyrius whispered. Gently, he pulled back on the steering apparatus. "No lights, no radar, no communications. That should keep us invisible."

"It *should*," Jon answered. "Except we've already been detected."

"*What*?!"

"Atlantean *Amur* ships, port and starboard." Jon said without emotion. "How fast can this vessel reach hyperdrive?"

"Mere seconds!" Tyrius roared, his thick fingers jamming keys. "Except she's not engaging!"

"Are the shields activated?"

"*No!*" Tyrius slammed more switches, letting out a low whistle. "We've got lift-off, and that's about all!"

"Show me which panels house the circuitry for the hyperdrive and the shields."

"Right behind you! On the floor." Tyrius pummeled the keyboard and Jon knelt over the mechanical panels as the ship shuddered. "I'll try to buy some time. Hang on!" With that, Tyrius threw the *Black Sprite* into reverse, gunning it straight back toward the Atlantean squadron. The oval craft's small size, ebony color, and absence of lighting made it both agile and challenging to see against the black backdrop of space – a difficulty the *Amur's* muscular ships, their gleaming silver hulls shaped like boomerangs, had never before encountered.

"What in the bloody Dark Heart –" muttered the *Amur 9* pilot to his lieutenant.

"Engage the lasers!"

"Are you *nuts*?! Not at this close range," the pilot shot back, slapping the squadron communication button. "Commander, this is *Amur 9*. We're under attack by an unidentified, undersized craft. No visible markings or lights. Awaiting advisement."

"*Amur* fleet, this is your Commander. I've been apprised. I'm ordering each of you to maneuver out of close range of your squadron, then pursue and destroy."

"Yes, Commander." The pilot banked left, creating a wide berth between his ship and the others. He glanced at his grimacing co-pilot. In mere seconds, both men had gone from arrogant assurance that they'd destroy the diminutive vessel to concern they'd get out of this battle alive.

Evenly spaced along each *Amur* ship's curved leading edge glowed multiple crystalline-powered lasers, which had been designed for practically any type of warfare – except extremely close range. Having served as a fighter pilot in his youth, before rising through the ranks to command the Great Central Sun's elite *Infinite* starships, Tyrius was well aware of this one weakness in the mighty Atlantean fleet's armor. Now his one thought as he floored the *Black Sprite* directly toward the closest *Amur* vessel was how their situation seemed perfectly captured by the euphemism "trying to kill a gnat with a sledgehammer." A maniacal laugh escaped his lips, as he reminded himself that's not easy to do.

Like a crazed hopping gnat, the *Black Sprite* darted and dove among the sleek warrior vessels. Tyrius maneuvered so quickly, so brazenly – heading straight for one laser after another – that his actions took the Atlanteans by surprise. His moves stayed swift, unpredictable. And he knew the *Amur* pilots risked destroying one of their own ships if they fired at such close range. Out of the corner of his eye, Tyrius saw the cabin filling with sky-blue light. But he couldn't focus on that at the moment. Up, back, and sideways he lurched, spinning and rotating as he wove in and around the twelve ships trying to adjust to his aeronautical acrobatics.

"Try the hyperdrive now." Jon's voice sounded so casual. "And then engage the shields."

"All right." Tyrius bit his lip as he once again slammed the ship into reverse. He hit another button, and suddenly they were moving at lightspeed – still in reverse. "It works! Jon, how did you –"

"Try the shields now," Jon interrupted, his words quiet but insistent. Tyrius slapped more switches and bellowed a battle cry.

"They're working!" Tyrius' fingers flew over the keyboard. "We sustained structural damage to the port side, but I think we can live with that. Until we reach Alpha Centauri, anyway."

"We're not out of the woods yet. Three of them are tailing us."

"How do you know –"

"Two are starboard, one coming up on port," Jon replied evenly. "Are your lasers engaged?"

"Yes, but –"

"Tell me what controls the lasers."

"Joystick just to your right, in the raised panel, is what you aim with." Tyrius dipped the ship sharply left. "The red buttons are what you fire with."

"Got it." Closing his eyes, Jon settled into his seat just as another hit rocked the craft. While Tyrius dropped and swerved, Jon's steady hands rested on the joystick and buttons. Tyrius glanced over as Jon twirled the stick and pressed a button – and one of the *Amur* ships exploded. Incredulous, Tyrius gaped at Jon, who'd just taken out one of Poseidia's premier war vessels. With his eyes closed.

"Are you kidding me right now?!" Tyrius breathed, as Jon rotated the stick. Again, he pushed one of the red buttons, and the second ship flamed apart. Before Tyrius could do more than blink, Jon once again spun the stick. The third time he pressed a button, the last ship burst into a fireball. For a moment, neither spoke. Tyrius gawked at Jon, whose eyes stayed shut, his face as serene as if he'd been meditating in a meadow instead of destroying sophisticated war machines.

"We're alone," Jon said at last. "For now."

"Holy Highest Light, Jonastus!" Tyrius roared, a loud, belly-quaking cackle that heaved his barrel chest. "How did *that* just happen?!"

"Just what you said." The slightest smile curved his thin lips. "Holy Highest Light."

"You're serious."

"Quite."

"But how –"

"Faith is never about the 'how,'" Jon answered. "It's about the 'how deeply do you believe.'"

"Then you, my friend, must believe all the way to your core."

"I do."

"Do you think the *Amur* got wind of our mission?"

"No," Jon sighed. "Nor do they know Father has reached Zacktronymus. They are simply stationed there to watch for him. Or anyone looking to assist him. Because they've known he *will* come for the essences." He shook his head. "Although we've definitely raised some suspicions. And more than a few eyebrows, I'd say."

"I suppose it didn't turn out to be the get-in-and-get-out-unseen scenario we'd envisioned," Tyrius remarked.

"Not exactly."

"Well then. Now that we have the essences, is it safe to chart a course for Alpha Centauri?"

"Safe or not, it's what we must do," Jon replied. "Of course, they will be broadcasting images of our ship far and wide across the galaxies. Portraying us as rogues of some sort. Perhaps traitors or criminals."

"Yes," Tyrius growled. "And, yet I don't know what exactly we can do about that."

"Simply another matter for Highest Light to resolve."

"I'm not following –"

"Can you get any of the ship's cameras to send you an image of the exterior?"

"Sure, but –"

"Please do so, Tyrius," Jon urged. "I want you to see something."

"Okay." As Tyrius punched codes into the control panel, multiple images filled the screen. And his eyes bulged at what he saw. Every picture clearly showed a large, silver-colored, bullet-shaped ship that looked absolutely nothing like their small, dull craft. He turned saucer eyes on Jon. "So what have we *here*? More of Highest Light's handiwork?"

"Indeed."

"Jon, you astound me!"

"I'm merely an instrument and a messenger." He smiled his cherub-like grin.

"Perhaps." Tyrius' eyes twinkled. "But I'd be honored to have you ride shotgun with me any day of the week."

"Thank you, Tyrius."

"You know, all my life I've heard it's wise to watch out for the quiet ones," Tyrius mused. "Your still and silent nature is a perfect camouflage for your ... unshakeable belief. And as solid and dependable as I know you to be, I simply never thought ..." His voice trailed off, and then he shook his head.

"The ancient teachings all say thinking is what brings you to the mountain," Jon said in his soft tone. "And faith is what brings you to the top."

"Indeed, my friend!" Again, Tyrius chuckled. "Well, we certainly climbed that summit, thanks to you and your Highest Light commitment." He clapped Jon on the shoulder good-naturedly. "Of course, it didn't hurt having you morph into an engineering wizard with a side of assassin, either."

"Divine will always finds a way, Tyrius. Always."

"Well, Divine will certainly brought me an engineering-wizard-assassin when I most needed one," Tyrius chortled. "Perhaps our dire straits are behind us, though. Let's see if the rest of the trip to Alpha Centauri can be a little less ... eventful." Together they laughed, as the *Black Sprite* hummed along toward their destination. The one place holding a sliver of hope that the essences could be restored, the Ahlaielians resurrected. And Atlantis redeemed.

THREE

In the depths, Elysia stirred. The hawk's shrieking pierced her stupor as crows cawed through her awareness. And on the heels of that cacophony came her horse friends' whinnied warnings.

Willing herself to breathe, she thanked her animal guides for their concerned cries – and Source for sparing her life. Opening eyes that felt long sealed in wax, she found herself staring at the palatial bedroom's gold ceiling. One of her last remembrances was Gadeirus dragging her into this bed. But that was before giving herself over to thoughts of Alaric, of his flesh fusing with hers. And before she blacked out. Yet she couldn't think of Alaric now. Not until she'd freed herself from this predicament.

She rolled to the side. Everything swirled and spun, so she shut her eyes and breathed into stillness. When she again surveyed the room, she moved her head gingerly, being careful not to agitate wafer-altered senses. The chamber's many sconces flickered still, lit just as they'd been since the king's guards carried her here. In the luminescence, she could see Gadeirus beside her. He lay face down, matted hair obscuring his raven's eyes. He breathed heavily, mouth open. Relief flooded her that he remained dressed, in a white silk shirt and the black and gold pants he'd worn to the dinner. Craning her neck, she saw she still wore her ballgown as grateful tears splashed from her lashes.

Slowly, ever so carefully, she pulled herself upright. She felt rusty, achy. A piercing headache pulsed as if it were trying to split her skull. Yet sitting was such a victory; it emboldened her to ease to the bed's edge. As she dangled jelly legs toward the floor, she spied the cuff enslaving her wrist, its green light continuing to flash. Elysia willed herself to think of the band as an instrument of Highest Light. After all, it had helped her ground an immense amount of love within these very walls just hours earlier.

Buoyed by breath, she wobbled on bare feet across cold marble. Dizziness threatened to topple her as she groped for the wall. She clawed red silk, feeling her way to the foyer where two hallways led in opposite directions. It was the nearer one that beckoned her intuitive sense.

She stumbled along, downlights winking on to illuminate her steps. At the passageway's end, she found herself standing in the king's massive dressing room.

Walls of waistcoats and cloaks and boots loomed before her. She took a deep breath and started slipping shirts from silk-covered hangers. Opening drawers stacked with leggings and undergarments, she grabbed handfuls as she eyed leather bags and pouches draping rosewood knobs. Another vertigo wave washed over her. As her head cleared, she snatched a black leather pack and stuffed it. Near the door hung multiple riding helmets and equestrian gear. Tucking some riding gloves into the bag, she hurried back to the foyer and along the other hall, which led to the lavatory. Once inside its alabaster expanse, she caught sight of herself as automatic lights brightened the floor-to-ceiling mirror. She nestled the pack onto the marble basin, taking in her straggly updo, smeared mascara – and swollen lips.

She pressed bruised skin and shuddered. Blood caked her mouth. She grimaced at her paleness, and felt grateful all her teeth were intact, as she remembered bone and flesh colliding. Determined not to think about it now, she set about the task of removing the ballgown. Trembling fingers tugged its fastenings as flashbacks flooded her mindscreen. She marveled at how this experience was such a far cry from Alaric's freeing her of a similar frock just three nights ago. From her deepest heart space, she sent him love, as a wild wondering shuddered her. What time was it? Had she slept past midnight, which was their "Plan B," the last agreed-upon time of communication? Again, she wrenched her thoughts from him, and stepped from the dress. As she undid the bustier's laces, she prayed for the best plan of action – for the safest way she could slip from Gadeirus' chambers – without waking him or alerting the guards.

Finally she stood, bare and trembling. Grabbing a shirt from the pack, she raked an arm through one of its white sleeves, as a moan echoed from the next room. She froze, heart thudding her chest. Agonizing seconds passed in slow-motion stillness. Yet as she jerked the other sleeve onto her shoulder, she heard an unmistakable voice.

"Elysia?"

Knowing the cuff kept her from speaking, she couldn't yell back. She felt she had no choice but to face him. There wasn't time to dress before he might awaken further – and that was something she couldn't risk. Praying for guidance and protection, she threw off the shirt and strode into the royal bedroom. With each step, she channeled as deeply from the balanced queen as possible. Stopping just shy of the bed's platform, she stared into Gadeirus' black eyes.

"What beauty awaits me," he whispered groggily. Elysia watched him teeter a shot glass onto the bedside table. He fumbled a disk into his mouth before sinking deeper into silk pillows. His half-mast eyes somehow still grasped the entirety of her nudity. Ascending the bed's platform, she breathed from her inner cave. She slipped beneath scarlet sheets, looking into a face filled with lust. And torment. Reaching a trembling hand toward her, Gadeirus cupped her cheek – and then traced a tapered finger over her lip. She gasped as he flinched.

"Damn me to hell," he mumbled. His thick lashes dripped tears. "I so deeply and humbly apologize, my lady. I never meant to cause you harm." Had she been capable of speech, his words would have rendered her mute. Gazing upon such anguish, she felt compassion – and the birthing of a plan. Moving closer, she caressed his face. For a moment his eyes squeezed shut. With her other hand she clasped his fingers, interlacing them with hers, as she continued to channel her queen. And as she used dolphin sonar to map his hand and fingerprints, which she knew she could use to free herself from the cuff – as well as perhaps escape the palace.

He shook his head as if to clear it. Devouring her with his eyes, he drew her near, and she allowed herself to be drawn. With surprising tenderness, he kissed her. Yet even the lightest pressure of his mouth made her wince, causing him to recoil. Again and again, he looked from her lips to her eyes as he lay beside her.

"You will think me a childish schoolboy," he mused, stroking her hair. "But no matter how many times I've envisioned you in my arms, I feel surprisingly awkward and tongue-tied in your presence." Sadly he smiled, as he studied her face. "Now finally you're here, but only because I've stolen you from your marriage bed. And only after I've inflicted agony upon you." He glanced away as more tears drenched his sallow cheeks. Then his eyes fell upon the cuff, and he cackled, a sound devoid of humor. "Everywhere I look is evidence of my selfish cruelty." With a wave of his hand, the band opened, and he hurled it across the room. The bracelet bounced off red silk and onto the marble below, clanging and spinning before coming to rest beneath her portrait. "With all of my heart, I want you, Elysia. But not if I have to use force. Or torture." Quaking fingers raked his hair. "Light damn my soul, I've used enough of both on countless others. But you ..." His voice trailed off. "Can you speak now that I've removed that hellish coil?"

"Yes," she croaked. She cleared her throat. "I can speak."

"Truly, I don't wish to silence your smarts – or your self-esteem, for that matter. In spite of my wickedness." Quivering, he reached across her and popped another disk in his mouth. "You do realize I'm vile, do you not?"

"Gadeirus –"

"It's all right, my lady," he said, and she noticed his words slurring. "I know it's the truth. I'm quite corrupt. I've done bad things, you know."

"Everyone has moments –"

"You don't understand, Elysia," he said, chuckling. "I've done *really* bad things. Or had them done, in my honor. Horrendous and horrific things." He shook his head. "My soul is irreversibly depraved, such that hubris is perhaps the closest quality I possess to a virtue. You see, for all of my devilry, I yet dare to love an angel." He clasped her face between his hands, his raven's eyes imploring hers. "You are this kind, unearthly creature. A pure, untaintable cherub. And though I myself am eternally damned, I do love you – and all your abiding goodness." Slowly, sweetly even, he kissed her cheek and her neck, as he unbuttoned his shirt. Flinging its sleeves from his fingertips, he explored her with trembling lips. She could hear heavy breathing as he freed himself from his clothing. For a moment he paused, drinking in the sight of her, as if he wished to commit her every curve to memory. "You are the most ravishing woman I've ever laid eyes upon," he said thickly, his speech becoming increasingly indistinct. She could see his eyes blur upward, nearly closing, when he pulled her to him. In spite of her pain, she drew his lips to hers, as her heart filled her eyes.

With all the unconditional love she could channel, through all her layers and from every dimension of her feeling space, she kissed him – deeply and slowly. Gasping, his eyes widened, before he fell into the depths of her gaze. Within her full and balanced power, she held him spellbound. Deeper and deeper she took him, her eyes enticing as her lips seduced. Gradually, his body relaxed. His hands slipped from her skin, and he collapsed against the pillows as she studied his face. His eyes were shut, his breathing shallow. But there was a peacefulness she'd not seen before – a softening. As she arose from the bed, she could sense him descending into dreams.

By channeling so much love, her body and mind felt grounded and clear as she raced to the lavatory. She tossed on the shirt she'd thrown off minutes before, knotting its hem at her waist. She scooted into black leggings and corralled her wild mane with a black scarf, stuffing the ballgown and her undergarments into the pack. In her reflection, she realized she looked dwarfish in Gadeirus' clothes, but she couldn't worry about that now. Scurrying about in his oversized attire was preferable to maneuvering in a heavy ballgown, she reasoned. And it was certainly more practical.

She fled the bathroom, her feet swift and silent on the foyer's black marble. Then she pressed her palms against the entryway's gilded doors. As she sonared the hallway, she sensed two guards, which meant leaving through the front door was not an option. She realized she hadn't noticed any windows at all, in any of the rooms she'd been in – just as she'd found no timepieces. Across the chamber, she spied the balcony, and her gut screamed that was the way out. She sprinted for the double doors and tripped. Her eyes bulged when she saw she'd stumbled over one of her own golden slippers. Desperate prayers and tears flew in equal measure as she searched everywhere for its mate. Then Gadeirus mumbled, a sound that pummeled her heart so hard she knew he would awaken. At last, she spied her shoe beneath the bed, sole up, so she grabbed it and ran. Lurching to a stop just shy of the glass, she eased onto the balcony. Moments passed in stillness. She cradled the pack, cramming in the pumps while her eyes adjusted to darkness. Gone were the candles that had lit the palace windows for the ball; on this night, only rooftop downlighting offered soft illumination, making it challenging for her to assess her surroundings. Not twenty feet away, she could make out her hawk friend observing from the balustrade, those wise, russet eyes radiating encouragement – and respect. Flanking the hawk, dozens of sentinel crows perched. She could feel their ebony gaze upon her, these otherworldly messengers, holding supportive space. And she knew what a profound moment it was for the hawk and ravens to unite in this path of service. Their actions moved her deeply. Her eyes misted as she sent her winged assistants her overflowing heart's love and thankfulness.

Slipping into the corner, where balustrade met wall, Elysia studied her plight as best she could in the shadows. She still needed to find Hunter and the others, and she yet hoped she wasn't too late to hear from Alaric. But before she could think of these things, she had to find a way off the balcony – and out of the palace. Tracing icy fingers over polished limestone, she prayed. The word "window" whispered on the breeze. As she looked out across the castle façade, she surmised she stood perhaps thirty feet from the nearest window. The wall itself had no discernible openings or grooves for climbing. There were, however, colossal rose canes crawling out of the limestone between the balcony and the window. Stepping back, she spied matching blooms leading to an identical window on the balcony's other side. One grouping had been mercilessly pruned into a perfect replica of the castle's coat of arms; the other unfurled as the Atlantean flag. From each design, a red rose border extended across the front of the palace – and, she presumed, encircled it in its entirety.

For several moments, she examined the flowers. Their border formed an angle with the balustrade before dropping to the next level of windows, and continuing in another straight line, paralleling the one where she stood on the fifth floor. She couldn't tell for sure in the shadows, but it seemed likely the roses embraced the palace on each of its five stories – and it appeared they might be the nearest window's only access point. She reached into the floral border and gasped. Not only did toothy thorns bite her palm; a honeybee buzzed forth from the disturbed blossom. As she oozed blood and fear from this little experiment, she knew she was unprepared for the agony her full weight resting on the canes would bring – not to mention the torment awaking bees could unleash. She realized socks and gloves would only entangle her in thorns, perhaps prolonging her painful journey. Sighing, she decided to bare her skin and surrender to roses and bees and the coming torture – while also accepting that she would be balancing five stories from the ground, in wafer-altered unsteadiness – in the dark.

Terror seized her, and for a moment she shut leaking eyes, searching for her inner queen and that heart of a lion she knew she possessed. As she took centering breaths, determination welled up from her core. Accompanying her courage came a clear message from all the hive queens with worker bees in the roses before her. The royals assured her their legions would only inject healing venom to help suppress pain from the inevitable suffering these thorns would inflict. Elysia sighed and thanked the queens, knowing a honeybee can only use its stinger once and then dies. She felt humbled beyond words at their sacrifice; such selflessness reminded her how compassion bears anguish gracefully while answering Highest Light's call.

She assessed both the flag and the coat of arms. It seemed she would have more hand-hold options within the royal family's intricate insignia. Tightening the backpack around her shoulders, she climbed upon the balustrade. Gingerly, she stepped onto the canes forming the red rose border, as she groped for a grip.

Taking one more breath in prayer, she eased her weight onto the roses beneath her left foot. The canes felt surprisingly solid. Then thorns slashed her sole and blood dripped, and she settled her right foot beside the left – while bees punctured each arch. Her mouth opened involuntarily in a silent scream. A flash of vertigo nearly sent her plummeting to the ground. Yet just as suddenly, peace filled and steadied her. With all of her intention, she refocused her breath and began moving one tiny step at a time – as she willed herself to ignore every piercing.

Methodically she moved, in a meditative No-Mind state. Though thorns shredded her body and bee-induced welts erupted everywhere, she'd anchored her heart in appreciation. Sacredly, secretly, silently she inched along in pitch blackness, with what grew to be all of the island hives supporting her efforts. The ravens and her hawk friend kept watch from the balcony. Below her, the horses nickered. She channeled the balanced queen with all her might, drawing from her inner cave, such that only the awareness of breath remained.

She'd just passed the midpoint when she heard voices. Willing herself to an even deeper surrender, she paused in painful suspension, five stories in the air. She ignored her trembling arms and listened.

"Light damn it, Galenius!" The young man's desperate whisper assaulted her ears in the still night air. "What're all these bloody birds *doin'* out here?!"

"I'll be Light damned if I know," a deeper voice replied. "But we got bigger problems. We gotta figure out what to do and be quick! Birds or no birds, we'd best do any jawin' right here. From what I heard, this balcony's the only place in the palace those hellfire witches won't hear us."

"I just can't wrap my mind around murder. I mean, he's wretched and all, but I can't help likin' him." Elysia stopped herself mid-gasp. "And maybe I'm just a sucker for a pretty face. But I don't wanna frame that dame we dragged to his room, either. Hounds of hell!"

"I'd just as soon leave the princess out of it, too. And as for Gadeirus ... well, so he's a cad. But he's a likeable one. Generous with buttons and smokes. Remember that time he shared those dames when he was flyin' high?" Galenius and the other man snickered, while Elysia digested all that had been revealed.

"It's a helluva thing deciding a man's fate based on his willingness to get us schnockered or sexed up, ain't it?"

"These are twisted times, Horasius. But what would that whore Lorelei do for us anyway?" Elysia bit her tongue at the mention of Lorelei. Could they possibly be speaking of the jealous teen who'd tried to take her life so many centuries ago?

"I don't see 'er helpin' us get high or get laid, if that's what you mean," Horasius muttered.

"Me neither."

"I wouldn't mind saddling that pretty little pony," Horasius added. "But I don't wanna kill no king. Not for the likes of 'er."

"So have we decided?" Galenius asked. "Do we blow off a direct order from the Dark Heart whore herself? And bring her wrath upon us?"

"Wrath is gonna rain down one way or the other, brother, no matter what we choose right now," Horasius whispered. "Of that you can be sure. But yahhh. I say we ignore that bloody bitch. And tell Gadeirus in the morning that Lorelei's put a price on his head."

"I'm good with that."

"Alrighty, mate. Let's get back and wait for first light." The balcony door hissed shut. Once more she was alone in shadowy stillness. Breathing relief, she stretched gouged and swollen fingers toward a new grasping place and shifted her feet. In spite of the pain, it felt good to be moving again. Little by little, she hobbled toward the window, losing track of how long and how far and how sweaty and how slippery it all felt. In each moment, there was only her breath and a steadfast belief she was progressing.

Eventually, she drew near enough to stretch sticky toes onto the window ledge. With as much strength as she could muster, she pushed off from the canes with her right arm. But she launched herself with such force – and with the wafers still playing with her equilibrium – she lost her balance. Teetering on a ledge slickened by her own secretions, she grasped one of the iron bars adorning the window. For agonizing minutes, she simply held on. The limestone's cool smoothness comforted her battered body. She sank beside the bars, ignoring red streaks leaking from her fingers onto the sill. Reaching for the latch inside, she swung squeaky hinges open, allowing herself to nestle deeper into the window. As she pawed with numb and puffy hands along the frame, she realized the window was locked. Sighing into sobs, she rested her head against the glass – and understood a long night had just become even longer.

FOUR

Creaking hinges aroused Alaric from *advaita*, the blessed No-Mind state, where he'd been praying for guidance – and preparing. As the arched oak door swung open, he looked up from his seat – cat-like, muscles taut, ready to spring. His gold-green eyes bored into Linasia's flirtatious leer. A bun now restrained her blonde tresses, her heavy makeup had been freshly layered, and she'd exchanged the negligee for a low-cut gown.

"I hope I didn't keep you waiting long." Hips first, she flowed her curvaceousness into the dungeon.

"Not long."

"I got ready as fast as I could." Kicking off red sandals, she lifted a taffeta skirt and plopped once more upon his lap. "I was hoping you would pleasure me before I leave."

"Linasia, we already agreed –"

"Please?" She batted false eyelashes at him, their extravagant length lacquered in mascara. "I can promise you it won't take long."

"Once you return," he replied, as she kissed him hungrily. "That's the deal."

"Maybe I've changed my mind," she cooed between kisses. "And maybe I can change yours."

"Maybe you can honor our agreement," he hissed. Taking her by the arms, he arose, lifting her easily from his lap. He peered unfeelingly at her as he set her on her feet, until she snickered.

"My, my, we're in a mood, aren't we?" She eyed him carefully while smoothing her skirt.

"I told you time is of the essence," he whispered. "Quenna has already transitioned. Or have you forgotten?"

"Of course not." In an instant, her tone changed. Gone was the coquettish floozy. Before him stood the gatekeeper, the shrewd business-woman. He could feel her trying to read into him, to see if her sharp eyes were missing something – anything that should make her back out of their arrangement. "I'll not be long anyway."

"I didn't think so." He glowered at her. "Five, ten minutes tops?"

"Something like that," she purred, her eyes wary as she studied his face. "I do have a short matter of business to discuss with someone while I'm there. But even so, I should return within fifteen minutes."

"Fifteen minutes in return for hours of pleasuring," he murmured. "I should think you'd be quite pleased with our bargain."

"Oh, I will be, lover." Her tone oozed sultriness. "I *will* be." Pirouetting, she sauntered to a desk drawer on the room's far side. She removed a set of keys and strolled to where the tubes sat caged. Circling to the back of iron bars bolted to a table, she jangled a key free from the others, then inserted it into one of the bars. Screeching, the cage door split open into two equal halves. She grabbed the tubes, carelessly clinking them together. She opened another drawer and groped for something. Unceremoniously, she seized a mesh bag and dumped the tubes inside, as Alaric winced.

"Don't fret," she teased, tossing the tubes to the floor, where they clanged against her pumps. She smiled at his pained expression. "These tubes are made of clear sapphire. Virtually scratchproof and impact resistant. Your darling wife is safe with me."

"Even so, have Jack send me an imprint – both when you give him the essences and when he delivers them to Jonastus."

"But that cuff will prevent –"

"Nothing will block an imprint, Linasia," Alaric said evenly, shaking his wrist bound by the gold and crystal cuff. "Not even this bauble."

"You really don't trust me, do you?" Her sticky red mouth curved into a smile that never reached her eyes.

"Trust is a strange word coming from those lips." Like a panther preparing to pounce, he stalked her. Stopping shy of where she stood, he scowled down at her. She caught her breath at the unbridled allure – and unmistakable danger. "Trust a woman who made me marry her daughter while forcing me into her own bed?" His voice was as smooth and soft as silk. Taking her by the shoulders, he pressed her back from the table, until he'd pinned her to the wall. "Trust a woman who for a thousand years has made a tidy sum, selling my body again and again to the highest bidder?" He leaned in close, and it filled her with lust to see this side of his passion – even if it bordered on rage. "Trust a woman who endlessly wants me to free her deepest carnal desires ... from a cage?" For long moments, he looked from her eyes to her lips and back, and she was sure he would kiss her. Certain he would at long last express a need and a desire for her – something he'd never done in all the centuries he had pleasured her. She trembled and turned starving eyes upon his unreadable face. But instead he smiled, a chilled curving of his sensuous lips, and released her. Turning his back, he dismissed her, as he resumed his reign upon the throne-like chair where he'd been perched.

"You wound me, Alaric." She sashayed across the room to stand before him. "I'm the only reason Elysia is alive right now. I arranged for her to have a second lease on life all those centuries ago. And earlier tonight, I spared her again – as well as kept your whereabouts secret from the Atlantean regime." Pouting into his icy countenance, she shook her head. "I should think you'd be grateful."

"I've always acknowledged my indebtedness," he replied in his velvety voice. "By honoring my word to you. And I will do so again once you've fulfilled your promise to me."

"Fair enough." She bent provocatively to slip on her sandals and scoop up the bag. "Would you like to wait for me in my bed?"

"I'm fine right here."

"Well, you shouldn't stay in the dungeon –"

"What difference does it make?" He glared at her. "You won't be gone long enough for it to matter, one way or the other."

"Suit yourself," she sniffed. Again, she scrutinized him. Some part of her simply knew he was waiting to trick her in some fashion, and yet she could think of no conceivable way he could possibly outsmart her in the span of fifteen minutes. "Then I'll go ahead and leave."

"Good."

"What – no goodbye kiss?"

"I think you'll have me kissing you for hours when you return," he replied in his smooth tone. "That should suffice."

"If you insist."

"I insist you have Jack send me an imprint." He showed no emotion as she rolled her eyes. "Once you give him the essences. And again when he delivers them to Jonastus."

"Yes, yes, of course," she snapped. "You've become so demanding." He flashed back to Elysia teasing him about being so demanding just two mornings ago, after their first hours of lovemaking in a thousand years. For a moment, despair deflated him, a deep sadness Linasia's eagle eyes spotted. "Come now. I haven't offended you, have I?"

"No," he said quietly. "I'm not easily offended."

"All right." She paused, giving him the opportunity to say more and perhaps reveal something she should know. But he remained silent and still. She sighed, realizing she should accept by now she'd never really known him – or effectively read into him. "I'll return shortly." And with that, she disappeared.

Closing his eyes, he took a deep, centering breath. Then in one graceful movement, he gained his feet. He crossed the length of the dungeon in easy strides, slowing to a stop in front of the three-headed dog pack. They watched him with guarded interest. Upon his approach, the leader rose from his bed. He sat at attention, his fiery eyes scorching Alaric's, as he awaited this strong alpha male's command.

"*Agatah*," Alaric murmured. The leader came without question. Alaric reached down, petting the beast's three heads, letting each mane's swirl of serpents writhe around his fingers. Kneeling before the dog, Alaric held up his wrist, letting the Cerberus smell and explore the cuff. He peered into the three sets of eyes, sending a clear mental image of what he desired. "*Khandayati*," he whispered, holding his wrist toward the middle set of the beast's massive jaws.

The dog opened his cavernous mouth, revealing large white teeth. With fierce precision, he gripped the band between clenched jaws – and began to bite. Alaric floated in No-Mind as he stared into those three red pairs of eyes. His breath remained deep and slow, even as the dog began to whimper. Sparks shot from the cuff, causing the Cerberus to cry out, and yet he continued to clamp down. Then the beast pulled hard – once, twice – and the band flew apart. Part of it struck the adjacent wall, clanging against the stone before rattling to a stop on the floor. Part of it flew in the other direction, rolling under one of the opposite wall's tables.

"*Ativa sadhu*," he said, his heart filled with gratitude, as he again stroked the dog's three heads. It appeared the beast was uninjured, in spite of how he'd cried. Glancing at his wrist, Alaric saw he was gushing blood from where the dog's teeth had pierced his flesh. He knew he shouldn't take time now to look for anything to bandage the wound, so he ripped off his shirtsleeve. Quickly he wrapped his wrist, then rose to his feet. Before he could take a step, though, he heard Jack's words in his heart. That deep, husky voice he would know anywhere, in the form of an impossible-to-fake imprint. The same technique he hoped he could soon use to contact Elysia. He could feel the truth in Jack's words – his old friend really was in possession of the tubes. Which meant he must move swiftly, as Linasia would be returning any minute. Willing himself into No-Mind, he closed his eyes and thought of his desired destination. And prayed.

In a heartbeat, the light shifted. Alaric opened his eyes and found himself standing in the middle of a high desert plain. Beneath the sky's cherry moon, he sank to his knees, thanking Highest Light for answering his prayers – and for keeping the door open to his and Elysia's happily ever after. Gazing about him, his reptilian eyes could see quite clearly. He noted the deep impressions left recently by a small craft just to his right. There were also two sets of boot prints leading from where the ship had landed to an area directly in front of him. Relief and hope filled his heart, as he realized Jon and Tyrius had indeed intercepted the essences he'd teleported here.

Within the stillness of these barren lands, he sensed a multitude of psychic eyes and ears attuned to the planet – and the oppressive presence of the Atlantean *Amur* fleet waiting for him. He realized he would have to be even more exceedingly cautious now. Linasia would not take kindly to his sudden departure, and he knew he could no longer count on her to help shield him.

While contemplating his next move, he caught sight of the blood-soaked sleeve binding his wrist. He understood the dangers of such a bite, even for immortals – as well as the perils posed by seeking a remedy. Yet the threat was so great he really had no choice but to take a detour before heading to Alpha Centauri. Perhaps his unexpected change in plans might be safer anyway for Jon and Tyrius – and the essences – if any of these psychic spies would in fact be able to detect him.

But before he left, he tuned his heart to Elysia's. At long last he allowed himself to feel into her, so he could imprint her with his next intended point of contact – and tell her he loved her. Yet what he felt was what he'd feared all along. She was in the king's lair, under a potent elixir that prevented him from making any contact she would recall. Sobbing in silence, he cradled his head in his hands. Yet he knew he couldn't long dwell in the luxury of an emotional melt-down. Straightening his spine, he again breathed himself into stillness. When he raised his head, he sent an imprint to another, to the only one he could think of who was far enough removed from Elysia as to not be watched – and yet he knew he could trust.

Once more he closed his eyes. He set a complex, sonar-like code in place to scramble and hide his vibration. Then he disappeared, heading in search of the one he knew was most capable of the healing he so desperately needed, but would be most reluctant to render it.

FIVE

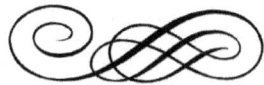

Gliding along the grand hallway, Lorelei moved as surely as the approaching witching hour. She carried herself regally in a striking scarlet gown. Ebony curls fell in obedient ringlets to her shoulders. Her makeup was tasteful and applied with a skilled hand, a lovely accent to her oval face and cupid-bow lips. But beneath her polished exterior, she seethed. She'd been beyond angry ever since her earlier conversation with Linasia. She knew so many puzzle pieces were in place, so many things were going her way. And, yet there was a splintering at hand she couldn't deny. Poseidia encompassed so many diverse and ego-driven forces. She could feel the factions beginning to break, splitting off in selfish distractions from their original unified intention – which was to rule this galaxy and beyond, once and for all.

She realized it fell to her to make a course correction, to hold intact the bigger vision they all once shared. And to that end, she found herself in Gadeirus' never-ending pleasure palace. Its non-stop parties and all-night orgies were indulgences Gadeirus graciously extended to members of his entourage as well as Poseidia's political leaders. Not to mention his staff, which made him popular with practically everyone, but also increasingly difficult to rein in. She knew the ever-flowing alcohol and endless hallucinogenic highs had so far thwarted her political camp's best efforts to remove him from the throne. It was a dilemma the Atlantean High Council certainly hadn't anticipated. Especially the weakness among their own ranks, as every day more and more members were coming under the influence of all the temptations Gadeirus readily made available. Yet problem solving was one of her specialties, so she'd stepped forward to bring order from this chaos. Although she'd made it clear she expected to be rewarded for her efforts – and handsomely. She knew when the High Council agreed to her demands they were either exceedingly confident in her abilities – or desperate.

In many ways, she thought it seemed natural for her to be the one sorting out this mess. Leading undeniably coursed through her veins. Like Alaric, she was a shape-shifter – or rather, she had been once, until she'd been stripped of those privileges. Even now, thousands of years later, she still missed those abilities. The lack thereof only served to deepen her bitterness. She, too, had grown up on Moldaaris. And like him, she descended from a royal snake lineage, the oldest, most distinguished shape-shifting ancestry in the universe. Yet thoughts of Alaric only fueled her rage. Even after the passing of thousands of years, she had not forgiven him – nor had she forgotten.

As she traversed the second floor, which Gadeirus had turned over to the psychics in residence, she knew she needed to bury her feelings. Alaric was the single greatest distraction she could have, and yet the one thing she could never quite drive from her mind. Usually, she kept thoughts of him subdued, hidden well beneath consciousness, in a mental realm even the best clairvoyants couldn't navigate clearly. But now, after Linasia's crushing veto, she felt vulnerable. There remained a few minutes before she would reach the seers' central vision room, so she allowed herself the luxury of wallowing in her long life's most painful memory.

Throughout the centuries, she'd never fathomed why he couldn't love her. They would have been the ideal couple. They *should* have been teenage sweethearts. And they *should* have married, growing up to rule Moldaaris together. After all, they'd been born to different families within the same lineage, so they possessed between them the ideal genetic profile to produce offspring unequaled in talent, strength, and allure. Her whole life she'd seen so clearly this unrealized potential. In her mind's eye, all she'd ever envisioned involved him falling madly in love with her and them living happily ever after. Even as a child, she'd coveted him. Butterflies fluttered her stomach whenever he stood near. His handsome face – and those eyes! Not to mention he'd been the most brilliant of anyone in school – academically superior even to gifted students who were years older. And well before adolescence, it became clear he'd one day possess a body any female would tremble to touch. To her, he'd always embodied perfection, and she worshipped flawlessness. Shaking her head, she blinked back tears. Yet they fell anyway, stinging her amber eyes. She knew on some level he must have been deeply dysfunctional not to see how ideally suited they were for one another. But what could have been never transpired. His heart had always and forever belonged to Elysia.

Thinking of it now, she felt exquisite jealousy. With aching clarity, she recalled how her early life had unfolded, yearning for him. Their parents had been good friends, and there wasn't a time when she hadn't known Alaric. Though she'd looked for excuses to seek his company since the age of four, he'd remained aloof. Polite but distant, as he was with mostly everyone. Until that day at school – what was called Wisdom Camp – when she and Alaric were both fourteen. That day, everything changed.

On Moldaaris, children from age seven to eighteen attended Wisdom Camps, held in various regions across the planet. Within this academic structure, those from different hybrid backgrounds were encouraged to mingle as part of the teachings, fostering love and harmony amid a staggering array of diversity. In fact, intermingling was so encouraged that every few weeks, children were rotated among these scholastic settings, traveling great distances at times in order to develop a sense of being comfortable in changing environments, with different companions – a guiding philosophy that also nurtured the Moldaarin values of patience, tolerance, and self-confidence.

Looking back, she could still appreciate how what she'd learned in the Moldaarin educational model had prepared her well for life. She remembered how much she'd loved those early years of Wisdom Camp. Until one warm spring day, when they introduced the latest group of seven-year-olds within her region. The older children were always encouraged to welcome the youngsters, to help them have a positive experience. Yet as a nervous teenager, she'd cared nothing about setting a good example. It had mattered not to her what the younger ones may have been feeling. Her first priority, every day, was looking her absolute best. She obsessed over every outfit, every ringlet; she applied with painstaking precision the minimal makeup her parents allowed. Once she felt she'd made herself presentable, her next priority was finding a way to sit next to Alaric. Many times, she'd even turned her ample powers of persuasion on other children, hypnotizing them with her amber glare so they'd relinquish a spot beside him. But on this day, she got to the crowded classroom just a little late, so she found the closest she could come was a space behind and to the left of him. She told herself at least she'd be able to keep him in view and steal glances at his sable and gold locks. Although she'd been unprepared for what unfolded next.

As was customary, the new students lined up in front of the school. Then each child was introduced by name and assigned an older student to serve as a guide for the first year. Not only did this protocol help the younger ones transition to the learning environment; it also cultivated leadership within the older children. In this particular year's fledgling group, there were eleven youngsters. When they stood before the student body, Lorelei's critical gaze was drawn to the third child from the left. Right away, she knew the girl was a dolphin hybrid. Not only was she beautiful, with long red hair and green eyes. But she absolutely beamed happiness – a trait all the dolphin hybrids shared – and her smile was delightfully infectious. Lorelei peered bitterly about her, as she heard others near her snickering and whispering how adorable the little girl was. Everywhere she looked, Lorelei saw people smiling and admiring the child, and a raging jealousy the likes of which she'd never felt before fouled her soul. As the first two children were introduced and paired with a mentor, Lorelei barely heard anything that was said, as she couldn't take her eyes from the little redhead. And then the girl was introduced. Her name was Elysia, and she smiled and waved to the assembled scholars, as if she were already an accomplished performer. The students erupted with applause, even though that action betrayed standard etiquette. But to Lorelei, watching this joyful girl was for some reason more than she could bear. And then she thought to look at Alaric. She was sure his impenetrable nature would be the only one besides her own that remained unmoved.

To her horror, Alaric was grinning, a smile she could feel radiating from the depths of his heart. And when she looked from his euphoric face to Elysia's, she watched the child wink at him before blowing a kiss. The flirtatious act evoked whistles and clapping. Practically everyone present was enjoying how this precocious girl had not only charmed the whole school, but especially the overly serious Alaric.

And then, before Elysia's student guide could be announced, Lorelei's jaw dropped as Alaric arose from his seat. Clearly, he intended to mentor the girl. And since he was so favored among faculty and students alike, Lorelei knew no one would challenge him. With easy grace, he walked to the front of the room, where he knelt beside Elysia. Offering his hand, he whispered something. She nodded enthusiastically while students thundered applause. Tears leaked onto Lorelei's cheeks, as Alaric led Elysia back to where he'd been sitting.

Lorelei reminded herself she *could* do more than watch. Drawing from rage and rejection, she channeled darkness directly at Elysia's heart – and the girl collapsed. In one agile movement, Alaric caught her before she hit the ground. He eased himself onto the floor, cradling Elysia, as worried instructors hurried to their aid. A hush fell over the student body, who began holding space in the supportive way they'd been taught to do when facing misfortune.

As the vision room came into view, Lorelei paused. She leaned against the gold silk wall, willing her eyes shut. Sometimes she wondered why she tortured herself so with these unpleasantries. And why she seemed powerless to stop – especially when she'd allowed herself to relive the story.

In her deepest recesses, she could still feel Shanta's firm hand on her shoulder. Her teacher's touch had broken her concentration, lifting the spell. She'd looked up into unblinking gold eyes. Shanta was the region's only teacher descended from a royal snake ancestry. And as such, she was perhaps the only one in the classroom besides Alaric who could see the sophisticated energy patterns Lorelei had wielded to hurt Elysia.

The incident abruptly ended her schooling – and indeed her life – on Moldaaris. Her horrified parents agreed to transfer her to the Atlantean school Shanta recommended. But not before Lorelei appeared before the school's disciplinary board, who decided her shape-shifting abilities must be destroyed since she'd used them with murderous intent. Just before she left for Atlantis, she was forced to undergo psychic surgery, which forever muted her genetic gifts; this alteration left her with no choice but to learn to rely upon a crystal ball for something as simple to a shape-shifter as mind-messaging.

In spite of all she'd lost, though, she retained immortality. And so, she used the luxury of time to forge new ways of channeling, which had been the gift she missed most. Down through the centuries, she'd taken her penchant for perfection and honed her Dark Heart methods. She'd been fortunate to finish her schooling in Atlantis, actually, because her teachers had been intrigued instead of mortified with her mindset – and her remaining talents. They'd helped her embrace brutality and direct depravity into a subtle, effective, and deceptively dangerous energy technique. An approach that, in its earliest form, had done no lasting harm to Elysia. But as Lorelei had cultivated and refined her theories, she'd created a lethal metaphysical weapon – as well as an outlet for passion and fury and insatiable ego. Having been cast down by Highest Light, she embraced Lesser; she'd birthed Dark Heart power and nurtured it, growing it into a hell realms' arsenal and army that had no earthly equal. Whispers begat rumors that grew to legends. Her legacy spread, one that ultimately captured the attention – and then the affections – of Helionel.

Not that she'd desired him. Yet he'd been the one person in the universe she knew that shared not only her ambitions – but her feelings. Helionel, like Lorelei, viewed Alaric and Elysia as *durga* or "unattainable" in the Old Tongue. The king had long realized he and Lorelei were bonded in the same wound, so he asked her to marry him. And while she was tempted by the promised title, she knew she could not long endure being pleasured by someone who frankly left her cold. Long-standing sexual frustration only hardened her resentment toward Alaric. She'd always blamed him for the lonely, miserable trajectory of her life. If only he'd loved her, as he *should* have – as all logical indications and sound reason indicated he would. Then she'd be sharing his bed and his kingdom right this minute instead of ambling along a darkened hallway to fix yet another crisis.

When she was being honest with herself, she could admit she felt damaged by Alaric – broken in a way that only his death would assuage. Yet she knew killing him remained a remote fantasy at best. And though she'd relished many of the cruel schemes Helionel had concocted for centuries to inflict pain and punishment upon him, in her heart of hearts these sufferings never seemed severe enough. She could appreciate the wicked irony of selling his beautiful body over and over again to women who would never be Elysia – and yet to her, this detail of his Linasia deal hardly seemed traumatizing. Nor did it seem so bad to marry him off in a loveless union to Carinnia. Even forcing him to share Linasia's bed – which did fill her with envy, as Linasia was the one woman who could, at the very least, count on being pleasured by him – didn't make up for the agony she'd endured herself. She knew she'd never be satisfied in Linasia's position, however, because she could never be happy as his whore. Though it had rankled her for eons to know that's all she could ever really be to him, even if she forced herself upon him. Slowly, she shook her head. No matter what, his lot in life just didn't seem that bad to her. Especially now, since reconnecting with Elysia mere days ago. In spite of everything, he wasn't alone, Lorelei reasoned – something she *had* been since Helionel's death. Not that there hadn't been offers. But there'd been no Alarics, and in her perfection-driven mind, nothing less would ever do.

Pushing herself from the wall, she gulped several centering breaths as she again hurried along the hallway. Thoughts of what had transpired in the last 72 hours, with Alaric and Elysia reunited, begged to surface. And, yet she simply couldn't bear thinking of their newly wedded bliss at the moment. When she reached the vision room's entry, she waved her hand across the keyless pad beside the handle, then swung open the double doors. A smoky haze greeted her, blanketing any hopes for a speedy resolution. Willing herself to remain patient, she entered the vast foyer.

Originally, the chamber had been decorated as a guest suite. But the beds and armoires had been replaced by tables and chairs – and several large crystal balls. As Lorelei marched across the gold silk rug, she noticed a seer near the window peering into a glowing orb; the clairvoyant's tapered fingers caressed the sphere as it rested upon a gilded stand. Two other psychics sat in trance-like states on a black settee. Everyone else, though, seemed otherwise distracted in meaningless chatter. And from what Lorelei could sense, incredibly altered.

"Hi, gorgeous," a deep voice growled in her ear. She looked up into Abigor's swarthy face. Since Gadeirus' coronation, the king had drawn to Poseidia the best-known psychics – and Abigor had been his top choice. All Lorelei saw in the hell realms' notorious grand duke was a flirtatious jokester. Wearing well-tailored pants and a black silk shirt, he caressed her cheek. "Come. Let me pleasure you."

"I'm not here to be pleasured," she hissed. His laughter indicated she hadn't offended him.

"But you should be." Mirth danced with lust in his orange eyes. "Some pleasuring would do you a world of good."

"Abigor, I –"

"I see I've struck a chord, and for that I apologize." He lifted her fingers to his lips. One by one he kissed them, his eyes never leaving hers. "If you've not come for pleasuring, then why are you here?"

"This is the central vision room, is it not?" Her voice sounded breathless even to her own ears. He smiled, moving his muscular body against hers, as he kissed her neck.

"It is at that. Why?"

"Because I need to make sure all the seers are on the same page." She realized he was no Alaric, but his broad face pleased her.

"You wouldn't really want that now, would you?" Softly, he touched his lips to hers, and she felt a stirring inside. "If everyone's on the same page, something is bound to be missed."

"Well –"

"I'm in charge here, you know." He feathered long fingers down her arms. "You'd trust me to take care of things, wouldn't you? Thoroughly and completely?"

"It's not a matter of trust –"

"Sure it is." Deeply, hungrily, he kissed her as she gasped. "Let me show you just how skilled I am. Why I'm in charge." Again, his mouth ravished hers. "And how I can take charge."

"But –"

"Not here," he murmured in her ear, and she realized he must have read her mind. "My room, down the hall. Where we can be alone."

"But I need to make sure the psychics –"

"After." His tongue explored her neck, quivering her. "Anything you need to say to them is fine with me. But only after I've pleasured you." He grinned wickedly. "Thoroughly and completely."

"I don't know what to say."

"Say yes," he whispered. Pulling a disk from his front pocket, he pressed it against her lips. "Just say yes."

"But I've never ... indulged." She gaped at him, her eyes guarded.

"That's why you should," he coaxed, and for a moment she wondered why she'd always been so prudish – why she'd been denying herself, since Alaric would never be hers. Awkwardly, she opened her mouth, and he smiled as he slipped the disk onto her tongue. "Come on, gorgeous." He clasped her hand and led her through the foyer door before escorting her along the hall. She felt so strange as she moved by his side. When he waved his hand across a nearby room's keyless entry pad, Lorelei realized her heart was hammering her chest. She wondered if it was the disk beginning to take effect – or just nerves. "Here we are." Abigor held the door for her. He followed her inside, then as the door shut, he swept her into his arms. Whisking her to the unmade bed, he laid her against red pillows and unbuttoned his shirt.

"Abigor, I think you should be aware I've never –"

"I know." He slipped onto the bed beside her.

"But how –"

"I really am psychic, you know." He laughed, his lips again finding hers. As he pulled her close, he felt trembling. "Hey." He lifted her chin and saw eyes widening to saucers. "It's all right. I'll be gentle."

"I appreciate that. It's just ..." Her voice trailed off, and she looked away. She could feel an internal mellowing she knew had to be from the disk, and it made her want to sob.

"I realize I'm not him." She could feel her face flushing.

"Who?"

"Alaric."

"*What*?!" She jumped up, and he caught her by the shoulders, easing her back onto the pillows.

"Did you think I wouldn't see that, either?" He swept onyx curls behind her ear, letting his lips fondle the hollow of her neck.

"I'm not sure if I'm mortified," she muttered, as he unfastened her gown. "Or relieved."

"Considering how long you've kept that bottled up, let's go with relieved." He lifted her, peeling the dress from her body.

"Thank you for your kind regard."

"*Kind regard*?!" With practiced fingers, he undid the bustier laces. "I know what you're thinking, Lorelei. But Light damn it, I didn't bring you to my bed out of any sense of 'kind regard'! You're no charity case. Of that you can be certain. You're here because you're smart and talented and stunningly beautiful. And any man who can't see that, well ..."

"He could never see that," she croaked, her words beginning to slur.

"He sees nothing but her," he scoffed, sweeping silk stockings from her thighs. "And *you* need to see that every other blood and bone male in Atlantis would *so* want to be *me* right now." He looked up as tears dribbled from her lashes. Slipping from his pants, he pulled her beneath silk sheets and into his arms. "But that's enough about him. Remember, I'm in charge here."

"Thoroughly and completely." She managed a smile as his lips and hands and body began showing her what she'd been missing for the last few thousand years.

SIX

Collapsed against the window frame, Elysia cried herself to quietude in the dark – and prayed. Five stories separated her from the ground, while mere glass barred her from this chamber beside the king's. Yet breaking the panes could draw attention and most definitely would leave a trail – evidence she'd have neither the time nor the means to hide.

As she weighed options, she noticed something dripping like candle wax down the window bars. When she realized it was her own blood, she examined her hands without emotion, noting how both bees and thorns had pierced her. Fresh wetness oozed as she flexed and stretched sausage fingers. But turning her attention to her hands brought more than pain – it made her recall her dolphin sonar. She reasoned the same ability she'd used to scramble her energetic signal and map Gadeirus' handprint might just do something else – something akin to picking a lock.

Hope flooded her as she scrunched by the window. Scanning the suite to make sure no one waited inside, she bit her lip and felt for the frame's keyless lock. Then she channeled into the tiny mechanism. She could feel her energy align with one crystalline code after another until she heard an audible "click." Her pulse pounded her temples as she pressed against the window. When it creaked open, tears of relief wracked her ribcage.

Still sniffling, she swam through layers of velvet and tulle drapery before her toes finally touched the floor. Once she wobbled onto polished marble and collected herself, her body quivered. She couldn't quite believe what she'd just accomplished – or rather, what Highest Light had orchestrated. As reality sank in, she realized she needed fuel. Thinking back to the dinner, she figured she'd had a mouthful or two of soup and salad before all the resulting drama. In her head she could hear Alaric's admonishing words. Fastening the window, she fluffed its heavy curtains and perused the sumptuous surroundings.

She found herself entering a cavernous suite as the high ceiling's motion-sensing downlights drifted on. Silk-covered walls and floral carpets harmonized with the gold-striped bedspread and rosewood furnishings. On a low bureau rested a lemon water pitcher, and she salivated. Splashing hydration into a waiting glass, she gulped until breathless. She refilled the vessel and glanced around for something – anything – she might eat.

Her eyes fell on a buffet feast engulfing the foyer. While that much food delighted her, she knew with a sinking heart this chamber had been prepared for a party who likely lingered at the palace dinner – guests that could return any minute.

Scurrying to the table, she gobbled berries and nuts, being careful to leave the dishes looking undisturbed. She sloshed steaming bone broth into her water goblet. Downing that, she tossed nuts and crackers into the empty vessel with quaking fingers; she kept spilling the snacks and giggling at the compounding ridiculousness. She realized her feet and hands were leaving bloody prints, so she rummaged in the pack for fresh clothes and gloves and socks, still smiling at this lunacy. Once she'd changed and hastily wiped away traces of her passage with the shredded garments, she gentled them and the cup into the pack and raced to the door. Sonar revealed a hallway as quiet as a crypt.

Tuning into the keyless entry pad, she hacked it herself rather than relying on Gadeirus' handprint. She figured they monitored palace doors opening and closing – certainly ones the king entered or exited – so she wanted to ensure she only used his energetic signature if there remained no other choice.

As she'd done with the window lock, she beamed sonar into the keypad. This mechanism proved more sophisticated than the window's. Yet one by one, each code synced with her channeling, and she again heard an audible "click." Cloaking herself in concealing energies, she slipped into the corridor.

Gadeirus' suite loomed perhaps thirty feet from where she stood – a much less harrowing distance than it had felt from the outside. The guards she'd overheard on the balcony now lounged in the royal doorway, their attention riveted on a card game. Praying for protection, she turned and tiptoed away. She forced herself to keep moving in spite of debilitating pain, hobbling along and breathing herself again and again into No-Mind. Ahead lay a juncture where one hall intersected another; intuition led her, loping, to the left. Halfway down this hallway stood an elevator. Yet she knew hopping a ride bore heavy risks – too exposed for one, with its crystalline sides – and perhaps soon to be in demand, with departing dinner guests. She wished she could learn the time and found it odd there had been no clocks anywhere on this fifth floor. But she couldn't think about that right now.

In the sconces' soft illumination, she finally spied a stairway sign – just as the light above the elevator winked on. In seconds, someone – or maybe several people – would be stepping from that shaft. She gritted her teeth and sprinted, her gloved hand at last grabbing the stair door handle – only to find it locked. Her heart hammering, she sonared the keyless entry pad, praying she could match the lock's internal cylinders in time. Wild eyes glued to the elevator, she heard chiming as it paused on the fourth floor. As her energy matched code after code, another chime sounded. Then the elevator doors parted just when she heard the lock "click."

She wedged through, easing the door closed. Crazily, she stumbled down slippery rock steps as the sound of men and women laughing and the drone of idle chatter echoed around her. It crossed her mind who all these guests could be that had been invited to the king's private floor at this hour. But she had no time for pondering. Elysia lurched down the black passageway, hurling forward until dizziness would catch up and she was forced to rebalance before throwing herself once more down the steep stairwell.

She'd hurtled past the third-floor landing when she heard trudging below. Scrambling and sliding back up to the doorway, she groped for the handle, hoping against hope it would open – but it didn't. She sonared the lock as heavy footfalls and men's voices loomed louder. The walls' lit torches showed silhouettes rising toward her. As their heads popped into view, the door clicked and she pushed with pulse-pounded fingertips, guiding it closed before tearing off down yet another hallway.

Realizing the men were likely heading to this floor, she made a drunken turn and staggered down an intersecting passageway. Behind her, the stairway door squeaked open, and the men's low chuckles jolted her. She bolted left into the next hall and crashed into the first doorway. A quick scan showed the room was empty, so she sonared the lock, wondering if the cylinders might now be tumbling faster. As if to prove her right, the lock yielded its audible "click" immediately. Breathless, she entered and eased the door shut, listening wide-eyed while weighing options.

Their voices reached her easily enough. She prayed, her pulse thrashing her temples, as she crouched behind a coat rack. Seconds passed with her heart bursting her chest. She heard them just outside, then their words trailed off as the adjacent room's door swung wide. Once that door closed, she sonared the lock beside her, yielding a knowing that all the locks shared a base energy pattern. Her system had now mapped and remembered this sequence, allowing immediate access. Gratitude buoyed her as she crept into the corridor.

Tiptoeing, she wobbled on shaky legs toward the stairway sign ahead. She snuck through the door, and silence greeted her. Then she grasped at the wall as she skidded to the second-floor landing. Stumbling down the last few stairs, she began to feel around her, yet she sensed no one ready to enter. Taking a deep breath, she paused on the ground level to collect herself before stepping out into yet another hallway.

Gazing about, she recognized this corridor as one of many joining the main foyer. Only a few guests stood chatting together to her right; she cloaked herself energetically and headed left toward the lavatory. As she opened its wide gilded door, she breathed a sigh of relief there was no one by the sinks or preening in front of the enormous mirrors.

Entering a private stall, she dropped the pack. Here in the stillness her teeth chattered, and she realized she'd been chilled for some time. She tugged at the gloves and Gadeirus' shirt and leggings, yet dried blood had sealed her wounds with fabric. There was no time to do anything except add extra layers, so with ham hands, she buttoned a fresh shirt.

Stepping from the stall, she caught her battered reflection in the mirrored wall. Grabbing from a stack of fresh towels, she held cottony softness under hot water and added dispenser soap. Then she washed off all the smeared makeup. Dabbing her skin with a dry towel, she straightened the hair scarf. All things considered, she felt ready to face whatever may come.

She devoured some nuts and contemplated her next move. Tucking baggy leggings into the socks made the silky material fit better, which helped her feel more presentable. Though she looked deathly pale, she was thankful she didn't appear so outlandishly odd as to call attention to herself.

Taking a deep breath, she heaved the pack over her shoulder and left the lavatory, praying for guidance – for a plan. She knew she must find Hunter and the others, and so she asked for the clarity to choose her steps wisely.

As she crossed the foyer, she recalled a clock near the ballroom – and knew once and for all she'd learn if she'd missed her appointed time with Alaric. If by some miracle it was still before midnight, she could yet hope for his words in her heart very soon. But if it was later, as she feared, then she'd simply have to surrender it all to Source.

Head held high, she channeled the balanced queen and willed herself to go unnoticed as she ambled across the foyer. Guests had gathered here and there, chatting and laughing. Feeling a sea of inebriation, she realized their altered senses rendered them less likely to see her. Ahead, mounted on the marble wall, she spied the clock she'd been seeking. As she approached its gold engraved case, her heart dropped – serpentine hands pointed to half past two in the morning. Swallowing this crushing blow she knew she couldn't let herself feel, Elysia allowed instead a deep, centering breath. Before she could take another step, though, she felt someone's focused energy fast approaching from behind. Whirling to meet whoever so clearly had spotted her, she glared into Arianna's wide eyes.

"Elysia," she whispered, her gaze absorbing the unusual attire – and cudgeled appearance. "I've been looking for you."

"Yes, well ... I was detained." She smiled, being careful not to move her lips much, and channeled concealing sonar.

"Please come with me," Arianna urged. Elysia thought she still looked so lovely in her sage green dress and elegant jewelry. "Perhaps we can finally have that conversation."

"Where?"

"My chambers. On the fifth floor."

"I've put forth quite an effort extricating myself from the fifth floor," Elysia muttered. She noticed Arianna studying her gloved hands. "And I'm afraid at any moment the palace guards will again come for me – once they realize my whereabouts."

"You will be safe with me." Her tone was firm, and Elysia could feel she meant what she said.

"No one is safe here," Elysia whispered. "Not even Gadeirus. Perhaps especially not him," she added, sensing Arianna's confidence faltering. "There is much I need to tell you. But quickly, as I must also find my friends. Is there somewhere we could go where we'd likely not be ... overheard?"

"I hadn't thought of being ... overheard," she murmured.

"Would you come to the stables?" Elysia asked, knowing horses would have a calming and grounding effect. She also reasoned it was less likely the eyes and ears so keenly focused on the palace would turn their efforts toward a barn. "I could meet you on the bridle path."

"Yes. Of course," she replied. "Would you allow me to get you some ... proper clothing before we leave?"

"I would welcome that most sincerely." Again, Elysia smiled at her, and she could see how her fattened lips troubled Gadeirus' sister. "Although I think it best if I go on ahead and have you meet me there. I wouldn't want ... certain factions to see you with me."

"All right," she sighed. Grasping Elysia's arms, she squeezed her gently. "I will meet you there just as soon as I change out of this gown and pull some things together for you."

"Thank you, Arianna." Elysia beamed with all her heart's gratitude. "You have no idea how much I appreciate your help right now."

"And you've no idea how deeply I regret that you need assistance in the first place." Tears blurred her kind, dark eyes. "I will see you in a few short minutes."

"Okay." Elysia turned and crossed the foyer to the open entry doors, where only two guards were stationed. She smiled at the closest one as she passed. He nodded, and she realized he probably thought she was a servant going home for the evening.

Slipping into darkness, she gulped the salty air – and prayed pure gratitude. Her quaking legs gathered strength as she hastened along the castle's facade. Before long she reached the rose gardens, their perfume heady beneath a blanketing dew. Had she not loved the fragrance, it may have been overwhelming. Yet she adored it, inhaling deeply and feeling blessed for such a simple pleasure. She felt nearly free of the palace, so much so that her steps seemed sprightly, in spite of all she yet must do this night. As her feet touched the path leading to the stables, she heard a familiar nicker and glimpsed Dara's obsidian coat flashing in the moonlight. Then she met the nervous gaze of one she never expected to see astride the black mare.

"Charlaeus?"

"*Elysia*?" Charlaeus dismounted and raced toward Elysia. Seeing her swollen face, she caught her breath. "You're hurt!"

"It's all right," Elysia whispered. Without thinking, she touched her mouth, and Charlaeus' almond eyes bulged.

"You're *bleeding*!"

"I'm okay. What are you doing here?" For a moment Charlaeus paused, eyeing Elysia uncomfortably.

"Alaric asked me to come."

"Well, I'm most grateful. And really glad to see you." Her words brought a smile to Charlaeus' full lips. Elysia felt herself bursting with unasked questions. She was desperate to hear any word from Alaric, but she knew she couldn't think of that now. "Tell me, how well do you know whoever would be tending the palace stables at this hour?"

"It would probably be Ben in charge tonight," Charlaeus replied. "I don't know him well, but he's a friend of Dehk's. As for the other stable hands, I know not."

"The reason I asked is I'm supposed to meet Arianna along the bridle path in a few minutes." She sighed as she watched Charlaeus absorbing her pummeled appearance. "And while I'm not sure if any of the help can be trusted, I knew the vicinity of the stables had to be a safer choice than speaking with her in the palace."

"I see." Charlaeus was about to say more but halted when horse hooves pounded the path behind them. Elysia caught her breath as Avalon galloped into view. He tossed his mane and slid to a stop. Nostrils flaring, he snorted and blowed – and as she stared up at him, she could see the wild whites of his eyes.

"Hey there, big guy," Elysia murmured. He blew on her face as she petted his high withers.

"He insisted on coming," Charlaeus explained. "Once I saddled Dara, he was inconsolable."

"Let's see if he'll let me ride him to the stables."

"But there's no saddle or bridle. And he's not exactly a beginner's mount –"

"I know." She met the gray gelding's gaze. "Since regaining my memory, I'm not exactly a beginner."

"I don't understand –"

"You will. Very soon," Elysia replied, her eyes never leaving Avalon's as she silently bared her heart to him. *Please. I'm in danger and I need you to carry me. But I can't pull myself up. Will you kneel for me?*

Avalon nickered, dropping to his knees. Mind-messaging her appreciation, Elysia hobbled onto his back. She knew it would only cause more bleeding if she grasped his mane, so she simply centered herself. He eased onto his legs and waited for her command.

"Well, I'll be," Charlaeus said dreamily. "How did you *do* that?"

"I just asked," Elysia whispered. "Because he really, *really* likes to be asked." She smiled at Charlaeus' stunned face. "Are you ready?"

"Yes."

"Let's ride." Again, Elysia asked a question of Avalon; this time, she inquired if he would merge with her. He answered by prancing to Dara's side. Then beneath a bright moon, the horses raced off, their legs parting the path's gathering mist, as Elysia smiled at this aid from the most unexpected of places.

SEVEN

Through jungle cacophony the jaguar sprinted, navigating foliage and fallen logs with equal grace. Here in steamy Jangala, the never-tamed Pleiadian cousin to the elegantly obedient Seven Sisters, wilderness ruled with detachment. Nature's eyes and ears, in all its diverse forms, watched and listened as the big cat bounded by. No whisker twitched nor muscle flexed without notice. And when he twisted mid-air, somersaulting to avoid another big cat, the whole of the rainforest hushed.

Intending a surprise attack, the jaguaress had leaped from a towering Kapok tree. She snarled as the larger male observed and circled. Though a graying muzzle betrayed her age, she regrouped quickly, springing toward him again at top speed. Easily he turned, tripping her with a swish of his three-foot tail. And then he was upon her, pinning her to the forest floor, his gold-green gaze never leaving hers. He held her while her growls softened to grunts. When she quieted, he released her. As she studied him, she changed to an elderly woman wearing a serpent headdress and brown tunic with bone closures.

"Hello, Alaric." In an instant, he morphed into his Moldaarin form. Dressed in a black shirt and pants, he crouched across from her as he rolled his sleeves to the elbow.

"Hello, Ixchel."

"I must be getting old," she muttered in a throaty voice. "Even with a Cerberus bite, you still bested me."

"But I couldn't for much longer. I need your assistance."

"Humph," she snorted. "You shape-shifters are always needing something."

"It's been a thousand years since I've asked for your aid," he whispered.

"Yes." Her golden eyes flashed displeasure. "And you've not forgiven me in all that time."

"Feel into my heart, Ixchel. And you'll know it was never you I was holding in contempt."

"You were the best I ever trained." Her eyes grew distant as she reflected upon another time. "Not that you even required tutelage. Just a little guidance here and there."

"You helped far more than you realize."

"I realize far more than you know." Tears drizzled her sunken cheeks. "And I'm deeply sorry for the anguished centuries you endured because I could not help your beloved. As well as the ... bondage." She shook her head. "Being enslaved is surely those of our kind's worst nightmare."

"I consciously chose to be chained," he replied. "Because it was the only way to protect her. With Elysia and the children gone, my heart was already walled off. What difference could it possibly make if I lived out my existence in a cage?" Jangala buzzed and hummed and chattered to life again, filling the void as he paused. "I cared not what became of me. Rage and little else drove my actions. For a very long time."

"I see that's changed." She smiled knowingly at him. "And so, Source has returned Elysia to your arms."

"It's a long story –"

"Or perhaps it's more accurate to say you've another opportunity before you to save her now very mortal soul." She looked through him. "But then again, you've been saving her for a thousand years. So you're well practiced."

"Practiced, perhaps. Yet not perfected. And I need to get it right this time, Ixchel." Tears misted his gold-green eyes. "I've been alone for a thousand years. But so help me, I'll not spend eternity without her."

"With that Cerberus bite, you could also choose to join her in death, you know."

"Yes." He raked trembling fingers across his brow. "Although I still hope for our happily ever after, here in physical form."

"Of course you do." Wickedly, she laughed. "Any two people who enjoy the flesh as much as you and Elysia *should* be embodied." A smile curved his lips as her eyes again grew distant. "There's to be another child, you know."

"Such a gift would bless us both beyond words." More tears overflowed his lashes. "But Elysia will not long survive if I can't get her essence restored." He looked down at his wrist, at the blackness oozing through the bandage he'd conjured. "And neither will I, if I can't stop the poison leaking from this lesion." He raised raw eyes to hers, and in the few thousand years she'd known him, she'd never seen him look more vulnerable. "Will you help me, Ixchel?"

"It will take time, Alaric," she cautioned. "That's no bee sting."

"I haven't the luxury of time."

"Need I remind you a Cerberus bite bears the most lethal venom in the universe? And that in attempting to extract its poison, it also can summon every hellish experience from your past or present – as well as potential evils yet to come?"

"I'm aware. And, yet my snake lineage offers some protection."

"Yes. *Some* protection. Which is why you're still walking and talking. And trouncing me on my own turf." She rubbed her wrinkled chin. "I've not tried to hurry this process before. In fact, I dread such healings, avoiding them whenever I can. Because they are exquisitely painful. And a shaman feels everything."

"I know."

"If anything, trying to speed things along will only make it a more agonizing experience."

"I'm prepared, Ixchel. As I hope you are," he murmured. "But I'm needed in Alpha Centauri. My help is required to transform Elysia's essence. So, the healing must be finished by nightfall."

"Impossible! You'd be lucky to pass through this shadow in *three* nightfalls."

"It *is* possible." His tone was smooth and relaxed. "It's just never been tried."

"In the name of Oneness," she breathed. "You know not what torment awaits."

"Oh, but I do." He smiled, and she was reminded how impossible it was to refuse him. "I had a mentor once, who schooled me in all the ways of excruciating energetic extractions. She helped prepare me for anything."

"Not for this, *maneesh*." A complex look of respect and abiding affection – and dread – deepened the lines of her face. "Even all your Light-given genius cannot help you fully understand what lies before you."

"I don't need to understand, *devanagari*," he said. In one elegant motion, he was on his feet. And then he kneeled before her, cradling her cheeks. "All I must do is surrender."

"You've always surpassed even my impossible expectations." She smiled, placing leathery hands over his. "And I've never seen your equal, in skill or bravery." Her expression grew serious. "But you will need every ounce of your considerable gifts in order to face this torture. Especially in such an unreasonably short period of time."

"Then you will help me?" His gold-green eyes implored hers, and she sighed.

"Yes, *maneesh*. I will help you."

"Thank you," he whispered, bowing his head before once again meeting her gaze. "Let me know how I can repay this debt, as I realize currency holds no value for you. What can I possibly offer as payment?"

"I see the worry behind your eyes, Alaric, but I assure you there's no need for it," she replied. "Your body is indeed a thing of beauty, but I'm still just as firmly anchored in Right Action as ever. Unlike those from your centuries of servitude, who desecrated your hallowed perfection for their own selfish gratification."

"Ixchel, I –"

"Yours is a temple where Elysia alone should worship," she continued. "I would prefer a more cerebral merging."

"I'm listening."

"Teach with me." The slightest smile crinkled her lips. "When all is settled, and you have once again found your happily ever after, return here periodically. And help me with the seekers who keep coming, thirsting for knowledge. You have much to offer them – as well as me – in the giving of yourself in this way."

"You have my word." Again, he bowed his head. "I would be honored to assist you."

"Very well then." She struggled to stand, and he lifted her to her feet. "I'll need you to come with me to my cave."

"All right." She looked smaller than he remembered. Frail, even. But when she placed her hand on his arm, there was no mistaking the energy powering through his body. In an instant the light shifted, and he found himself in a cave he'd not visited for more than a thousand years. The middle of the chamber held a firepit, where the memory of the morning's blaze still smoldered. Along the limestone perimeter stood stones and crystal clusters. Sacred objects such as feathers and bones and dried plant bundles lined the walls. Multiple headdresses hung in neat rows. Outside the rounded entrance, perhaps a quarter mile in the distance, he could see Lake Maya, Jangala's largest freshwater body. Her lapis expansiveness seemed an appropriate talisman for this undertaking, he thought, as Ixchel wasted no time in setting herb jars and spoons and assorted other items on a nearby table. "Tell me how I can help."

"See to the fire," she instructed. "Fill the kettle with water and bring it to a boil. And then choose a blanket and feather bed. There are flat ones and plump ones and offerings in between." She paused before continuing. "Select your bed wisely, Alaric. You'll be in it a while. And any small measure of comfort it brings is all the ease you'll have once the healing begins."

Without another word, he hoisted the cauldron from its trivet beside the firepit – and hauled it outside to where he remembered her well to be. He filled the kettle and returned to the cave, where he shoveled ashes and stoked the fire. Once flames were flickering, he hung the kettle on the iron bar above the firepit. Then he carried two big barrels from the cave's entrance to the well. He filled those also, returning with a barrel balanced on each shoulder. Carefully, he set them down, and

Ixchel smiled at his strength – and thoughtfulness. She'd not asked him to refill the water supply she liked to keep handy. It was a time-consuming chore of dragging buckets for her, one that seemed to take longer and longer these days. Yet in a matter of minutes he'd given her a week's worth of water, and her heart swelled with gratitude. Watching as he selected a mat from the stack along the wall, she prayed that this time she'd be able to help him.

As the water bubbled, she shuffled toward the kettle, carrying a paddle and knotted linen pouch filled with herbs. Dropping the pouch into wispy steam, she stirred and chanted in the Old Tongue. Alaric covered his chosen feather bed with a blanket and kneeled at her side, bowing his head. She noted his focused presence, and realized in all her very long years, no one had ever held space for her more powerfully. She asked for guidance, to be a clear, pure channel of Highest Light – to be a conduit, a vessel leading him once more to Divine immortality. She asked for swiftness, to be able to carry him with the speed and strength of hawk wings. And she gave thanks, before turning her eyes to his.

"Take the cauldron from the fire," she murmured. She was in a prayer-altered state of clarity, and from this centered space of No-Mind she observed without thought or feeling as he grabbed two thick mitts from the table. He placed the kettle on its trivet as she whispered another prayer. Ladling the decoction into two waiting chalices, she then stirred in a thick liquid she'd mixed separately. Handing one cup to Alaric, she wrapped gnarled fingers around the other. "Drink of this elixir, *maneesh*. It will open and soothe your energetic system for what we are about to do. Be aware – I have no anesthetic that can reach to the depths we're about to explore. But these herbs have some sedating properties, and I will be coaxing you to drink from them periodically as we journey together. Do you understand?"

"Yes." He downed the liquid in two swallows as she sipped from her goblet. Laughing softly, she prepared him another cupful, which he drank just as readily.

"All right. Remove your shirt, as I'll be placing healing amulets on your skin. And lie back on the blanket." Shedding his shirt, he eased himself onto the mat and closed his eyes. She took a knife and, clasping his wrist, slayed the bandage, which she tossed onto the fire. Then she studied the wound's tar-like weeping, as she held the knife blade to the flames. "Breathe deeply, Alaric – as you so masterfully know how – into a state of No-Mind. And realize there's no way for me to soften what I'm about to do." For a moment she held the knife's fiery tip in front of her, as she said one last prayer – and as she allowed him to reach *advaita*. "This is going to hurt," she whispered.

With a surgeon's skill, she seared an "X" across the wound. Alaric willed himself to float above the agony. As he relaxed into No-Mind, his body stilled to the sound of Ixchel's Old Tongue prayers. And though she continued to flay his wrist, periodically scooping out black bloody pools, he neither cried out nor moved.

In his mind's eye, he saw himself standing with Ixchel by an ebony reflecting pool. He held her withered hand, and she squeezed his palm. She gestured for him to peer more closely. He smiled, releasing her as he knelt alone by the mirrored water. And in its glassy surface, he began to see images coming fast and hard, of all his life's heartaches – interspersed only with the faint awareness that Ixchel was having him drink more of the herbal remedy from time to time.

Most of his early life was missing, as he'd largely moved through the world in a happy and fulfilled way then. But most of the last thousand years was replayed, in excruciating slow motion. Starting with the explosion that decimated Moldaaris, before crawling forward to him having to say goodbye to the children once more. Then it seemed like another eternity passed as he again felt himself holding Elysia's lifeless energetic body in his arms, trying to find her a peaceful resting place even as he did his best to deal with his own devastation. Once he saw her being reborn in Ahlaiele, he bore wave after wave of bitter defeat. And loneliness, despite all the surfacing images of the forced company he'd endured over the last several centuries.

He knew not how long he looked upon these horrors, as the venom driving them transformed within his system. He had no conscious awareness his body had been drenched in sweat for hours, or that his chest had been covered at various times by scorpions and spiders and centipedes, and once by more than a hundred dragonflies. But at some point, his seemingly endless past yielded to the present. He revisited his awkwardly painful first meeting with Elysia in Atlantis. He faced her anguish when she met Charlaeus and learned of his relationship with her. He endured her words cutting him anew as they stood on the dock by *Red Lotus*, when her fears of other women clasped hands with his worthiness issues. And he felt his heart nearly break as he watched himself disappear from the boat's bow, knowing not how long it would be before he'd again hold his wife in his arms – yet realizing he once more had no choice but to leave her, if he were indeed going to save her.

Deeper and deeper, he peered into the still waters, thinking perhaps they had finally run their course, as he'd just relived his life purely from the vantage point of pain. But as he continued to gaze into the obsidian mirror, he began to see things unfamiliar to him. Things that perhaps were summoned from his deepest fears of what lay ahead – or were images of what could be happening now. He witnessed Elysia's nude body being kissed and touched by none other than Gadeirus. He eyed her swollen lips and noticed her mapping the king's handprint in order to secure her freedom. In agonizing slow motion, he observed her climbing along the roses outside Gadeirus' balcony – and gasped at every thorn and bee sting. He knew her torment when she sobbed outside a locked window. And he could sense the psychic eyes and ears upon her, before experiencing the depth of angst only continual pursuit can conjure. He suffered a slow descent into rooms of surgical implements and bright lights and blood and terror and jar after jar of unspeakable atrocities. He bore gut-wrenching pain. He sensed dizziness and disorientation in what seemed like unending blackness. Images of fleeing through forests and streams and hiding in caves and crowded markets flashed across his mindscreen. Scenes of the technological wonders that once built an empire being turned toward its destruction despaired his soul. Alliances no one would believe – and the strange bedfellows such allegiances made – shocked and awed him. He gaped at what his inner being revealed, part stunned, part surrendered, part stricken. And then, with a gulp and a shudder, he awoke. For a moment he knew not where he was, thinking perhaps this was the beginning of yet another torturous vision. But he caught sight of Ixchel's welcoming smile and realized he lay in her cave. It was shadowy here, and he saw she'd lit several candles along the room's periphery. The candlelight seemed to flick gold dust into her eyes as she studied him.

"Hello, Alaric," she croaked. "I'm glad to see you emerge. And so soon!"

"Soon?" He managed the barest whisper as he struggled to sit. Yet she pressed him back against the mattress, holding a cup to his parched lips. "I've experienced an endlessness I know not how to fathom. And as such I know not if it's been one night or three."

"It's only been several hours, *maneesh*," she clucked as she wiped a cool cloth across his forehead. "It may seem dark in here to your eyes, but I assure you it's not quite sundown. You've completed your healing as you desired. In a timeframe I thought impossible." She caressed his cheek. "You bore your afflictions alone, as you allowed me only to hold space – and not share in your burdens. But while you spared me any suffering, I cannot imagine what you have endured." She shook her head. "I have no words for the courage you've displayed."

"I assure you I had no awareness of courage." He stared up into her golden gaze. "Only the continual need to surrender to what is. And what is yet to come."

"That is one way of describing true courage."

"Perhaps." He observed his unmarked wrist. "I'd expected a scar at the very least."

"Not on your immortal flesh!" She laughed as he grasped her hand, kissing it. "You are, for all intents and purposes, good as new."

"I am most grateful to you, Ixchel."

"Then show me. By eating something." In one graceful movement, he sat up. Placing a steaming stew bowl in his hands, she ladled one for herself before settling beside him. "You're not the only one who frets if a loved one won't eat."

"Indeed." He smiled as he devoured the soup. "You'll see I don't need encouragement."

"You never did."

When the meal was over and he'd helped clear and wash the dishes, he took a dip in Lake Maya. Emerging from cobalt waters, he felt mostly renewed and refreshed. There were those lingering wretched whispers, though. He dried himself, refocusing his breathing to distract his mind from the horrific visions he'd experienced, images of what Elysia was bearing in his absence – and what they all would soon face.

As much as he longed to be with her, to rush to her aid, he simply couldn't allow himself to make that choice. Not until the essences were secure within Centaurus' sheltering constellation and he'd played his part in their restoration. Only then could he risk exposing her to even greater danger by his very presence – a bet he'd only wager to bring her to Alpha Centauri's primary healing planet for the psychic surgery she so needed. He would not chance attracting Lesser Light eyes and ears to their whereabouts, just so he could indulge in the feel and the sound and the smell and the taste of her.

Donning khaki pants and a cream-colored shirt he'd materialized, he rolled the shirtsleeves to his elbows. As he headed for the cave to say his goodbyes, he promised himself this would be the last unexpected detour. The last wrong turn on the way to happily ever after. The last time he'd allow himself to ache for her.

Instead, he vowed to think only of her laugh. Of her silky skin and gentle heart. The devotion in those deep green eyes. The way her hair teased his shoulder when her body rose above him. And the feel of her opening to receive when she lay beneath. Such thoughts allowed no loneliness or worry. Just a small, satisfied smile.

EIGHT

Energetically cloaked in silver, the *Black Sprite* sped on through light-years of space. When at last the craft entered the constellation Centaurus – the home of Alpha Centauri's star system – Tyrius felt his breathing deepen. And once the greenish planet Rohati came into view, he realized his brow had unknotted. Glancing at Jon, he chuckled.

"Almost there, Jon."

"Yes."

"Anything you're sensing that I should know about? Because you've been quiet. Even for you."

"All bodes well for us to proceed as planned."

"And Alaric and Elysia?" Tyrius prodded, sensing something behind Jon's smooth countenance. "Are things boding well for them, too?"

"Things are being perfectly orchestrated, as we speak," Jon replied, though neither his words nor his cherub-like grin did much to ease Tyrius' mind.

"I know that's your way of telling me Source is running the show. And though it may look dark and dreary to the non-believers in the audience, everything is eventually going to work out in the end. And all us actors will be singing and laughing and dancing our way off the stage, to live happily ever after. The end." His deep belly laugh rang the ship's walls like bells. "Am I right?"

"Indeed, you are," Jon murmured. "Father and I have been sending coded messages via the heart, hence my stillness. You'll be relieved to hear he's freed himself from his ... difficulties. Now he's en route to an unexpected destination, a detour he must make before joining us on Rohati. But he's coming. Just a little later than anticipated."

"Oh, I'm glad, Jon! I'm so glad! And Elysia?"

"At the moment, there's nothing for me to report."

"But you'd let me know if I needed to worry, right?" He gripped the ship's steering column. "Or if I should turn this baby around, head for Atlantis, and start cracking skulls?"

"It's all right, Tyrius," Jon answered in his reassuring tone. "I don't believe skull cracking is going to be necessary." Tyrius nodded, and both men fell silent. In his heart, Jon accepted without doubt that what he'd just said was true. And, yet he knew more than he'd shared. He realized Tyrius' fierce and loyal nature would most likely cause him to re-route the ship for Atlantis if he knew the darkness Elysia was now facing – a bleakness both Alaric and Jon agreed they must not feed with their own fears. And so, in order to best help his mother, as well as deliver the essences as planned, Jon again turned his thoughts to accepting that all was in Divine order and unfolding at the ideal time.

Outside the *Black Sprite's* viewport, Rohati's jade green surface tumbled toward them. Scattered white clouds hugged and released the ship, punctuating views of amethyst mountains staggered amidst sapphire lakes. Just then the communications receiver blinked.

"We're being hailed." Tyrius tapped the keyboard. "Prepare for landing, which will happen in one minute and thirty-nine seconds." Jon settled his lanky frame into the seat and fastened its safety harness, holding a prayerful appreciation that they'd arrived.

The ship descended toward Heera, the capital city. As a pink sunrise broke open its rosy glory, rainbows reflected off towering quartz spires and multi-faceted geodesic domes.

"She's the most beautiful city I've ever seen," Tyrius gasped.

"Yes." Jon lit up as he scanned the horizon. "I was born on Anji, on the other side of Alpha Centauri, but my family often visited here. And I always looked forward to coming, because I thought it was simply the most magical place."

"I can see why." Tyrius pressed a button to lower the craft's four stabilizing legs, and the ship eased onto solid ground. "Well, we've arrived in this most magical of places. Finally!" He cackled as he clapped Jon on the shoulder.

"Indeed." Jon unhooked the harness and opened the stowage compartment at his feet. Gingerly, he removed his pack, as Tyrius stilled the engines.

"Anything your visionary eyes have seen that I should know before we leave this ship?" Tyrius asked, one eyebrow raised.

"No." Jon beamed his cherub grin at Tyrius. "Here you can relax. The Rohatians are Highest Light beings, with pure hearts. I can assure you they'll make us feel most welcome."

"Glad to hear it!"

As they squeezed themselves toward the tiny ship's hull, it parted. A ramp extended, kissing the pearly stone landing surface. Waiting beyond the ramp stood two tall women dressed in lavender.

"Welcome, Jon!" The taller female embraced him, sheer bliss emanating from her almond eyes. "It's been too long."

"Yes, it has." He released her, grinning his seraphim smile. His fingers traced her brown cheek. "Reena, this is Tyrius."

"I'm so pleased to meet you, Tyrius."

"My lady, it's an honor."

"I've missed you, Jon!" The shorter female giggled as she threw herself against him.

"And I've missed you." He cradled her dark curls against his chest. "Tyrius, I'd like you to meet Beeja, who is Reena's sister."

"It's an absolute pleasure, my lady." Beeja hugged him like an old friend as Tyrius chortled.

"Shall we arrange to have your ship detailed?" Reena smiled politely at Tyrius. "Our engineers could easily repair those damaged sections."

"I'd be so grateful for the assistance, Reena." Tyrius bowed before her.

"Very well, then. I'll see to it right away." Reena grasped both men by the elbow. "Shall I accompany you to the palace? Lochana awaits your arrival."

"Of course," Jon responded. Tyrius watched emotion ripple his friend's face, but before he could think what it might mean, the four of them were walking toward a translucent hovercraft. The vessel had no steering wheel or obvious means of maneuverability – only a thin clear rail, shaped as an outline of its oval base, which hovered three feet above the platform. No bars connected the crystalline pieces. When they approached the disk, a railing section opened, and they boarded. Then the rail floated back into place as the vessel whirred to life, lifting into the air.

As the sun climbed sleeping mountains, they neared the palace. Tyrius marveled at Heera's skyline. Quartz wands and orbs mirrored geometric prisms of pink sky. Gazing about, he noticed the city streets and walkways seemed to be fashioned from gold. He felt he'd only begun to drink in Heera's loveliness when a large sphere came into view. Its perfectly rounded sides bore a flower of life engraved patterning. The craft slowed and dropped, and in a matter of moments, they disembarked in front of the building's circular entryway.

Inside, they were bathed in rainbows of light, whose reflections changed continually with the rising sun's trajectory. Skylights shaped in sacred geometric symbols directed sunshine into exquisite patterns upon the golden quartz floor. At the center of the foyer flowed a shimmering screen of water. To either side, along the far walls, crystalline stairs spiraled to upper floors. Reena motioned to the right, and they ascended the staircase.

Once they reached the first landing, Reena led them along a hallway, which opened into a vast chamber. Plants bearing lush foliage and flowers hugged the room's perimeter. Stained-glass windows, portraying sacred geometry patterns, dotted transparent outer walls, through which the exterior's flower of life etching reflected. In the middle of the room sprawled a silk rug, woven to match the windows' colorful symbols. And upon the rug sat an enormous crystal ball, cradled in a gilded frame. Nine elegant chairs circled the sphere; each seat had been honed from clear quartz with purple padded seats and arms. A woman wearing a gold crown, embellished with the flower of life, arose as they approached. A gold belt cinched her pink silk tunic; warmth radiated from her sable eyes.

"Make yourselves at home, my friends," she called out in a clear voice. Her ebony skin glistened. Dark tresses fell in waves reaching her waist. She clasped hands with Tyrius before embracing him. "I am Lochana."

"Your Highness."

"Please," she grinned, her lips parting to reveal perfect teeth once she released him. "Call me Lochana."

"All right. I'm delighted to meet you, Lochana." Tyrius watched her gaze turn to Jon. And he began to suspect the nature of the emotion that had crossed Jon's face when he'd heard her name.

"Hello, Jonastus." She closed her eyes and sighed as Jon's arms enveloped her.

"Hello, Lochana." He pulled away, just far enough to shine his angelic smile at her. "It's been too long."

"It most certainly has." She caressed his cheek, her eyes lingering on his, and then she gestured toward the chairs. "Please, Jon. Won't you and Tyrius sit with me?"

"Of course." He held her seat until she perched regally upon it. Then he slipped into the chair next to hers, as Tyrius sat beside him.

"You've brought the essences?"

"Yes." Jon fingered the pack at his feet. "They're in here."

"Good." She relaxed in her chair. "I thought Alaric would be with you. Our team is planning to collaborate with him."

"He's been delayed. But he most certainly is coming. I expect him by morning."

"Very well." Just then Reena and Beeja returned, carrying platters with crystal teapots and delicate cups. "Thank you, ladies."

"You're most welcome." Reena smiled as the sisters poured steaming liquid into vessels. "Gentlemen, may we offer you some of our golden lotus tea?" Both men nodded, and the siblings filled teacups with a fragrant elixir as Reena glanced at Lochana.

"Is there anything else we can do?"

"Yes. Would you ask Nayaka to join us?"

"Of course." Nodding to Jon and Tyrius, the sisters hastened from the room.

"I'm eager for you to meet Nayaka," the queen said, eyeing her guests. "He leads our Berdaches, the two-spirit souls, who are our most revered healers."

"I'm very much looking forward to meeting him, as somehow, I never have. Despite all my years visiting here," Jon mused.

"Doesn't it make you wonder what else you've missed by your long periods away?" Lochana grinned at Jon, and Tyrius barely stifled a laugh as Lochana's eyes widened in loving recognition. "Nayaka! Please join us, my friend."

Nayaka seemed to glide across the room. He was tall, with brown skin and straight black hair brushing his waist. As he approached, Tyrius could see that the Berdache leader exhibited both male and female characteristics. His shoulders were broad, his muscles beautifully defined, and ample breasts swelled beneath his belted white tunic. His silver eyes shimmered at the queen.

"Good morning, Lochana," he said in a deep, soft voice.

"Good morning, *triyasti*." Lochana rose from her seat, embracing him. Moments later he released her, turning his neon smile to Jon and Tyrius.

"Hello, Jonastus." He took Jon in his arms, as Tyrius wondered how Nayaka had known his name.

"Hello, Nayaka. Please call me Jon."

"All right, Jon." Nayaka then hugged Tyrius. "And hello, Tyrius."

"Pleased to meet you, Nayaka. But how did you know –"

"Your name vibrates off of you in a tonal pattern," Nayaka explained. "I simply read the pattern is all."

"Nayaka has many surprising gifts." Lochana beamed at the healer. "He and his team of assistants have skills that are unique among any I've encountered. Which is what will allow them to restore the essences."

"I'm aware Alaric is in the midst of a necessary detour," Nayaka murmured. "He rests in *advaita* like no other I've met, which facilitates rapid renewal. That's why I requested his presence. But it matters not. We will begin before he arrives." He shifted his glittering gaze to Jon. "May I?"

"Of course." Jon handed the burlap bag to Nayaka, who unwrapped the glowing sphere of Great Central Sun Source energy Alaric had channeled to protect the essences. As Nayaka floated the orb in front of him, he studied its five pearlized essences – and a gleeful smile lit his face.

"That grin tells me all seems to be well with the essences," Tyrius observed.

"Indeed," he whispered. "Better and yet more delicate than I'd anticipated." He glanced at the queen. "I must begin right away."

"Certainly," Lochana replied. "Is there anything I can do or provide for you, *triyasti?*"

"All has been provided, Lochana." The luminous glow his body had been emitting grew brighter. He smiled reassuringly at Jon and Tyrius. "I will be in the Grand Temple," he added, before he and the sphere disappeared.

NINE

When the palace stables loomed into view, Elysia mind-messaged Avalon. The gelding slid to a stop along the tree-lined bridle path. Dara slowed and stood by his shoulder, and Charlaeus met Elysia's gaze.

"This is close enough," Elysia whispered. Before she could say more, her hawk friend screeched, and Avalon fidgeted as galloping hooves echoed in the distance. "On second thought, it's too close. We need to get off the path. *Now!*"

"This way!" Charlaeus whirled Dara, who raced side by side with Avalon through thick ferns. Just as they breached a clearing encircled by ancient oaks, a palace guard regiment thundered by. Elysia realized her senses had all been heightened ever since coming under the influence of Gadeirus' magic wafers. She clapped her hands over her ears, squeezing her eyes shut as the sound tore through her body's sensory receptors.

"Are you all right?" Charlaeus asked once the guards galloped past. Her large, dark eyes bulged with concern.

"I believe so. Just give me a moment." Elysia dropped her hands and closed her eyes. She could hear and smell and even feel things she knew she normally wouldn't be able to discern. Things like Avalon's tiniest muscle flinches – which once seemed like reminders of connection – now felt like little whips against her legs. Things like the rose scent permeating these lands; it had always been a perfume she adored, yet suddenly its sweetness sickened her. Things like the pleasantries being exchanged between one of the guards and the stable manager. She'd always had keen hearing, but what she could pick up at a distance right now astonished her. At the stables, it seemed the guard was showing her picture, because he'd just asked if either the woman in the image or Arianna had been there. When the manager said he'd seen no one, the guard demanded he message him immediately if either woman showed up. There was a moment's hesitation before the manager agreed, and then a heavy stillness until hooves came pounding back toward them. Once the sound faded, Elysia glanced at Charlaeus' worried face. Before she could say anything, though, rapid footfalls caught her breath. "Someone's approaching." She turned her eyes upon the bridle path, and her now-enhanced vision showed surroundings lit up as if she were wearing a headlamp. In an instant, she honed in on Gadeirus' sister. "Wait here." Slipping from Avalon's back, she crept through ferns and saplings until she emerged in front of Arianna, who gasped.

"You startled me," she whispered.

"I apologize." Elysia stared at this kind woman with her heart's raw sincerity. "I simply needed to intercept you before you got to the stables, as the king's guards just left."

"*What?*" For a moment she looked down, brow furrowed in thought – and anger – before again meeting Elysia's eyes. "Why? Especially at this hour?"

"They were looking for us."

"But ... how can that be?"

"It's a long story," Elysia sighed. "One I'd like to share with both you and Charlaeus, who's waiting on horseback not thirty feet away."

"All right." Resolve hardened her face. "Where do you suggest we meet? Where we won't be ... overheard?"

"Perhaps Charlaeus will have an idea, as clearly anywhere near the palace is being watched." She sent a sonar-scrambled image to Avalon, who trotted through tangled greenery to stand by her side. Dara matched him step for step, carrying Charlaeus.

"Hello, Arianna," Charlaeus murmured.

"Hello, Charlaeus." Arianna flashed a welcoming grin. "It's always a pleasure seeing you. Although I must admit these circumstances are ... surprising. And most unusual."

"They are indeed." In one nimble movement, Charlaeus dismounted and stood with the other women.

"We were discussing where it might be safe for us to speak." Elysia said in a hushed tone. "Right now, I'm surrounding us with signal-disrupting sonar, which should help keep us concealed. Although with so many psychic eyes and ears trained upon these grounds, the sonar at best slows their efforts. But clearly it didn't stop them from deciphering that Arianna and I were planning to meet at the stables." She looked at Charlaeus. "You know this island like the back of your hand. Is there any place where we'd likely not be discovered by Gadeirus' seers?"

"I've never before considered being under surveillance, so let me think for a moment." Charlaeus grew quiet, biting her full lips in focused concentration. "What comes to mind is an area I won't name here. But we could reach it quickly with the horses."

"Good," Elysia replied. "Is that okay with you, Arianna?"

"Of course."

"Then we must leave at once." Before Elysia could mind-message

Avalon her desire, he knelt at her feet. "Arianna, would you like to ride with me? I can promise Avalon has one of the smoothest gaits you'll likely experience."

"Certainly." She smiled at the gray horse. "How on earth did you ever train him to do that?" A quizzical look crossed her face as Elysia and Charlaeus chuckled softly.

"Avalon has a reputation for having a mind of his own," Elysia explained, adjusting her shoulder pack before straddling his back. "But all the training in the world has never impressed this horse who already knows everything anyone wants him to do. I've found he just really likes to be asked. And appreciated."

"Amazing." Arianna slipped onto the gelding behind Elysia, and then Avalon arose.

"We'll follow where you lead," Elysia said. Charlaeus nodded and urged Dara into the forest, where shadows stretched deep. Sheltering hemlocks and cedars swallowed any evidence of their passage. A light mist blanketed ferns and vines, stirring into foggy swirls as the horses brushed by. Elysia sensed they'd slipped from the palace grounds once they crossed a stream and emerged in another clearing. Hugging the tree line, they ascended a steep passageway parting a forest and roaring creek. Charlaeus circled Dara around black cliffs until dismounting at last in a grassy meadow. Avalon knelt beside a grazing Dara so Elysia and Arianna could slide off. Charlaeus motioned for the women to follow before leading to an opening in the rocks.

Inside the cave, a dark and cool quietude welcomed them. Elysia could make out several ceiling-to-floor stone pillars. To the far right bubbled a hot spring. She and Arianna followed Charlaeus to an old fire pit surrounded by boulders serving as seats. Sinking onto a smooth stone, Charlaeus watched as Elysia and Arianna settled beside her.

"It should be safe to speak here," Charlaeus said in a low voice, which nonetheless reverberated in the room. "This is one of the island's many vortex centers, which eons ago fell into obscurity in favor of better-known ones closer to Poseidia's downtown."

"And, yet potency remains," Elysia murmured, as energy hummed her body.

"Yes," Charlaeus replied. "A vortex should be able to disrupt or distort any signal emanating from within its field of influence. Considering time pieces and crystalline tabulators and other such devices don't work properly here."

"Exactly what we needed." Elysia turned grateful eyes on Charlaeus. "Thank you for leading us to this place."

"You're welcome." Charlaeus began gathering wood that had been split and stacked nearby. "I'm glad I could assist. I'll start a fire, as its warmth will prove even more helpful."

"You've already helped far more than you realize," Elysia whispered. "Before I continue with all I need to share, I'd like to inquire about your children. Are they settled somewhere safe this night?"

"Indeed, they are." Charlaeus smiled as she lit kindling with matches from a weathered metal chest. "Thank you for asking. When I got Alaric's message, I brought them to my mother's and told her I was needed on urgent business."

"I'm glad to hear it." Elysia swallowed hard, realizing her mouth was dry. "There is so much to tell you both –"

"Elysia, please," Arianna interrupted, her husky voice particularly raspy. "Before you say anything else, I'd like you to be able to change into fresh clothing, if it would please you." Taking a bundle from the pack she carried, she offered it to Elysia.

"Thank you, Arianna." Elysia pawed at the package clumsily with gloved hands before sighing into giggles. "I tried to remove these mitts at the palace with no luck. Perhaps I should first immerse myself in the cave's hot water, so I can ease from this apparel."

"Absolutely." Arianna nodded as Elysia turned and limped toward the steaming spring. Even clothed in the shadows, Elysia bore painfully obvious wounding; the punctures and swellings she'd endured appeared as if her milky skin had been beaten with barbed wire and painted in blood. The women nurtured a growing fire while Elysia hobbled fully dressed into the water. At one point, the Moldaarin queen gasped. Arianna and Charlaeus startled, their heads jerking to see Elysia tugging at ripped material glued to puffy gouges. And then they stared uneasily at one other. Arianna clasped Charlaeus' hand and squeezed hard; they sat in silent solidarity in front of crackling flames until Elysia at long last emerged from the mist, dressed in fresh clothing.

"I simply must know about your ... wounds. And your lips," Arianna muttered as Elysia perched beside her. "Did my brother beat you?"

"He struck my face." With ham hands, Elysia struggled to finish buttoning the brown shirt already glued to her gashes. In the darkness, Charlaeus squeaked, throwing both palms across her gaping mouth.

"Oh, no!" Arianna gasped. "Did he have you removed against your will from the dinner as well?"

"Yes." Elysia could feel the king's sister searching for a considerate way to uncover more of the evening's unpleasantries.

"Now I know not of a delicate way to ask you this," Arianna continued. "But I need to know so I can take appropriate action. Did Gadeirus ... force himself upon you?"

"Not exactly." Tears leaked from her lashes as she recalled her relief at waking fully clothed. "At the dinner, he grabbed my wrist and locked a cuff around it, which rendered me mute and made it impossible to mind-message anyone. He demonstrated how he could cause great pain by waving his hand across the cuff, which encouraged me as much as possible to stay within my spirit and not resist. And then he had his guards carry me to his chambers."

"What happened then?"

"He began to drink heavily and consume multiple wafers he procured from several bags in an armoire," Elysia replied. "He coerced me to drink a potent elixir, most of which I was able to spit out. And then he made me ingest two wafers. I awoke from a heavy sedation, fully clothed, on his bed. He was passed out beside me – also completely dressed. As I prepared to escape, he awakened. He was still quite drunk but expressed remorse for his actions and in fact released me from the cuff." She swallowed hard. "He wished to ... consummate our interaction. And, yet by the grace of Oneness he fell asleep – at least long enough for me to escape out the balcony."

"The *balcony*! But that's five stories high!"

"Yes," Elysia whispered. "I got these lesions from climbing the roses connecting the balcony to the nearest window. While honeybees sacrificed themselves, stinging me repeatedly to help numb the inevitable wounding's pain."

"*What*?!" Arianna's hands flew to her heart.

"Oh, Elysia!" Charlaeus cried out.

"It's all right," Elysia began. "Guards were posted right outside his door, so I did what I had to do –"

"It most certainly is *not* all right!" Arianna snapped. "I'm appalled. Though he's my brother, and I love him dearly, I cannot condone such cruelty. Especially from a king! One I know was raised to be better than this." She shook her head. "May I arrange medical treatment?"

"I so appreciate your concern," Elysia replied. "But there's much more at stake right now. I still don't know where my friends were taken, yet I fear they're in grave danger. I'm also worried about your safety, Arianna – and yours, Charlaeus. Based upon what I overheard Gadeirus' guards saying, I'm not sure who remains to be trusted. And anyone who is allied with me, I'm afraid, will be a target."

"What exactly did they say?" Charlaeus asked.

"They came out onto the balcony as I was climbing," she answered. "They called each other by the names Horasius and Galenius. Then they debated whether or not they should kill Gadeirus in his sleep – and make it look like I'd done it. Apparently, Lorelei had given them a direct order to do so."

"*Lorelei!*" Charlaeus spit the name like bitter melon. "But I thought she was Gadeirus' biggest supporter –"

"I'm sure she's made it appear that way," Elysia murmured. "But her allegiance is to securing her own bid for the crown."

"Did you hear whether or not the guards made a decision?" Arianna asked, her sharp tone wavering.

"They decided they liked Gadeirus better than Lorelei, because he let them get high or get laid whenever they wanted," Elysia answered. "And, his generosity with wafers and women spared him his life this very night, as they said they would tell him of Lorelei's plan once he awoke in the morning."

"I ... just can't believe what's happening. I mean, I –" Arianna stammered.

"Believe this – Gadeirus must be warned," Elysia continued. "I'm not sure what will happen to the guards once they disobey Lorelei's order, as I don't know how much political clout she may have garnered in support of ousting him."

"You would trouble yourself with him after what he did to you?" Dumbfounded, Arianna shook her head.

"Yes." Elysia smiled at Gadeirus' sister. "I see and feel the goodness in him. And I believe much of his wickedness has to do with a ghastly past that led to addiction. Clearly, he needs help." She thought to herself how much he'd softened within the matrix of love and hope she'd channeled throughout his chambers. "He may yet become the wise and honorable king I know he can be. Though not if he's murdered in his bed."

"You amaze me, Elysia." Arianna sputtered at last. "I can't believe the depth of your forgiveness."

"Nor can I," Charlaeus whispered.

"In antiquity's teachings, forgiveness isn't about condoning behavior," Elysia replied. "It's about releasing ourselves and others from whatever has transpired. So we can be free of bitterness that otherwise would fester. And so, we can ultimately still trust in grace and kindness, and that everything is always working out for our best, highest good." She paused as both women gaped at her. "I've released Gadeirus – and myself – because I aspire to an untainted heart – and to yet believe in magic."

"From the moment we met, I felt drawn to you," Arianna said wistfully. "I thought perhaps we would become casual friends, as is so often the case in the life of royals. Acquaintances are generally of a shallow and superficial nature." She laughed. "But you embody depth and wisdom. And you hold a chaste heart, despite my brother's best efforts to the contrary." She again shook her head. "I would welcome a friendship with you, Elysia. I hope you'll let me foster that connection now, by offering my aid and influence, in whatever way I can."

"Your words touch me, Arianna," she replied. "I very much could use your help right now. I fear my friends have been taken to the dungeons somewhere beneath Poseidia. To the ... laboratories. And I know not how to get there. Nor how to gain access once I do."

"The dungeons aren't ... typically discussed," Arianna sighed. "All I know of the labs is what I've gleaned from parties and gatherings. Namely drunken whisperings and paranoid speculation among those seeking to explore conspiracy theories. Hypotheses that indeed seem to become more rampant with every passing day."

"I've been hearing more murmurings about the labs as well," Charlaeus added. "Though it's like you said, Arianna. Often among the inebriated or those looking to gossip. Yet I can't deny the hearsay has grown louder. Particularly since Gadeirus ascended the throne."

"What's my brother *doing*?" Arianna squeezed her eyes shut. "Though I know that train of thought won't be helpful right now." She turned determined dark eyes on Charlaeus. "Perhaps you're aware of more specifics than I? Such as where the entrance might be?"

"I've heard access may be gained beneath the Tuaoi Stone." Charlaeus' almond eyes held a deep uneasiness. "Mostly I've heard that's the only way in. Or out. But there are some who say the city's sewer system offers many access points. Which would make sense if you believe all the conjecture about the ... experiments. Because they would need to be able to dispose readily of ... unspeakable things."

"Yes." Elysia's green gaze was focused on a distant horizon, as thoughts and feelings and impressions flooded her. Such psychic clarity she hadn't felt since her days on Ahlaiele, and she wondered once more what might have been in Gadeirus' wafers. "I feel the truth of what you say, Charlaeus. The official entrance is beneath the Tuaoi Stone. But there's a vast availability through the sewers. An underground network, if you will. And the city's bowels afford the better opportunity to come and go unnoticed."

"Are you suggesting –" Arianna began.

"I'm saying I plan to enter the dungeons. And I'll do it through the sewers," Elysia interrupted. "It feels to me as if one of the main access points nearest the palace would be the best place to begin." She looked at Arianna. "I see a steep stairwell leading from the palace kitchen, a door behind a pantry door. Those stairs descend into tunnels excavated from Poseidia's black bedrock. It's a veritable maze, a subterranean city beneath the city. Have you seen this doorway of which I speak?"

"Yes," Arianna whispered. "I remember it from the first palace tour we took, right before Gadeirus' coronation. My sister Gwenesia was being her usual exuberant self. I believe she in fact opened most of the cupboards as well as the multiple pantries when we were being shown around the kitchen." For a long moment, she paused in reflection. "She'd just investigated the pantry closet you mentioned, Elysia, when she reached for the next door's handle. And that's when the head of housekeeping threw her a stern look and shooed her away. She suggested Gwenesia shouldn't be looking into all the castle's dusty corners." She shook her head. "At the time I didn't think anything of it. But reflecting on it now, well ..."

"From what you've shared, it's clear that the pantry would be as closely monitored as the Tuaoi Stone. So for our purposes, these entryways wouldn't be viable options," Elysia observed. "Yet I'm sensing a sewer grate behind one of the greenhouses. On the west side of the palace, just beyond the rose gardens. Near where the hovercrafts park."

"Is that the best entry point?" Charlaeus asked.

"Yes." Elysia's face held no emotion as she remotely viewed the grate. "It's locked, as are all the grates across the city. But I'm good with locks, so that won't be a hindrance. And if I go while darkness cloaks Poseidia, scrambling my signal with sonar, I should be able to get in and out without attracting attention. That is if I move quickly enough."

"You realize I'm going with you, don't you?" Arianna asked, her eyebrows arching.

"As am I," Charlaeus added.

"You both have no idea how much it means to me that you'd offer such a thing. But –"

"No 'buts,' Elysia." Arianna's voice held compassionate conviction. "You could use our help. Our hands and eyes and ears. And perhaps, if need be, our influence."

"Arianna, if you're seen with me –"

"So be it," she replied. "As it stands now, I am still the king's sister. And that small privilege may yet prove invaluable."

"I can't deny that," Elysia whispered before turning to Charlaeus. "Yet I can't let you risk your life, Charlaeus. Not with such young children. And I know not what being part of this plan could do to your career. Should we be discovered –"

"I didn't join the High Council to play it safe," she stated simply. "I believe all it takes for Lesser Light's triumph is for Highest Light watchdogs to do nothing. And now that I'm aware of the evil at hand, I simply cannot sit by and do nothing."

"But your children –"

"If we don't stop these horrors, my children's lives are already forfeit." Tears spilled from her long lashes. "Truly, it honors me – and my children – to assist you."

"I'm nearly beyond words." Elysia's voice broke. "But thank you. Both of you. From the bottom of my heart."

"You are most welcome, my friend." Arianna's broad grin returned. "Now that we have our alliance, Elysia, do you have an idea of how you'd like to proceed?"

"I do. Or rather, I did ... until I waded into this cave's healing waters." Taking a deep breath, she continued. "My dear friend Khrestes is the Ocean's Oracle. Do you know of her?"

"Only the legends," Charlaeus answered. "She and the merfolk are said to keep watch over Poseidia's waterways."

"I've not heard of Khrestes," Arianna chimed in. "Please enlighten me."

"Khrestes is the merbeings' queen, and she rules alongside my dolphin ancestry to keep not just Poseidia's – but the world's – waterways balanced and healthy."

"Does she really live in an underwater paradise?" Charlaeus asked. "I've seen ancient books bearing detailed color drawings. Magical images of gilded palaces with coral and crystalline gardens."

"Yes, what you've seen is accurate."

"How amazing!" Arianna exclaimed.

"Khrestes herself is even more amazing," Elysia explained. "Source crowned her with equal parts integrity, alchemy, and foresight. She sees through Lesser Light's many veils."

"And so, what did her oracle eyes see and share with you in the hot spring?" Charlaeus asked.

"News that hurts my heart."

"What news?" Arianna leaned closer, her eyes shining coals in the firelight.

"She brings word of a trap. All the psychic eyes and ears turned toward Poseidia are now laser focused on finding me – and thwarting any efforts to aid my friends."

"Oh, Elysia," Charlaeus sighed. "It's not even daybreak, and the hunt has begun."

"Indeed." Elysia smiled, cheering the women's sad faces. "But it's okay. All is unfolding according to Divine timing."

"Then we must abide," Charlaeus whispered.

"Yes."

"What about me?" Arianna asked. "Surely the king's sister may yet prove helpful in some small way?"

"I believe it's best if you visit your brother as soon as possible," Elysia replied. "You should be able to get past his guards – especially since Horasius and Galenius are likely still playing cards outside his door. They will let you into his chambers if you mention Lorelei's plan. Then wake Gadeirus from his drug-induced slumber, if need be, and share with him what I've told you. My concern is I know not who remains within his camp – and who's pitched a tent in Lorelei's. And that wariness extends to Desineus, by the way."

"All right." Arianna nodded. "I should get going. First light will come quickly."

"Agreed," Elysia muttered. "I'd like to suggest that you ride Dara back to the tree sanctuary. Then ask her to wait at least until nightfall for your return. If you are delayed beyond that, tell her to head to Dehk's – she'll know what to do."

"I understand."

"Good. And then after you've met with Gadeirus, if all seems okay, mind-message me the word 'love' and return to meet us here. If for any reason something goes awry, message the word 'split,' and we will come to your aid – psychic trap or no psychic trap."

"Okay."

"Rest assured, I'll be blanketing you in sonar, to help shield your steps – and hide our communications."

"Very well."

"Meanwhile, Charlaeus will wait with me here. At least until Khrestes gives us the go ahead to leave for the sewers." With steady eyes, she held both women's admiring gazes. "Any questions?"

"I think all is perfectly clear," Charlaeus answered.

"As do I." Arianna pulled paper-wrapped bundles from her pack and placed them near the firepit. "I brought food from the palace."

"Thank you," Elysia whispered.

"You're so welcome." Arianna arose and walked toward the hot spring. She retrieved the ripped clothing Elysia had peeled from her lesions. "I plan to show my brother these consequences of his deplorable actions."

"I hear you. As I hope he can," Elysia murmured.

"We shall see." Securing the shredded material inside her backpack, she swung the bundle over her shoulders. "I will take my leave then." Elysia and Charlaeus followed Arianna from the cave. Beneath the moon's golden glow, the horses shone like carved stardust grazing beside the pond. As Arianna approached Dara, the mare raised her head and moved toward her. Moments later, after all three women had hugged, Arianna lifted herself into the saddle. Looking down at the others, she smiled. "I will be in touch – hopefully with a 'love' message – as soon as I can."

"Indeed." Elysia grinned while Charlaeus waved, and then Arianna turned Dara onto the narrow ledge leading back toward the palace. For a few moments, the two women stood in a silent stillness only broken by Dara's fading footfalls. Then Elysia took a deep breath, willing herself to calmness as she at long last had an opportunity to speak with Charlaeus alone. "There's something I'd like to discuss."

"About Alaric?"

"Yes," Elysia sighed. "Honestly, I don't quite know what to say. Except it was never my intention to cause you pain."

"I know," Charlaeus whispered. "It's taken me a minute to work through my own feelings. But I truly see you've always been meant for him." Her eyes misted as her lower lip quivered. "For as long as I've known him, he's been madly in love with you. Even though it seemed he could never again be with you, it mattered not to his heart. And I knew that. I went into our relationship with my eyes wide open – or so I thought. But I foolishly allowed myself to do what I swore I would not. I fell in love with him. In spite of the fact that he'd told me from the beginning he couldn't give me what I sought."

"Charlaeus, I'm so sorry –"

"It's okay," she continued, as tears dripped down her chin. "I don't know how I would have survived the death of my husband if it weren't for Alaric's support. Especially in those early months. After Robaeus died, I felt so lost. So ... alone. And Alaric so deeply understood such a loss. He was kind and gentle and empathetic. And present." She fell still, her gaze on distant days Elysia sensed still close at hand. "He was ... perfect. I'm sure you know what I mean."

"Yes," Elysia replied, her voice breaking. "Yes, I do."

"And, yet there was his impenetrable shield," she continued. "His walled-off heart. He would only allow me so close." Softly, she laughed, a sound bereft of humor. "Besides Jon, I believe I'm the only person he told that you would be coming to Atlantis, in human form. When he spoke of you – even the *possibility* of you – his eyes, his face, his very body burned with a depth of passion I'd never come close to experiencing with him. And though he said you wouldn't remember him, I knew in his mind it made no difference."

"At first, I didn't remember him," Elysia murmured.

"Considering what he said had happened to you, I'm not surprised." She shrugged. "And then when I met you at the gathering, I saw how you treated him no differently than the multitudes of men vying for your attention. So, I knew you couldn't possibly recall who he was." Momentarily she paused, and Elysia wondered again at how she could have been feeling such strong emotion for Alaric at the gathering, and yet Charlaeus had no idea of the depth or nature or even the existence of those feelings. "But I saw his eyes. The way he looked at you. And on some level, even though I didn't want to admit it, I realized a love so strong, so steadfast, over so many centuries, would eventually awaken your memory. I also knew he'd never have to say a word to you. Soon enough you'd hear how he felt, because his whole body, heart, and soul kept screaming how much he loves you."

"Oh, Charlaeus –"

"Do you know he never once told me he loved me?"

"No," Elysia whispered. "I didn't realize that."

"It's because he seems unable to speak anything less than the truth." Charlaeus sighed deeply. "The truth is, Elysia, you're the only woman he's ever loved – completely and forever. And I wanted you to know that, in case you've ever had even the shadow of a doubt."

"Oh, my dear friend!" Elysia hugged Charlaeus hard and sobbed. They cleaved to one another, ribcages heaving, until their breathing stilled. At last, Charlaeus pulled back, the smallest smile curving her full lips.

"Thank you, Elysia. I think I needed that."

"I know I did." Tenderly, she brushed dark curls from Charlaeus' forehead.

"There's one other thing I must mention."

"I'm listening."

"I told you before how Alaric messaged me at midnight when he couldn't get through to you."

"Yes." Closing her eyes, Elysia let out a long, trembling breath. "I knew something had prevented him from contacting me earlier, as we'd initially planned."

"All he said was he'd been delayed," she continued. "And he knew you couldn't hear him because of a potent drug's influence. Which is why he got in touch with me – and why he asked me to help you."

"I'm just so grateful you came," Elysia murmured through tears. "Did he say anything else?"

"He said he'd message you when he could be sure he's not being traced, and yet he couldn't be more specific than that." She clasped Elysia's hand and squeezed it reassuringly. "But he wanted you to know he loves you. And the essences are on their way to where they will be restored."

"*Yes!*" Elysia squeezed Charlaeus once more. "That at least means he escaped the initial danger. The one that had me so worried."

"Yes. He sounded relieved."

"On that high note, I suppose we should settle in and see if we can sleep." Charlaeus nodded, and they walked side by side back to the firepit. Reaching for one of the bundles Arianna had left, Elysia fumbled it open to reveal bread and cheese and crackers. "But I think we should have at least a little nourishment before we rest."

As they shared the palace provisions, Elysia felt full of her own thoughts. She wondered how long they'd have to wait until Khrestes gave her blessing for them to disappear beneath the city. Yet even when they could begin their descent into those hellish tunnels, she knew it would only be the first step – one inch forward in a thousand-mile trek. But raw weariness only fed forlornness. She recognized that in this vibrational universe, where like attracts like, she'd never see the answer as long as she kept staring at the problem. She prayed that sleep would stop her obsessing over not only finding her friends – but finding them in time.

TEN

Arianna hurried without appearing to hasten along the palace's fifth level. As far as she knew, this floor had been reserved for Gadeirus and his immediate family. Yet she couldn't help noticing all the "do not disturb" signs hanging askew from several doorknobs. She wondered whom he would have invited up here for the night – and why.

Ahead, she spied two guards camped outside her brother's chambers. Just as Elysia had predicted, they were sprawled on the floor, playing cards. Apparently absorbed in the game as well, because she got within ten feet of them before either looked up. Once they noticed her, they tossed the cards in a heap and scrambled to their feet. Their sloppy stewardship left Arianna aghast. Yet shock boiled to rage once she glimpsed bloodshot eyes.

"Hello, Horasius and Galenius."

"Good morning, Lady Arianna," they mumbled in unison as they bowed clumsily before her.

"I'm here to see my brother."

"I'm sorry, my lady," Galenius replied. He had short brown curls and a stocky build. "We've orders not to allow anyone in until he wakes up."

"I'm not just anyone." She spoke with unsettling authority. They shifted their feet, and then fair-haired Horasius smiled.

"Indeed, you're not, my lady. And, yet I'm afraid this is a ... delicate matter." He bowed his head before his glassy gray eyes once more met her gaze. "You see, the king is not alone. And he wishes not to be disturbed."

"I'm well aware he's not alone," she said evenly. "And I know who was dragged in there against her wishes. As well as who dragged her."

"My lady, let me explain –" Galenius began.

"I don't require an explanation – only his audience." She moved closer, dark eyes boring their ashen faces. "You see, gentlemen, I also know what Lorelei commanded you to do. And I'm here to make sure that's one order you disobeyed."

"Please, Lady Arianna –" Horasius sputtered.

"The only thing that will please me is you opening that door," she replied. "Right now." They gaped at each other, and then Horasius shrugged.

"All right, my lady." Galenius' face flashed disapproval before finding the polite smile of his training. "Please be aware. He doesn't take kindly to being awakened."

"I spent most of my youth making sure he got up for lessons and commitments, so believe me, this is nothing new." As Galenius reached toward the keyless entry, she touched his arm. "There's one more thing, before you unlock this door."

"Yes, my lady?"

"I expect you and Horasius to disappear for twenty minutes, once you allow me into his chambers."

"Forgive me, my lady, but I don't understand –"

"I need to be able to get the lovely red-haired diplomat out of here in as discreet a manner as possible," she murmured. "I'm sure you can understand that."

"Well, I, uh –" Horasius stammered.

"The less you know, the fewer questions there will be for you. The fewer ... possible implications, if you will." Horasius protested until Galenius grabbed his forearm, silencing him.

"Of course, my lady." Galenius extended another civil smile, one that never touched his eyes. Waving his hand over the lock, he inched the door open before turning to Arianna. "We will return in twenty minutes."

"Thank you, Galenius." Slipping inside, she shoved the massive door shut and marched through the foyer. A gagging bouquet greeted her – the sickening stench of cigarette butts and stale wine and ale souring in steins. Crossing the expansive floor, she spied half-empty beer mugs among a drained decanter and multiple silk bags littering the bedside table and bureau. As she wondered just how many wafers had been strewn across these rosewood surfaces, the large painting watching over this mess drew her eye. She gasped as she gaped at the most beautiful rendering of Elysia she could imagine. When she saw her brother depicted as Elysia's partner, her mouth fell open in surprise – as well as dawning comprehension.

Crossing to the balcony doors, she eased them open before gazing upon Gadeirus. He lay sleeping, his head tilted to the side. As she moved nearer, she saw peace on his face – a contentment she'd never before witnessed – not even in childhood. Ascending rosewood stairs to his lofty bed, she settled her pack at its foot and stroked his matted hair.

"Good morning, little brother," she whispered. He slumbered on, undisturbed, continuing to breathe deeply, rhythmically. She grasped his shoulders and shook him. "Wake up, Gadeirus. I need to speak with you."

"Hmmm," he muttered.

"Wake up," she insisted, her hands jiggling him. "Please. It's urgent." His eyes struggled into slits. For a moment he peered at her, unseeing, bewildered. And then his raven's eyes opened wide. He caught his breath, whipping his head to the other side of the bed, and she realized he was searching for Elysia.

"Damn it to hell, Ari!" She watched him reach across the bed, groping for the nightstand wafers. Popping a few in his mouth, he struggled to sit up straight. "What are you *doing* here?!" he grumbled as he slid from the bed.

"We have to talk."

"Light damn it! Right *now*?" He stumbled as he stepped into his pants. "It must still be the middle of the night! What Light-damned thing is so urgent –"

"Stop swearing." Her curt command stifled him. He scowled while he sized up the room. "And you can quit looking for Elysia. She's no longer here."

"How did you know –"

"I know much more than you'd like me to, little brother," she murmured. "Much more than I care to know, actually."

"I see." He climbed back onto the bed. "I'm listening."

"Come outside with me."

"Why?"

"Please. I need some air. It's rather ... oppressive in here."

"All right." Yawning, he strode to the balcony's parted double doors. Throwing them wide open, he sauntered into a serenity only the edge of daybreak commands. She followed, watching him stretch beneath moonbeams. A breeze carried the sea's scent, washing their hair with it, and she felt grateful for this cleansing. In the distance, she heard birds singing and knew daylight was fast approaching. Gadeirus then lounged against the stone balustrade. She closed the doors and joined him, resting her elbows on cool gray stone.

"I wanted to speak to you out here, because it may be harder for your seers to pick up on our conversation," Arianna began.

"Go on."

"There is much you should know, and no easy way for me to say any of it," she continued. "This very night, Lorelei issued an order for your guards to murder you in your sleep. And make it look like Elysia had done it."

"*What*?!" She noticed his eyes had sharpened since she first awakened him. "I thought for sure Lorelei was in my court," he muttered. "So far, I've given everything she's asked of me."

"Everything but the crown from your head," she replied. "Which is what she wants."

"So what stopped them –"

"The guards prefer you to Lorelei." She observed his greenish countenance, his tangled hair, those somber eyes. "They've grown quite fond of the way you give them female company and let them get high. As they are right now which – by the way – if there really was a threat at your door, neither Galenius nor Horasius is in any shape to deal with it."

"How do you know about Lorelei?"

"Elysia told me."

"Elysia?" She watched concern crease his brow. "What happened to her? Did anyone hurt her in any way?"

"It's an odd thing for you to worry about her being harmed." Tears misted her eyes. "I saw her face, Gadeirus."

"I know, Ari." He shielded his eyes with his hands. She heard broken breathing. Then he looked at her, his lashes wet. "I'm horrified by what I did."

"And, yet in spite of how you treated her, she remains concerned for your safety." She shook her head. "I still can't grasp how pure she is – how loving – to be able to overlook your mistreatment and believe in your inherent goodness."

"She is an angel," he sobbed as he looked out over the city lights. "And Light damn me to hell for wanting to drag her into depravity with me." Moments passed, and he quieted, raising raven's eyes to his sister's calm stare. "How did she ... escape? I can call it nothing but that, for I had her brought to these chambers against her will in the first place."

"Before I answer you, I should tell you the guards still believe she's here with you. I sent them away for twenty minutes when they first let me in, as I told them I had to get the foreign ambassador out of here in as discreet a manner as possible."

"I understand."

"That being said, you won't believe what else I'm about to utter, so I'll show you instead." Arianna grasped Gadeirus' shredded clothing from her pack and spread it over the railing. He studied the white blood-soaked shirt she placed on top.

"What is the meaning of this?" he whispered.

"She took this clothing from your wardrobe and escaped out this balcony," she muttered. "She crawled five stories in the air, across those climbing roses – all the while suffering thorns and bee stings – until she reached the nearest window."

"But how –"

"How could anyone endure that kind of pain?" Arianna arched her eyebrows at him. "Or for that matter, how could anyone prepare to inch forward for that long – while five stories above the ground?" He winced, and she leaned closer. "I saw her body, Gadeirus. Not just her hands and feet, but her whole body is swollen and gouged and bleeding. Because of you."

"Ari, please – I –"

"She overheard the guards, who discussed Lorelei's orders on your balcony while Elysia was clinging to your castle," she continued. "I happened to see her once she'd reached the ground, and I was shocked at her appearance. We agreed to meet someplace, as she was worried your seers would overhear us. And in fact, it wasn't long before a regiment on horseback came looking for us, right where we said we'd be."

"I didn't sanction that, Ari." Anger flamed his obsidian gaze. "I have no such orders issued."

"Well, *someone* did," she whispered. "Someone the guards are obeying."

"Damn it to hell." He squeezed his eyes shut. "Desineus had similar concerns when I met with him a few days ago. Misgivings I dismissed as paranoid." He shook his head. "I should have listened."

"You need to find out who is still loyal to you. And who isn't."

"Indeed," he replied. "I will meet with Desineus at first light. It's likely he's already begun this investigation."

"Be wary even of Desineus, little brother," she cautioned. "You need to be exceedingly careful."

"I've certainly heard that before." He sighed. "It's not my nature, you know. But I see my very life may depend on developing this attribute."

"It would make me happy if you did." She placed her hand on his, and he clasped her fingers. "There's something else that would please me."

"What is it?"

"Have the Ahlaielians released from where they've been taken."

"I wasn't aware –"

"You mean you didn't have them arrested at the dinner?"

"No," he whispered. "I was rather ... inebriated. And all my focus was on Elysia."

"Gadeirus, someone has been orchestrating quite a lot behind your back." Apprehension flooded her features. "And even many things right under your nose."

"Apparently."

"So, where would they be?"

"The only logical place would be the dungeons." His eyes pierced hers. "There is a vast ... prison network, beneath the palace and stretching far across Poseidia."

"Can you have them released?" Her eyes beseeched his, and again he sighed.

"If you'd asked me that yesterday, I would have said absolutely." He shook his head. "And, yet at the moment, I'm utterly unsure if I can. If I still have enough of the ... absolute authority of my office."

"Then you can do nothing?" He brought her fingers to his lips and kissed them.

"Officially? I'd say there's very little I can do, until I can determine just how damaged I am politically." He grinned pure mischief. "But *unofficially*? I have this acquaintance, you see. And I believe he can help very much with this ... situation."

"I'm almost afraid to ask about this ... acquaintance," she began, and he chortled. "You're not calling him a friend, so how well do you know him? And what makes you think you can trust him?"

"Jack is a rogue, associated with all yet affiliated with none," he explained. "He's a hybrid. Mostly human, a tiny part shape-shifter – although he can't truly change form. In fact, he's bereft of many shape-shifting skills. But he's good with messaging. And he can think on his feet, so he's an unbeatable messenger for hire. He always makes it clear his allegiance is to himself and the job, so he's the perfect type to be trusted. That is, if you pay him." He cackled again. "And I've always paid him handsomely. I've also ... indulged with him before. In all instances, I've found him to be refreshingly candid." He glanced at her eager face. "He's long been associated with Alaric as well, so I'm sure he wouldn't mind a job helping Elysia and the Ahlaielians."

"Will you contact him?"

"I'll do it now." Closing his eyes, he sighed once more. Arianna peered out across Poseidia as dawn tugged at the night's ebony blanket. In the distance, the city's pearly bridges lit passageways to the markets, and she marveled at how she never tired of her native land's beauty, no matter the time of day. Just then Gadeirus chuckled, and she turned quizzical eyes upon his crazed face.

"I'll be Light-damned if Jack isn't here on a job as we speak."

"So he's available?"

"Yes."

"And you've hired him?"

"Yes. He will contact you within the hour."

"Thank you, little brother." She embraced him, and he nestled his chin against her shoulder. "I cannot explain it because I've only known her briefly. But I already care deeply for Elysia."

"She has that effect."

"I do not mean to pry, Gadeirus, so you don't have to answer me," she whispered. "Yet I sense you have strong feelings yourself for Elysia." Softly he laughed, releasing her and lounging against the balustrade. Folding his arms, he peered into her.

"What gave me away?" Shaking his head, his lips curved into a self-deprecating smile. "Was it the painting? The one I admired so much when I moved here that I simply had to have myself rendered as the one holding her?"

"Well, I –"

"Or maybe the fact that this very night I stole her from her marriage bed? Beyond furious she'd gone ahead and married Alaric not long after I lost my temper – and my one chance to woo her myself?"

"I didn't realize –"

"I have my obsessions, Ari," he murmured. "And my addictions. Yet if I'm honest, she's the most potent drug that's ever held sway over me."

"Oh, Gadeirus." Tears splashed from her lashes. She laid her hand upon his folded arms. "I'm truly sorry."

"You don't know the half of it," he croaked. "I've planned and plotted and schemed and seduced – and things much, much more terrible – all in the name of bringing her to me. To make her my queen. So I could possess her. So I could satisfy this hunger I've never been able to feed." Running trembly hands through his hair, he shook his head. "I'd never once considered her feelings. What she may want – or whom."

"It sounds as if you're having a change of heart." She cupped his cheek. "A softening. Or maybe an opening."

"Something most definitely has shifted." He clasped her hands. "In spite of my cruelty and barbaric behavior, on this very night she kissed me. With all the goodness and love in her heart. She extended herself to me, and for the first time in my life, I became aware of depths and feelings and ... sensitivities I must have long ago rejected within myself." Tears misted his eyes. "She's healed something within me, Ari. With just the sweetest touch of her lips, somehow, she's quelled the hunger so I'm no longer ravenous."

"I'm really glad to hear that, Gadeirus." Moving closer, she embraced him, resting her head against his chest. "I so want you to be at peace."

"I never before felt peace was possible," he murmured. "But it is, Ari. Somehow, she's made me *feel* that it is." He hugged her tightly. "And though I'm still crazy in love with her, I'm resolved I'll not cause her any more pain. I will choose, instead, to help her in any way I can. Just as she's helped me."

"You've never made me prouder than this night." She pulled away far enough to beam at him. "I should go, and let you prepare to meet with Desineus. Which makes me think to ask, little brother ... do you believe you can trust him?"

"Desineus?"

"Yes."

"He's my oldest friend, you know."

"Yes," she smiled. "I fondly remember us all growing up together. And he always looked up to you. Even then."

"I realize that." He released her, turning once more to look out over the city. "Desineus has had my back through every phase of my life. From the playground to planning Poseidia's future. And during all our long years together, not once have I questioned his loyalty."

"These are unusual times, Gadeirus." She leaned on the balustrade beside him. "I'm not saying he's capable of betrayal. But in light of all we know is going on –"

"And all that we don't know," he added.

"Yes. Just promise me you'll be observant."

"You have my word, Ari." Wickedness cracked his lips. "And though you haven't asked it of me, I want you to know I plan to curtail my ... indulgences. All of them. As of right now."

"You don't know how happy it makes me to hear you say that. Or how relieved."

"I *want* you to be happy. And to have no need for relief." He shook his head. "For too long now, I've given you cause for angst."

"You know how I worry –"

"But not on my account. Not anymore." He brushed her cheek with his fingers. "So, you will be seeing Elysia?"

"Yes."

"You're venturing into the tunnels, then?"

"Yes." She started to mention Khrestes, but on second thought, it seemed best to hold her tongue.

"Not without some measure of protection. Wait here." He disappeared into his chambers; she breathed cool salty air and felt grateful for all the positive changes transforming her brother. When he at last returned, he handed her a wrapped bundle.

"What's this?"

"A measure of protection," he murmured. "Each letter bears my official seal. Inside is written *mira asirvada*, which means 'my blessings' in the Old Tongue." He lazed against the bannister on one elbow, his eyes intent on hers. "It's a code allowing its bearer essentially a free pass. The ability to proceed, to move forward with an intended action, with the crown's full support."

"But what exactly –"

"Present one of these letters to anyone questioning you in the tunnels. Or anywhere else in Poseidia, for that matter. Any guard, or anyone acting in any leadership capacity, will recognize its message, and allow what you're requesting or doing," he said. "That is, if they're still loyal to me."

"It appears I may soon be finding out firsthand who continues to support you."

"Yes."

"Thank you, Gadeirus." She cradled the bundle before tucking it into her pack. "You've brought me a measure of comfort with this unsettling task at hand."

"I simply can't allow you to descend into Poseidia's deep pit without as much assistance as I can provide." He placed a hand over hers. "And that includes Jack, who'll meet you as soon as you confirm you're on your way."

"Very well then."

"I'd like nothing more than to accompany you myself," he added. "To see to it you are safe and unimpeded in your journey. Yet I must meet with Desineus and see what's down Poseidia's rabbit hole of betrayal."

"It's going to be all right, little brother." She hugged him hard. "You weren't murdered in your sleep this night. So, we may move forth with our eyes and hearts and minds wide open toward a solution. Which I hope will bring your kingdom reigning peace."

"Yes. That is my hope as well." Gently, he released her. "You must promise me you will be careful, Ari."

"I believe I've always been the careful one in our family, have I not?" They both laughed, and he brushed her cheek with light fingers.

"You have at that."

"Should I mind-message you later?"

"No. You'd be too easy for any number of parties to trace." He eyed her carefully. "Only have Jack contact me. He knows the art of untraceable messaging."

"All right."

"If you run into any resistance whatsoever, have Jack let me know." His black eyes bored into hers. "I don't want you fretting, as I will find a way to help you."

"Indeed." She kissed his cheek. "I love you, Gadeirus. With all my heart I do."

"I love you, too, Ari." He watched as she slipped through the balcony doors. When she disappeared, he spied the shredded material strewn upon the balustrade.

With quaking fingers, he lifted the bloody tatters and breathed deeply of Elysia. The smell that had swallowed him as he caressed her in his bed. The sweet scent of an angel. Collapsing in tears, he buried his face in soiled silk. He'd meant what he said to Ari, that he would cause Elysia no more torment. No matter how excruciating that choice would be to him personally, he would abide. He realized he must stop thinking of her, as that attention would only keep reopening his wounds. But not before allowing himself to mourn her loss, and all she'd allowed him to taste with that one delicious kiss. By holding her, he now knew what it felt like to hold the world. And for once – even for his swollen ego that had overstretched an already ambitious life trajectory – it was enough.

ELEVEN

"Are you asleep?"

"Mmmm-hmmm," Charlaeus mumbled.

"I know it's late," Elysia continued, kneeling upon the bedroll beside her own. "But Khrestes just messaged me."

"What? Really?" Stifling a yawn, she propped herself awake on one elbow. The firelight sparkled in her eyes. "What did she tell you?"

"She said on this thirty-third night we've sheltered within this cave, a portal opened. An opportunity to move forward." Elysia held her hands in prayer position. "The Ocean's Oracle says we may make our way into Poseidia's underbelly."

"At last," Charlaeus sighed.

"Yes. Are you ready?"

"Can one ever be ready to descend into hell?" Charlaeus shook her head. "Yet waiting to ride into war is worse than battlefield sword-swinging. I'm grateful Arianna keeps checking in on my children. And I accept that it's time to go."

"Agreed." Rummaging inside her pack, Elysia grabbed wrapped bread and nuts Arianna had brought on her most recent visit. "Here. I think we should have a little nourishment before these wee hours unfold." As they chewed, Elysia settled more supplies into the pack while Charlaeus folded their bedrolls and stowed camping gear. Dousing the fire, the women hugged and then heaved packs across their shoulders. As they walked out into moonlit shadows, Elysia messaged Avalon. The gelding trotted up and lowered himself, letting Elysia slip easily onto his back. Once Charlaeus climbed behind her, Elysia asked Avalon to carry them to Poseidia. To the palace rose gardens, where the women would disappear into the city's bowels – and where this inevitable journey's next leg would unfold.

Winding through sheltering trees, they heard owls hooting encouragement while Elysia's hawk friend screeched support. Their passage felt timeless, surreal, engulfed in fog as dew kissed their chilly cheeks. Hours passed and the terrain softened; they rode by the palace stables and freed Avalon in the tree sanctuary before creeping toward the rose gardens' western edge. Beneath bright moonbeams, Elysia and Charlaeus at last knelt beside the sewer grate. A dull bronze cover camouflaged its grassy location. Elysia shivered as she stared at the metal's engraved spiral design. She couldn't help thinking how such beauty mocked the horrors stirring beneath. Elysia scanned the covering, feeling into its invisible mechanism, until the lock yielded.

"Help me slide it," she whispered to Charlaeus. Together, they heaved the cover open enough to squeeze through. "Wait here. Sonar will show what's ahead." Elysia descended a ladder fastened to the black rock below, and minutes crept by. Charlaeus felt alone hearing her heart's hammering, as the reality of what they were doing – and where they were going – seeped in. Just as she feared she might panic, she heard Elysia's light steps. "The way is clear and quiet. At least for now," she murmured from below the grate. "It's dark, though, so you won't be able to see much. But I can find our way forward with echolocation."

"All right." Charlaeus felt relieved Elysia would be leading. "Once I climb onto the ladder, should I pull the grate closed?"

"Yes," Elysia replied. "As tempted as I am to leave it askew, to allow for a fast exit, if need be, I'm more concerned about someone noticing it's been moved – which could be the littlest thing that prompts our discovery."

"Of course." Charlaeus edged beneath the grate, her feet groping for rungs as Elysia guided her boots. Then she tugged until the cover thudded into place.

"Great," Elysia whispered. "Now just keep climbing down. When your feet touch bottom, you'll be standing on a stone ledge. I'll reach for your hand. Remember that I can feel what's around us. But in general, we'll need to keep our backs to the wall, as the ledge is only about a foot wide. Then there's a drop-off of a few feet, and below that is the water. Be prepared, as we're entering a sewage system. There's a foul odor. And sounds echo crazily down here. So, the splashing may take some getting used to."

"I understand." Charlaeus lowered herself along the ladder. She wasn't sure how far she'd dropped before her feet reached stone, but it seemed to be at least thirty feet, judging from the number of rungs she'd grasped and released. Elysia helped ease her against the wall, then they clasped hands and inched sideways together in pitch blackness. The stench stung Charlaeus' eyes. Every so often she flinched when the fluids rushing by gurgled unexpectedly. She noticed Elysia's hand stayed steady. Here in Poseidia's bowels, Charlaeus had no concept of time. It seemed they'd been easing their way along the ledge perhaps for hours, when Elysia finally paused.

"Ahead is a chute, one of many the labs use to dump waste," she whispered. "I've sonared it, and nobody seems to be anywhere near it right now. From what I sense, it's much closer to us than the nearest maintenance stairs leading down here. And it's not terribly steep, at least until the very top, which is to our advantage. So, I'd like for us to climb up through it. But I must warn you ... it is slick with ... substances we dare not imagine. Can you possibly be okay with that?"

"As okay as I can be."

"All right. Follow me." Elysia squeezed into a metal tube. As sonar had informed her, the chute angled upward. Her hands slipped along greasy walls. The chute smelled of death and all that can lead to it. Praying and surrendering, she kept inching upward while Charlaeus crept along behind.

When they reached the last few feet, the chute curved into a vertical pipe. Elysia braced herself with one foot against the angled section. She explored every foothold imaginable, then realized the only way she might be able to ascend through the slime was with bare hands and feet. She stuffed gloves and shoes into her pack as Charlaeus followed her lead. Bit by bit she moved upward, until she was close enough to sonar the tube's covering. It was a metal grate much like the one behind the greenhouse – only smaller. Feeling along the grate's frame, she sonared its lock mechanism until she heard an audible "click," and then slid it aside.

Wedging through the cramped opening, a feat made easier due to chute slime greasing her body, Elysia hoisted herself into a seated position. From there, she slipped each leg free. Sensing in all directions, she determined it was at least safe enough for them to proceed. She shoved the grate wide before helping Charlaeus through. Together, they heaved it back into place before blinking at their bright white surroundings; they found themselves standing in what appeared to be a surgical suite within Poseidia's vast underground city.

As opposed to black bedrock and slimy sewer darkness, this room radiated sterile cleanliness. Downlights flooded the seamless white quartz walls, floors, and ceiling. Crystalline cabinets bore glass jars brimming with rainbow-colored liquids. In lower cabinets, multiple shelves held clear trays; Elysia's eyes bulged at all the chisels and scalpels, scissors and saws, and probes and picks. One tray's large needle assortment looked to be composites of copper, silver, and gold. On the lowest shelves, white tunic tops and matching pants had been stacked beside bins of surgical gloves, masks, and shoe/hair coverings.

In the middle of the room rested a metal table, with foot pedals on one end and restraining clamps on the other. Elysia and Charlaeus grimaced at these instruments of torture before realizing just how much reddish sludge was pooling around their feet.

"We need to ... clean up a bit," Elysia whispered.

"Yes."

Elysia spied a hose within arm's length of the grate. It seemed designed for washing things down the very drain from which they'd emerged. She opened its nozzle, and the two women washed their extremities in icy water.

Next to the cabinets hung a host of clear face shields. Crisp lab coats draped the wall by the room's double sink. On its countertop rested two stacks of folded towels and a soap dispenser. Elysia snatched some towels, and she and Charlaeus wiped themselves and the floor. Right next to the counter, a curtain stood ajar, exposing three shelves holding more orderly supplies. She glanced at Charlaeus, whose wide eyes bored into her. But before she could say anything, she sensed activity outside the door on the far side of the room.

"People are coming." She hurried Charlaeus into the closet, fumbling its door shut as the room's entryway slid open. The women's hearts raced while they heard a scuffle and something being dragged. A female's muffled crying ensued when the door glided shut. Charlaeus grabbed Elysia's hand as two men laughed.

"This one's feisty!" A deep voice complained amid sounds of struggling.

"I seem to get all the feisty ones."

"Well, I seem to get the half-dead ones. And I much prefer feisty." The men cackled again, a sound that chilled Charlaeus' spine. She squeezed Elysia's hand.

"What's this one in for?"

"Lemme look." There was an audible beep. "Third-eye removal."

"What time?"

"In half an hour."

"Then we better get to prepping her." Again, the men chuckled while the women prayed. Elysia and Charlaeus had no choice but to hear two men taking turns violating their captive.

"I could get used to feisty," the deep voice sighed.

"You're not numbing her, right?"

"No, mate. I've always been told they want 'em fully awake – and able to feel."

"Just making sure." Cabinet doors whirred. Metal clanged and feet shuffled before the entry once again opened and closed. Elysia barely breathed in the crypt-like quiet. She sonared the hallway, which appeared empty, before pushing the door wide.

She and Charlaeus emerged to a naked and trembling female strapped to the table. Seeing them, the red-haired woman gasped and moaned in surprise. Elysia hurried over, motioning for her to be still as she sonared calming signals. The woman, who was once a mermaid, settled down. She looked at Elysia, her green eyes curious – and perhaps the slightest bit hopeful. She had a sparkling indigo jewel embedded in her third eye. Her body bore barely discernible surgical scars from where scales had been removed, and where human-looking legs had replaced what once was her tail. Elysia waved her hands across the table clamps, opening them. She took the gag from the woman's mouth and helped her sit up.

"We don't have much time," Elysia whispered, and the woman nodded. "We'll open the sewer grate for you in the floor, which is how we came up into this room. If you slide down, you'll come to a ledge, and the sewage water runs about three feet below that. I know that liquid's not pleasing, but it will lead you to the sea if you can bear it."

"I can bear it," the woman croaked. "It will be nothing after what I've borne here."

"Can you still breathe underwater? And is your sonar intact?" Elysia asked.

"Yes," she replied. "Within these walls, my sonar's been blocked so I couldn't wield it against them. But it hasn't yet been surgically altered."

"All right then. I just have two more questions for you, which I'll ask while we get you over to the drain." Gently, she and Charlaeus carried the woman to the hatch. Then the woman leaned on Elysia as Charlaeus slid open the grate.

"Okay."

"Have you seen three men and a woman who were brought in a month ago? One of the men is tall, and he has ... our green eyes."

"I have not, but the labs sprawl like a huge maze. I've only been here a few days," she replied. "New inmates are brought to the holding area first, then assigned to a section based upon the ... intended experimentation."

"And do you know how we would find the holding area?"

"It's near the middle of the complex," she whispered. "If you search for it by sonar, you'll know it by the sheer concentration of bodies that are housed there, in cramped quarters."

"Heading north?"

"Yes."

"One other question," Elysia murmured. "Would we be likely to walk about unnoticed if we donned lab coats?"

"Yes," the woman muttered. "Most of the techs are dressed that way. But you'll need a crystal badge, or you're likely to draw attention pretty fast."

"Where would we get badges?"

"One of you can have mine." She plucked a white triangular button from her skin. "It adheres magnetically to your energy field. Just sonar any badge to reset the programming. Mine is set to 'Inmate.' But you could just as easily set it to a name and add 'Tech,' which is what the staff does. Although they lack sonar, so they use their computers to redo these."

"Thank you." Elysia took the badge, and then she and Charlaeus helped the former mermaid slip artificial legs into the tube. "I'm surrounding you with Highest Light, my friend. May your journey be swift and safe."

"I don't know how to thank you –"

"You can thank us by living long and happily." Elysia smiled as she embraced the tearful merbeing. "Now go – and be quick." The woman nodded and slid into the pipe, and then Charlaeus repositioned the grate. "I'll clean the floor if you'll select some things for us to wear," Elysia suggested.

"Sure." Charlaeus grabbed surgical tops and pants while Elysia swabbed the white quartz. She tossed the soggy linen into a nearby bin of bloody towels before they donned the new attire. "What about our clothes and packs?"

"I've been thinking about that," Elysia replied, as she sonared the badge. It chirped once, and then she typed "Dara Avalon, Tech" on its tiny virtual screen. The badge beeped again, showing off its new message. She handed it to Charlaeus, who held it to her tunic, where it adhered as if by magic. "There's a small laundry cart in the corner. I was thinking of putting extra towels and gowns and the like in there, in case we need to disguise our friends. And we could just have our packs at the bottom, covered by supplies."

"Sounds like a plan." Charlaeus smiled as she helped Elysia fill the cart with their gear and supplies.

"You know they'll come looking for us sooner than expected, once they realize the woman we freed is missing."

"Yes."

"Are you ready anyway?"

"I am."

"All right. Let's go. And if I start talking to someone, it's because I'm looking to get a badge." Charlaeus nodded, rolling the cart into a wide hallway. Workers in snowy lab coats scurried here and there. Techs jockeyed for position with gurneys bearing gagged beings. Then the women approached a dark-haired male who dropped what looked like surgical gowns. Elysia bent to help, and she noticed him admiring her.

"Do I know you?" She smiled as she handed him the last garment.

"No, but you're going to," he cooed, his eyes raking curves barely disguised beneath her tunic. "I'm Tomanicus."

"And I'm Selenius." She leaned toward him, her heart in her eyes, and his ogling stare softened. "Perhaps we could meet sometime after work," she murmured as her hand clasped the badge from his chest.

"Absolutely," he whispered, his blue gaze glued to hers. "I'm free after nine this morning. Meet you at Harmony Falls?"

"Sure." Elysia smiled once more and turned away. She could feel him gawking after her before he again ambled down the hall.

"Quite impressive, Selenius," Charlaeus whispered, a grin splitting her face.

"You liked that?" Elysia sonared the badge so it reflected her chosen fictional name before adhering it to her top. "Let's just hope our exit strategy doesn't take us by Harmony Falls. Or else I may have some explaining to do."

Not for the first time, Elysia wondered why just about everything was white in these labs. She supposed the color of wedding gowns and dove's wings and high priestess robes brought the image of purity or sanctity to what could never be purified or sanctified.

At a hallway intersection, they wheeled left, past chatting men sporting "surgeon" badges. The doctors wore metal-belted ivory tunics. She couldn't help noticing their hands – soft, smooth, and pink like a child's – with delicate fingers. She wondered how such loveliness could perform the atrocities occurring every hour in this place. She realized she couldn't think about that, however; she needed to focus her sonar north and look for clues leading to her friends.

Ahead, the corridor widened into a circular desk area. Support staff buzzed about, some clearly in a rush. Several touchscreen monitors floated above employees operating state-of-the art workstations. Glancing at the wall beyond the workstations, she spied a clock. It was just after six – a little past daybreak. She felt her pulse quickening, as they were rapidly losing any advantage of remaining unseen that the early hours had afforded them. But before they could slip beyond the desks, a chime sounded. Several techs scrambled down the hallway, and then a lab-coated staffer grabbed Charlaeus' sleeve.

"You two!" The woman wearing a coiled bun barked at them. "Code Indigo in Tank Room B. *Stat!*" Charlaeus opened her mouth to reply, and the woman squeezed her arm, gray eyes narrowing to slits. "I don't want any lip about ends of shifts or panties in a wad, do you hear me? We're short staffed as always. Now *go!*" Launching Charlaeus down the hallway, the woman gestured for Elysia to pick up the pace – and then the Moldaarin queen and Charlaeus sprinted away.

Elysia's sonar detected a disturbance halfway down the corridor. She and Charlaeus joined a stream of techs swimming through a quadruple-doored entry. The closely pressed bodies swarmed a vast chamber, its ceiling spanning at least three stories. Black lights running vertically up the walls separated glass tanks filled with fluid and mysterious shapes. The lighting made all the tunics and lab coats and whites of the eyes and flashes of teeth in the room neon bright. At first, Elysia wondered what the purpose would be – why there'd be a need for the black light spectrum – before a growing grisliness dawned.

Inside the floor-to-ceiling tanks floated human forms and body parts. Catching her breath, she glanced at Charlaeus, who was gaping about with glowing eyes. Turning her attention back to the tanks, Elysia could identify both males and females – perhaps tens of thousands of them – stored in solution. Peering into the tanks, she saw certain areas glowing more brightly, or in a different color altogether, beneath the black lights. It was then she realized they were using the lighting – together with the special tank fluid – to pinpoint the most potent energy or gifts a particular part contained. Elysia realized the ancients had long spoken of various talents emanating from specific body areas; in humans, she knew clairvoyancy was tied not only to the third eye, but also the liver, gut, uterus, and ovaries. She wasn't surprised, then, to cast her eyes about the room's vast collection and see row after row of psychic tissues.

Before these horrors could sink in, a lunatic's laugh drew her attention across the room, where she and Charlaeus began to understand what a "Code Indigo" meant. Facing the gathered techs, which numbered in the hundreds, a naked hybrid female staggered. Her glassy-eyed swagger spoke volumes about her drugged state. She stood eight feet tall and appeared half human, half hawk. Magnificent, mottled wings towered above her, their ebony edges contrasting white, gray, and rust feathers. Her face had been pierced at the third eye – and her right wing was split open. Blood poured down her nose and spine. Her wounding looked all the more pronounced because the gashes glowed in the room's black lighting. In spite of her injuries and inebriation, no one approached to apprehend her. Elysia saw a crystalline scalpel in one clawed hand – and a vial bearing luminous green liquid in the other.

"You *cowards!*" she screeched, the sound reminding Elysia of her hawk friend. "Not one of you has courage. Either meet me in battle or free me!" she cackled, the brazen guffaw of one with nothing to lose. "You just didn't think, did you?" Her voice quieted, hushing the chamber. "One descended from the Hawk of Achill stands before you. One who will never bow. One whose energy is regrouping – renewing in front of your very eyes. In spite of your best efforts to disable me." She pumped a bloody fist in the air, taunting the crowd with the test tube. "Oh, but I could disable *you*. All of you know what's in this vial. One drop is all it will take. One drop hits the ground, and you will breathe your last. I guarantee it."

Along the room's perimeter, more techs filed in. Elysia saw the surgeons from the hallway huddled and whispering. With her enhanced hearing, she learned they were thinking of evacuating the room to release sleeping gas, which would render the hybrid unconscious. Elysia prayed, asking for the greatest degree of love to unfold. And then, as if the hybrid were directly answering her prayer, the hawk-woman spoke again – as if to her heart alone.

"All I need is a boost," she pleaded. "I can almost reach No-Mind – nearly touch the messenger realms – but for this filth in my veins. Just a helping hand. Will *none* of you aid me?" Before the hybrid could say more, Elysia dropped within the heightened sense of power she'd been feeling since being subjected to Gadeirus' hallucinogenic disks – and pushed.

In a golden light flash, the hybrid vanished. A collective gasp and murmuring rippled the crowd; Elysia felt their fear and confusion over this loss of control evolving into panic. She met Charlaeus' wide eyes.

"Let's go," Elysia whispered.

"But you're –"

"Not so fast, sweetheart." A well-muscled arm draped her shoulders, and Elysia looked up into familiar blue eyes fringed with velvety lashes.

"*Jack*!" she hissed. "What are you doing here?"

"Keeping you from drawing any more attention to yourself." He steered long black hair to the side of his face as he assessed her. Pulling a handkerchief from his doctor's tunic, he pressed it to her nose.

"What –"

"You're bleeding, El." He flashed a half-smile in Charlaeus' direction. "I'm afraid niceties will have to wait. But for now ... I'm Jack."

"Charlaeus." Her smile lit her eyes, and Elysia could feel she found Jack attractive.

"A pleasure." Grasping their elbows, he escorted the women from the room. Halfway down the hall lay the cart that was no longer hiding their packs; in the Code Indigo chaos, somehow it had been overturned. Jack leaned Elysia against Charlaeus, then righted the cart and reloaded its contents. He motioned for Charlaeus to wheel it while he half-carried Elysia along the corridor. "If we're lucky, this nosebleed will get us where we need to be. And without any questions." He grimaced at the bloody handkerchief smearing Elysia's nose. "That was quite a shove."

"Yeah, well ... a lot of things seem a bit ... distorted since Gadeirus fed me his wafers," she whispered. "I hardly seem to know my own strength."

"So, *that's* what you think –" he began, before breaking into chuckles. "I see we have lots to chat about. Once I get you out of here."

"I'm not leaving without my friends –"

"I'm well aware, sweetheart." His striking eyes scanned each chamber they passed before whisking the women through a doorway near the elevators. "This one's clear, at least for now. Come with me."

"But –"

"I've got to get this bleeding under control," he said as Elysia and Charlaeus gazed around a room identical to the one where they'd freed the former mermaid. "I can't have you getting dizzy. Nor do I want my costume spoiled, as it was a bit tricky to come by on such short notice." Gently, he lifted Elysia onto the examining table. "Charlaeus, will you get me some cotton strips from that cabinet's lower left side? Along with gauze and bandages. And a little of the brown powder, fourth shelf up." She nodded, parking the cart by the wall while she grabbed supplies.

"You seem to know a thing or two about doctoring," Elysia observed.

"I get paid to be acquainted with my surroundings." He dumped brown powder over the cotton Charlaeus handed him.

"Did Alaric send you?" Elysia winced as he pressed powdered cotton against her nostril.

"No."

"Then who –"

"Gadeirus."

"*What*?!" Elysia fought his grasp. Powder dirtied the floor as he grabbed her wrists.

"Hey, come on now," he whispered. "Feel into me, El. I'm not here to hurt you."

"But –"

"I have strict orders from Gadeirus that not a hair on your pretty head is to be harmed. In any which way. Period."

"What?" She could feel the truth of his words. Tears misting her eyes, she slumped on the table. "Can this be so?"

"But of course. It's quite simple." He grinned, plucking freshly powdered cotton from Charlaeus' fingers. "You have a way with kings I've never before seen. When you inspire rulers to such depths of devotion, how can it be otherwise?"

"Seriously, Jack –"

"I *am* being serious, sweetheart." He dabbed clean gauze at her skin. Then he secured a bandage beside her nostril and wrapped her head with more gauze. "We can continue this conversation later. For now, it looks as if the bleeding's stopped. But I've made your wound look bigger than it is, which should prevent anyone from stopping us." He steadied her as she slipped from the table. "So, we'd best get to your friends, before it gets any later. Or before you decide to shove somebody else."

"All right," she whispered, taking a deep, centering breath while Charlaeus opened the door.

"Lean on me a little. For effect," he urged, as Charlaeus rolled the cart beside them. "And rest your sonar. I know where they are."

"I don't know how to thank you, Jack." She sniffed grateful tears, feeling his sheltering strength around her shoulders.

"All in a day's work," he murmured. They passed the elevators, and he led them through the next door. Elysia thought perhaps they'd be taking the stairs, but instead they walked onto a boarding platform. She counted eight sleek trams whizzing by in either direction as they approached. Jack paused behind a painted symbol, and in seconds a train whirred to a halt, hovering mere inches above the stone where they stood. A sensor recognized the cart, extending a ramp so Charlaeus could load the cart easily. Then Jack and Charlaeus grabbed support straps suspended from above as the rapid transit vehicle accelerated. Seconds later, they plunged into darkness. Overhead lights blazed on, blinding them, before the tram slowed and stopped; its automatic ramp extended access to a cart they'd never claim. Instead, Charlaeus dug out their buried packs while Jack whisked Elysia to the platform stairs.

Gone was the antiseptic whiteness; they'd emerged in Lesser Light's underbelly. Cage-like sconces cast grim shadows on the surrounding sable stone, features Elysia recognized from the palace stairwell. There was a chill here, a dampness she felt to her core. As they descended dank stairs, she felt anguish and torment and fear weighing more and more heavily on her heart. Yet on some level, there was relief, on this knife edge of reaching her friends. With Gadeirus' blessings and Jack at her back, she could feel the grounding of Highest Light strengthening. And that gave her the one thing she most needed – hope.

TWELVE

Lorelei's eyes bulged as she bolted up from a nightmare. She felt trembly and weak, two indulgences she never allowed herself, and she wondered how else she would suffer from those Light-damned disks. In the tangled sheets, she spied what she could only see as deflowered rose remnants. The sight inflamed her cheeks with shameful thoughts of her behavior with Abigor.

"Lords with swords!" she muttered, clawing through red petals in search of stockings and undergarments. With fumbling fingers, she dressed, angered by fuzzy thoughts and a wobbly stance once she'd staggered into her shoes. She grabbed a bureau for support and stared critically into the room's full-length mirror. The Dark Heart queen wondered with horror if she looked different – if, in fact, everyone would be able to tell what she'd just done. And what, despite devilish tempting, she'd still been unable to yield.

"Thoroughly and completely," she hissed, assessing her makeup – or what little was left of it. Her stomach dropped as it dawned on her she'd brought nothing to this room. No purse, no makeup. Not even a hairbrush. She seethed as she scrutinized tangled locks, wondering what in the hell realms she'd been thinking. And she realized, for the first time she could ever remember, she hadn't been.

Sighing to quell stinging tears, she closed her eyes and gathered scattered energy. She could no longer morph into other beings, but eons ago she'd perfected the ability to draw Dark Heart energies into herself and utilize their power for her own benefit. She might not have blush or lipstick at her disposal, but within moments of channeling, her pasty skin bloomed rosy and smooth. A stunning light filled her eyes. Within Dark Heart depths alone, she felt safe surrendering. And that deep trust she shared with no other allowed her to reanimate and refresh, such that her swagger was apparent when she marched from the room.

Down the hall she strode, toward the suite turned psychic command post. Flicking long fingers at the keyless lock, she thrust the door open. Choking smoke again enveloped her, but this time she'd centered herself in the Dark Heart instead of stumbling through in a state of should-have-beens. She headed for a group with hands splayed across one of the room's centerpiece crystal balls, as the lightest touch brushed her spine.

"Hello again, gorgeous." Abigor's orange eyes searched her with curiosity – and lust. "Back so soon?"

"I didn't get what I came for the last time."

"Is that right?" He seized an opportunity to grope her. "I could have sworn your needs were met. Thoroughly –"

"And completely," she interrupted, flinging herself from his grip. "Yes, yes, I suppose you would see it that way."

"Good." He moved to kiss her as she recoiled.

"I'm here to learn what the psychics have discovered."

"I'm in charge, remember?"

"Not at the moment. Not when I have business here." She spewed icy words over him, even as the Dark Heart ignited her eyes. "I won't be interrupted again."

"I see." His gaze sobered and he stepped back. "You realize I won't take no for an answer for long."

"I realize no such thing."

"The hell you don't," he hissed. "You can't run from me. Or hide. You never could. But especially not now."

"I don't know what you're insinuating –"

"Light damn it, woman!" Eyes flaming, he leaned down so his nose nudged hers. "Don't think for a moment you can shut me out! I will not *allow* it!"

"You allow *nothing* when it comes to me," she seethed. "*Nothing*. Are we clear?"

"What's clear is how afraid I have made you," he muttered. "How vulnerable. How –"

"Ridiculous." She straightened her spine. "Now step aside."

"What I should do is throw you over my shoulder. And take you to my bed." He reached out and cupped her chin. "Because you ... need."

"I need *nothing*!" She whirled from him, onyx curls lashing his face. She heard him chuckle as she channeled the Dark Heart to wash him from her awareness. Turning her focus to the psychics, who all sat gaping at her, she felt cold fury knowing they'd seen far more than she'd planned. Fuming as she circled them, she assessed their nervous swallows and shifting feet while electric pulses fizzled from her fingertips. No one spoke in the ever-expanding awkwardness.

"Must I ask the obvious?" Lorelei's voice dripped quiet contempt. "Is there none among you who can tell me what I need to know?"

"My lady," a slow, steely voice chiseled the agonizing stillness. Lorelei's head swiveled toward an insect hybrid's iridescent orb eyes.

"You wish to know above all else if Alaric has been ... detained."

"Yes, that's right."

"And his plans uncovered."

"Yes."

"The short answer is 'no' and 'no,'" the hybrid replied, its silvery antennae flicking in time with Lorelei's twitching brow.

"What did you just say?" Lorelei's lips trembled with rage.

"No. And no," the hybrid repeated calmly.

"*What –*"

"He's no longer on Zacktronymus," the hybrid interrupted. "And his plans remain his own, as he quite skillfully concealed his exit. I've been working to trace the ethers and even alternate timelines for any sign of his energy. But so far –"

"So far, you've failed," Lorelei whispered.

"So far, I've not tracked him," the hybrid scoffed, ignoring its superior's cutting words. "But it's just a matter of time."

"Time, you simpleton, is something we're running out of."

"My lady –"

"Don't 'my lady' me!" Dark Heart energies flooded her, fueling her fist pumping as she swore in the Old Tongue at the quivering psychics.

"Here," the hybrid beckoned, its needle-like pincers pointing to the gazing ball. A gray cloud obscured the crystal, and then rapidly changing images appeared. "Look."

Lorelei leaned in, impatient to dismiss this annoying beast. Yet when she caught sight of Alaric's body, she couldn't look away. She gawked as Linasia unbuttoned her dress. Her gaze stayed glued to the gazing ball until she watched Linasia disappear, and then the ball flashed dark. When the scene reappeared, Alaric had vanished. Lorelei turned accusing eyes toward the hybrid.

"What does this mean? Why have you lost sight of how he vanished ... right when she left?" Her eyes narrowed as the hybrid began chortling.

"My dear lady," the insect mused between chuckles. "Have you forgotten this is Alaric we are watching? A master shape-shifter, if I may say so. A legend –"

"You fool," she muttered. "Of course, I know Alaric's gifts. Much more keenly than you can imagine."

"Apologies, my lady. I meant no disrespect."

"You meant every disrespect." Contempt contorted Lorelei's face. "With a side of disregard and a whole plate full of disinterest. But it matters not."

"Madam, I assure you –"

"It matters *not!*" she sneered. "Continue as ordered. I expect full details of his departure and whereabouts when I return this evening. At the very least, I know he's one step ahead of you and all the others gathered here. I shouldn't need to explain how costly your ineptitude is to our mission."

"Yes, my lady. But –"

"No 'buts.' Find him. Any more failures will not be tolerated."

"Yes, I understand, it's just ..." Lorelei whirled from the hybrid, no longer listening to the disappointments leaking from its lipless mouth. She simply couldn't bear to hear more. Or to lose. Not this time. Not to Alaric. Not in front of an intergalactic audience. Her pride had already been dealt every imaginable blow. Now it was time for the Dark Heart to beat for all to hear. As she stamped from the room, she affirmed her commitment to her dream. It had been such a long time in the making. And she'd been stuck such a long time in the suffering. Yet now her star was rising, and all she'd had to do was sell a soul that had only ever brought her misery. Now, at last, she would reign.

"Thoroughly and completely," she whispered into the castle's echoing chill as she hurried toward a destiny only the Dark Heart could have secured.

THIRTEEN

The foyer's rushing fountain flooded Alaric's awareness as he materialized inside Heera's palace. Stepping from behind a crystalline staircase, he emerged to echoing laughter and friendly chattering. He heard a gasp and footfalls racing nearer. Then a chortling Tyrius barreled into him, arms outstretched in a bear hug.

"Alaric!" Tyrius boomed. "My friend, I'm so glad to see you! So very glad!"

"As am I to see you." Alaric embraced Tyrius for several moments, his gold-green eyes locking on Jon's as his son approached. "Your efforts to bring the essences here have assured the initial victory we needed. I am forever grateful."

"Anything to help!" Releasing him, Tyrius slapped his shoulder before Alaric trembled to tears in Jon's arms.

"Am I really here with you now?" Alaric sobbed, clutching his son to his chest.

"Yes, Father," Jon whispered. "Welcome to Heera. I'm beyond words except to say I love you so much."

"I love you, too, Jon." Alaric held him at arm's length, absorbing the peaceful certainty Jon radiated. "Despite a minor detour, our plan is yet alive and well."

"Assuredly, it is." Jon sensed Lochana's quiet presence. "You remember Lochana?"

"Of course." Alaric released his son and knelt before Lochana and the six attendants flanking her. "My queen. Thank you for all you continue to do to honor Highest Ljght."

"Alaric, please call me Lochana," the monarch murmured, bowing her head. "Your presence honors all of our people. Welcome to Rohati."

"I appreciate you, Lochana." In one graceful movement, Alaric arose and clasped hands with Heera's ruler. "It's my deepest honor to be here."

"I hope you'll allow for some rest and nourishment." Lochana eyed the Moldaarin king's snakelike calm that so convincingly cloaked weariness. "Please. We've prepared a meal and a resting chamber for you."

"There is much we need to discuss –"

"Indeed. And we shall. After some self-care, yes?"

"Yes." Alaric grinned. "Some self-care is assuredly in order."

"Very well then. Please come with me." Lochana offered her arm, and together she and Alaric ascended the quartz stairs. Tyrius and Jon bowed to the attendants, who motioned for them to follow. As the entourage reached the third level, a brilliant pink brightness showered them.

"My queen!" Tyrius gasped. "What blessed beauty is this?"

"A precious gift from Atlantis. Feel free to touch these structures." She turned toward Jon. "Do you remember, Jonastus?"

"All too well." A serene smile parted Jon's lips; he watched Tyrius run meaty hands over one of the fiery pink pillars lining the grand hall's quartz walls. "Heera's High Council had been looking to refurbish parts of the city's infrastructure. Many buildings had been damaged eons earlier, in the last reported fighting within her borders. A visiting Atlantean delegation promised aid. And returned promptly with a generous gift – enough ruby lavender quartz to rebuild all the weakened walls and broken bridges."

"I don't know this quartz," Tyrius mused. "And I've never before seen this exquisite rose-purple clarity in a stone."

"Lovely, isn't she?" Lochana's tinkling laugh twinkled her eyes. "Who'd ever guess this quartz that carries a commanding feminine force of unconditional love would be a lab-created reject?"

"*What*?!" Tyrius shook his head. "How could that *be*?"

"Ruby lavender was once thought to embody the alchemically perfect mixture of rare molecules that would manifest whatever was desired, anywhere in the universe," Alaric explained. "Atlantean researchers made her. They carried out one painstaking experiment after another. At first, they were impressed, because she was so easily programmed. Then they were baffled because ruby lavender would flawlessly deliver any heart-centered request – yet refused to cooperate in creating war or oppression of any kind."

"A stone with a conscience?" Tyrius asked.

"All stones have a conscience, yet this crystal has a mind of her own." Lochana beamed at the translucent 22-foot-tall fuchsia columns surrounding them. "She proved to be incorruptible. Not even the realm's most gifted seers could get her to do their bidding if the intention didn't serve Source."

"But how did she wind up here?" Tyrius looked quizzically from one to the other in their party when they began chuckling.

"Throughout the galaxy all the known governments and commercial markets who'd been clamoring to invest and exploit her abilities soon learned she could not be coerced," Lochana explained. "Field test after field test, demonstration after demonstration, failed miserably. What ruby lavender did exasperated her Atlantean creators beyond measure. She was consistent. She would demonstrate she *could* manifest what was desired when the request was spawned from the love vibration. She made flowers grow. She healed wounds. She aligned anyone and anything placed within her field of influence with the Divine."

"But what happened with Lesser Light requests?" Tyrius asked.

"Nothing," Jon said, his cherub face lit like a candle. "Absolutely nothing."

"Her creators couldn't explain her behavior," Lochana added. "From a purely scientific point of view, none of it made sense. Of course, they were only observing her from a purely scientific point of view. So they missed her spiritual, alchemical transformation. Grace spawned something greater than her elemental makeup, right under their noses. And she had evolved to the point where she became a liability because she was no longer marketable. Investors pulled out. Governments mocked the demonstrations and made the Atlanteans look foolish – something they loathe beyond all else."

"They tried to destroy her," Jon continued. "I witnessed their final effort, as a member of the Diplomatic Relations Committee. Kenaseus and I were brought in as damage control, after the scientists discovered their attempts to dissolve or disassemble their greatest creation proved futile. They'd already fabricated large pillars of her, and yet every effort to crumble her failed. Which made her creators eager to hear the idea I put forth – to send her here. To help a small planet rebuild its infrastructure after a devastating war. It would be a humanitarian act and a public relations success; it would prove to the intergalactic community that Atlantis cared not for greed and manipulation but would offer its bounty to a civilization in need."

"Lords with swords!" Tyrius guffawed, slapping the scarlet columns.

"Divine wisdom's tranquil beauty touches my heart every day that I walk through Heera." Lochana placed her palms together in a prayer position. "The best gift that was beyond any of our wildest dreams came unexpectedly – and arrived exactly when most needed. And now, that gift serves us moving forward. Because we serve Source."

"Indeed, we do." Alaric raised his fingers in a pyramid shape above his head, apex pointing first upward and then downward as his hands passed his heart. Tyrius watched the entourage mimic his motion, with everyone's hands finally resting in place below the navel, over the belly's Lower Dantian, their triangled fingers pointing to the ground. Tyrius himself performed the gesture, and loving energy flooded him from crown to toe.

"What magic is this?" Overcome, Tyrius swiped at tears washing his face.

"That, dear friend, is the love vibration." Lochana crossed her palms over her heart. "The very life blood of Highest Light. And what we are here to serve and sustain – in ourselves and others." She glanced at Alaric. "And speaking of serving and sustaining ... Alaric, isn't it time you had some nourishment and then rested within this ruby lavender sanctuary?"

"Yes." Alaric studied Lochana's sweet countenance, fresh tears misting his gaze. "I am so grateful."

"As am I," she replied. "Please follow me. A buffet awaits!" Lochana clasped Jon's hand. Together, they skipped along the ruby lavender-lined hallway, leading a hopeful group among yet another gift that promised all was unfolding perfectly and in Divine timing.

FOURTEEN

Three thuds shuddered the entrance, startling Gadeirus from a strung-out reverie. Sweat slicked his shirtless torso as he glared at that Light-damned painting, the one that had begun his life's latest and greatest painful chapter. He wondered if current circumstances might also write his legacy. He faced a grim reality; whether he remained Poseidia's supreme ruler was anybody's guess. He'd lost track of recent days, ever since the disciplinary board had suspended him over the Elysia debacle. Combing shaky hands through his tangles, he knew a deeper, darker reality kept surfacing as well. He was losing by the minute even the memory of peace Elysia's kisses had brought weeks before. The old hunger again consumed him; his body ached with the need to feed. Yet at the moment, he had no time for indulgences. He needed clarity and he needed his wits about him, and he needed it all now, because once he unlocked those chamber doors, his every word and deed could lead to his demise.

"So be it," he muttered, snatching a wafer from the nightstand and a robe from the bedpost where it had dangled by a sleeve. Marching to the bedchamber's gilded entry, he flung its double doors wide open. On either side of the entrance, two guards stood erect in crisp ebony breeches and high-collared waistcoats. And across the mahogany hall lounged Desineus, ivory tunic unbelted, head tilted back. Sandy hair fell in waves around a face etched with duty. Beside his sandals lay a leather satchel. As Gadeirus' bloodshot eyes burned into his, Desineus noted the unkempt hair and pasty green complexion. Propelling himself from the wall, Desineus retrieved the satchel, his fingers skimming crimson-veined black marble. He brushed past Gadeirus and entered the royal quarters. While the guards closed the doors, Desineus sighed, the resigned exhalation of a friend long tired of making excuses.

"Are you lucid enough to hear me?" Desineus pivoted to stare at the king. "Because there is much we need to discuss."

"Yes," Gadeirus answered. Cinching the sable robe's belt, he strode to the rosewood bureau beneath the painting. He splashed lemon water into a glass from a waiting decanter before fixing his gaze upon

Desineus. "I'm listening."

"Your suspension caused you to miss the cabinet meeting. The one where you were supposed to sign the lab expansion decree. We also voted to increase funding for crystal weaponry research and development – as well as officially endorse the frequencies your seers have devised in order to reprogram the Tuaoi Stone."

"Damn it to hell," Gadeirus breathed, gulping from his glass. He slammed the empty goblet back onto the bureau. Sloshing more water into the crystal vessel, he peered at Desineus. "Has the disciplinary board appointed someone to act in my stead? Or did you bring the decree for me to sign?"

"I was able to persuade them to let me collect your signature."

"Good." He hastened to the bedside armoire. Hurling open its carved doors, he fumbled for a stamp, a candle, and red wax. Desineus noticed he also popped a thin wafer from a pouch into his mouth. "I will affix my seal immediately."

"You should know the psychics and the scientists are at odds." Desineus watched Gadeirus dump the candle and implements onto the bureau. "Both sides want control over the experiments – and the weaponry R & D. And they each desire a voice in deciding the particular Lesser Light energies the Tuaoi Stone will soon beam around the globe. So, today we heard their arguments. Yet who will ultimately be in charge of what remains your decision."

"*I* will be in charge," Gadeirus fumed at Desineus. In large swallows, he drained the lemon water. "Or is that something my brief absence has made you and the rest of the cabinet members forget?"

"Gadeirus, please listen to what your advisors –"

"My advisors!" Gadeirus threw back his head and cackled, as Desineus shifted his feet. "What do my advisors have to do with running this island?! Poseidia was an absolute monarchy the last time I checked. Which means *my* power and *my* wishes rule the land. And they have no limits."

"Yes, but –"

"No 'buts,' Desineus. And no limits," Gadeirus whispered, his black eyes glassy as a smile split his face. He wagged a tapered finger that would look at home on a woman's hand at his closest confidant. "*No limits.*"

"Yes, of course." He bowed his head. "My apologies, Your Highness."

"Accepted." Gadeirus spilled more water into his goblet. Crossing the room, he shoved at the glass doors opening onto the balcony. "Please join me. I'd like to be updated on where we stand with our crystalline arsenal. And the Tuaoi Stone, since she's our greatest weapon."

"Certainly." Desineus settled the satchel on the bureau and followed the king outside. Perched five stories high, the balcony overlooked a view unequalled anywhere on the continent. He felt relieved trading smoky-stale air for the ocean's fresh breath. A mid-morning sun had yet to greet the castle's façade, so the men lazed against a cold stone balustrade. Its polished smoothness overlaid iron pickets, forged with roses to match the castle's coat of arms. Before them sparkled downtown Poseidia, her crystal and marble buildings alight beneath roofs of sun-kissed copper, silver, and gold. Her skyline had been meticulously planned, a chorus of pleasing geometric shapes voicing perfect harmony. Beyond her boundaries lay the city's concentric circular outskirts, each thin land mass hugged by canals and spanned with spectacular white bridges. All along the canals sprawled Poseidia's markets, where any type of indulgence – from foods to furnishings to other, darker desires – could be gratified, at any time of day. And past that lay the ocean's aqua expanse.

"The arsenal continues to grow. It's on target to meet our agreed-upon expectations," Desineus said at last. "I don't anticipate any problems."

"Good. I'm pleased something is going along without a hitch." He downed more lemon water. "Are the scientists and psychics at least on the same page about the army I wish to create?" His black stare scanned the horizon. "I need absolute compliance."

"I know. And we're working toward that."

"What seems to be the problem?"

"Are these walls secure?" He eyed Gadeirus, certain the king was much more alert as he pondered what might have been in that wafer.

"Yes, of course. Sonar scrambles any conversations, preventing them from being overheard – either conventionally or psychically." For several moments, Gadeirus scrutinized his chief aide's face. "You've voiced these concerns before. Why do you ask?"

"There have been too many surprises of late. Too many ... unexpected events." He shook his head. "I dare not speak of specifics beyond what was debated at the cabinet meeting, my friend. Because in spite of your claims to the contrary, I believe certain factions are listening. Unauthorized factions."

"Unauthorized?" Gadeirus broke into giggles once again. A laugh Desineus had never before noticed sounded utterly mad. "But you realize I have an *authorized* team of the best seers from all over the universe –"

"Yes," Desineus interrupted. "The absolute best there is. I'm aware."

"Then why are you worried?"

"Many reasons, of which I can go into detail at another time. In a more trusted location."

"Des, if I didn't know better, I'd swear you were paranoid."

"Perhaps," he replied. "But too many unexplained happenings speak for themselves. Like Elysia. Who keeps failing to meet her Angel of Death, despite our best efforts at an introduction."

"Well, surely all is not lost," he whispered. "As long as she's –"

"You had her removed from that dinner weeks ago," Desinius declared. "Forcibly removed, if I may say so. And you left with her and your guards."

"Yes."

"And you had her carried here, into these chambers."

"Yes."

"But there was no evidence of her departure, and you were of no help at all in that you had no answers for the disciplinary board's many questions." Desinius turned so he faced Gadeirus. "A month has come and gone, and still there's no hint of how she left – or where she went."

"I see."

"No, Your Highness. Clearly, you do *not* see." Desinius slapped the railing and paced behind the king. "You don't seem to understand at all that we've got a big problem."

"What am I missing? Please. Enlighten me."

"All right." Desinius leaned against the bannister. "At that dinner last month, one by one, the Ahlaielian delegation was taken from the celebration. In a manner that would neither draw attention nor create a public relations scandal. All except Elysia."

"So, you're blaming me? For botching a plan I had no idea was underway?" Gadeirus whirled toward Desinius. "Really?"

"Gadeirus –"

"Who authorized it?"

"Let me explain –"

"*Who authorized it?*" Gadeirus grabbed his aide's tunic, drawing him face to face. Surprise and fear bulged Desinius' eyes before practiced polish returned. "Light damn it, Des! Who in the bloody hell has the power let alone the *balls* to do such a thing?!"

"Your cabinet," Desinius muttered. "They have the power *and* the balls. And they *did* such a thing."

"When? And *why*?!"

"As soon as we learned the Ahlaielians landed alive."

"*What*?!

"For all of your brilliance, you're such a fool," Desinius grumbled. "Look at you. Do you think your indulgences and indiscretions and absences haven't been noticed? Not just by your cabinet. But the High Council and all of the committees in charge of our choices and our collective way forward."

"How dare you –"

"No, my friend. How dare *you*," Desinius hissed, the slightest smile curving his thin lips. "How dare you dabble in one risky behavior after another. Toying with Poseidia's future as if she were one of your intoxicants or whores."

"You're way out of line –"

"Oh no, Your Highness. *You* are the one that's way out of line. So out of line, in fact, that one more misstep will cost you the crown."

For one terrible moment, Gadeirus' face blackened into a rage that erased all he'd learned in the last month. All that had transpired with Elysia. All that Arianna had shared. And all he'd discovered in his own murky depths. In that moment, Desinius never wavered. His gaze and his energy aligned with the words he had spoken. And so, in the next moment, Gadeirus knew he must yield. He began by releasing his grip on the man who'd stood by him unquestioningly until now.

"All right." Gadeirus moved his hands to Desinius' shoulders. "My deepest apologies, Des. You've been my friend and ally since long before royal manners or political maneuvering mattered to either of us."

"Indeed, I have. Apology accepted."

"Good." Gadeirus smiled and turned once again to gaze upon the city. "So please. Update me on all I've missed. Starting with the whereabouts of the Ahlaielian delegation."

"Beyond the plan to detain them and being informed that they'd been detained, I know not where they are."

"Why not?" Gadeirus tracked a merchant vessel entering Poseidia's calm harbor.

"There's no real need to know." Desinius shrugged. "The Civic Security Council is in charge of such affairs. I'm sure Sammaseus could answer any questions you have regarding the preachers."

"Good. I'll speak to Sammy. As for Elysia –"

"The High Council as well as the Civic Security Council – in fact, all of Poseidia's political factions – are up in arms about Elysia. So many donors and influencers witnessed your little tantrum with her. It seems anyone who's watched her courting at court is a fan, and they'd all like to see her 'rehabilitated' so she becomes an obedient and loyal Atlantean."

"Good luck with that." Gadeirus smirked and shook his head. "She is recalcitrant. An extraordinarily difficult wench. As all beautiful women are."

"All the more reason to treat such a delicate matter ... delicately."

"Perhaps, but –"

"But nothing. You didn't hear the after-dinner uproar. Your cabinet sent extra guards to report back once it was discovered she'd left your chambers." Desinius let out a long sigh. "But no one saw her leave. How can you explain that?"

"I can't." The king chuckled. "It's true that I had her brought back to my chambers. It's true that I drank wine with her. But it's also true that I was nervous and took too many wafers. I passed out cold, and when I awoke, she was gone."

"Gone?"

"Yes."

"But how?"

"I didn't see her leave, so I really can't say." Gadeirus shook his head. "She's some sort of witch, you know. Perhaps she used magic to cloak her exit."

"Perhaps." For a long moment, Desineus studied Gadeirus' face. "And perhaps you don't wish for me to know more."

"Do you need to hear more depraved details?" Gadeirus laughed. "Hell's bells, Des. It's embarrassing enough that I stole her from her marriage bed in front of Poseidia's most influential citizens. And then I passed out before I could do more than spill some wine on the carpet before her."

"Spare me, Your Highness." Desinius slapped the king's shoulder. "So, you really don't know when or how she left?"

"I really couldn't tell you."

"I see."

"And so, it's helping us politically to have imprisoned the Ahlaielians?"

"Speak no more of it." Desineus' cobalt eyes flashed a warning. "We must accept the Civic Security Council's choice to do so and make our plans accordingly."

"Which means?"

"Watch everyone," he insisted. "And trust no one."

"We're doing that already, are we not?" Gadeirus asked, and both men laughed.

"We are," Desineus answered, looking out over the city. "And, yet we need to be more careful."

"You mean *I* need to be more careful." The king's voice was soft. Vulnerable even.

"Yes, my friend." Desineus unleashed the persuasiveness he mostly kept tethered. "*You* need to be *much* more careful. Especially when it comes to *her*." He shook his head. "I've never seen you so consumed by a woman. Normally, I wouldn't object, as I want you to be happy. You know that."

"I do."

"But she's pure, Gadeirus. The very essence of Highest Light. And you're anything but that. Not to mention, you know she's *his*." He leaned closer. "You realize such differences make her the enemy. Make her cloud your head – and your purpose."

"Desineus, I have my ... moments," Gadeirus confessed. "When I indulge myself. And at times I admit she ... occupies me. She is, after all, the most intoxicating of agents. Yet I assure you, I'm committed to our shared vision. To Poseidia's rise to ultimate power." He swigged lemon water. "Tell me if you will, if you feel you can bear the unauthorized ears you fear so much upon these grounds. What of the Dark Heart energies? Are they holding?"

"Yes," he murmured. "The incorruptible has been irreversibly tainted. Of that you can be assured."

"Good. So –"

"So, the Tuaoi Stone is another matter. One we must address." Once more he amputated the king's words. Desineus watched, unfazed, as a shadow bled over Gadeirus' face. "Everyone wants a say in how it's wielded, for obvious reasons. Of course, some made stronger cases at the meeting than others."

"Who?"

"Lorelei, for one."

"*Lorelei*?" Shaking his head, Gadeirus chuckled, though to Desineus it sounded more like choking. "So, our Dark Heart whore wants even more power, does she?"

"She does," Desineus confirmed. "And considering what she's been able to do, I believe she's earned it."

"Clearly, the Dark Heart is a key to our expansion," Gadeirus mused.

"Yes."

"Then we will do what we have to do to keep her happy. At least for now."

"Agreed."

"Good. So, in regard to any other matters –"

"I'll handle them," Desineus said.

"And Alaric?"

"Wait and watch." Desineus realized the king's focus was now piercing. Laser-like, even. Again, he wondered about that tiny wafer as Gadeirus grinned, a smile that never touched his newly whitened and brightened eyes.

"What are you not telling me?" He stepped closer, and Desineus could feel simmering intensity.

"Nothing you don't already know," he replied. "He's impossible to track. Even your best seers must be saying that."

"Yes," Gadeirus whispered. "I've been warned. Over and over. And over again."

"Unlike you, he's exceedingly cautious," Desineus observed. "But with the evangelists imprisoned, he will let down his guard. It's inevitable."

"All the psychics say the same thing." Gadeirus sighed, rubbing his eyes. "I'm simply not a patient man, Des."

"Throughout time, the finest women, fiercest battles, and most savored spoils have all been won through patience." Instinctively, he recoiled as a hawk's wings clipped the balustrade.

"Indeed, patience is a virtue." Gadeirus chugged the last of the lemon water. "But as you so readily point out, I'm much more vice than virtue."

"Perhaps vice *is* your virtue. It's gotten you this far," Desineus suggested. "Besides, look at what all that virtue has done for Ahlaiele."

"It does appear purity is no match for the ways of the Dark Heart. Truly, we're fortunate to have its keeper within our midst. And under our influence." For a moment, he studied his glass. "Yet it would be a mistake to underestimate the delegation. Even under ... compromised conditions."

"Yes," he muttered. "They've sent their very finest. Who were once their most powerful. And gifted." Once more he turned and faced the king. "Tell me the truth. If we find her and can reprogram and rehabilitate her successfully, are you prepared to meet the new Elysia?"

"What a question!" Again, the king cackled, circulating doubt through Desineus' veins. Then the raven's gaze grew serious. And when his face looked thus determined, Desineus could see a monarch capable of ruling the world. "Perhaps no man can ever fully be prepared to meet his destiny. Yet he must at all times be ready to embrace her." A wicked gleam lit his eyes. "And I am most ready to embrace her."

FIFTEEN

In bleak quietude, Elysia reminded herself to breathe. She expected one horror after another to leap from the shadows. It felt surreal, creeping after Jack with Charlaeus, through Poseidia's infamous and hellish-smelling bowels. Yet here they trudged. Eerie echoing drips drowned the sounds of every footfall. Forged from obsidian in some ancient time, these tunnels made her think of large worm holes, excavated in darkness and covering covert operations that most would never understand or even know about. She wished with all her heart she didn't know about such things. For one tortured moment, her whole being ached for Alaric and all the anguish Poseidia had for centuries wrought upon her and her family. But she knew she couldn't allow such thoughts to occupy her. Not when their mission hung by a thread and Alaric's whereabouts and well-being were unknown. Not when her friends could be anywhere down here, in any kind of shape.

"Stop," she whispered, before she realized she'd spoken aloud. Jack and Charlaeus froze, and she could sense rather than see their uneasy expressions. "I didn't mean to say that out loud."

"No worries, sweetheart." Jack's voice readily reached their ears, the tone of someone long accustomed to speaking in secret places. "We're taking the back way. Which is the long way. Prepare yourselves, ladies."

Elysia shivered at Jack's warning and resolved to think of her body's instinctive reaction as a way of shaking off current circumstances. Everywhere she let her feeling sense penetrate reflected fear and anger. She appreciated this contrast for revealing in stark clarity what she did not want. Then she shifted her focus to more pleasant thoughts so as to draw pleasantry her way. She believed without a doubt in an attraction-based universe. Her long years had proven over and over again that finding a way to feel good – in any way possible – was key to good things happening. She also knew without question that she alone had created the dark reality she now faced; dying in fear centuries earlier when Moldaaris exploded had etched her soul with lower vibrations, frequencies kept suppressed as long as she'd been buoyed by Ahlaile's

Highest Light culture. Yet in Atlantis – with its heavy Dark Heart infiltration and where she again embodied a human form – her point of attraction and resulting experiences were vulnerable to how she alone was feeling. So, she realized she hadn't the luxury of negative thinking if she wished to reach happily ever after once again with Alaric – and if she hoped to find her friends alive and able to be helped.

To lift her spirits while tramping through these hell realms, she understood she must focus upon more general "feel-good gratitude" – on anything she readily appreciated – that came naturally and flowed without effort. Eagerness swelled her heart when she thought about how their intention to plant the love vibration must be working on some level, since Gadeirus had softened – he'd even summoned Jack! And all the angst she'd felt around Charlaeus had morphed into a trusted alliance. A small smile spread Elysia's lips, as she pondered Arianna offering aid and the fact that food and supplies and a plan and, in fact, everything needed kept showing up. She felt so happy that Jack knew where to find her friends – and that this journey kept confirming how things ultimately work out if staying positive is the priority.

"Look." Charlaeus pointed to the nearest metal-encased sconce. A flickering flame spotlighted the most unlikely guest. A pink butterfly, its translucent wings flicking the stale air, alighted upon Charlaeus' outstretched finger. Elysia stifled a squeal as the butterfly then fluttered up onto Charlaeus' forehead. The two women exchanged grins when the insect departed for Jack's nose. He rolled his eyes, making Elysia and Charlaeus nearly double over to keep from laughing. When he offered his hand as a platform, the butterfly readily boarded. Jack then touched the sconce and returned their new friend to the fixture. For a long moment, they stood watching it hover and spin, as if it danced in delight. Elysia felt thankful for this little bit of brightness before Jack motioned them onward.

Further into the tunnels, deeper and denser pools appeared upon their path – and a stronger stench. Elysia heard the others sniffling like she was from noxious fumes burning and tearing their eyes. Jack handed the women big black handkerchiefs, which they tied over their noses and mouths even as they quickened their pace. Agonizing minutes ticked away, and then Jack threw up his hands; they gathered around a circular hatch in the obsidian wall. He pressed a nearby button, and the hatch popped open.

"Through here," he murmured, offering Elysia and then Charlaeus a hand.

The hatch led into a secondary tunnel system. Its rounded halls were also crafted from obsidian, yet they were wider and dryer than where they'd just been navigating. The smell wafted more faintly here; in scant minutes, they felt relief as eyes and noses cleared. More cage-like sconces bearing lit torches dotted these walls at frequent intervals. Flanking the passageway, rows of heavy dungeon doors stretched for as far as Elysia could see. In the shadows, Jack continued to lead them forward. Suddenly, Elysia sensed Hunter close by. His energy felt thready and weak, but she'd know it anywhere. Something else occurred to her, too. Something that swelled her belly with dread. She swallowed hard when Jack waved what looked like a name badge across a door sensor. There was an audible "click," and then the three of them slipped inside.

"Well, butter my butt and call me a biscuit," a raspy drawl chuckled from the floor.

"*Will!*" Elysia clutched his outstretched hand and fell to her knees. In the dimness, she spied Ava and Hunter lying motionless beside him. They were nude, their heads shaven. Elysia squeezed Will's bony fingers, tears splashing from her lashes, as Jack ducked out the door.

"It's okay, honey," he whispered.

"Oh, Will -"

"I see nobody's licked the red off your candy, and for that I'm grateful."

"Oh, my goodness! Are you -"

"Here's the long and the short of it," he interrupted. "You can see Ava and Hunter are no longer present and accounted for."

"Yes."

"They took Kendrick first, and we've seen neither hide nor hair of him since."

"When?"

"Time's a funny thing. We hadn't been down here but a short spell when they dragged him away."

"Lords with swords!" She cradled his hollow cheeks. "How have you survived?"

"They've been experimenting," he sighed. "We get injections, not food. And we all have different ... reactions."

"Is that why Hunter and Ava -"

"Yes." Slowly, he shook his head. "They both sank into a catatonic state ... must've been yesterday. After the injections. But somehow, I still have my wits about me."

"I'm so ... grateful you do," she stammered.

"They'll be coming soon." His sunken eyes bulged at her from a blood-crusted face. "If you've got a plan, El, let's get to it."

"Staying one step ahead of them is the plan." She rubbed his icy fingers, trying to warm them. "Remember Charlaeus from the Gathering? She's here to help."

"My lady."

"Hello again, Will. I'm so sorry -"

"It should be me who apologizes. The fact that our predicament has brought you to Hell's Half Acre is another slap up the side of my now very bald head," he quipped, as Charlaeus grinned.

"That was Jack who got us through the door," Elysia continued. "I think he went in search of our next move."

"He went to find the tools he'd left nearby," Jack said, sliding back into the small cold cell. Tossing a backpack to the floor, he looked at Will. "There are scrubs and some bread in that pack. Have a bite and get dressed." Will was already unzipping the bag when Jack turned to the women. "El, I'd like for you and Charlaeus to help me get the others and then Will onto the gurney. We can fold and tuck sheets and blankets around them to make it look like one dead body we're bringing to the morgue. Which is our exit strategy, by the way."

Jack stooped and scooped Hunter's gaunt frame from the floor while spinning the gurney into position with his boot. Gaping at his graceful precision, Elysia wondered just how many bodies – and most likely dead ones – Jack had moved. Yet she reminded herself this was simply another spiritual lesson in not holding judgment. Instead, as they nestled first Hunter and then Ava and Will onto the gurney, Elysia realized she'd found something she thought had been lost to Lesser Light's recent maneuverings. And that something was faith.

SIXTEEN

Opening gold-green eyes, Alaric sighed as he stirred. Above the sleeping chamber where he lay shone a series of chakra lights; each ray emitted a changing cadence and shade in response to the level of balancing his body required. For a long moment, he observed without emotion as the lights kept returning to his heart chakra. He realized recent traumatic experiences had triggered his old patterns, the ones that had kept him functioning without feeling all those eons without Elysia. And he knew it was a razor's edge where he teetered, between keeping his feeling sense from freezing over again and plunging into despair. He knew he could not sidestep the duties at hand and risk all that hung in the balance by rushing to Poseidia to save her. Because saving her physical body would not preserve her immortal spirit, and it was this harsh reality that kept bringing him back to the present and his breath and the increasingly difficult task of trusting that Highest Light would prevail.

In one elegant motion, he slid to his feet, exasperated that he'd awakened in such a morose mood. Gone was the renewed sense of hope the Cerberus bite's healing had bestowed. Though he still sensed his friends' earlier excitement – the tight hugs and quick congratulations for beginning to right all of Lesser Light's wrongs – what stretched before him just looked like another long day. One endless series of meaningless moments he could no longer perceive as Divine unfoldings. It all seemed instead like a wicked courting at court drama, where any rare appearance by honor or truth or love gets checked at the door. Where nothing but playing and being played opens purse strings and pant zippers as the reigning powers that be laugh and look on after one shallow distraction or another.

Centuries of such fakery and fornication had left Alaric feeling powerless to conjure a happy face for any of it. All he could muster now resembled stomach-churning angst – the kind of mental mulling-over weariness that only someone from a snake lineage could appreciate. The kind of subsisting he knew all too well. Yet for good or ill, it remained a path he still knew how to navigate.

He knew something else, too. He had to get himself out of his head and this mindset. Going back to sleep would do that, yet there was no time for slumber. He needed to meet with Rohati's High Council soon and discuss the plan moving forward that would restore the essences – and return Elysia to him, if all went well. And so, he prayed for the power to surrender when he couldn't quite bring himself to do so. Closing his eyes, he fell inward as he took three centering breaths. Using the disciplined focus he'd cultivated for centuries, he opened to a meditative No-Mind state that rerouted and then rebooted his thinking. Minutes later, when he gazed about the room, he radiated peacefulness. While it wasn't all-out joy, it was enough of a vibrational lift to get him going without dread dragging every step.

After a hot shower, he toweled off and studied the many tunics, sashes, and belts left for him near the bed. He noticed there were no shoes or sandals or boots, and remembered how the Rohatians were a shoeless society by choice; this practice allowed their bodies to remain connected to their planet's benevolent, life-supporting frequencies. Rohati's weather remained pleasant and sunny throughout the year as well, so there was no need for foot protection or warmth, and as such the natives encouraged a custom of going barefoot. Realizing his own toes had been missing freedom, he felt noticeably lighter as he dressed without shoes in a belted silk ivory tunic.

On the bedside table rested a water-filled crystal teapot over a heating element. Alaric pressed a lever, igniting flames beneath the vessel. From among several tea blends, he chose peony and lotus petals to diffuse in a sparkling cup. Feeling deep appreciation for all the self-care tools the Rohatians had bestowed, he prepared to meet his friends while he sipped.

When he at last stepped to the sleeping chamber door, he took a deep breath as gleaming gold metal parted in the middle. He strode forth into ruby lavender brilliance. Light from a strengthening sun streamed through the central dome's quartz skylights; each facet had been cut into a sacred geometry shape. He'd only taken a few steps when Reena's bright smile greeted him.

"Good morning, Alaric!" She looked resplendent in a sea-green tunic as she offered him her hand. "I trust you rested deeply."

"Good morning, Reena. Thank you – I did indeed."

"Wonderful. I hope you're hungry. A morning feast awaits!"

"I would most appreciate some nourishment, my lady."

"Come with me, then." He slipped his arm in hers. Down the fuchsia corridor they strolled, bathed in pink luminescence and Reena's bubbly chitchat. They descended three flights of stairs and crossed the palace foyer before entering a grand banquet hall. Floor to ceiling windows overlooked a calm cerulean lake. Aqua and tangerine marble floors and selenite walls studded with aragonite vibed pure positivity; the welcoming space brimmed with delicious smells and chuckly chatter and clinking glassware. Alaric grinned when Tyrius' laughter boomed from a far table. A large center buffet draped in teal offered fruit and just-squeezed juices and roasted vegetable delights. And then an open-armed Tyrius was hurrying toward them, his thunderous voice echoing off crystalline walls.

"My dear Alaric!" The men embraced as Tyrius clapped Alaric's back. "Did you sleep well? And are you hungry? Because there's a feast fit for kings upon us!"

"Good morning, Tyrius," Alaric smiled, his voice silky soft. "I did, and I am."

"Fabulous!" Tyrius turned to Reena with a bow. "My apologies, Reena. How are you, my lady? I forgot my manners when I saw this big guy alive and well – and I realized his well-being was not last night's wild dream."

"No worries at all, Tyrius." Reena beamed and hugged him. "So, the food is to your liking?"

"Oh my, yes!" Tyrius patted his round belly. "I'm nearly stuffed, and I haven't yet sampled many of these delicacies." He pointed to the back table. "Come join us! After you've filled some plates, that is." Grabbing a glass of purple juice, he drank deeply as he perused the nearby heated dishes.

"Please," Reena said to Alaric, gesturing toward the buffet. "Help yourself to whatever appeals. I need to attend to some details for the upcoming meeting."

"Thank you." He kissed her hand, and Reena nodded before retreating through the arched entryway. Grasping a plate he stacked with colorful selections, Alaric exchanged pleasantries with everyone at Tyrius' table and sat down. In the short time since landing, Tyrius had already made fast friends with many Rohatians. Alaric quietly watched Tyrius gesticulating and guffawing with locals. While the Moldaarin king chewed, he felt such appreciation for these gentle beings who were so in tune and aware of his desire to stay silent.

When he'd eaten his fill, Alaric nodded farewell to those seated nearby. Tyrius was lost in a lively debate with a Rohatian elder seated opposite him, so Alaric slipped unnoticed from his side and left the banquet hall. In the foyer, late-morning sunshine showered sacred geometric symbols upon the polished floor. Breathing in this beauty, Alaric stepped outside, onto Heera's golden quartz sidewalks. Hovercrafts darted about as vendors peddled wares from carts and tables lining the street. Purple and pink trees formed flowering rows as far as he could see, their branches bent beneath songbirds screaming joy. As he paused to drink in all this loveliness, he heard drumming and instruments and singing in the distance, and he lit up knowing that the High Council would be meeting – but only after they danced.

Moving to the deep drumbeats, Alaric allowed his soul to be lulled. He hadn't visited Rohati in centuries, but he recalled how dancing here was no courting at court staged production. This celebration was not about playing to the crowd, but about playing in earnest and purely for the fun of it. He giggled in spite of himself when he glimpsed Heera's downtown park ahead, its daily devotional in full swing.

Alaric could feel Source lifting his funk, bringing hope – and a spontaneous groove to his moves. Dancing without care or choreography, Alaric whirled and glided his way through the park's gilded entrance, into a cacophony of laughter and gyrating bodies and heart-thudding music.

Lining a central white quartz sand courtyard stood several massive drums. Hollowed from tree trunks with hand-laced hide drumheads, the instruments rested on metal platforms; multiple drummers wielding mallets struck the hides as they danced. In between the largest platforms moved musicians playing smaller drums along with gongs and chimes and maracas. Weaving in and out of the crowd, people playing flutes, horns, and other instruments added to the festivities.

Spraying powdery sand, bare feet in all sizes stomped and spun to the lively beat, and Alaric added his voice to the call-and-response chant. In the Old Tongue, the first group sang *lokah samastah sukhino bhavantu*, meaning "may all beings everywhere be happy and free." The second group replied with a simple declaration of peace – *om shanti shanti shanti*. Someone threw Alaric a tambourine and he joined in, the very picture of feline grace as he crouched and leaped and twirled. Minutes unfolded in a timeless bliss the powerful sound frequencies allowed and encouraged.

Mesmerized by his moves, the crowd cheered and stepped back. Soon, Alaric danced solo. The drums slowed to his rhythm. Then he prowled the courtyard, fist in the air as he rebel-yelled "I am love!" three times in the Old Tongue – *aham prema* – until all gathered chimed in with an answering *om*. Keeping time to the chanting with the tambourine above his head, Alaric worked the throngs into a frenzy. Motioning everyone to follow suit, he then tossed the tambourine to the sand. As instruments dropped everywhere, all joined hands. A sultry tempo swirled Alaric, and he began leading an age-old Divine celebration. Hip-swaying eight small steps, first left and then right, the dancers next turned toward the center. Raising clasped hands as they sashayed forward, everyone slapped hands all together in the middle before hip-swaying back into a circle. Each dancer then spun to the right three times, pausing to clap hands with the person on either side before thrice whirling left. They then slapped neighboring hands once more before the routine repeated. Alaric led them through three rounds before Lochana and Jon appeared. It wasn't long until the group noticed their queen. In unison, everyone dropped to one knee. A gleeful Lochana grabbed Jon's hand. Giggling, she waved her people to their feet again and joined in. Then the celebratory ritual repeated until, minutes later, the rest of the High Council filed in.

Alaric looked up to see a dozen men and women slip into the circle throughout its circumference. The only thing marking them as High Council members was a purple sash belting their flowing tunics. Gratitude hummed his whole being, while a planet's ruling elite moved with its subjects as one. For what could have been eternity or mere moments, everybody danced. Within this sheltering circle of sound, Heera streamed a solitary love force, its integrity intact and thus its power unmuted, uncompromised, unleashed.

SEVENTEEN

Sashaying rounded hips across the palace foyer, Linasia ignored ogling guards and smoothed her braided blonde bun. She'd just left the lavatory after tidying caked makeup – and rehearsing options. Fury filled her. She couldn't believe how fifteen minutes had changed not only her own life; Poseidia's plans now hung by a hair. She'd never been so stunned, so caught off guard as when Abigor mind-messaged her minutes after Alaric's escape. And it wasn't just that demon seer's delivery of the facts that had so unsettled her. Abigor had belittled her; he blamed her for letting Alaric slither from her grasp, even though all the best and best-known psychics had missed his move, too – including Abigor.

A month had passed, and painfully so, she sighed to herself. Linasia realized all of the realm's power players were still reeling from this latest revelation, and not just Abigor would be prickly. Her stomach dropped at the idea of this most unpleasant meeting that was upon her. Yet she could see no way of avoiding Lorelei at this point. Deep in her own musings, she nibbled shiny red lips and ascended a darkened stairway with a confidence she didn't feel. Reaching the second story, she marched down a smoky corridor until she spied a gilded entryway guarded by four Poseidian sentinels. She dismissed them with a mani-cured wave when they bowed and opened the double doors.

Inside the shadowy suite, Linasia breathed black orchids and bella-donna. Candles glowed from every corner and chandelier and candela-bra, and as she met Lorelei's scorching gaze, she nearly cackled aloud; what a perfect metaphor for two difficult women at odds, she thought crazily. The Great Central Sun's gatekeeper could hardly believe how badly her own cinnabar lipstick clashed with Lorelei's long gown and the whole crimson-cabernet chamber.

"Hello, Linasia."

"Hello, Lorelei." Stopping short of circled rosewood chairs where the Dark Heart queen perched, Linasia bowed. "My lady, it's good –"

"You silly bitch," Lorelei hissed.

"I beg your pardon –"

"You heard me. As this realm's chief gatekeeper, you more than disappoint me."

"Take a number," Linasia shot back. "Abigor was first in line. And for a bloody month now, Poseidia's influencers have all been whining to me."

"Yes," Lorelei muttered. "Because of your epic failure."

"Nobody saw this coming –"

"Must I point out what is eye-rolling obvious?" The picture of unhurried grace, Lorelei arose from her silk seat to face Linasia. "You have long been paid – and paid handsomely – to guard what Poseidia deems most precious. And now ... our most coveted prize ... has been lost."

"Oh, he won't be hard to find –"

"Don't jolly me, Linasia. I'm really not in the mood."

"There's your problem, honey. Maybe if you lost the chastity belt –"

"*Enough!*"

"Oh honey, you clearly don't get enough –"

"Linasia –"

"Don't get me fired up, dear," she cackled. "Oh wait, that's *your* problem, is it not?"

"You cannot –"

"Oh, but I can. And I have," Linasia crooned as she moved closer, clearly enjoying herself now. "And I do so with gusto. And release. Wouldn't you like to know a thing or two about release?"

"You –"

"Silly bitch. Yes, I heard you before." Thrusting ample cleavage forward, Linasia stood eye to eye with Lorelei. "But I would rather be silly than spend the rest of eternity wondering what he felt like."

"I never allow anyone to –"

"I know, honey. It's written all over your face." Looking the Dark Heart queen up and down, Linasia laughed again. "Maybe you should allow someone that knows how. And lords with swords, Alaric knows how."

Whipping away from the sultry laughter Linasia spewed, Lorelei seethed with a singular desire to kill the gatekeeper. Just lash out with Dark Heart frequencies and hope to end this floozy's vulgar existence. Yet as she remembered her breath and her stolen gifts that would make such an assassination impossible – as well as her own promised Poseidian path moving forward – Lorelei stilled herself.

"You've never had his attention or felt his desire," Lorelei whispered. The insinuation that she herself had once experienced those things lay between them like a moldy blanket. "You've never even been his whore, because that little word 'his' implies he gives at least a damn about you. Which he does not."

"Perhaps. But at least I know what it's like to be pleasured by him."

"You especially don't know that." Now it was Lorelei who laughed, and she felt true glee watching a cauldron boil beneath Linasia's icing face. "Performing is not worshipping. You. Silly. Bitch." To her astonishment, Linasia cackled.

"You don't like me much, honey," she cooed at last. "And it goes way beyond our obvious differences and character flaws. And silly bitchiness." She settled herself into the plush chair where Lorelei had nestled minutes before. "It's a woman thing, I suppose. We loathe anyone who occupies our men. But here's where it gets absurd." She drummed glossy nails against the rosewood armrests. "Neither you nor I occupy an ounce of space in Alaric's heart. On that point, I believe we can agree."

"Yes." Lorelei sighed in spite of herself. She hated to admit it, but in truth her respect was growing for this woman who clearly felt unafraid to say bold things and to hell with the consequences. Despite their differences, the gatekeeper shared the same hunger – a hole in the belly that neither of them, for all of eternity, would ever fill. "We can agree on that point."

"And I believe we can agree on something else as well." Linasia leaned forward in her chair, as Lorelei slipped into the seat beside her.

"I'm listening."

"Men and not women rule Poseidia, yes or no?"

"Yes."

"Men who've stood by and stayed high for the most part ... as all of our hopes and dreams and hard-earned plans for a more powerful Poseidia rot on the limb. Like so much low-hanging fruit. Yes or no?"

"Yes."

"Then perhaps it's time we take it back. Our power. And Poseidia. And if we do that, we can lure Alaric back as well."

"Go on."

"Hear me out, my lady." Linasia shifted in her chair, a slight smile spreading her sticky lips. "We are ripe for a takeover. Before the low-hanging fruit draws flies as it ferments in our faces."

"What do you suggest?" Lorelei's eyes sparkled with an intensity Linasia had never seen in any Atlantean king.

"Even as we speak, the men who are truly in power here are plotting against you – though they have professed to your face to offer you the throne."

"Everyone lies," Lorelei replied. "It's nothing new or, for that matter, unexpected."

"Perhaps. But did you realize there are women elsewhere in this realm that would align with us?"

"Us?" Lorelei laughed. "You make it sound as if you and I have an alliance."

"We do, of sorts."

"With all due respect, Gatekeeper. We do *not*."

"But we *do*, honey." Lifting herself from the thick seat cushion, Linasia sauntered to a decanter set upon a nearby bureau. "May I?"

"Yes, of course." Lorelei watched Linasia pour plum-colored liquid with a barkeeper's finesse. Linasia handed her a shot glass, and Lorelei shook her head. "I couldn't possibly."

"Sure, you could. And you should, you know." Linasia downed a shot and studied Lorelei's wide-eyed stare as she shoved the other glass in her face. "It would do you a world of good to be pleasured. But it would serve you even more to accept how this realm really works. How it's the backroom barters and drink-and-drug-laced deals that drive the whole lying, stealing, and whoring machine."

"Yes, but –"

"Those two little words have brought more empires to their knees than you'd care to know," Linasia muttered. She held the glass firmly in front of Lorelei's nose. "Drink up, buttercup. We've got work to do."

EIGHTEEN

In torch-lit shadows, Elysia cringed at the gurney wheels' high-pitched protests. She couldn't understand why the sound affected her so deeply. It felt beyond annoying; the frequency rubbed her raw, like nails clawing chalkboards or knives scraping plates. As if reading her mind, Jack turned abruptly and muttered into her ear.

"They all squeal down here, sweetheart. Because nobody cares how it sounds when throwaways are being thrown away."

"Okay." Scabs from the balcony escape bled into Elysia's surgical gloves every time they had to stop and muscle the gurney through rotting flesh – which was frighteningly often. At first, she didn't know if she'd ever stop retching. Charlaeus seemed more resilient; her quiet determination inspired Elysia to a deeper surrender. It wasn't that Jack hadn't warned them. In fact, he'd been eerily accurate in describing the tunnel atrocities they'd face, and Elysia couldn't help but wonder how he'd known such things.

Wearing white protective jumpsuits and face shields, they sloshed through an ever-changing hallway maze strewn with medical waste and corpses – many in pieces – for she knew not how long. Behind every drab dungeon door, she sensed horrors she would rather not feel. Every so often she glanced at Charlaeus, who simply kept pushing beside her. And she prayed, even as she struggled for her deepest breath. This terror felt like what she imagined a blindfolded free fall would be. And mid-fall, there really was nothing left to do but trust that one of two Divinely inspired things would happen; either a soft landing of sorts would greet them, or they'd sprout wings and fly.

Suddenly Jack stopped, and Elysia's heart hit her throat. He held up his hand, freezing the women in sludge. Elysia heard chatter and snickering. Ten feet from where they stood, their hallway intersected another, and echoing male voices told her perhaps 10 yards yet separated this inevitable meeting. Holding one finger to his lips, Jack adjusted his security badge and moved forward once again. When they reached the new corridor, he swung the gurney wide and to the right before stopping. The white-suited men quieted, and for long moments, the only sound was their squeaking gurney getting closer.

"G'day, mate," the shorter, stockier man called out in a raspy voice. He waddled along at the gurney front, tugging hard to propel a massive sheet-draped shape through the slime.

"Hiya." Jack nodded to the second man, who was leaning into the gurney to push from behind. Both workers eyed the women warily as they halted, and while Elysia's pulse raced in her ears, Jack continued in a carefree voice. "What is it today, mate? Already battled a bloody half-breed. Look at my helper!" He pointed at Elysia's bandaged face. "Lords with swords!"

"It's been weird a long time," the taller man grumbled, his deep-set eyes scouring Jack's badge in the gloom. He shrugged thick shoulders and laughed, a sound that sent chills up the women's spines as it echoed off the blackness. "But now it's getting creepy weird."

"I hear ya, brother." Jack shrugged a mirroring gesture. "Bad creepy."

"Say, why ya got womenfolk down here?" The shorter man's eyes kept darting from Elysia to Charlaeus. "You know the rules. Two goons and a cot. That's it."

"Yeah, well. Light damn the rules when ya save a pregnant woman from a hybrid ready to blow this whole facility to Orion and beyond." It was Jack's turn to laugh, as Elysia and Charlaeus closed their eyes so they might breathe more deeply through whatever Jack was going to say next. "What else could I do, mate? I just couldn't leave the lasses up there with a Code Indigo going down."

"Bloody hell," the shorter man scoffed as he spit into the dark. "It's all gone to *sevaka*."

"Aye."

"Best get to it, Herc." The tall man was clearly done chatting. "G'day."

"G'day, mates." Jack wrenched the gurney into motion behind the men. Then the two groups plodded along, bearing squalling stretchers to the morgue

Elysia focused on her breath and her steps, tuning out as best she could the suffering behind the cell doors they passed. She could feel Charlaeus doing the same thing. There really was no other choice now, as they navigated Poseidia's bowels. Focusing on their present circumstances, Elysia knew, would only hurt their chances of getting out alive – as well as feed the energies allowing these evils to continue in the first place. And so, she prayed as the women followed Jack's lead, traversing one dank tunnel after another. Elysia had lost all track of time and space and even the tunnel sights and smells and wheel sounds by the time Jack signaled them to stop. Stirring from her reverie, Elysia looked up to see the men ahead standing before a black double door.

"One gurney is allowed per security code entry, so we wait," Jack whispered, as the shorter man slapped his badge at a keypad that parted the doors. "Make sure your nametags are visible. They monitor everything."

Pausing just long enough for the doors to close, Jack waved his badge at the lock, and again the entryway opened. Once they'd maneuvered the gurney inside the well-lit and noticeably colder all-white room, Jack led them toward a waiting security guard dressed like them. Looking up from a small desk where he'd been typing, the guard's face showed he'd expected just another routine gurney delivery. But when he saw the women, he set aside his crystal tabulator and keyboard so he could address this procedural breach. As Jack launched into the dramatic tale about escaping a Code Indigo, Elysia felt into the guard – and knew he was the type who reported everything that went against protocol, no matter how convincing the story. She sensed his doubt and suspicion growing, and then he arose, fingers grasping his holster. And so, Elysia dropped into No-Mind, tuning out everything but the energetic field that allowed her third eye to cradle this man. His gaze softened as he approached her, and when he spoke, his voice came liltingly to her ears even as she heard Jack sigh.

"Are you injured badly, madam?"

"It's just a flesh wound, sir," she murmured. "Some were not so lucky."

"That's regrettable." His eyes never left hers as he turned off his headset microphone.

"I've experienced such a string of unfortunate events," she whispered. "Would you like to help me find a bit of good luck in this day, sir?"

"Of course, my lady." A goofy grin split his thin lips.

"I appreciate you. What's your name?"

"Evestus, my lady. And yours?"

"Pleasure to meet you, Evestus. My name is Selenius," she said evenly, recounting the name he'd already studied on her lapel.

"The pleasure is mine, Selenius." He eyed her from head to foot. "Anything I can do to help, I will."

"Anything?"

"Yes."

"Would you be able to help me get back to the surface without traveling through those nasty tunnels again?" She smiled, and his grin widened. "It was so frightening."

"I'm afraid there's no way out of this hellhole that's not ... hellish," he muttered.

"What would you suggest?" Elysia donned her most flirtatious face, and the guard's eyes bulged. "I trust a strong and smart man like yourself knows just the right way to do many things."

"I'd like to do many things right now," he slurred, his eyes raking Elysia's body, whose shape was no less perfect cloaked as it was in protective gear.

"The day's young, sir. Time for many things ... after I'm free of this place." She touched his arm. "What's the best way for me to get free of this place?"

"There are only two ways out. Go back. Or go beyond."

"Back means the tunnels?" He nodded. "What's beyond?"

"We only go beyond when there's a problem with going back." He shook his head. "Nobody likes going beyond."

"Why not?" Elysia smiled again. "What's beyond?"

"We call it that because it's beyond all reason to use. Trust me, it's not someplace you wanna go. If you thought the tunnels were bad ... Selenius, you have no idea."

"Tell me, so I have more than an idea. Tell me so I can make a choice. To go back or go beyond." Jack shifted his feet, and Elysia knew another gurney would soon arrive. She moved to look directly in the guard's eyes. "Tell me."

"Beyond is what the witches use."

"I'm listening."

"There's a ... graveyard of sorts there."

"Graveyard?"

"You think we haul these half-breeds back to the surface?" He chuckled without mirth. "You wouldn't get it. Some are dead when they're brought here, but not all. Truth be told, most aren't. Even when they *are* dead, they're not really gone. They're somewhere ... in between. And they're more powerful when they're in between. Seems like when they're all used up, the brutality loses its effectiveness. Because these are souls that know how to navigate once they can drop the body. But the witches have so many hybrids they need to work on. We don't have the space to leave 'em until they're not just dead, but their souls have gone, too. So, when they come here, we toss 'em in the graveyard ... until their rotting flesh releases its final grip on their spirits."

"I see. So, how do the witches use the graveyard?" Sonar told her a gurney would stop outside the morgue's door in mere minutes.

"You wanna dance? You strike a deal with the fiddler," he croaked. "The bloody witches have a bargain with the otherworldly realms. They've made the graveyard a portal. Soul exchanges happen constantly with half-breed ancestors from all over the universe."

"I need to strike a deal, Evestus. And I need to do so now. Because that doorway we came through is going to open soon, and another couple of goons with a gurney are going to occupy you. Such that you will turn on your headset to chat with them and forget this little exchange with me. In fact, you will forget my name and that you ever saw us or this stretcher. And in exchange for that kindness, you will go on to have a most beautiful day." Elysia's eyes blazed like fiery emeralds as the guard gawked at her. "Deal?"

"Aye."

"What direction is the graveyard?"

"That way, my lady." He hoisted his arm like it weighed a hundred pounds and pointed. "That last door leads to a tunnel. And the grave-yard lies at the very end."

"Thank you. Please return to your post and prepare yourself to re-ceive the next cot as well as to have a fabulous day. And don't turn again to look toward the graveyard for at least another hour."

"Aye, my lady." Dragging his feet, he lurched back to his desk. Ely-sia watched as he turned on the headset and resumed typing, his eyes never leaving the keyboard.

"Follow me," Elysia whispered, her eyes meeting her companions' gaping gazes. "I know a thing or two about 'beyond.'"

NINETEEN

Freshly bathed and dressed in a favorite crimson waistcoat, Gadeirus owned the palace foyer as he strode forth in cabernet boots and flowing teal pants. Flanked by four guards and feeling wasted on wafers, the king simmered inside, a fury that even his most potent elixirs had done little to quell.

In his short reign, he'd already chained himself to the hell realms and all the pompous Poseidian power players. He'd orchestrated atrocities that would forever damn his soul. And, yet for all of that – for all that he'd given, which was all that he had – he trusted no one; nothing real remained that he could count on except an ever-deepening spiral of mayhem and misery. Except for that kiss. That one unforgettable moment of bliss. The only high he'd experienced that actually lived up to what he thought it would be. He knew she belonged to Alaric. He knew she was pure. Yet even after he'd harmed her deeply, instead of refuting him – she chose to taint herself, to share from a well of love he'd always longed to taste. Surely, she sprang forth from some ethereal essence, the likes of which he'd never before known. She so clearly was as star-studded in Highest Light as he was buried in all that was Lesser. And that polarity pulled him like the magnet it was. Yet he knew his own wickedness and his obsessive nature, and the truth was everything he'd ever bested or possessed soon lost its sway over him. Perhaps it was simply that she was forever out of reach that made her endlessly captivating. But it was what it was, and at the moment he knew he couldn't keep thinking about her. As he strutted into a palatial meeting hall, he straightened his spine and flashed a boyish dimpled grin at the assembled Civic Security Council.

"My king," Sammaseus said in a honeyed voice, as the council stood.

"Hello, Sammy." Gadeirus waved everyone back into high-backed chairs and sat at the head of a long rosewood table. "How's that sailing vessel coming along?"

"Craftsmanship takes time, Your Highness." Sammaseus' hair framed his handsome features in willowy blond wisps. "She's nearly seaworthy. But not quite."

"No doubt a worthwhile exercise in patience and endurance."

"Indeed." The council chairman's hazel eyes flicked briefly around the room before once again resting on Gadeirus' greenish pallor. "And so, Your Highness. We understand your suspension was lifted this morning."

"Yes."

"I was then informed you wished to meet with us. I did manage to assemble a quorum of our members, which is quite fortunate on such short notice."

"I see." Gadeirus noted the defensive postures of the half-dozen men gathered around the polished table. "So, is a 'man-cave moment' upon us? It appears the ladies have all decided to sit this one out," he quipped to muffled chuckling.

"Hardly," Sammaseus replied in a smooth tone without smiling. "You said it was urgent. And we have a quorum of those who were readily available to meet with you." He leaned his lanky frame forward in his chair. "Please tell us, Your Highness. What matter of urgency brings us together?"

"The matter of the Ahlaielians comes to mind."

"Does it now?"

"Yes."

"Funny thing about that," Sammaseus cooed. "As I recall, you missed that meeting weeks ago. The one where we decided their fate."

"It seems I didn't get the memo."

"It seems you didn't get out of bed or the bottle for the entire time we were wondering what in hell's fury we should do about them." Sammaseus' anger flared the orange flecks in his eyes. "*Your Grace.*"

"It seems you're out of line," Gadeirus murmured.

"*I'm* out of line?" Sammaseus' laugh dripped syrup like his speech. "I'm a member of your cabinet, and I chair this council. Perhaps it falls to me, then, to inform you, Your Highness. That you've been so out of line for so long that you may soon find yourself out of a *job.*"

"Really?" It was Gadeirus' turn to laugh – a maniacal sound that had even his guards shifting their feet. "Did my father get that memo?"

"It's beyond his control now –"

"Is that so?" Gadeirus' voice quieted, and as he rose to his imposing height, the council collectively squirmed. "Must I remind you that the sea is Poseidia's quintessential queen?" He circled the table, appearing as cold and hard as the black veined marble beneath his velvet boots. "Must I also remind you ... who rules the sea?"

Silence fell like a shroud over the assembly. Gadeirus hunted for anyone who would meet his raven's gaze. Not an eye raised to his, though. For many moments, the only sound was Gadeirus' heels clacking the polished floor before Sammaseus sighed.

"We realize who put you here, Your Majesty," the council chair grumbled at last. "We understand the political maneuverings behind your inauguration. And we abide by the High Council's decision. Even if we don't necessarily agree with it." Sammaseus reached for one of the table's ice water carafes and poured a glass. "So, you wish to know the preachers' whereabouts."

"Yes."

"Perhaps you can first tell us where Elysia is."

"I cannot."

"Cannot, Your Highness?" Sammaseus sneered as he sipped. "Or will not?"

"I know nothing of her whereabouts."

"Interesting. Especially since you made a spectacle of yourself with her just last month. And then your guards quite unceremoniously carried her as they followed you from the ballroom. To the horror of our wealthiest benefactors, I might add." He clanged his water goblet onto the tabletop, smiling without humor at Gadeirus. "As I'm sure you can imagine, I've been flooded ever since with messages about your ... indiscretions."

"What can I say, Sammy?" Gadeirus swept newly graying locks behind his ears. "Would you like the truth?"

"Yes, of course."

"You realize she's a bitch of a witch."

"Your Highness, with all due respect –"

"She's a shape-shifting, magic-wielding half-breed, and you know it." Gadeirus folded his hands behind his back as if he were perusing the palatial rose gardens simply to smell their sweetness. "She's also Light-damned gorgeous, and there's not one of you who hasn't dreamed of getting all nasty with her nude body in your bed."

"Your Grace!"

"Especially you, Sammy – you uptight closet whore."

"Lords with swords! I should –"

"Oh, you really *should*, Sammy," Gadeirus cackled, clearly enjoying Sammaseus' red countenance and the council members struggling to straighten their faces. "You really should join me in all of Lesser Light's pleasures. Your soul is every bit as bloody as mine, so why not be a complete dithery douchey?"

"*You cannot* –"

"Oh, but I *can*," the king continued to nervous laughter as the assembly could no longer contain their chuckles. "Clearly, I can. And, yet it's all in mirth, is it not? Because you know me, Sammy. I take so very little seriously. And nothing personally." He stopped and pivoted, flashing the self-deprecatory smile that had endeared him to Poseidia's masses. "You said you wanted the truth. And the truth is, Elysia was nude in my bed on that fateful night. As you all can imagine, she cast quite a spell over me. I experienced a bliss that's quite beyond what I could have conjured in my wildest dreams." Again, he laughed while the council members tipped forward in their seats, their faces bearing identical captivated expressions. "She left me in some sort of trance, from which I was only roused when my guards were ordered to open my chamber door."

"It was Arianna who made them allow her in to awaken Your Majesty." Sammaseus sputtered.

"Yes." Gadeirus' face sobered as he sank back into his seat. "Nothing like a sister's tongue lashing. Especially mine, after she'd witnessed my ... indiscretions."

"Indeed." Sammaseus straightened his black tunic's collar. "Now if I may redirect our discussion, Your Highness?"

"By all means."

"Wonderful." Sammaseus' lips snarled open, revealing small, perfect teeth. "So, you know not where Elysia is?"

"That's correct."

"And you know not how she escaped your chambers?"

"Also correct."

"Correct perhaps, yet odd," Sammaseus mused as he eyed Gadeirus. "Also correct?"

"Also correct."

"All right, then. Shall we move on to the matter of the other preachers?"

"Yes."

"We detained them as a matter of national – and, in fact, intergalactic – security."

"I see," Gadeirus replied. He glanced around at the gathered council members' practiced blank stares. "So, they're detained but unharmed?"

"Since when has their well-being become important?"

"I'm sure you already realize what I'm about to say," Gadeirus answered in his deep melodic voice. "The preachers' well-being is our most pressing matter of not only national – but, in fact, intergalactic – public relations."

"I would say instead, Your Grace, that the narrative we build around their well-being is of the highest priority."

"Light-damn it, Sammy. Do we have yet another scandal on our hands?" It was Gadeirus' turn to tilt his muscular frame toward the chairman. "Am I, myself, not enough of a lotharian lush to fuel Poseidian gossip? It's going to take me more than a minute of backroom dealing and baby kissing to get my own royal ass back into the influencers' good graces. And you know it. But these missionaries ... they're popular. Bless my swarthy heart, I even like that goody two-shoes Ava."

He pounded the polished rosewood, as Sammaseus sighed. "What in the hell realms is it now? Have you already bagged and tagged them?"

"We've begun that process, yes."

"Begun how?"

"By cutting off the head of the snake, of course."

"Kendrick?"

"Yes."

"You killed Kendrick?"

"Yes."

"Lords with swords!" He snatched the table's nearest crystal carafe and sloshed water into a goblet before gulping it dry. "Couldn't you have simply left him to die in some miserable way on his own with the rest of them? You know they're weakening by the minute."

"We couldn't risk that," Sammaseus mumbled. "You know as well as I do that something ... unnatural ... has been sustaining them. How else to explain why they aren't already dead?"

"Yet it's obvious they *are* dying, Sammy. And you know we're flirting with public outrage if whispers of this execution ever reach the hounds of gossip hell!"

"Let me brief you, Your Grace, on those *memos* you didn't receive." Sammaseus spit the words as if scolding a recalcitrant child. "Keep in mind that what I'm about to repeat is old news to the rest of us assembled."

"I'm listening."

"Something has destabilized the already volatile Mid-Atlantic Ridge. Seismic activity is increasing. And that deep current is crumbling Poseidia's infrastructure." Sammaseus tapped on a crystal tabulator, then handed its data-filled screen to Gadeirus. "Look at the numbers detailing what we've examined thus far. And then the images. Streets. Bridges. Buildings. Even this very palace. Cracks and fissures and holes are popping up everywhere."

"Indeed." Gadeirus' brow creased while he scanned charts and pictures. He thought the whole of Poseidia appeared as if she'd been placed inside a fracturing crystal. For several moments, he examined the data and even studied the meeting room, noting how hairline cracks crisscrossed the floor and climbed the walls. Then he turned the tablet toward a friendly face among the council members, a native Poseidian and master builder who was also a palace soiree regular. "Thomaeus, what do your skilled eyes see?"

"There's no observable cause driving this thermal movement, Your Highness." Thomaeus' portly frame filled his chair. He sported short straight hair as black as the king's had been a month earlier. "We have crews working around the clock. We've checked ocean temperatures and underground springs and gaseous rock deposits and everything else we could think of. Things like moisture, permeability, and corrosion are all within normal and expected ranges. In fact, nothing seems out of the ordinary. Nothing except the very real fact that deep molten rock is waking our long-slumbering Mount Tartarus. And Poseidia is splitting apart." He shook his head. "We just don't know why. And until we uncover what's causing the splitting, we won't know how to stop it."

"Have you brought in Maya?"

"The Crystal Keeper?" Thomaeus snorted as he chuckled. "No, Your Grace. We have not. But, if I may ask, my king – why would we?"

"My friend, it seems very much as if Poseidia's science is in order here," Gadeirus answered. "You've unbuttoned this city's bustier and lifted her skirts and, from a purely scientific perspective, she should perhaps be screaming in orgasm from so much focused attention – but not splitting." He glanced around at these mostly science-supporting members; they laughed, even as they once again paid him rapt attention. "But seers as well as scientists play a part in Poseidia's planning and research and development. If the science is on point, that suggests to me the issue will be found with some glitch in the crystalline frequencies."

"Yes, Your Highness." Thomaeus smiled and typed notes into his crystal tabulator. "I will message her as soon as we adjourn."

"Good. And Thoms?"

"Yes, Your Grace?"

"Please have her get the Crystal Weaponry Commission together, on my order. Tell her I will touch base with her by tomorrow morning to go over their findings. I want them to look at everything, just as you've done from the scientific perspective. But most especially, the Tuaoi Stone's newest frequencies. And any R & D weapon testing that's underway. It's possible the frequencies that seemed stable a year or even a week ago have somehow started splitting this island apart. Have her message me directly if there are any questions or concerns."

"Yes, Your Grace."

"Thank you, Thoms. Your patience and cooperation in working with the seers is most appreciated." The king grinned at the master builder before once again turning his raven's gaze on Sammaseus. "By my decree, hold off on harming any more of the half-breeds. I'm guessing you've imprisoned them in the tunnels?"

"Yes, Your Grace."

"Let's just observe them for the next 48 hours. Perhaps in that time they'll do us a favor and die of the natural causes we've already inflicted upon them. Although the narrative we can spin of our medical experts' Herculean efforts to save them will make us all look heroic ... nationally and intergalactically."

"Of course, Your Grace."

"Good. Is there anything else you need from me? Or are we ready to adjourn?"

"Quite ready to adjourn, Your Majesty." Sammaseus and the rest of the members stood with heads bowed as Gadeirus rose.

"Thanks, Sammy. Be seeing you." With a flourish, Gadeirus waved to the members while he called over his shoulder. "Hey Sammy! Be sure you get your bad self to the next party. Check that Light-damned tabulator for a memo with all the details!" Hearty guffawing echoed after him. Tailed by his guards, Gadeirus' still-buzzed mind was already busy strategizing. He couldn't let this minor victory make him complacent, though. It was a battle won, but a war was underway. Whether he wanted it or not, mattered not. Atlantis was splitting, and he needed to decide once and for all where his allegiance would lie before the shards started flying.

TWENTY

Seductive drumbeats slowed, rousing Alaric from the mesmerizing moves dancing through him. Widening his gold-green gaze, Alaric spied locals leaving the sugar-sand courtyard. Many stood hugging one another, or else they busied themselves gathering smaller instruments the crowd had played and cast aside. He noticed an area behind the big drums where tambourines and maracas and such were being nestled into metal chests. He also saw how everyone was taking turns, of how the hugging was deemed equally important to the helping. He could feel true heart-centered warmth in those lingering, life-giving embraces. The energies swelled his own chest to the point of bursting. He deepened his breath, allowing these loving frequencies to fill him. Then he settled himself into the sand, into a circle that was forming from High Council members joining him in the soft quartz seating.

"Welcome," Lochana said at last from her place opposite Alaric. She looked resplendent in a lavender tunic and baby's breath tiara. "Let's commence by uniting hands and hearts and voices to celebrate grateful happiness." She reached slender fingers toward Jon on her right and a eucalyptus-crowned man to her left. Singing in a clear, vibrant voice, Lochana led those gathered in an Old Tongue chant that meant "I am gratitude, I am compassion, I am bliss."

As they crooned in unison, Alaric and the others grooved to their voices' high-flying vibe. *Kritajna hum, karuna hum, ananda hum.* He knew not how long they sang and swayed. Yet at some timeless point, the rocking slowed, silence settled in, and another infinite moment unfolded with only the sounds of bird calls and a breeze gentling the leaves. When his spine stilled at last, Alaric looked up to see Lochana smiling at him.

"*Namaste,*" she whispered in the Old Tongue, acknowledging Source sparkling him like white diamonds.

"*Namaste.*" Alaric placed his palms together at his heart. He bowed his head before gazing into Lochana's warm almond eyes. "Thank you, Your Highness. For all of your kindnesses and aid. I don't know how to express the depth of my gratitude for all you've done and continue to do."

"All of Rohati honors what *you've* done and continue to do, Your Highness," she murmured. "We are united as we serve. Continuing to forge a way forward that uplifts this galaxy and beyond remains our common path."

"Indeed, it does." Alaric folded his hands in his lap. "Please tell me how I may aid the forging of this path."

"By letting the love vibration that's been cultivated here for millennia heal your heart," she answered. "Our planet exhales love. If you but linger in her presence for a little while, her vibration will breathe through and transform these traumas that still bleed you."

"My queen, I do hear you, and I know you speak Divine truth," he sighed. "Yet I haven't the luxury of lingering."

"I understand the urgency you feel, and I want you to know our most powerful Berdache healers are working with the essences as we speak." She grinned radiant reassurance. "As you're aware, Nayaka leads their efforts, and he is most eager to see you."

"Thank you, Lochana." Tears drizzled his chiseled cheeks. "I am beyond grateful. And I am honored to reunite with my dear friend and all of the Berdaches whenever it pleases you."

"I shall arrange it. As soon as we discuss anything you wish." A light-hearted laugh bubbled from her lips. "And dance!"

"*Dhanayavad.*" He expressed his gratitude once more in the Old Tongue, and then the High Council members introduced themselves one by one. As the assembly chatted and chuckled with him, Reena and Beeja appeared with trays bearing four large crystal tea sets. Inside the tea pots, Alaric spied purple lotus blossoms floating above the other flowers. He smiled when Beeja handed him a crystalline vessel. Once the fragrant brew had been served, Lochana raised her cup.

"My beloveds," she called out, as those gathered toasted the queen. "Let us drink to Highest Light. May we align with truth, peace, compassion, and love. And may all our choices, creations, and endeavors spring forth from the union of Divine Love and Right Action, here in the eternal now. And so it is."

"And so it is," the assembly replied.

"Splendid!" Lochana gentled her cup into the sand and clapped her hands. "Let us lift one voice, drink one elixir, join as one heart-mind-soul. We let go of all hope and confusion, so that we may receive with clarity the answers to our deepest prayers. And so it is."

"And so it is," everyone murmured.

"*Om tare tuttare ture soha.*" Lochana bellowed a mantra of liberation, of letting go of what no longer serves. As everyone roared in response and release, Alaric could feel the quartz sand recording the powerfully peaceful frequencies generated. He could also feel old tensions and worries slip from his own shoulders while he sipped and sang. He knew not how long they chanted, but as if by magic, their voices slowed and quieted as one into stillness. For long moments, they simply breathed in love and breathed out appreciation. And then Lochana tapped a crystal spoon three times upon her emptied cup.

"And so it is," she whispered.

"And so it is," the assembly purred.

"Thank you, Reena and Beeja," Lochana said, as the sisters circled with fresh hot tea. "Please join us if you wish." After all the teacups were refreshed, the sisters sat cross-legged on either side of Alaric. Then Lochana exchanged grins with the eucalyptus-crowned man seated beside her. "Everyone is free to express and share. I ask Abhasa, our Lead Source Reflector, to offer knowings as we proceed."

"It's my honor, Your Grace," Abhasa answered in a soft melodic tone. Hyacinth eyes shimmered his smooth cocoa countenance as he gazed at Alaric. "A great task has fallen to you, Snake King."

"Yes," Alaric whispered.

"A task of your choosing. Born of your unbreakable love."

"Yes."

"A task laden with burden and risk and sacrifice. With intergalactic importance in the face of impossible odds."

"Indeed."

"I can say nothing that you don't already know," Abhasa continued. "Yet there are reminders Source wishes to reflect to you."

"Thank you, Abhasa. I welcome these reflections."

"Some may seem unpleasant." Abhasa stared off in the distance, his face serene yet serious, as if he witnessed something foreboding. "Truth can feel harsh, especially when one has just sustained and overcome a Cerberus bite."

"I appreciate your gentleness, *atisakhi*," Alaric's velvety voice held equal parts strength and vulnerability. "Yet it is what it is. And here we are."

"Yes." The Reflector's voice softened as it slowed. "Here we are, in another causal looping of the space-time continuum. With yet another opportunity to shift events toward their Highest Light trajectory as opposed to a Lesser Light unfolding."

"Agreed." Alaric sighed. "We've long ridden this endless loop's coding. In fact," he added, raising his gold-green gaze to Abhasa's. "For what has already felt like eternity, we've lacked an exit strategy. Thus, we keep recreating and repeating its misery sequence because we've failed to upload instructions that will override the program. And yield a love-inspired condition."

"Aptly put, Snake King." The Reflector's kaleidoscope eyes shimmered purple to pink to blue in a dazzling display as he channeled.

"The coding repeats because Highest and Lesser are locked in a stale-mate with no legal moves left. I know you recall when Lesser Light first hacked the Akashic database."

"I do," Alaric muttered. "That's when Earth and many other planets were dragged from the Highest Light realms. Plunging all inhabitants into 3D brutality. Moldaaris strived – and yet failed – with our infiltration."

"Moldaaris lacked enough beings holding the love frequency consistently enough to override the programming."

"Indeed. The encoded fear was overwhelming. It paralyzed many of our people who moved among Earth and other affected planets." Alaric shook his head. "Fear is the most contagious blight."

"Agreed. They've embedded fear throughout their misery sequence instructions. Such that every time Highest Lighters have managed to hack in, we've lacked the numbers to sustain loving frequencies as we attempt to plant new coding. As such, we cannot get the program to ascertain the specified condition we are introducing. At which point, we fail."

"Yes. Over and over again."

"Although, a new day dawns." The Reflector grinned. "Causally looped events are once again presenting opportunities to effect massive change within the space-time continuum. Not legal opportunities, you understand. At least, not legal in the Lesser Light-created paradigm."

"I understand all too well," Alaric whispered.

"Yet there's a deepening of your understanding that needs to take place."

"I'm listening."

"Are you aware that intergalactic eyes have been watching your efforts?"

"My efforts to save Elysia?"

"More specifically, the soul growth you've shown throughout all these centuries of selfless actions made in the name of Right Action," Abhasa replied. "You've had a singular, unshakable motive. You've held the love vibration in its purest, most unadulterated form. And you've clutched it consistently. With all your heart and integrity." Sweet laughter danced across his face. "Nobody else has ever done such a thing."

"Perhaps nobody else has ever loved another in the way that I love Elysia." Fresh tears leaked from his lashes. "Although the matter of my integrity is indeed in question."

"Not from a Highest Light perspective, Snake King." The Reflector leaned forward in his lotus position. "And until you heal yourself and align with that Divine truth, I'm afraid we may miss the opportunity before us. The chance to open this closed loop. To implant the purest love frequency in the universe. But that frequency needs to be without origin and as such identical to the purest, strongest expression of itself throughout infinity. If it's not identical in past, present, and future timelines, it will be detected and deleted because it will vibrate an inconsistency that the program will find and terminate."

"What are you asking of me?" Alaric looked around the seated circle. Thirteen calm faces resonated loving empathy. Jon nodded his support when his beryl eyes met his father's pained gaze. And then, a regal woman who'd introduced herself earlier as Chela spoke.

"Your Highness, we mirror truth to you," Chela uttered in a husky voice. A sapphire tunic draped her smooth sepia skin. "And truth is like pregnancy, is it not?" A few council members snickered. "A woman is with child, or she is not. There's no gray area. No middle ground."

"No middle ground at all," Alaric replied. "And so, what do you wish me to bear?"

"Birth your own healing," she answered. "Because if you do not, then you won't be able to impregnate the Akashic Records with pure love's perfect frequency. You won't be able to rewrite the code and change the causal loop. You won't be able to liberate the universe of the pestilence that Lesser Light has begotten as its only offspring. And ultimately, you won't be free to have your 'happily ever after' with your beloved. Because her essence has long been embedded in low-vibration codes."

"You're saying Elysia's demise is doomed to be repeated forever throughout the space-time continuum." Alaric paused, drinking in the full implication of Chela's words. "Unless Lesser Light programming is terminated and the universe, in essence, is rebooted."

"Yes."

"I see." Moments passed in silence. The assembly anchored in as one, holding Alaric in the love vibration as he breathed and cried and settled at last into stillness. Many more minutes unfolded with Alaric joining the assembly, breathing and grounding in love even as he himself prayed for guidance. He asked for healing that would allow transformation of a trauma that not only bound him and Elysia to an unrequited forever; their wounding kept Source from righting all the wrongs that had long allowed only anguish to reign. In the quietude, he smiled across at Jon before glancing around at everyone gathered. "What shall I do?"

"Let me bring you to Nayaka," Lochana suggested. "The Berdaches can help you find your way to healing."

"All right." Alaric again clasped his hands in front of his heart as he gazed at all the hopeful faces. "I will follow the path they set forth." He bowed his head after his eyes met Lochana's. "Please take me to see my old friend."

"Once we dance," she answered. Rising from the sand, she crossed the circle and offered Alaric her hand. "Let's celebrate as if it's already come to pass, shall we?"

"We shall." Alaric smiled as he embraced Rohati's queen. While the others gathered instruments from the courtyard chests, Alaric offered a thankful prayer for these kind, incorruptible beings. Throughout the centuries, he'd had so many close calls and last chances, and yet Source still dangled hope before him. He knew he had to set his mind and heart upon his own healing with the ferocity of the love he felt for Elysia. He also knew that this time, with this many loving souls aiding and encouraging him, the destructive forces splitting so many worlds apart might just be overcome at last.

TWENTY-ONE

Leading the gurney along a torch-lit cavern, Elysia paused to sonar the walls. An unyielding harshness pulsed out over the obsidian floor, magnifying the dark crystal's mirror-like ability to reflect one's shadow. She felt more oppressed and overwhelmed than she had earlier in obsidian's presence; in this subterranean grotto, she felt weak and trembly touching the olive and forest green bubbled surfaces surrounding them. Her eyes met Charlaeus' as Jack donned a headlamp.

"What unearthly stone is this?" Elysia murmured. "It's so familiar. Yet something's off. I can't quite say what."

"It is indeed unearthly," Charlaeus replied as her fingers skimmed the cold stone. "It's called moldavite in Atlantis. But – well, it's just an old legend, really. Locals have long claimed it came from Moldaaris."

"*Moldavite*?!" Elysia gasped, her hands grasping the crystalline verdancy. "How could this *be*?!"

"What's wrong?" Charlaeus' eyes widened to black pools in the bleakness.

"Moldavite once made up the very bedrock of our planet. Even the home I shared with Alaric had moldavite gracing many chambers." Elysia's whisper hissed like wet kindling. "We honored her in ritual and ceremony as a Highest Light transformation tool. We created natural cathedrals from her formations, forged from the fires of ancient lava flows." She shook her head. "But this stone ... this stone has somehow become abusive where she was once assertive. Cold instead of reflective. Unforgiving as opposed to undoing the knots we tie that prevent us from our potential."

"The old stories teach how Moldaarins had programmed evil and corruption into their favorite crystal. Atlantean children have long been conditioned to fear it as a bringer of bad luck." Charlaeus sighed heavily. "And, then when Helionel ordered the surprise annihilation of your planet, Poseidia sent its agents on a highly publicized quest. A mission meant to rid the intergalactic community of the sickness moldavite debris was spreading, as they said at the time, like a virus."

"Of course he did," Jack muttered. "Helionel was nothing if not a master propagandist."

"Yes," Charlaeus continued. "And he filled his coffers from all the wealthy benefactors he frightened into believing moldavite was a scourge that needed to be collected and contained. The gathered stone shards were famously encapsulated in deactivating crystalline sheaths and paraded into Poseidia's laboratories, ostensibly to be imprisoned for eternity. For the public's safety and well-being, of course."

"Lords with swords," Jack harrumphed. "More atrocities have been sanctioned throughout time in the name of keeping the public safe than for any other lie." He beamed his headlamp across the swirly silica glass. "Yet clearly, they remade the moldavite somehow. Took the shards and turned them into these slabs."

"The bigger the crystal, the more energy it can channel," Charlaeus whispered. "These walls ... the power is palpable."

"It's something, all right." Jack's eyes darted about, a scowl wrinkling his brow. "Something for sure even has me feeling weird. And that's ... weird."

"That's not the only strangeness." Charlaeus pointed to the shadows stretching ahead. "I keep hearing ... something I can't define."

"Rats maybe?" Jack's stance straightened into high alert.

"That's no rat." Lights strobed the moldavite, and Elysia sonared coded shielding over her companions. When she stepped forward in the brilliant flashes, both Jack and Charlaeus saw blood streaming from her nose.

"El!" Jack yelled before a thunderous boom overturned the gurney and knocked him, motionless, to the ground. Charlaeus scrambled after Elysia, only to sprawl face down when the second shuddering rumbled through. In its wake, a cacophony akin to rebel war cries and raspy whispers and high-pitched squeals and deep, dark laughter trembled the earth. Yet Elysia plodded on, even as mist roiled the cavern, conjuring mud from wet debris and swirling the smell of death in its wake. From the foggy filth, a cyclone spun up into a shape-shifting specter.

"Depart. Or suffer departure," a throaty female voice purred. Her nude figure morphed and dissolved as if puffed from smoke. Twitching like an angry cat's tail, her knee-length plait flexed and stretched. Elysia could feel the passion with which this Netherworld witch wished to strangle her.

"Fish. Or cut bait," Elysia said evenly. "Or go ashore."

"Do you mistake these depths as Acheron?" The Daayan's delicate upturned nose belied her chin's immutability. Stretching her arms wide, she thrust ample breasts forward. "Do you take me for a ferryman?"

"You are a keeper of the dead, are you not?" Elysia eased closer, causing the chestnut braid to flick faster.

"This crypt is of the dead and the undead," she whispered. "The undead keep it."

"I'm looking for safe passage through your Patala, Daayan. For my party and myself." Elysia's emerald eyes shimmered in the shadows. "Will you arrange it?"

"You've nothing I want. Nothing I haven't already taken," she sneered. "Alaric has already pleasured me. And I him. Multiple times, you understand." Her tittering tinkled like ice swirling a glass. "He's quite amorous."

"Quite." Elysia deepened her breath as she surrendered to Source. Everywhere around her, she sensed movement and spirit exchanges taking place. All manner of ghastly beings materialized and vanished, bearing souls to the afterlife realms like cheap market wares. But something else stirred. Those who'd hovered near death were now crawling or clawing or dragging their way toward her – feeding off the energies she channeled as blood flooded her chin. "There must be something."

"You'd never concede it."

"Concede what?"

"Your baby."

"I really don't –"

"You really don't know, do you?" Mocking laughter split her thin lips. "How could you not know?"

"Know what?" Elysia's heart hammered her ribs as a deep truth began to surface.

"You're with child, Elysia."

TWENTY-TWO

The chamber's longcase clock struck eleven as Lorelei sipped from a half-empty shot glass – the same one Linasia had so rudely shoved in her face. In the scant minutes since Linasia left, Lorelei had pondered much. Yet the more she looked, the more of a debacle she found. A growing blemish now marred the face of her magnificent Dark Heart plan. She alone had envisioned the future that the whole Lesser Light brigade claimed to endorse.

"But do they?" she whispered. Turning amber eyes toward the near-by table's gazing ball, she peered into a psychic's world she could no longer see. Tears gushed from her thick lashes. "Do they really?"

Arising like the queen she'd never been, Lorelei sniffed as she pulled her crimson cloak close. She hugged herself as she paced, her brooding brow deeply creased. Rows of burning candles did little to warm the vast room's forenoon chill. Nor did they thaw the icy armor that for so long had been her sole support. She knew not how to lean on any-one. She'd grown up without confiding in or trusting another soul. Her world had contracted so much since she'd been stripped of her gifts. Yet she'd made the best of what she still had, and she'd forsaken the rest – just as the whole of Moldaaris had shunned her.

Shaking her woozy head, she only managed to muddle the self-damning thoughts flooding her mind. Somehow, she'd softened her vigilance. Perhaps her ego had let the influencers infiltrate her hold over Poseidia, loosening her grip on what was about to unfold. The morning's mishap with Abigor was simply the latest example of her plans gone awry – and also the last straw. Her cheeks flushed as she chastised herself once more for crumbling a cardinal rule she never should have broken. She knew better than to defecate where she dealt the cards. But it had been so long since anyone had taken notice of her or said anything kind. It had been longer still since anyone had em-braced her. She'd known he wasn't Alaric, yet she'd wanted so very much to be soothed ... and seduced. Her eyes misted hot as she realized Abigor had done neither. Her lower lip trembled with thoughts of his selfish needs syncing so poorly with her anxiety. He appeared to feel

139

into her accurately enough; he seemed to understand she feared intimacy. Yet for such a renowned psychic to be blind to her shameful little secret seemed incredulous. She wondered how he could be so clueless; how could he not see that she'd never experienced sexual release? Although, it seemed miscues and missteps abounded everywhere for her in Poseidia. Even now, when she knew Light-damned well she should have her wits about her, she was instead swilling an inebriating elixir. And she imbibed simply because it had been the politically correct thing to do when that swine Linasia handed her a glass. Now that she was tipsy, she just couldn't seem to find her spine or her spunk.

"Damn it to hell!" She pivoted and pitched the jigger into the fireplace. It shattered spectacularly, igniting molten embers and spreading satisfaction across her face. "Get hold of yourself, Lady Lei." Breathing deeply of Dark Heart energies with a practiced perfection that sobered her, she replenished herself in the candlelight. As she smoothed her ruffled edges, she became increasingly aware of a way forward. Of a Lesser Light prompting. Though it had been centuries since she'd been able to channel, she could still interpret imprints. She knew if she could center herself within the Dark Heart, its Cosmic Controllers would make contact. Slithering into a rosewood seat, she stared at the flames – and received.

For many minutes, she sat without thinking or feeling, as messages downloaded into her being. Once the transmission was complete, she closed her eyes and sighed. Over the millennia, she'd found the Controllers intuitively nudged her to reach out whenever she wavered or the plan waffled. Today, they called on her to orchestrate a course correction, one that would require her to keep her clarity and focus in order to be guided through this ever-changing maze of unfolding events. Although, much remained murky – including Alaric's whereabouts – she now knew more than she'd ever cared to learn about the Ahlaielians. About their childish attempts to Highest Light their way out of sorry circumstances. Still, the Controllers had cautioned her to watch carefully. It hadn't gone unnoticed at the realm's uppermost levels that something, somehow was amiss in the short time since the missionaries had landed in Poseidia. Somehow, they'd arrived alive. And somehow, in spite of how they should have already met their demise due to their surgically split essences, they kept regrouping. Something hidden was helping them. Something the Controllers would not concede as a Highest Light intervention, let alone a victory. And so, the task had fallen to her, once again, to find a way to fix things.

"Bless up, buttercups," she muttered. "You preachers will need all your Light-damned luck moving forward. Because the Dark Heart has yet to be unleashed in all her terrible beauty." Gazing into the fireplace embers, Lorelei maintained a No-Mind connection as she sifted and sorted options and opportunities. The longcase clock chimed noon and still she sat, unmoving and unfeeling, while her plan evolved. An unpleasant reality kept returning to her awareness. It wasn't just Linasia she needed to appease at this point. She would have to forge many uncomfortable alliances, partnerships she neither trusted nor liked, in order to steer the Dark Heart back on track. This unavoidable fact roused her from her reverie, leaving her sullen and sulking. For a moment, she allowed herself to succumb to victim consciousness, in a "woe is me" wallowing that she knew only served to make her vicious. The cold, hard truth that kept presenting itself throughout her long-suffering life had always been simple yet not easy. It had always been her destiny to endure the unendurable – while she overcame the insurmountable. All while moving unseen behind the scenes. Perhaps that last part is what rankled her the most. If she were honest, remaining invisible when her very being craved accolades and acknowledgment was excruciating. "How is a queen to be crowned, if her subjects know not who she is?" Again, she lifted herself from the seat's velvety cushion. "How can a queen be recognized, if her power is not visible?"

With a straight spine and lifted chin, she marched along the room's candlelit perimeter. Pausing before a gilded frame hugging a full-length mirror, she scrutinized her appearance. Though centuries of life experience had taught her that others found her attractive, she could only see in her reflection a complexion that was too pale. Eyes that were set too close together. An unevenness to her bottom lip's natural plumpness. Hair that was so curly it frizzed into a tangled mess in Poseidia's ever-present humidity. Curling slender hands into fists, Lorelei sighed as she closed her eyes against her ugliness. Breathing deeply of the only perfection she knew, she drank of the Dark Heart and looked again upon her countenance. Somehow, in this bolstered energetic stance, she couldn't focus upon her flaws. In this Lesser Light state, she only saw her unrealized, unborn potential. In this Dark Heart shadow, she alone could shine – if she but persevered. In this knowing, she still ached from her fall from grace and from all the personal wrongs she'd never before been able to make right. Yet in spite of all she'd suffered and survived, the Dark Heart lifted her from despair. It promised redemption – and revenge. And, to the soul she'd long ago sold, that comfort in and of itself wasn't ideal – but it was enough.

TWENTY-THREE

With feline finesse, Alaric crossed the Grand Temple's rose quartz foyer. Sunlight streamed through its three-story crystalline dome, shimmering his sable and gold locks and ivory silk tunic until he strode through the spherical sanctuary's back portal. Its archway had been fashioned from an amethyst geode, split into towering purple halves that led to an underground selenite cave. As he descended limestone steps into this jeweled womb, Alaric felt a quietude calming him. Lamp-lit selenite walls left in their natural formations protruded as sword points wielding Source. The further he slipped into these sacred depths, the bigger the crystalline projections became. Rounded doorways opened to either side of the spiraling stairway, offering glimpses into the Berdache chapels. And the longer he journeyed, the more intensely he felt Elysia's essence. He'd reached a meditative stupor by the time he stopped outside the chamber where her thready soul fragments quivered.

"Hello, my friend." Nayaka's soothing tone enveloped Alaric as the two embraced.

"Hello, *triyasti*." Alaric breathed back sobs. "I am just so grateful. For all you and the Berdaches have done. And all you are yet to do."

"I love and appreciate you." Nayaka's silvery eyes gleamed like the gold of his tunic belt, as he released Alaric. "Please come with me. There's much to share."

"Yes, of course." Alaric followed Nayaka to the chamber's center, where a massive, milky-white gypsum cluster anchored floor to ceiling in all directions. Each crystal trunk measured three feet in diameter and stretched in spikes more than 30 feet long. These angled supports cradled a translucent selenite slab, a natural altar which held a myriad of other stones and golden geometric shapes. Hovering among the sacred objects and above a copper flower of life grid rested the essence-bearing tubes. For a long moment, Alaric gaped at the crystalline vessels. Something was different. Something had begun to alter Elysia's essence. Something he couldn't quite believe or hope or dare to dream as even a possibility was now an energetic reality before him. "It cannot be," he whispered, and Nayaka chuckled.

"Oh, but it *can*!" Nayaka's gleeful laugh echoed in the cave, joined by a chorus of ringing crystals. "Congratulations, Papa!"

"In the name of Oneness," Alaric murmured, as fresh tears flooded his face.

"Yes." Dressed in a long lilac tunic, Nayaka raised one hand toward the essences. A rainbow swirled from his palms – pure positivity to support the tubes. The energy patterning kept morphing from one sacred geometry shape to another, in a healing matrix of codes. "Our work together has a surprising yet welcome development."

"I am beyond words, looking upon my wife's energy. And my daughter's." Alaric shook his head, his gold-green eyes never blinking as he studied the tiny essence spark that had joined Elysia's soul fragments. "Thank you, Nayaka. I know not how such grace has been granted."

"Because you are so aligned with your inner being when you are with Elysia." Nayaka moved closer to the altar, the colorful coded energy pouring from his hand continuing to circle the tubes.

"I hear what you're not saying, *triyasti*." Closing his eyes, Alaric seated himself before the altar. "I'm not aligned with my own divinity without her. Yet that's the ironic task before me, is it not? If I don't align alone, then I will spend eternity alone."

"Alignment is a continuing calibration." Nayaka eased onto the limestone floor beside Alaric. "It's like sailing. Minor steering adjustments are needed to stay on course. Because life, like the sea, is ever flowing."

"Stillness in motion," Alaric whispered. "It's effortless with her."

"When it's effortless within you, all resistance will disappear. The rough seas will calm." Nayaka's smile sparkled his luminous eyes. "I tell you nothing you don't already know."

"Yet knowing is a far cry from doing. And further yet from being." He sighed and bowed his head. "May Highest Light forgive my guilty centuries."

"There's nothing to forgive, Alaric."

"I can't seem to forgive myself. I've spent a thousand years ... unclean."

"Your soul is spotless," Nayaka said gently. "Source sees only your pristine essence. And so do I." The Berdache healer grounded loving frequencies around Alaric, watching as tears trembled the Moldaarin king. When Nayaka again spoke, his voice held a hushed prayer. "You know your inner being is pure and magnificent, do you not?"

"I realize 'yes' is the correct response." Alaric's stony gaze studied Nayaka's compassionate countenance. "Yet you so clearly see my heart. I feel anything but pure and magnificent."

"It's simply your practiced vibration, dear one."

"I once believed as you do," Alaric sighed. "But when Moldaaris shattered before my eyes, something split apart within me. Something I haven't in all these centuries since been able to heal. Something that keeps me from wholeness still. Something that keeps me from getting it right."

"Nothing is broken," Nayaka murmured. "Take these essences, for example. They're intact energetically. They've merely been split and regrouped physically. It's just a perception shift. A recalibration we're supporting in non-duality – in *advaita* – within this chapel. And that's all the Divine asks of you. Shift what you see. What you focus upon. Recalibrate. Redirect. Once you only see Oneness, the regrouping occurs naturally."

"I know you speak the truth," Alaric replied. "I keep recalibrating. I can so clearly feel my misalignment. I have a few good moments. A few hours at a time, perhaps. And then when I get off kilter, it feels like my old, deeply ingrained vibration envelops me. Overtakes me. And overwhelms me to the point where I can't find my eternal now."

"It's time to become a more deliberate creator again. That's easier to accomplish when you first become more generic with your thoughts." Nayaka placed one of his rainbow-swirling palms on Alaric's knee. "Point your compass toward a pleasant horizon that holds no triggering emotion. Perhaps focusing upon your 'happily ever after' with Elysia is too specific at times, when you aren't riding the highest-vibe frequencies. When you feel overwhelmed, it's good to go more general with what you're thinking about. I know you know what I mean. Focus on anything at all that holds no resistance and feels good. A forest floor's soft foot hug. Jasmine's sweetness. Dawn breaking. The ocean's ebb and flow." His broad face lit up even more brightly as he spoke. "Nature in all her vastness offers so many feel-good focal points."

"I appreciate these reminders, *triyasti*. So very much." Alaric again closed his eyes, his face visibly softening as he took centering breaths – and as the Berdache healer continued to hold space. When he looked once more at Nayaka, he had reached *advaita*. "I realize great power demands great responsibility. It falls to me to direct – and keep redirecting – my focus so I remain in universal flow."

"My dear friend." Nayaka's expression radiated peace. "All you really need to do is relax. Your immense energy is well trained to fight. To push. To make things happen." Quietly, he chuckled. "You're so afraid you won't get your way."

"Indeed!" Alaric laughed, and at last true mirth warmed his gold-green eyes. "You do see my motivations clearly. And kindly, I might add."

"Kings and queens and warriors and visionaries share a type of courage that, if focused, moves mountains and parts seas and creates worlds," Nayaka observed. "Your task at hand isn't to do more. It's to stop doing at all. And start allowing. Trust that you don't have to effort any of this. In fact, it's all this efforting that takes you straight out of *advaita*. And slows your flow."

"*Yes.*"

"You don't trust Highest Light, Alaric. You lost confidence in Source a thousand years ago," Nayaka whispered. "It's time to believe in more than your love for Elysia."

"She is my church," Alaric croaked. "I am a devout believer who happily worships at her altar. Yet again, you express truth. If I'm honest, I haven't trusted Source in so long. Not really. Not like my love for Elysia."

"I merely mirror your growing edge to you." Nayaka placed a reassuring hand on Alaric's shoulder. "Perhaps reflect upon it this way. You wouldn't be able to align so perfectly with Elysia if that perfection didn't already exist within you yourself. It's like sonar; you can't hear the frequency if you aren't tuned to that vibration. Yet you *are* flawlessly aligned with her. Such perfection can only be a direct reflection of Source – of Highest Light in its purest, most magnificent, and unadulterated expression. Such alignment can only exist because you are attuned to Source at your deepest essence level, yet you only allow this attunement with Elysia. With that being said," Nayaka paused, taking in Alaric's rapt attention. "I wish to make a suggestion."

"Please."

"Allow. Unconditionally. Just flow with what is, whatever it is. And if you meet unpleasantness or resistance within, redirect your attention. Adjust your sails if you will. And sail on."

"Ah, you offer wisdom, Nayaka," Alaric replied. "Yes. I've spent so many years perceiving my bow as broken, the helm locked and hull leaking. None of that type of thinking serves me. None of it." He shook his head. "With Source as my witness, I vow simply to allow. It's the only place of peace and prosperity within the eternal now. It's a place I know as well as anguish. *Advaita* always feels like home. I've simply been caught within my own wounded story. Yet here, in this place – and in your presence – I feel the beginning of a most welcome transformation."

"It's a beautiful thing to witness your awareness shifting." Nayaka folded his hands in a prayer position over his heart. "You know how these sacred stones assist with alignment," he continued, looking around at the selenite cavern. "Have you noticed anything else about the essences beyond the obvious change within Elysia?"

"I've been so struck by this baby's blessing that no, *triyasti*. I haven't observed anything else." Alaric turned his gold-green laser gaze upon the vessels. In the lamplight's luminescence, Alaric dropped into his inner being. There, in *advaita*, he was awash in the selenite structures' powerful pulsating. Their rhythm kept time with Rohati's heartbeat, and within that harmonic frequency, Alaric could see and sense the cellular regrouping for which Nayaka and the Berdaches had been holding vigil. He recalled the frailty of how the essences had felt in his hands just before he departed Zacktronymus. He remembered fretting as he left, hoping against hope that Jon and Tyrius would retrieve the vessels without incident and escort them to Rohati. The split energies had seemed so feeble, so fragile. Yet as he felt into them in these selenite depths, he sensed a strengthening. A coming together. A reworking and a regrouping that, for all its delicacy, felt inevitable. "I'm beyond words, Nayaka. All I can say is I'm witnessing a recalibrating."

"It's another celebration in the making, dear one!" Nayaka giggled as he stood, and the selenite chimed in response, echoing like church bells throughout the cavern. "You've honored us so many times before as we've danced and sung and offered ourselves to the Highest Light realms. And this time," he continued, gesturing broadly toward the crystalline tubes. "We party with the essences." He raised his hands over his head before bringing his palms together to rest in front of his heart. "Do you know that every time we celebrate with them, there's a quickening? The healing unfolds more rapidly. Every being in the universe thrives on joy." He turned gleeful twinkling eyes upon Alaric. "And so, will you join the other Berdaches and myself? As we have some fun?"

"The honor and the pleasure are most assuredly mine." In one elegant motion, Alaric gained his feet and hugged Nayaka hard.

"Splendid!" Nayaka held Alaric for several moments. When he released him, he grinned his brilliant smile. "But first, there's tea."

"I seem to recall how Rohatians begin every endeavor with tea." Alaric smiled at his friend, and he realized it had been a thousand years since he'd felt such relief.

"What better way to start any ritual ... than with one of the oldest rituals?" Nayaka threw an arm around Alaric's shoulders as they walked toward the chapel entrance. "Come with me to the tearoom, Papa. Let's see what brew you choose for this happy occasion!"

TWENTY-FOUR

Gadeirus lay nude on his palatial bed, twirling an empty pouch and staring up at that Light-damned painting. He'd just taken the last of his strongest wafers after sending his guards to get more from his favorite Artisan Market District vendor. A smile that never touched his eyes tried and failed to curve his numb lips. Nonetheless, he was amused at how shocked and appalled most of Poseidia's good citizens would be if they knew just how many wafers their king consumed all day, every day. And they'd be equally horrified to learn their beloved Artisan Market was a front for illicit activities of all kinds, from all over the galaxy – some of which even made Gadeirus squirm. He shook his head and reached for the second of three shot glasses he'd poured. The plum-colored elixir was the most potent Poseidia produced. Yet it hadn't put Elysia in the mood for his advances. Nor had it reached the deep pit he felt within. The abyss that missed the soul he'd sold long ago. The part of him that yet recalled he'd once had a conscience; a ghost that still haunted him whenever he sobered enough to its pure if puny presence.

"Lords with swords," he slurred. A wild thought occurred to him; for some reason, he wondered if Arianna might soon knock on his chamber door. And if she did, he would have no words to defend his present narcosis. On the heels of that revelation, he realized he didn't quite recall what he'd promised her. It felt like forever since he'd seen her anyway, the morning he'd awakened to Elysia's kiss. But he'd given her his word about something. More than likely, it was what he always swore he would do, which was curb his appetites. Although he was as foggy on those details as the double vision blurring his raven's gaze. "I'm so sorry, Ari. Better luck ... tomorrey!" He cackled, downing the shot before grabbing the third glass. He gulped from it, too, and then tossed the jigger onto the rug, where it landed among the once-fine carpet's many purple stains.

Gadeirus settled back onto the bed. He lay unmoving in sweaty sheets, though his thoughts never slowed. He was a visual thinker even when he hadn't indulged in hallucinogens. Memories smeared his mind like muddy pigments mixed with blood. One bled into the next as he fell into a reverie of childhood torment. Images flooded him of his elder brother, Atlas the Perfect, with his greater height, better face, longer legs, sharper wit. And those Light-damned dreamy blue eyes that always seemed to get him out of trouble – and into the bed of any woman he desired. Gadeirus had grown up in a constant state of angst and envy. No matter how good he was at anything – and he'd cultivated many talents in search of something, anything he could reign – he never bested Atlas. Even worse, his brother never competed against him. It had always felt to Gadeirus as if he wasn't good enough to merit attention as a contender. Although the deeper truth Gadeirus hated to admit was closer to the oft-repeated legend – Atlas lived up to his name's very meaning as a bearer of the heavens, a fountainhead of responsibility, and as such he was above one-upmanship. Yet Atlas appeared ruthless because he believed the end justified the means; he could always be counted upon to do what was right or what was necessary. Even his detractors admired his effectiveness – which was why it had taken the almighty Poseidon himself to hoist Gadeirus to the throne, since his big brother had long held sway in any Atlantean popularity contest.

As the potion infused the wafers, funneling him into the hole that offered the only respite he'd known besides Elysia's kiss, Gadeirus caught a fleeting glimpse of his mother's face. Her name was Cleito, and she'd been quite the long-suffering queen. Orphaned at an age when many suitors were storming Atlantis, Cleito had embodied a spirited regal presence and voluptuous figure that captured even his father's wandering eye. At first, the reclusive Cleito evaded Poseidon's best efforts to bed her. Yet their sparky rapport soon led Cleito into a tumultuous love affair, a union that provoked the possessive Sea God into building Poseidia's beautiful cage to contain her. In all, she bore him ten sons and six daughters during her mostly isolated existence; it was a life that drove her into addictive indulgences in an effort to quiet a feisty heart that no longer had any means of expression.

It wasn't long before the very liquor Gadeirus himself kept as a daily companion had befriended much of Cleito's mortal life force. As a child, Gadeirus had mostly known just the shell of a woman that in the past had kept an island kingdom wrapped around one of her lovely, tapered fingers. Rare were the instances when a flash of steely blue eyes emboldened her face, or where her walk took on the confident swagger that had once caused women as well as men to gawk. It was from Cleito that Gadeirus learned how to mask and medicate. He grew into manhood feeling his father's physical absence and his mother's mental vacuity. Wistfully, he'd witnessed Poseidon's fame grow from afar, even as countless goddesses and hybrids and mortal women kept bearing more and more of his children all over the galaxy and beyond. At the same time, he and his siblings were left with their mother fading into obscurity, a once-vibrant beauty long written off by Atlantean socialites as enviably lucky if increasingly disturbed. He stirred in his stupor, still pained by the sadness he so deeply felt that had kept his mother staring out the castle windows for hours on end. He'd often wondered what she saw with those unseeing eyes, what she had felt as she sat twiddling a crystal cup brimming with violet spirits.

The only things besides intoxicants that had fueled Cleito's interest later in life had been material in nature. Jewels. Dresses. Shoes. Sculptures and artwork from across the galaxy. And horses, although any that struck her fancy became pasture ornaments, as her riding days ended when her turbulent relationship with Poseidon began. Yet Cleito made sure all her children knew how to ride and would sometimes sit and watch their equestrian lessons with a filled flask and an empty stare – the same way she would observe some of their dancing or drawing or violin or sports or foreign language instruction. There but not there, as Gadeirus often thought to himself, even as he would hear his sisters quibble about their mother's coldness or unwillingness to hug them or say anything kind or supportive. On rare and random occasions, she would have the kitchen staff bake cookies or little cakes for them. Or surprise one but never all of them with gifts for no known or expressed reason, which left each of them wondering if the child showered with favor had done something to deserve it.

Growing up in such an environment – rich in resources but lacking emotional connection – fostered much drama and heartache among Cleito's offspring. Her youngest daughter Leucippe, who'd been named for Cleito's beloved mother, had inherited both her parents' good looks. Known as Leuci, she had Poseidon's stunning aqua eyes and Cleito's wicked tongue – and she used both to her advantage when she rebuffed suitor after suitor, until a wealthy Lusatian king sought her hand in marriage. Despite Cleito's objections, Leuci was smitten by the pomp and circumstance and lavish gifts; she thought all the attention had made her mother jealous, so as soon as she reached her mid-teens, she eloped with Lech to his palace overlooking the Vistula River. And there she remained, with just hearsay to fill in the details of how she'd fared in the ensuing years. Gadeirus' cheeks dampened as he imagined what Leuci looked like now – if she still had eyes like the sea. And if that spunk that had so loved to tease him still sparkled her world in the way it had once enlivened his own. It dawned on him that now, as king, he could inquire about her and perhaps even re-establish their relationship. In his altered haze, Gadeirus made a mental note to dive deeper into this possibility, although he had a passing awareness that this inspired idea would find its demise at the bottom of the bottle bearing the rest of his good intentions.

Before he could lament Leuci for too long, though, his mind's eye turned to another haunting face. That of Basileia, his middle sister. The brooding one. The one with auburn tresses and his mother's porcelain skin. The one whose death by her own hand at seventeen had been what drove him to his first hallucinogenic high. His brow furrowed with memories of finding her frigid body, one icy hand still gripping a mostly emptied golden cup of hemlock and honey. More tears drenched his clenched jaws as he recalled how Basileia's facial muscles had contracted, branding him with that last impression of his favorite sister's smile locked in a pained grimace. He tried and failed to shake his head, to throw off this horror that had forever changed him. And in his uneasy recesses, he knew his obsession with redheads had begun with Basileia's passing. He'd always tried and failed to recapture her presence in his life. And he'd never gotten over his rage at her leaving him; he'd played out that bitterness again and again, with one vicious act after another toward any gingered beauty that fell under his influence – or into his bed.

Then the floodgates opened with face after face of the lovelies he'd harmed. And the crimes he'd committed in order to claw his way to the throne. Blackmail and backdoor deals and bodies left as bloody messengers were powerful influencers, ones Poseidon himself routinely abused – and ones Gadeirus had called upon in perhaps the most brilliant move ever made against the Sea God. For once in his life, Gadeirus had held his father's rapt attention. Staring into the stormy eyes of the legend responsible for his miserable existence, Gadeirus felt momentary triumph when they at last met along Poseidia's outer canal. "Well played, Gade," Poseidon had thundered in the sexy growl that by itself had lured so many to his bed. He said little else, being a god of few words unless playing his player role. Yet there was respect in his chiseled expression, and something else – something worth the price of admission. Gadeirus could see that his father, on some remote level, felt guilty over being so uninvolved in his son's life. Perhaps the greatest victory Gadeirus felt that day was witnessing Poseidon having momentary regret over siring so many strangers. Gadeirus knew his own actions had forever stained his soul, but he had his intoxicants and his puppets – and at long last, he had the kingship. As he slipped ever deeper into his musings, Gadeirus sighed. For the millionth time, the question of whether or not it had all been worth it crossed his altered consciousness.

"*Audentes fortuna iuvat*," he croaked, his tongue refusing to form crisp consonants. He drooled and snickered at a preposterous idea – that of streaking buck naked through the palace, screaming this anthem about fortune favoring the bold. Though he realized neither his mouth nor his legs were cooperative components at the moment. More chortles ensued as he wondered if he could get away with prancing to the stables just wrapped in a fur cloak. He loved how free that would feel, hopping on a magnificent white carriage horse to bear him on this battle cry run – and Light damn the consequences. He'd set his thoughts toward a plan of sobering enough to sift through his royal robes when he heard a knock. He giggled, torn between answering in the buff or throwing something on. Either way, he knew he needed a little help to get on his feet. Slapping at the bedside table, he groped among its many pouches as the knocking continued. He popped a handful of the weaker wafers he had left and took three centering breaths. When he'd finished, his vision had cleared, and he stood without staggering. Grabbing a nearby robe, he covered himself and crossed the cavernous room. When he threw open the door, the most unexpected face was waiting with an unreadable expression.

"Hello, Gade," Linasia cooed, sizing up his sobering state as she clucked cinnabar lips. "Feeling a bit off, are we?"

"I'm great, Lin. Never better." He flashed a shark's grin, at once put off by her using Poseidon's nickname for him yet turned on by the idea that his father had slept with this woman who'd warmed his own bed as well.

"I see you're happy I'm here." Well-manicured fingers probed knowingly under his robe before she pushed by him into his bedroom.

"Always good to see you." Closing the door, he followed her curves into his chambers. "May I offer you something to drink?"

"It's early for the hard stuff."

"I didn't mean liquor."

"Honey, are you too high to miss the pun?" She eased onto his bed, swelling her breasts into her dress bodice.

"I've missed nothing, Linny." He threw off his robe and stood naked before her. "Just wanting you to get my point."

"I've got a couple of points ready to pique your interest." Sighing, she slipped her dress from her shoulders and nestled into his sheets. "Come here."

"Here, there, and everywhere," he cackled, as he lost himself in perfumed softness.

TWENTY-FIVE

For seconds that stretched to infinity, Elysia observed the giggling fiend. The Daayan was obviously amused by dropping such a bombshell of a revelation. Elysia had long known the warnings to heed when in the presence of these Patala hell realm witches. Once a Daayan cast an evil eye upon someone, her death stare heralded a bad omen rumored to extend to the victim's family. Yet Elysia stood in No-Mind, unblinking as she gazed into the oily eyes of this most powerful of all paranormal beings.

"Come now," the Daayan chortled, as her form billowed into the blackness. "Have you no words for this painful truth I have shared?"

"I'm in no pain."

"You're bleeding, Elysia," the witch snapped. "And you're dying even faster now that life – a life that can never be – grows within you."

"I'm not here to negotiate 'nevers,'" Elysia replied. "My party and I seek safe passage to Poseidia's surface. I know you can arrange that transit. And I'm looking to strike a deal here and now – not something rooted in a future that you just said could never be."

"I could take her here and now," she suggested, her long braid flicking feistily. "And then transport you and the others to the palace grounds."

"Look at me," Elysia commanded. Blood spurted from her nose in thick dribbles. "I'll bear no more severances from this body. Name another price."

"I've named what I want."

"Then name what you'll accept."

"My dear, I don't settle." She grinned, more snarl than smile. "I don't have to."

"I would ask nothing of you that I wouldn't yield myself." Elysia scanned the smoky sorcerer's energetic structure. "I'm so sorry your baby died."

"How dare you –"

"She was beautiful," Elysia continued, as tears choked her. "She had your long chestnut locks. And saucy eyes the color of midnight seas.

She loved turtles. And dolphins most of all. My ancestors adored her."

"Shut up."

"Poseidon fathered her. And named her Vatya, for her stormy nature. And those eyes."

"I said *shut up!*" The Daayan raised her arms, and more blood gushed from Elysia's nose.

"She was with my daughter, in the Realm of Immaculate Innocence," Elysia sobbed. Her tears trailed into blood, their reddish rivers flooding her neck and chest. "And now her spirit grows within me."

"You have no right to what's *mine!*" the witch wailed.

"Only Source assigns souls to be birthed, Daayan," Elysia whispered. "And she has been assigned to me."

"Then I will take her!"

"And you will lose her. Because she will die with me."

"*No!*" Fury flapped the sorcerer's plait, her fingers trembling from the flames she channeled. Fire engulfed Elysia's body, yet her emerald eyes never wavered while she stood like a Phoenix ablaze in the shadows. The Daayan howled her heartbreak before dissolving into mist. In her stead, a winged snake arose in a serpentine spiral. His gilded scales glistened as the fire encircling him danced against the darkness. Massive ebony and ivory-tipped feathers stretched to envelop Elysia when she collapsed.

"Hello, my *priya*," the serpent hissed, hugging her scorched body. Gold and champagne scales crowned his regal head, surrounding black and bronze knowing eyes "Day meets night, soul yet clings to substance, here at the *saanjh* hour." Iridescent energies bathed Elysia as the snake being held her close, sealing and healing wounds and transforming burned flesh to its former pale pinkness.

"Mmmm." Green eyes fluttering, Elysia stirred at last. "Nehabkau?"

"Yes."

"It's really you," she whispered.

"Yes, *priya*. Long years have come and gone, since I last gazed upon my queen."

"So much has happened, Nehabkau. So much to share. And so much to do –"

"In time."

"But –"

"Your irrepressible enthusiasm is alive and well." Nehabkau laughed. "*Jijivisha* favors you still, I see. And now, you add the blessings of a baby."

"I just became aware of her. The Daayan –"

"Yes," he murmured. "Your compassion helped raise the Daayan's frequency. Which fostered a healing that has placed her on a higher path. A vibration that lifted her right out of this place. Such a shift, in fact, that her spirit granted me access so I could assist you. And by the grace of Highest Light, my queen, I am here."

"So you are here ... because she allowed it?"

"Yes."

"For the love of Oneness." Fresh tears flooded Elysia's face. "As always, we've met the enemy, and that she-devil is us."

"Indeed. Let me help you to your feet."

'Thank you, *mitra*." Clinging to the serpent's outstretched wings, Elysia wobbled up. "Will you please lend your considerable healing powers to my friends?"

"Of course, Queen." Wrapping Elysia in a feathery hug, Nehabkau hobbled her through the shadows to where Charlaeus and Jack lay unmoving near the capsized gurney. Beaming a golden aura that radiated in all directions, the serpent's glow revealed the Dead and the Undead in faded green luminescence. As startling as these lower vibration beings appeared, they busied themselves in soul bartering and seemed to ignore all else. Yet it was the Gray Ones, known as Shadow Spawn or the Nearly Dead, who scurried and scrounged and snarled as they fought one another; and it was the Nearly Dead she saw feasting upon her friends.

"*NO!*" Elysia shrieked, breaking free of Nehabkau as a bloody ghoul bit Hunter's limp body. Sonar flew from her fingertips, jolting the goblin backward. Though the disfigured body hovered between worlds, something unnatural fueled it still. It stumbled to its feet, half human, half some sort of experiment gone awry. The screeching and spitting specter lunged at Elysia, and she sonared it again. This time, white hot sparks shot out as the ghastly being ignited. Aflame and screaming, this Lesser Light embodiment staggered forward once more, while Nehabkau zapped it with lightning. Its shrieks echoed into the blackness, and it disappeared. But before Elysia could tend to Hunter, the rest of the chamber's Nearly Dead swarmed her and the serpent. "*I said NO!*" she screamed, racing toward the lurching creatures who were dragging her friends into the gloom. Sonar pulsed from her core, emanating outward in electromagnetic waves that trembled the cavern and shook the demons from their feet. Elysia stretched her arms wide, channeling a sonic forcefield that flattened the Nearly Dead, while Nehabkau levitated the others to the entrance. Once their lifeless bodies lay side by side on the obsidian ground, Nehabkau used telekinesis to transport Elysia to his side. Together, they kneeled next to her friends. "In the name of Oneness," Elysia groaned, fingertips caressing each face of her beloved tribe. Even in the dim light, she could see bite marks and bleeding scratches covering their immobile forms. Breathing past this horror, she channeled the love vibration around them, even as blood once again poured from her nose.

"Listen carefully, my queen," Nehabkau commanded. "More of the Nearly Dead are arriving, even as I speak. We haven't much time."

"I'm all ears."

"Those trapped between worlds wounded your friends. These beings are neither living nor dead. When they draw blood as they've done here, then the bitten also move into shadow. And so right now, your friends are trapped in the ethers. In one of the Lesser Light dimensions. One of the hell realms."

"I understand," she replied, choking on tears, as more of the Shadow Spawn crept closer. She sonared a new force field around them all and wiped her nose with the back of her hand. "What do we do?"

"Focus with me on the divinity that is their true essence," he murmured. "And I shall move us to a safer place."

"All right." She breathed deeply into her core, dropping into No-Mind while Nehabkau encircled them all with golden energy threads. Then light flashed like the sun before dissolving to stardust, and in its wake, she found herself sitting among ferns, staring up into a deep forest canopy.

"Hold the vibe," Nehabkau urged, as he continued weaving sacred geometry into the complex energetic patterns he channeled. Elysia nodded, adding stabilizing and grounding frequencies to the codes Nehabkau created. Yet howling and growling grew closer. "Poseidia is splitting. Portals and dimensions are opening unexpectedly as the magnetic fields grow more and more unstable. The Nearly Dead are coming through the cracks in our wake. We must move quickly so they cannot follow." Before she could respond, the light shifted once more, and she knew they were inside the Grand Temple. Another light flash left her wide-eyed beneath the Tuaoi Stone. On and on the light shimmered and the scene changed, as Nehabkau dialed in different location code sequences to outmaneuver the Nearly Dead's pursuit. A veritable kaleidoscope of places morphed before her eyes, until at last, a black, cool dampness enveloped them. All she could hear was water dripping into echoes; all she saw was unyielding darkness.

"Where are we, *mitra*?"

"On Poseidia's outskirts, in her Cave of the *Nilakantha*." His whisper hissed as it reverberated through the cavern. "As you witnessed, it took many location key codes before we landed somewhere they couldn't follow. Here in serpent-king Vasuki's healing temple, we stand among the holy *amanita muscaria*. And here we shall regroup."

"Ahhh, Nehabkau." Elysia's eyes widened when she saw thousands upon thousands of colorful mushrooms emitting rainbow light everywhere she looked. "Do you recall the Moldaarin strains of *soma rasa*? Our 'Highest Light Nectar'?"

"Yes." Nehabkau's black and bronze eyes shimmered, and he

smiled. "*Amrita*, our 'Magic Tea.' She was most magical."

"She was at that." Elysia's eyes misted with memories. "*Amrita* nourished us so deeply. Body, mind, and spirit. Fueling us with pure light frequencies."

"Indeed."

"The life force emanating from this strain is unbelievable." Elysia held her hands toward the fruiting cultures. "They're feeding me deeply, even without me ingesting them."

"Yes, my queen." Nehabkau reached a golden-clawed hand gently into the glowing mushrooms. "These sacred beings hold the frequencies of joyful expansiveness and loving kindness. One's inner well always fills easily from such a fountain, as long as Nature is left to govern as she pleases in the process. And, yet," the serpent paused, eyeing Elysia thoughtfully. "We're dealing with something unnatural here."

"Yes, I'm aware."

"I'm afraid, Elysia, that you don't know the half of it."

"Well, it wouldn't be the first time." She laughed weakly. "Tell me. What am I missing, *mitra*?"

"Ahhh, my queen," he murmured. "As I began to tell you before, we've saved your friends from the tunnels' immediate dangers. Yet they've not been spared the hell realms."

"Go on."

"Bites from the Nearly Dead carry a venomous form of Lesser Light gui," Nehabkau continued. "With that inoculation, those bitten are brought to a bridge between worlds from which there's no easy exit. Your friends have crossed over into Shadow. Into the Borderlands. Where the rules that govern the realm are vastly different from the laws overseeing reality as you've experienced it in Poseidia."

"In the name of Oneness." She sank to her knees, her senses alert to the look and feel of her friends. They lay motionless and with eyes closed next to one another. An odd luminosity lit their faces and exposed skin. In the month since being captured, Hunter, Ava, and Will had not surprisingly withered. Yet she felt horrified at how gaunt Jack and Charlaeus already appeared. All her friends' cheek bones protruded, their eye sockets had hollowed and blackened, and Elysia smelled rotting fruit and sewer stench coming off them in waves. The realization of all that had just transpired was slow to sink in. She felt numb and nauseous, yet she hadn't the luxury of reacting to these dire circumstances. She couldn't let gui feed from her any longer, so she willed herself to breathe deeply and to release all she saw in her surroundings – and to recalibrate herself to something, anything that would tune her to a higher vibration. In her mind's eye, she saw Alaric, and she knew most beings in the universe had never known the kind of unbreakable love she had always shared with her Moldaarin king. Her heart swelled with gratitude for being reminded of a higher point of attraction upon which to focus, and as tears streaked her cheeks, she looked again at her friends. They needed her wholeness and her commitment to Right Action now more than ever. "I've long trusted your counsel, Nehabkau. Please direct me, as you once did, toward the best course of action to help my friends."

"We are fortunate to have *amanita muscaria* and her sister strains as allies," he answered. "Let us continue to cloak our whereabouts with frequency coding and allow Nature to work her miracles. Do you see the blue light emanating from the far reaches of this cavern?"

"Yes."

"Those are the *entolomas*, the gatekeepers of the inner fringes. The bridge-location guardians and stewards of sacred passageways. Their cerulean color radiates truth and lights the way to integrity within, to alignment of body-mind-soul. They vibrate the way back from the hell realms toward wholeness and Highest Light embodiment." For a moment, he observed Elysia's calm countenance. "Much like crystals do, all *soma rasa* beings work as a family. Here in this healing temple, *amanita muscaria* anchors the love vibration, while the *entolomas* weave the way back from the Borderlands."

"Yes. I feel the truth of your words."

"There's more, Queen."

"Of course there is." Again, she chuckled, shaking her head. "What else must I know?"

"That choice determines fate," he murmured. "Each of your friends must now choose between healing and the hell realms. Which, of course, sounds like an easy choice to make, since your companions serve Source. Except Jack. As you may know, he serves the Borderlands, and as such, he may already be lost to the hell realms, unless he makes a new choice."

"He navigates easily where others fear to tread."

"Yes. He is fearless. Yet he's prone to temptation." Nehabkau turned his black and bronze gaze upon Jack's bloodied face. "He plays all sides against the middle, which is a particular talent that will either gain him a quick departure from the Borderlands. Or permanent hell realm residency."

"Lords with swords." Elysia sighed deeply. "What I'm seeing in my mind's eye is a plane of existence filled with distractions."

"Yes."

"That delight the senses."

"Yes."

"Where everything's for sale, and everyone has a price."

"Yes, Queen." He looked at her somberly. "Even those whose souls were never before in question – whose very existence had previously been governed by Highest Light alone – find temptations in the Borderlands. Wicked itches. Because that realm reads where someone is in lack or otherwise pinched off from Source. And brings beautiful baubles and bodies and soul-altering substances that feed false feelings of being, having, and doing whatever is desired. It can all seem blissful for a moment – long enough for the deal makers to extract a steep and heavy price. One that can be so costly that all inner resources become bankrupt. At which point, soul death is certain."

"Soul death?"

"Yes, *priya*. I'm not referring to the dropping of the body. That's a normal mortal experience in realms where the soul opens to another dimension upon reaching a transitional phase of the life journey. I'm talking about true soul death. It means only remnants are left of the essence, since the soul has made choices that leaked its love-based life force to the low vibrational point where it can no longer hold together as an individual spark of the Divine. As such, these soul fragments revert back to being part of the collective consciousness energies – and more often than not, they are of such a low vibration that they are a perfect match for the Borderlands. And become forever trapped there."

"I see," she rasped. Slowly, she rose, stepping back from her friends' unmoving forms. Nehabkau watched her take a few deep breaths and square her shoulders. "Then we must take them to this cavern's far recesses. To lie among the *entolomas*. Shielded by our protective coded energies while we uncover the Divine path moving forward."

"The path forward has split unexpectedly." It was Nehabkau's turn to sigh. "So much that's happened since you survived your ship's hijacking has been Source intervening. I know I don't have to remind you how you've been protected and guided and loved – and sometimes lifted – so that your journey continues on a Highest Light trajectory."

"I don't need reminding, *mitra*."

"Yet I cannot accompany you where you must go. If I do not hold together energetically the threads worn bare here, then Poseidia's gilded seams will rip apart. And if that happens, dimensions will shift and portals will open such that nothing will prevent the hell realms' fury from raining down on this island – and this planet as a whole."

"We won't be able to save Atlantis if that happens," she agreed. "Or Gaia, the Earth Mother herself."

"We will not."

"In the name of Oneness." For a long moment, she bowed her head. Eyes closed, her body radiated pink luminosity as she summoned the love vibration and allowed it to pulse through her being. "Though I have such clarity around my mission here, I still long to drag this ignorant world kicking and screaming into vibrational awareness."

"I know," the serpent laughed, his deep voice booming off the cavern walls. "You wouldn't be the leader you are if you didn't have such a longing."

"Yet I know our only hope is simply to do the work – sacredly, secretly, and silently. And those with eyes to see and ears to hear will join us."

"Of that you can be assured."

"It falls to me, Nehabkau. To go on alone."

"You're never alone, my lady."

"You're right. And I do know that. I appreciate the gentle reminder, which your counsel has always offered. Truly, Source has remained the steadfast companion that's carried me thus far." She patted her abdomen. "And by the grace of Oneness, I'm now carrying a daughter."

"You carry the weight of this world on your shoulders, *priya*. Even as you hold her hope in your womb."

"Without hope, we have nothing," she murmured. "Hope is the matrix for all the higher frequencies. Love, joy, gratitude – we can't hold them unless we first embrace hope. It's like a tree. All the higher vibe leaves and flowers bud from hope's trunk and branches."

"Aptly put, Queen." Nehabkau beamed at her. "Come. Let's get your friends resting comfortably among the *entolomas*. And then I'll see to it that your next steps set you firmly upon Right Action's path."

"Thank you, *mitra*." Elysia hugged the serpent. "You showing up at this time – and what allowed for your appearance – is reassuring confirmation of how absolutely everything is unfolding perfectly, in Divine timing. And according to Source's plan."

"Yes, *priya*." He held her fiercely. "Things are always working out, though at times they may not appear to be."

"But it's especially those times when Highest Light is working its magic," she whispered into his feathered chest. "Sacredly. Secretly. And silently."

TWENTY-SIX

Latching her chamber's gilded door, Lorelei straightened her spine. Fumbling icy fingers over a fresh frock, she barely felt its scarlet silkiness as she obsessively rehearsed yet again the script set forth by the Cosmic Controllers. She hurried along the hallway, her frantic steps revealing more about a desire to flee than any eagerness to tend to the business at hand. Yet she was not one to run from responsibility. Though she longed for a reckless abandon she never allowed herself, she knew such carelessness was a fool's playground – and she'd vowed centuries ago not to play the fool ever again. So, she pressed onward, passing door after closed door that blocked the palace psychics' activities from her disapproving eyes if not her awareness. Smoke wafted along the corridor, carrying incense and a hallucinogenic haze to her flaring nostrils. "Light damn them to hell," she muttered, quickening her pace to get past all the nonsense before she lost her already shortened temper on some silly witches.

Taking the stairs instead of the stuffy elevator she knew would reek of mind-altering vapors, Lorelei trotted down the single flight of steps. With ruby heels bashing polished marble, she pounced across the palace foyer, ignoring the roped-off areas where masons worked to repair splitting stones. Raking Arianna's unreadable body language with a harsh amber glare, Lorelei purposely slowed herself as she approached Gadeirus' sister.

"Hello, my lady." Arianna's husky voice extended a warm welcome that matched her pleasing smile.

"Hello, Arianna." Lorelei used courtesy titles only when a situation forced her hand. Looking upon Arianna's kind face, she knew she needn't bother with such formalities. "Thank you for seeing me."

"Of course."

"May we speak somewhere privately?"

"Certainly. I had a room prepared. Please come with me." Gesturing toward one of the hallways branching off the concourse, Arianna turned to walk side by side with the Dark Heart mistress. Much like Ava, Arianna had the gift of gab, even with awkward communicators like Lorelei. Arianna's friendly rasp echoed off the alabaster walls as she spoke of architectural details and Gadeirus' palace upgrades and plans in the works. Lorelei paid only enough attention to be able to offer a clipped response when necessary. To Lorelei, the short walk to the nearest conference room seemed unbearably long. By the time Arianna opened the arched double doors and motioned to the rosewood table and chairs before them, Lorelei felt cold irritation after so much cheerful chatter.

"Please sit, my lady," Arianna suggested as she pulled out a tufted armchair for Lorelei. "May I have any refreshments delivered?"

"No." She spied the table's ice-filled pitcher. Grabbing a frosty goblet from several stacked in a crystalline beverage chiller, Lorelei poured herself lemon water and then sank delicately into the offered seat.

"Very well, then." She tugged the heavy doors closed and sat next to Lorelei. "What do you wish to discuss?"

"I'll come right to the point." Lorelei begrudged the king's sibling her perfect updo and matched pearl accessories. Jealousy pricked her as she noticed how perfectly Arianna's curves hugged her sea-green dress. "Poseidia is in a shambles. The worst of her long and illustrious history. And I, for one, will not tolerate her being brought to her beautiful knees because of incompetence and weakness and lack of focused leadership."

"With all due respect, my lady –"

"I give respect where it's due, but that isn't here. Not when Atlantis is fast becoming the laughingstock of the civilized universe."

"I can appreciate your upsetment, Lorelei. Truly." Arianna reached for the water pitcher and filled a goblet. "Yet we are in the midst of massive changes here on this island. Changes that are widespread and that, ultimately, will prove beneficial. But change by its very nature is chaotic. We're in the phase of having broken the eggs to make the omelet, but the pan is just heating up. So, the dish is a long way off from being served."

"If a commercial kitchen is unclean, it will never pass inspection," she hissed. "Your 'broken eggs' have dried and hardened all over the stove. I would think you'd be wiping up that mess instead of sitting around waiting for the skillet to warm."

"Patience is needed. We can't possibly –"

"Don't speak to me of 'can't.' That's a Light-damned copout," she scoffed. "And I've *been* patient. I've been sitting on my hands while your brother leads us along a drug-induced downward spiral." Lorelei's laugh held no humor. "I ask you truly – how much longer do you expect me to wait and not act?"

"Perhaps I'm not the best person to address your grievances," Arianna murmured. Her dark eyes held steady under the Dark Heart queen's piqued stare. "Shall I message Desineus? He would be better suited to help you than I am."

"I'm afraid Desineus has been running interference. He won't grant me an audience with Gadeirus." She shook her head. "If you have Desineus' ear, then yes – I would meet with him immediately." Rising from her chair, Lorelei subtly raised a finger to her lips, an action that yielded its intended effect when a wide-eyed Arianna nodded once that she understood. "It's rather suffocating in here, don't you agree?"

"Yes."

"If you will help me get through to Gadeirus, then I'm satisfied this meeting has been most productive." She pulled a crystal tabulator from her skirt pocket, quickly scribbling something before holding it so Arianna could see. "Here's my schedule so you can jot down a few opportunities of my availability before I take my leave."

"Of course, my lady." Arianna sipped from her glass, pulling a crystalline writing tablet from several stacked on the rosewood table. Lorelei watched her write in flowing flourishes as the king's sister continued the conversation. "I will message you as soon as I hear from Desineus. But first, please check that I've noted your schedule accurately before I relay this information."

"Yes, everything looks correct," Lorelei replied as she read from the tablet.

"Very well, then. Is there anything else I can do for you?"

"No, thank you. You've been most helpful."

"My pleasure. Perhaps we may meet for lunch soon?"

"Yes, that would be fine." Lorelei thrust open the double doors before pivoting to look once more at Arianna. "I'll be seeing you."

"I'm looking forward to it." When Lorelei closed the massive doors, there was an echoing clang, and for several moments, Arianna sat still. She shut her eyes, willing herself to breathe deeply, and it took all of her diplomatic presence to regroup in the conference room quiet. "*What absurdity is afoot?*" she thought to herself, aware that speaking aloud may be overheard in this palace that seemed to be monitoring whatever was unfolding within its walls. A nagging uneasiness nipped at her consciousness – a knowing that Poseidia was splitting before her eyes. Her beloved city was breaking into unpredictable and unreadable factions – such that friend and foe had become indistinguishable. How else to explain Lorelei's shocking revelation – if it was indeed true? How was it possible that the Dark Heart queen herself had just extended a message about protecting Gadeirus through making the High Council think she was going to have him assassinated? Yet Arianna knew she couldn't dwell upon this development; she realized focused attention would open her more easily to the psychics and bring closer a reality she didn't wish to be hers. And so, she turned her mind toward surface niceties that her years of being in a politically connected family had taught her how to do so well. She arose from the table with generic pleasantries as focal thought points. The smell of the room's fresh flowers, and sunshine pouring through its leaded glass windows. The taste of tart lemon water wetting her lips. And hope swelling her heart that perhaps she had just discovered the help she, Gadeirus, and Elysia all needed – in the most unexpected face.

TWENTY-SEVEN

Strolling along Heera's outskirts, Alaric and Nayaka chattered away while the city's gleaming crystalline structures morphed into forest majesty. Not long after the woods swallowed them, a double gate appeared that so perfectly blended into the greenery it remained unseen until it parted. Above this arched entryway was written *suswagatam*, which meant "welcome" in the Old Tongue. The way forward, through an ornately carved wooden fence, served as passage into a secluded courtyard. Afternoon sunshine peeked through the grounds' pine and maple canopy, dappling steppingstones that wound through the landscape toward a tea house that was as yet hidden from sight. On either side of the garden path lay mossy meditation areas sheltered by ferns and rock formations. Bamboo poles engraved with sacred geometry and healing mantras in the Old Tongue walled off bath facilities nestled below a path that would eventually lead to the rustic building's entrance. Water features abounded, and near the tea house, the steppingstones culminated in a large flat rock placed before a washing basin.

"Here, my friend." Nayaka gestured to the low rounded stone, its hollowed bowl swirling with water from a bamboo pipe. A wave of his hand lit a nearby lantern. "Let us kneel and purify ourselves, in preparation for entering sacred space."

"Indeed." In one graceful motion, Alaric slipped to his knees. Following traditional Rohatian practice, he lifted the basin's ladle and doused his hands to wash them. Then he cupped water to his lips, rinsing his mouth as he whispered prayers. Bowing his head, he rose to his feet and stepped aside so Nayaka could similarly ready himself.

"Shall we?"

"Yes." Alaric followed Nayaka across a wooden footbridge spanning a bubbling brook. The cedar overpass sloped in a gentle curve over the water before dipping to a small courtyard beside a bamboo lattice and framed gate. Alaric knew it was customary to wait to be escorted inside. As they paused, he focused on deepening his breathing and appreciating this consciously created sanctuary.

It wasn't long before a petite woman with white hair pinned into a bun appeared. Her azure eyes sparkled in joyful recognition. The men bowed their heads, hands clasped at their hearts, while she opened the gate.

"Hello, Nayaka. And what a wonderful surprise to see you, Alaric!" She tinkled laughter and hugged them, her crisp white tunic sleeves flowing like ship sails around their backs. "Welcome back to Caya."

"Thank you, Sneha," Alaric grinned down at this Rohatian high priestess' timeless beauty. "It's been way too long since I shared tea with you."

"The way of tea always brings us to the eternal now, does it not?" She smiled, her eyes closing to crescent moons. "That means you're perfectly on time."

"Agreed." Alaric bowed his head once more. "I am honored to be in this eternal now with you."

"The honor and the pleasure are mine." She clapped them good naturedly on the back before handing them hair ties from her pocket. "I appreciate how you're both barefoot and in communion with Rohati as such already. Please pull back your lovely locks. And be sure to place any jewelry in the special treasures vessel found upon our table before we begin." A tittering laugh lit up her rounded features once more. "Come with me. Our tea gathering awaits!"

Alaric and Nayaka grasped the black silk ties from Sneha's outstretched palms. After securing flowing manes, they followed her graceful form through frosted glass double doors that slid apart as they approached. The opening was intentionally low, requiring entrants to bow once again in order to enter as a sign of remembering to be humble and defer to the Divine in all things. Inside was a vast open room covered in woven reed mats. The mats' cloth brocade borders bore sacred geometry symbols in soft colors. Pearly walls with wood borders provided a peaceful backdrop for silk scrolls bearing nature scenes. Everywhere Alaric gazed radiated tranquility. Gesturing toward a short table set with tea ware and a vase with a single blossoming sprig, Sneha smiled as her guests settled onto flat cushions.

"Thank you," Nayaka whispered, removing gold and gemstone jewelry, while Alaric nestled his wedding ring inside the special treasures vessel.

"Of course!" Sneha knelt before them. "Shall we sink into *advaita*?" They nodded and bowed their heads, mirroring Sneha's reverent posture. For several minutes, three breathed as one in an altered state of appreciation for all that is. Then Sneha lifted the pottery piece by piece, wiping each cup and saucer with a cloth and a dancer's wrist flourish. She stoked a gentle flame flickering beneath the nearby fire pit's grated surface. As Alaric and Nayaka continued their meditation, she heated a kettle and then whisked steaming water into porcelain vessels bearing jade-colored powder. She placed the frothy tea before them and settled herself back onto her knees with a filled cup before they stirred. "Let us sip to the satisfaction we feel as love, gratitude, joy, and freedom." Her knowing eyes watched a shadow swallow Alaric's face. "I see the negative emotions you feel instead."

"Yes."

"You know what you want. Yet you focus on its absence – the very thing that keeps you wanting and not having."

"Yes." Alaric studied the tea before sampling it. "I know what I must do."

"Then do it."

"For all these centuries without her –"

"Do you see how your words speak only to current circumstances? To the absence of what you want? To the problem and not its solution?"

"I do, Sneha," he murmured. "My practiced vibration is nearly perfected. At keeping me caught within the wound."

"Then stop it." Alaric and Nayaka laughed while her grin lit the room. "I tell you nothing you don't already know."

"Indeed." Alaric sighed. "Although reminders are welcome."

"I see your dilemma, my dear friend," she said gently. "You've experienced perfection in the eternal now. You've lived it. And that feeling of perfection shattered with the Moldaarin shards that slayed your family."

"Yes." His voice broke with the weight of truth she'd spoken. Alaric squeezed his eyes shut, but he couldn't block the sorrow stealing his breath. Nor could he stop the streaming tears that had defined most of his time thus far on Rohati. "I am ashamed to say this. But I almost wish I'd never known such alignment, such peace. Such love. Because I've fallen so far from grace, into this gash and all the self-loathing its shame mirrors to me. Its reflection has blinded me to the magnificence I am well-versed in saying is within. Yet I can no more feel its presence than I can hold my wife in my arms."

"I know." She sipped tea as Nayaka placed a steadying hand on Alaric's knee. "Words don't comfort or teach. A healing touch such as Nayaka's will balm many hurts. But not all. And not this."

"No. Not this," he whispered.

"May I make a suggestion?"

"Of course, *adhyapaka*. Tea time with you has always taken me beyond the wisdom you impart and into a state of *being* these knowings."

"All right. Then reframe how you see the wound," she urged. "And not only will it look different; your experience of it will change."

"Perhaps you will suggest a new view." Tears drizzled his face, and Sneha watched as water and emotion froze his cheeks into icy cliffs.

"For all the thousands of ways I have gazed upon this chasm, I find it an ugly pit stretching in every direction. And brimming with all I do not want." He paused, swallowing hard. "I know it's true that I simply must stop this wicked momentum. That I must recalibrate and hold those high vibrational thoughts that will flow my heart's desires to me once more. But I don't believe I can bear you saying that right now."

"Ah, Alaric. I hear you." For a long moment she paused, savoring the tea. "How you feel when you take your attention away from something is the vibrational imprint you leave with that subject in the eternal now." Again, she raised the cup to her lips, while her visitors sipped in silence. "Wounding is just a thought and a feeling we continue to think and feel around circumstances we have experienced. That's all it is. And so, to reframe how we perceive a wound, we must first remember that every affliction has a gift to offer. Once we receive that gift, our perception inevitably shifts – and the 'wicked momentum,' as you call it, subsides. So, we must bring a better-feeling thought to the unsettling topic, you see. And only turn our attention from those circumstances when we are holding the gift, which our better-feeling thought allows us to receive." She held Alaric with sparkling eyes. "We can't keep feeling the hurt as we turn our attention from a painful subject and expect it to go away. Because it won't."

"You speak the truth," Alaric whispered. "Yet I know not how to align with a new perspective in relation to this subject matter. And leave it in the eternal now while I hold peace in my heart." He stared, unblinking, into her calm gaze. "I'm broken, Sneha. I –"

"No, Alaric. I cannot allow you such a convenient lie."

"My apologies for being so prickly, *adhyapaka*. But what happened to my planet, my people, and my family was neither convenient nor false."

"I'm well aware your circumstances have felt so challenging. You get tripped up by them over and over again, such that the momentum you've built around suffering has become almost unstoppable." She set down her cup and clasped his hand. "*Almost*, Alaric. You're so powerful. So smart. And so dedicated to the memory of what happened. Those normally admirable qualities, ironically, keep you chained to the pain. Because you keep reliving the trauma. And that feeling state is preventing you from feeling better consistently enough to be able to draw to you once more a life that you love."

"Agreed," he sighed. "What would you have me do?"

"Change the subject. At least for a little while," she urged. "Find something else – *anything* else – to focus upon that feels better. And keep your attention there."

"But all my life's pleasures involve Elysia." He shook his head. "Every single one."

"Then that's your problem, dear." She met his cold stare with kindly directness that triggered more tears. "That's you placing your happiness in her hands and out of your own. That's you tethering your ship to another vessel in rough seas and not Highest Light pilings in a safe harbor. And that choice is neither stable nor sustainable." She paused, releasing his hand as she held the pure frequency of unconditional love. For several moments, the only sound was the room's bubbling bamboo fountain. "We cannot ask another growing and shifting and changing soul to place all focus on our well-being – that is Source's job alone. Such a request stifles the other and stops us from drawing from Divinity's well, which is the only place we can find continual replenishment. You well know how that type of energy arrangement benefits neither you nor Elysia."

"What I know is it seems all of my actions for a thousand years have been for naught." He swore in the Old Tongue beneath his breath and then laughed, a sound devoid of humor. "So, you're saying I am forever headed in the wrong direction if my only love is my life's unerring compass point?"

"Yes, that's what I'm saying." She swallowed tea while Alaric squirmed upon a woven straw cushion. "You can't get where you want to go from where you stand and the direction you face. You can't see a solution while staring at the problem, because solutions and problems are different frequencies; you can only tune to and hear one or the other. But not both."

"I do hear you, but –"

"No 'buts,' Alaric. You realize how simple it all is."

"Simple, but not easy."

"There you go with the 'buts' again," she chastised with a grin.

"Ah, Sneha." He smiled sadly. "The struggle is real."

"It's real for you because you allow it to be. And because you only think about and feel the hurting, you keep getting more pain."

"Yes. But how do I find a focal point that doesn't include her?" He paused, swallowing hard. "She's my everything."

"I speak only from love, Alaric. Truly, I relay nothing you don't already know," she murmured. "But that's a dysfunctional belief. One you must let go of in order to again experience your own Divine awesomeness. And one you must release before you can ever draw all the cooperative components needed to recapture a life you love."

"All right." Minutes passed in silence, as Alaric sat without moving. Sneha watched shadow and surrender ebb and flow across his countenance. He stared off into a distant horizon only he could see. At last, he brought his attention back to the tearoom. With softened eyes, he glanced at Nayaka before meeting Sneha's gaze. "Then tell me exactly what I must do, and I will recommit myself to that task." His voice cracked as Nayaka wove healing energies into his weary heart. "In the name of Oneness, I shall get and keep my vibration right this time."

"This subject is too volatile right now for you to bring a better feeling thought to it with much success. Once you get some momentum around feeling better in general, then you can return to thoughts of Elysia," she suggested. "And only then can you leave this subject while holding peace in your heart, which will heal your eternal now. And tune you to the frequencies that allow access to all you desire."

"And so, I must raise my frequency to the Highest Light realms, where I will vibrationally already be experiencing my happily ever after," Alaric replied. "Before I can ever taste it and touch it and hear it and smell it and see it and feel it here in physical form once more."

"Yes."

"Thus, you are suggesting that feeling good should be my only priority. Which will keep my vibration high enough to reach the Divine doorways that stand open to all I desire."

"Yes!" She laughed and nodded. "That's exactly what I'm suggesting. Because those doors are open and waiting for you to feel good enough *for long enough* to not only go inside – but to begin living the vibe that allows all your dreams to come true."

"So, I must train myself not to think of Elysia."

"Yes. For now."

"All right." For a third time, Alaric sighed.

"It would be easier for you to feel good consistently if your focus is on anything that makes you feel good," she replied. "Just for a little while. Until your practiced vibration is held steadily enough within those Highest Light frequencies to bring peace to your thoughts around her."

"You're suggesting I focus on something – anything – that makes me feel good?"

"Yes."

"Something like dancing?"

"*Yes!*"

"Or the way sailing sprays salty goodness upon my lips. And the wild thrill my soul feels while teleporting."

"Yes, precisely!"

"Okay." Alaric held the teacup to his lips, his gold-green eyes taking in the wood-trimmed walls and hanging lanterns. "I'm reminded of that old adage – *one who wants a rose must respect the thorn*. And so, even if my fingers get pricked daily, I must be thankful for that sharp nudge to get me back to inhaling even more deeply of the sweetness that makes such minor inconveniences so worth it."

"Well said!" Her chuckles brought grins as Nayaka threw a comforting arm around Alaric's shoulders. "You have such a gift with words,

Alaric. And I know it's no accident you should bring up roses."

"Thank you for the kindness," he murmured. "My words are indeed intentional."

"I realize that. Just as you will acknowledge that – for a thousand years – the rose has symbolized your heartache," she observed.

"Yes."

"But it can come to represent your redemption."

"That would be a most welcome gift, *adhyapaka*."

"Then let us hold ceremony around you receiving this bounty." In one fluid motion, she stood and pattered across the mat-covered floor to a wall with a built-in bureau and shelves. With nimble fingers, she plucked dried petals and stems and root clippings from sealed amber jars. Placing the flower parts into three small bowls alongside a glass teapot, she prepared utensils and arranged them with the teapot onto a serving tray. She then carried the tray to the fire pit and added a small steaming kettle before returning to the table, where Alaric and Nayaka waited with closed eyes. She could feel them resonating *advaita* as she resumed her seat. "Let us begin by remembering that the only difference between a flower and a weed is a judgment. And let us acknowledge that many of the most powerful plant medicines come from those decried as weeds," she said as she removed the teapot's infuser. "Just one example is the dandelion, whose tea helps to heal anger and bitterness despite the plant's pesky reputation. And so today, we shall call upon dandelion to serve as a soothing agent, to be the releaser of festering emotions – and the bridge allowing harmony to be restored between the Royal Houses of Rose and Lotus."

"And so it is." They bowed their heads as Sneha placed the bowls before Alaric.

"On your left is a vessel bearing mostly red rose petals, which represent the love vibration – the highest of the Highest Light frequencies. Just a touch of the flower's balancing and grounding leaf, stem, and root have been added to symbolize wholeness," she murmured to the Moldaarin king, whose gold-green gaze pierced the dissected rose as a thousand emotions flooded his face. "On your right is a vessel bearing mostly red lotus petals. As with the roses, just enough leaf, stem, and root are blended in to reflect the Oneness we are honoring." She watched as Alaric turned focused attention to the cup containing lotus pieces, and she could feel him melting as he opened himself to one of his life's enduring touchstones of unconditional love. "And between the rose and the lotus rests the dandelion, serving as bridge and gateway and way shower to all that you already know – that love is really all that is."

"Yes," he whispered.

"Your eyes reflect that truth, and so does the symbol forged as your wedding ring," she continued. "Do you see, then, that the point of all conscious life is to grow and expand and create from love?"

"I do."

"And do you see how all wounding happens when beings pinch themselves off from love – from Highest Light? When they create with eyes turned from Source, they only feel Lesser Light feelings. And if they get others to join in with their illusions of separation, to hop on their band wagons that keep beating the drums of sadness and anger, then the resulting power and percussion of collective consciousness just keeps tapping out tunes of misery. And not magic."

"Yes, I see that," he muttered, his voice husky with tears.

"Let me remind you, Moldaarin King, that with great power comes great responsibility. And there's no greater responsibility, as Lesser Light realms and realities split and spin, than to hold the line. To cleave to the love vibration. And bear her truth forward. Not to drag with you those who are kicking and screaming at Lesser Light illusions. But simply to love. Sacredly. Secretly. Silently."

"*Samadhi!*" he cried out in the Old Tongue. Sneha and Nayaka held a space of pure, positive energy as sobs wracked Alaric's big body. For minutes on end, there was only the bamboo fountain's flowing and Alaric's weeping to break the stillness. When his tears quieted, Alaric looked upon Sneha's calm countenance and sighed once more. "I'm shaking with the truth of all you reflect to me. Truly, I see how I've beaten myself up for so long. With each strike of the drums of anger and sadness I've played self-righteously – and relentlessly – for a thousand years." He swallowed hard. "Help me to leave all of it here at the altar of the eternal now. And offer myself up as the Highest Light in physical form that I really am."

"And so it is," Sneha and Nayaka replied.

"And so it is," Alaric whispered.

"This is your ritual," Sneha murmured. "Your recalibration with Source, to carry out as you feel called. In any tea ceremony, hot water facilitates the alchemical blending of all the cooperative components present into Oneness elixirs." She lifted the heated kettle and placed it closer to him. "I wish to remind you of one more thing."

"Please."

"Millennia ago, in the free-will-based Atlantean empire, Lesser Light forces chose for the king's coat of arms a symbol that had long represented the Highest Light realms. This choice was an example of controlled opposition at its finest, of taking something inherently high vibration and manipulating it to further Lesser Light's agenda. At that time in Atlantis, rose gardens had been cultivated for centuries throughout Poseidia – so what better symbol to seize for brainwashing the masses into thinking certain carefully constructed thoughts? And doing so by first getting them to accept without question that the royals possessed this exquisite flower's inherent gifts." She paused, clearing her throat before continuing. "Rosebuds open into layered blossoms, which honor how spiritual wisdom unfolds in our lives. A rose's strong, sweet scent and soft petals in practically any color speak to her powerful reflection of all of Source's majesty. Let me remind you how, intergalactically, the rose is often described as the fairest of flowers, with the highest vibration of all. Yet we know a deeper truth, do we not?"

"Sneha, must we –"

"Yes, Snake King – we must." Her ocean eyes glistened as she leaned toward him. "You are so much like your beloved lotus. Which is just as lovely as the rose and arguably more powerful, since her vibration is many times higher. Yet she is largely forgotten in such worldly comparisons, as all sacred things are in a Lesser Light-dominated paradigm." She laughed as she rolled her eyes. "As if being rooted in mud and destined to move through shadow before blooming in the light somehow sullies her essence!"

"I can assure you it does not," Nayaka added. "Just as your own essence remains gorgeous and pure, Alaric, as you sit here rising through this core trauma's mud and murky waters. I see the energetic reality of you. The wholeness behind the victimization. And you are stunning."

"Agreed, Nayaka. Energy never lies, and the beauty of which you speak shines forth in all its glory in this king's aura." Sneha beamed at Alaric for several moments, letting him remember how to absorb the joy she felt in appreciating him. "To offer yourself up as Highest Light incarnate, you must honor all of who you are," she continued. "And who you are is the closest embodiment of *samadhi* that's ever been birthed. Before –"

"Sneha, please. That was long ago," Alaric whispered.

"It's here – right here – in your eternal now," she scolded. "You know I love you so much. But it's time to put away the victim. And straighten that crown."

"Straightening won't polish what's tarnished."

"No, but you'll never buff that crown if you don't first muster the backbone to straighten it." She sipped the tea, her eyes alight with the fire blazing back at her from his gold-green gaze. "As I was saying, you're the closest incarnation of *samadhi* there is. And before the wounding that wobbled you into centuries of Lesser Light slavery, you walked through life embodying the highest of Highest Light's emotions – love, joy, gratitude. And freedom. And you uplifted anyone you encountered simply by your way of being. And you did it sacredly. Secretly. Silently. So, what better target than yourself for Lesser Light to set its sights upon?" She squeezed his hand. "Alaric, please. Acknowledge that those looking to wield darkness for egoic gain have always focused their formidable power upon ruining the best, the brightest, the highest flying, the most gifted, in their self-serving war to unseat all that is Highest."

"For my part, I am no deity," he muttered. "I've known alignment and spent centuries within that perfection. Which it was my honor and duty to uphold for all, so everyone within my sphere of influence could have not simply a model of – but a guidepost to – such bliss."

"And that answer, dear friend, is why you are *samadhi* personified. For all of your gifts, you are humble."

"Ahhh, Sneha," Alaric said at last, raising her thin fingers to his lips. "One of my life's great blessings is you always calling me out on my number one nonsense."

"I'll drink to that." They all laughed as one, and she placed three earthen cups from the table's tray in front of the flower-bearing bowls. "That is, if we may continue your tea ceremony while the kettle yet steams."

"It would be my pleasure." Alaric cradled the bowl bearing rose petals and pieces. "I'm nearly beyond words to express my gratitude. For both of you holding loving space, as I recalibrate to the highest and best expression of myself." He shook his head, his chiseled features half in shadow in the tearoom's soft light. "Saying 'thank you' feels inadequate. Yet I so appreciate all you are doing in our mutual quest to once more crown Highest Light as this realm's sovereign ruler."

"Hail to Highest Light!" Nayaka exclaimed. "And hail to you, Moldaarin King. For walking the talk. For holding the line. And for surrendering any less-than beliefs to the eternal now."

"I've long known my attitude needs adjusting." Alaric spooned lotus parts atop the rose pieces in the teacups before him. "There's simply no room in the eternal now for wounded beliefs and behavior. Not when I bear the responsibility of the greater awareness I possess. And not when I have finally faced – and with your help, embraced – this realization."

"Yes, acceptance is key." Sneha studied Alaric's energy as he added dandelion to the rose and lotus mixture. "You've relaxed, my friend."

"I feel a deep peace." He reached for the kettle. "Let us drink to putting down the sword and the struggle. And picking up new ways of seeing things. Of realizing each moment breathed in boldness is an opportunity to celebrate something." He grinned at Sneha, and she was struck by the reclaimed power radiating forth. "So, let's celebrate flowers yielding tea. Friends holding space. And fortune favoring the bold."

TWENTY-EIGHT

Elysia opened her eyes, finding herself face to face with the luminescent Tuaoi Stone. Its otherworldly glow pulsed through her from where she rested against its rounded radium-walled housing. The walls' acoustical insulation encapsulated and magnified the hexagonal crystal's unfathomable strength. Energy coursed through its immense height; frequencies funneled up from the earth emanated out through a point that was simultaneously receiving sound and light from throughout the universe. Above the crystalline tip hung human-inspired hands crafted from orichalcum; these detailed appendages had been formed from Poseidia's most conductive metal. For millennia, Tuaoi Stone guardians had changed the channeling crystals cradled by these enormous fingers several times daily, depending upon the weather or the energies needing to be transmitted or gathered. The orichalcum's right hand sent forth energies to sister quantum converter crystals around the planet and across the universe, while at the same time, the left hand drew in beneficial intergalactic signals.

As she gazed about the structure, which had been the agreed-upon teleportation spot Nehabkau had helped her reach, Elysia realized much was amiss. Many disturbing changes had transpired since she'd last set foot inside this former sanctuary. When she and Alaric had long ago frequented Atlantis, they always made time for rejuvenation sessions within this structure; its original design had included specialized wall chambers for replenishing physical vitality. Yet the rounded openings that once led to healing beds appeared melted; charred drippings of what looked like black candle wax blocked the doorways. The ruby in fuchsite floor, which had served to enhance the earth's life force-restoring energies, lay split into uneven slabs. In her mind's eye, Elysia saw the psychic spells that had been cast to debilitate the Tuaoi Stone. While the tower still sent and attracted signals, the captured energies were being siphoned into a massive quartz spire resting upon a wired electrical box near the entrance. The box's electrical circuitry flashed and hummed with the powerful vibrations it was collecting. Still cloaked in Nehabkau's concealing energies, Elysia observed without emotion how huge wire bundles had been threaded through holes in the wall to somewhere outside. Everywhere she looked around the electrical box, selenite shards and quartz pieces and a multitude of colored stone splinters littered the floor. Clearly, Poseidia's Dark Heart regime had been doing everything possible to curtail the Tuaoi Stone's healing capabilities, while at the same time draining its power for Lesser Light purposes. Sighing, she closed her eyes against the devastation that would keep dissipating beneficial energies not just in Atlantis, but across the universe. For several moments, she prayed, asking to see the way forward. Minutes passed as she waited for illumination. She breathed herself deeply into No-Mind, allowing Oneness to soothe and satiate her, until the entry door slammed open.

None other than Gadeirus himself strutted into the strobing lights. Dressed in lilac breeches and a tailcoat trimmed with gold brocade lace, he snorted as he stared up at the Tuaoi Stone. Elysia's mouth fell open at his markedly changed appearance. In the month since she'd escaped from his chambers, his hair had continued to whiten; a skunk stripe now streaked the center of his crownless head. His greenish pallor and blackened eye sockets looked more ghoulish than kingly. Yet Elysia saw how his raven's gaze missed nothing. She could feel him taking in every detail despite some form of drug altering his consciousness. Suddenly, he stopped, his heeled violet boots clacking to an echoing halt, as he peered right at her invisible form.

"Light damn me to hell," he muttered. "But I would swear on a stack of Dark Heart spell books that the Moldaarin queen herself is near." Catching her breath, Elysia realized how Gadeirus had appeared before her last courting at court affair as an unlikely answer to Highest Light prayers. Here, in the Tuaoi Stone's shadow, she felt once again that Source was showing her how foe and friend are one and the same, depending upon circumstances and perspective. Straightening her spine, she lifted herself from the floor, and allowed herself to be seen.

"Perhaps nearer than you knew," she whispered.

"My lady," he gasped, swatting at salt and pepper bangs sweat had stuck to his brow. "You shouldn't be here."

"Many things in this world feel as if they shouldn't be," she replied. "But here we are."

"Indeed. Here we are. But really – you shouldn't be in this Light-damned building." He shook his head. "These very walls are poisonous."

"This was a sanctuary –"

"And now it's a tomb." His raggedy whisper hissed off the walls. He circled toward her, one hand's slender fingers tracing a path along the radium-lined perimeter. "Destructive energies are radiating out into this room and the universe as we speak. Although you already know that. I see in your eyes that you're aware of one of Poseidia's dirtiest little secrets."

"I'm aware that Dark Heart spells are misusing the Tuaoi Stone." Elysia met Gadeirus' gaze as he approached. "And I know the lengths Lesser Light will go to in order to realize a new intergalactic order."

"You don't know the half of it." He cackled, a shriek that shivered her. "You are blinded by Divine delusions. Which you also know I've had a hand in shaping."

"What I know, Gadeirus, is that I stand before you now because Highest Light has brought us here."

"Why would you think that?" He stood not two feet away, and Elysia felt the bottled intensity bubbling within him. "It could just as easily be Lesser Light that's led you to this place."

"You're not wrong," she replied. "I would suggest that Highest and Lesser Light co-create this realm. And the dance between the two brings us a choice. Lead or be led."

"Ah, my lovely." Again, he laughed, but melancholy and not mirth flooded his features. "You always think Source is asking if you'd prefer rainbows or unicorns. But those rose-colored glasses blind you to the truth."

"What truth?"

"That we're all being played."

"I know."

"With all due respect, Elysia," he continued. "You do not know the depth or breadth or height of all that is transpiring here."

"I know all that I need to know."

"You're not even aware that you're bleeding." He flicked a monogrammed handkerchief from his breast pocket. "Your endless optimism, even as life force leaks from your nose, is exasperating."

"Your caring nature, even as you continue to be consumed by the Lesser Light narrative, is uplifting." She dabbed at her nose as Gadeirus rolled his eyes. "Thank you."

"Of course." He smiled at her, and this time genuine warmth lit his ebony eyes. "I am a scoundrel and a whore and all sorts of Dark Heart madness. Yet I haven't ever been able to harden myself against you."

"Do you see how we aren't so very different, you and I?"

"You know, I meant 'harden' in the emotional sense, my lady. You must be aware that the physical part of me –"

"Gadeirus," she warned.

"I mean every part of my physical vessel –"

"Gadeirus!" She shook her head and giggled. "I hear you."

"Then hear me fully."

"All right." Elysia looked up into a worn face that had softened with his tone.

"I struck you, and for that I'm deeply sorry. In fact, I hope you'll forgive me."

"I already have." She realized, as she stared at this broken king, that he didn't remember his earlier apology. "You have such gifts. A son of the Sea God himself and his Atlantean queen. You could do much good here if you choose to."

"My choices were made long ago." He glanced about the structure, taking in its splitting perfection. "My fate is sealed."

"No," she whispered. "That's not true."

"Oh, but it is." His chortling showed her how he teetered upon the knife-edge of sanity. "When you have as much blood on your hands as I do, eventually you have to accept inevitable consequences."

"Nothing is set in stone, Gadeirus. Everything is fluid. Every choice brings a new reality."

"Lords with swords!" His stare pierced her, and she dropped even more deeply beneath her breath. "Why do you still see the good no matter what evil stands before you?"

"Because I choose to." He whirled from her, hands in his tangled locks, as she raced after him. "And because all our choices keep changing things. They *matter*. Now more than ever!"

"You impossible *bitch*!" Spinning on slick heels, he stopped, and she slammed into him. He broke her fall by twisting onto his back while she toppled on top of him. He smelled of tobacco and decay as he whispered into her ear. "Don't fear me, my lady. They cannot hear you when you are this close – and only when you are this close. I had that little bit of privacy built into their prying and spying so the specifics of my whoring wouldn't feed the gossip machines any more than they already have."

"All right." She looked into bleary-eyed exhaustion, but for all of his self-ruining insistence, she could still see strength and cleverness in equal measure. "What now?"

"Forgive me if my mind wanders momentarily to all the wicked ways I wish to have you." He grinned, and the truly benevolent nature emanating from him teased a smile to her lips. "I'm beyond redemption, but not past reason. Not just yet anyway."

"Go on."

"First of all, that kiss is all that happened physically between us." He sighed, a sound that trembled his body against hers. "I want to reassure you about that. For what it's worth, you have my word."

"Thank you," she whispered, as tears drowned her lashes. "When I first awoke next to you, I thought –"

"Yes, I know." He cleared his throat. "But I assure you. You've not been tainted by me."

"I appreciate you saying that."

"Then let me say this," he murmured. "I know not who remains loyal to me. We are in uncharted waters, my lady. Where ally and adversary are making the strangest bedfellows, as the very bedrock of this island splits and separates."

"That's it exactly." For a moment, she marveled at how he'd come to the same conclusion Source had shown her. "So what now? And how long may we speak like this before someone gets suspicious?"

"Not much longer. When we arise from this floor, I want you to talk to me like I have just defiled you."

"*What*?! But –"

"While I have not touched your gorgeousness in any of the ways I would like, I regret to inform you that I *have* sullied your reputation." With gentle fingers, he whisked a ginger lock that had fallen across her widening eyes. "I had to ... mislead ... the Civic Security Council. They didn't buy it when I told them I had no idea how you escaped from my chambers – after so many influentials had reported back to them that you'd been carried to my quarters. Nor did they believe me when I told them I knew nothing of your whereabouts."

"Oh, Gadeirus –"

"Yet they *do* believe in my vile nature," he continued. "They believed my insinuation that I bedded you against your will. And they will believe that I came upon you here and wished to have my way with you again."

"Oh, my goodness –"

"Rest assured, the psychics already know as we speak that we are here together. The only saving grace we have is the narrative I've already created. That I've finally turned you into one of my whores."

"Are you kidding me right now –"

"Not at all, my lady."

"And so, you're telling me that many of the influential Poseidians I met last month now think you've slept with me."

"Not many of them, Elysia," he said evenly, as relief flooded her face. "I daresay all of them."

"In the name of Oneness!"

"I know you're upset, my lady. And rightly so. But we really don't have time right now for you to call me out on my unreasonably outrageous behavior."

"Ya think?" Softly, she chuckled, in spite of herself and him and this turn of events. "This is highly unusual. And most ridiculous."

"I know. But it may be the hatching of a plan that saves us both. And what's left of Poseidia."

"I won't argue," she sighed. "Tell me what we need to do."

"Moments from now, I will ask you if you're ready. And when you tell me you are, then I want you to get up, and I want you to find the tears that so naturally flow from those exquisite emerald eyes. Pretend I have forced myself upon you, fresh from your marriage bed. And then, I want you to cry and tell me you're bleeding and so you're heading back to the palace for aid. But I want you to find your way instead to the stables. And wait for me in the trees just outside the back paddock area. Is that clear?"

"Yes."

"Are you ready?"

"Yes."

"And Elysia?"

"Yes?"

"Forgive me." With lightning speed, he grabbed her face and kissed her passionately. Before she could react, he thrust her from him. "Now get up and give me some drama!" As if on cue, hot tears sprang from her eyes, and as she began a tirade to rival any of her courting at court performances, she thanked Source for the clarity of knowing nothing at all anymore was what it seemed.

TWENTY-NINE

As dusk deepened to darkness, Arianna asked Avalon to pause beneath the red-tinged sky. Sunset's rapidly fading afterglow yet reflected its coral loveliness in the metal stables' silvery sides and copper roofs. For a long moment, the king's sister breathed in the stillness that was Dehk's sanctuary. Yet uneasiness consumed her as she looked out over the empty pastures. She noticed Avalon's ears pointing in the direction of an approaching figure. Soon, she recognized the thin man moving toward her as Kevonious, Dehk's right-hand helper. But he didn't throw up a hand the way Kev normally did in greeting. Then Avalon pawed at the ground, and she knew that whoever this stranger really was, he wasn't Kev.

"Hello, my lady." It sounded like Kev's gruff voice calling to her. It looked like Kev's shoulder-length brown hair and impossibly long legs standing not ten feet away. Although a chill shivered her spine as she stared down at his sober face. "We need to talk."

"All right."

"Please come with me." The man's blue eyes caught hers, and then he brushed a slender index finger across his lips. She placed her palm on her midsection in the gesture Lorelei had demonstrated earlier – during a secret second meeting in the rose gardens – when she'd told her Kevonious would be waiting here for her. He motioned for her to follow and turned toward Dehk's biggest barn. There was only the sound of Avalon's hooves on packed earth until this Kev lookalike led them inside the barn and tugged its double doors closed. Arianna slipped from Avalon's back and, as this mysterious man pivoted to face her, she noticed an emerald and gold pendant shaped like a merkaba flicker in the stable's soft lights. Before she could say anything, Avalon squealed and lunged at the man. Calmly, the stranger raised one finger, and a lightning bolt crackled into the gelding's chest. Avalon snorted and pawed the ground before staggering to a standing stillness. Arianna hastily checked the horse to see if he might be hurt, but she saw no injuries – so she petted his neck and mane while pondering what could possibly have happened. She felt at a loss as to how to address this awkward development and her growing discomfort with this unknown being. Before she could think of anything to say, the man bowed his head before her.

"My apologies. I didn't mean to frighten you. I've some experience with spooked horses – and I merely used channeled energy to soothe and settle him."

"I was quite startled," she admitted.

"Yes. I hope you can see he isn't harmed."

"He seems okay." She continued to run her hands along Avalon's chest and legs, weighing the very real impulse she had to jump on his back and ask him to gallop as fast as he could from this madness. Yet she knew there really was no escaping the insanity unfolding everywhere around her beloved Poseidia. So, her well-conditioned inner diplomat spread a smile upon her face and gave her words to smooth over this strangeness. "Horses can spook over just about anything."

"Indeed, they can." He smiled and pointed toward two square hay bales facing one another. "I know this setting's not fancy, my lady. But I hope you won't mind sitting here with me."

"Not at all." She saw what she hoped was kindness soften his face. "May we speak plainly now?"

"Yes."

"You look like my dear friend. Yet you most assuredly are not Kevonious."

"I am not."

"You know I am Arianna, sister to the king?"

"Yes."

"And you are?"

"My name is Anahata. In the Old Tongue, that means –"

"Unbroken," she interrupted. "It can also mean 'unstruck,' as in the sacred, silent sound."

"Yes."

"I see. And, yet frankly, I don't," she murmured.

"I understand, my lady. Perhaps our meeting shall provide illumination. In more ways than one."

"I hope so, Anahata. I really do."

"I do, too." As Anahata stared into Arianna's eyes, a bright light flashed; his physical form sparkled and morphed into a radiant green. She gasped and he laughed, a tinkling, joyful chuckle, and she wondered why her impulse had been to fear him. "I chose Kevonious' physicality because it is familiar to you – and because it allowed me to travel unnoticed to this place."

"I see."

"Do you also see how these are strange times? And that, energetically speaking, nothing that once was ... is?"

"I feel the truth in your words. My eyes have been opened to new perceptions in just the last month."

"Yes. That has been the plan."

"Whose plan?" She peered more closely at the swirling silver orbs that had overtaken what had looked like Kev's eyes moments before. "What exactly is going on here?"

"Nothing is at it seems. Nor is anyone who is anyone in Poseidia standing in integrity."

"Yes," she sighed. "My brother –"

"Your brother wavers moment to moment," he replied. "In this moment, he has put everything on the line for Highest Light. For he's had a revelation regarding unconditional love."

"Does this have to do with Elysia and –"

"Yes."

"Is she okay?" Arianna leaned forward.

"She is adapting."

"But is she overcoming?"

"She is improvising. In the face of ... unexpected challenges."

"In the name of Oneness." Arianna sighed again. "Since you know so many unknowable things, can you tell me if she has found her friends?"

"Yes." Anahata's eyes shimmered as tears spilled from Arianna's lashes. "Yet their fate is uncertain. Much is at stake. All of Poseidia – and beyond – is poised to fall. If Elysia fails in her mission."

"How can I help?" She shook her head. "I know not anymore whom I can trust."

"That's because all who were trustworthy ... have been eliminated."

"Killed?" Arianna's eyes widened to saucers.

"Or worse, my lady."

"What are you *saying*?"

"I'm saying there are worse things than death. And many who'd held true to Highest Light have discovered that truth."

"This cannot be," she whispered.

"Oh, but it is."

"So, Kevonious –"

"He's dead."

"*What?*"

"Dead, my lady. And so, I know your next question is about Dehk."

"Yes. Is he –"

"You may not have known just how deeply involved Dehk has long been in Poseidian politics."

"Are you *serious*?" Arianna gaped at him. "You do realize how deeply I, myself, have been involved in this island's political maneuverings? And for how long?"

"Yes, of course. Yet you've been a cog in only one wheel of one vehicle. That tends to blind one to other cogs in other wheels of other vehicles. Surely, you must realize that Poseidia has an armada in her service. And Dehk had a whole fleet under his command."

"Had?"

"Yes, my lady. Dehk has met a fate worse than death. He met it nobly, and without so much as blinking, I might add."

"What are these horrors of which you speak?"

"It matters not, Arianna. Details will only lower your vibration and derail us further from what we need to discuss."

"Okay." She swallowed hard and took a deep breath as she gazed about the deserted barn. "Where are all the horses?"

"They were Dehk's guardians. So, their fate was sealed to his."

"Lords with swords!" She leaped from the hay. For several moments, she paced along the empty stall-lined corridor. The smell of leather and feed she'd known her whole life did little to calm the tears she couldn't stop. Finally, she returned to the square bale across from Anahata. She beseeched those orb eyes as she sank once more onto the dried timothy seat, while Avalon stood motionless nearby. "I asked you before, and I need you to tell me. Whose plan is undermining Poseidia?"

"It's complicated, my lady."

"Said every politician ever."

"Yes. Because every life experience funnels its way from the top down. And politics, like any theatrical production, gives us glimpses of truth. Of the strings being pulled. And who is pulling them."

"Agreed. But you still haven't answered my question." Again, she sighed deeply. "Who is running this realm? If I may speak so boldly ... last month, I thought my brother was at the very least in charge of Poseidia. A few hours ago, Lorelei led me to believe she had taken control in secret, since Gadeirus admittedly has been unstable at best. Yet," she paused, peering carefully into his swirling, silvery eyes. "I don't know what to believe. And quite frankly, I don't even know why I'm sharing all of this with you. Except I am. There's just something about you that compels me ... to talk to you."

"What choice do you really have, Arianna? Except to surrender to what is before you." He smiled, a grin that flickered his glowing green countenance. "I am a messenger from the stars. Shape-shifters, we are, traveling via stargates that open to and through the heart."

"All right," she muttered. "Whose heart granted you passage here?"

"Dehk's, my lady."

"Ahhh, I see. Please go on."

"Truth, you see, is the great balancing sword here," he continued. "When tempered by love, it cuts through all the untruths or half-truths Lesser Light forces keep weaving. Falsehoods that serve to make the earth's inhabitants believe in anything except the One Truth, which is that love is all that's really real." He fell silent as he watched her digest his words. "Many of my kind before me have unsheathed the One Truth's tempered blade before many of your kind. I am here because none who've been offered the opportunity to wield it have done so."

"And why is that?"

"Because free will allows many who access this realm to reward those who keep its illusions."

"Forgive me, Anahata. I'm sure I appear like a child with all my curiosity and continued questions. But who is really in charge here?"

"Each soul is sovereign, my lady," he murmured. "Each is free. Yet I see in your eyes you do not believe these words."

"How can I? Have you looked about you at all?" Arianna shook her head. "I cannot even bear to witness the oppressions that seem to grow worse by the hour. The sight of the pearl divers alone is enough to bring tears."

"Yes, I understand. Yet have you considered how everything you see about you is old news? How the energy that created what *is* has long since passed?" His hypnotic eyes radiated a warmth that quieted Arianna's heart, even as his gaze brought fresh tears. "The evils you see are nothing you can fix. Do you understand what I am saying?"

"I believe I am beginning to," she sniffed.

"Getting humans to focus their attention almost exclusively upon whatever wrongs are unfolding is precisely what Lesser Light has gotten so right in this realm."

"But ... I mean, well –"

"Do you see, my lady, how dramas playing out big and small serve only to distract and derail humans from making deliberate choices? We can only affect things positively when we are feeling positive and in our power. And the only empowered place to stand and make a choice is right here and now."

"In the name of Oneness." She clamped her mouth with both hands, letting his soothing energies continue to balm her frazzled heart. She ran trembling fingers across well-manicured locks and, for what felt like the hundredth time in recent hours, she sighed. "What do you ask of me, Anahata? How can I truly serve Poseidia when I'm realizing I barely have a grasp of what's going on here?"

"Take up the One Truth's sword," he urged. "Join Elysia not merely as an aid, but as an accomplice in breaking this paradigm. So a return to a Highest Light paradise is possible."

"How?"

"This island is splitting apart. Have you seen what the unseen forces at work have already wrought?" He leaned closer. "Poseidia's bedrock is giving way. The palace itself is crumbling, and none of the scientists or engineers can explain why. They fear Gadeirus' seers may be to blame, and so while they spin excuses and point fingers, a window of opportunity exists. One Elysia has already seized. Yet she needs help."

"I hear you. And I will be Elysia's accomplice. Tell me what I must do."

"Accept a transmission from me. An energetic download, if you will, that will help hold your heart in the face of what is coming." He grinned, and her heart tingled. "The hell realms have opened here, my lady. The only way to navigate them wisely is with a steady heart."

"I see," she said dreamily. Avalon whinnied weakly, and Arianna found she couldn't tear her eyes from Anahata's. In fact, she felt blissfully at peace as she delighted in the glittery rainbows now emanating from his body.

"Do you accept my transmission?"

"Why yes, of course." She cocked her head and giggled. "You keep changing before my very eyes. Now you look quite like a mythical unicorn. With kaleidoscope eyes!"

"I know that you associate unicorns with kindness and purity." Anahata waved his palm across Arianna's face, and she slumped. "Me? Not so much." Rising from the hay, he invoked an incantation as he raised his arms and hovered above Arianna's motionless form. Then Avalon stumbled forward, nostrils flaring; he lost his footing and fell onto Anahata. The shape-shifter rolled to escape the wildly kicking gelding, but not before two hooves had bloodied his face and arms. Anahata shrieked, while Avalon scrambled to get up. Red light enveloped the horse, and Avalon roared in agony, bolting at a full tilting run as he slammed into the barn's double doors. The old wood groaned and split into jagged spears, leaving a stunned shape-shifter momentarily dazed while Avalon galloped into the mist. Anahata wiped his gushing nose with a dirt-caked sleeve and swore in the Old Tongue. "Well now. This is a most unexpected development."

THIRTY

Smoothing a perfect updo with one hand while the other felt for imagined flaws in the third silk dress she'd donned since dawn, Lorelei paused before the entrance to yet another palace conference room. She took a deep, centering breath before opening the door to yet another secretive meeting of unreadable intention and, she was certain, questionable purpose. She dared not speak aloud, nor let her true thoughts wander here in the belly of the psychic beast Poseidia had become. Long ago, she had trained her mind to communicate even to herself in code as a way to prevent anyone from picking up on what she was really thinking. And so, her self-talk – to the psychics who kept tabs on every aspect of her brain's cortical excitability – left them wondering how such gibberish occupied the Dark Heart queen's mind almost exclusively. There were always whispers about her playing any number of tricks, of course, yet it was well documented how ages before she'd publicly been stripped of all her meaningful psychic gifts; so, for the most part, many wondered privately if that severing had perhaps also left her quite mad. She knew from playing all sides against the middle that everyone who was anyone in Poseidian politics agreed she remained as useful as she was elusive. Regardless, she felt confident that no psychic seemed interested enough to try to crack the meaning behind the mysterious mindscreen images and words that flowed endlessly from her. A smug smile creased her cabernet lips as pictures of prancing unicorns trampled her imagination. She felt certain nobody would ever guess that was her way of telling herself she was amidst fools, who were once referred to as *murkhas* in the Old Tongue.

"My lady." She turned toward Desineus' familiar voice, letting a proverbial flock of unicorns stampede her. The sheer lunacy of it all brought a broad grin to her face as he bowed. "It is good to see you again."

"And you as well," she replied. In her mind's eye, unicorns were tripping all over one another in some crazed dance, and she nodded in his direction. "Shall we?"

"We shall." He opened the ornately carved door for her, and she slipped through with the effortless elegance inherent to all those with a Moldaarin snake lineage. Looking up from a high-backed chair at the head of the polished conference table, a silver-haired woman smiled in recognition. "My lady, it's always a pleasure. How are you?" Desineus kissed the delicate hand she extended.

"Wonderful, dear friend. Never better, in fact." She turned small, wide-set eyes upon Lorelei, and as always, the Dark Heart queen was struck by their icy blue clarity. "And how are you, Lorelei?"

"Oh, I'm living the dream, Maya," she quipped, as images of sheep jumping fences leaped across her mindscreen. Sheep always appeared as her conditioned response to annoyance, and they dominated every conversation with Maya. Since they first met eons ago, Lorelei and the Crystal Keeper had personified oil and water. Maya never addressed anyone using appropriate titles, and that always irritated Lorelei – even though she herself extended such courtesies only if her hand was forced. As a woman with harsh judgments about appearances, Lorelei felt largely superior to Maya in terms of attractiveness. She hated Maya's short silvery coiffe, with its lone skinny braid reaching ridiculously to her waist. But those snowflake eyes of hers were as extraordinary as ever. "Thank you for coming."

"Of course." Maya gestured toward the carved wooden chairs to either side of where she'd perched herself. "Please join me."

Desineus pulled one of the heavy seats out for Lorelei, and she flashed a coquettish smile at him that she could feel brought an inner eye roll to Maya's outwardly steady gaze. The Crystal Keeper busied herself with pouring a glass of lemon water from the table's chilled decanter, as Desineus slid into the chair opposite Lorelei. "Care for a cold beverage?"

"No, thank you." Lorelei sniffed as she surveyed the room. "I'd been hoping for hot tea."

"That could easily be arranged, my lady," Desineus offered. "I'd be happy to –"

"No worries," the Dark Heart queen said with a smile that brought another internal eye roll from Maya. "I'm fine for now. Shall we get down to the business at hand?"

"Indeed." Maya sipped from a crystal goblet, amusement and something akin to arrogance in her icicle eyes. "What exactly *is* the business at hand? I got a cryptic message earlier from Sammaseus. Something about Gadeirus wanting to know more about the various Fire Stone frequencies we're using among our crystalline towers. Most notably the Tuaoi Stone. Yet for all of my messages to him, Gadeirus has remained silent."

"The king has been busy with the engineers and scientists," Desineus explained. "And so, it falls to me to broach this subject with you both, since you each lead various factions that may be able to come together to help unravel a growing mystery." He reached for the decanter. Only the sound of ice tinkling in his goblet broke the room's heavy silence. "Have either of you become aware of Poseidia experiencing a deep splitting in her bedrock? After much investigation and analysis, the scientific experts have no explanation for the growing seismic activity they've detected beneath Mount Tartarus. Yet she is awakening. And whatever has stirred her to toss and turn is shaking our island to its core."

"Splitting? Shaking?" Maya's quartzlike eyes narrowed. "You're saying ... what exactly? Because what I'm hearing is that the scientists think this island is breaking apart. And that Gadeirus must be in agreement with them."

"His Majesty is not in agreement with any theories thus far. He is in fact-finding mode. And he is committed, as am I, to getting to the bottom of this disturbing development."

"I've noticed the palace is full of fissures," Lorelei muttered. She turned curious amber eyes on the chamber's crimson-veined black marble. "These walls and floors show the same stress fractures as the suite where I'm staying."

"Yes, my lady. Every room inside the palace is cracking."

"So, it feels like the scientists may be pointing fingers at the quartz coders," Maya fumed. "Is that fair to say?"

"And perhaps throwing the psychics to the wolves as well," Lorelei added.

"Ladies, please," Desineus held up his hands in a gesture meant to settle the room's rising tensions. "No one is saying –"

"No one has to say anything," Maya interrupted. "The coders are all psychic, you know. Lorelei and I may have our differences. But I think it's fair to say we trust the knowings and not the science. Would you agree, Lorelei?"

"Yes." Lorelei leaned forward in her seat. "What is the real question you wish to ask of us, Desineus? Do the scientists think we have made an error in our frequency calculations? That would be a grievous accusation."

"Agreed. Our camps do work together to monitor and adjust those frequencies," Maya sniffed. "Not just daily, I might add. But hourly."

"Indeed." Lorelei nodded at Maya before turning her glare on Desineus. "So, I shall ask once more. What is your real question?"

"Let me put it this way." Desineus sipped lemon water, his sandy locks shining like burnished gold in the chandelier's glow. "How would you look at this matter if you were the king? Or for that matter, a Poseidian resident? Surely, you can appreciate how this as-yet unexplained phenomenon is troubling. People are noticing the shifting and splitting streets and sidewalks and bridges and downtown buildings. Our administration is beginning to get questions from citizens who fear a cataclysm may be underway. And so far, we have no answers. But we need to find out why our biggest volcano is exhibiting unusual thermal movement that's fracturing this island. Only then can we fix it."

"Fix it?" Maya threw her head back and laughed, blowing silvery bangs about her forehead. "Come now, you can't be serious."

"Oh, but I am. Quite serious. The king and all of our administration –"

"Are fools." Fire leaped from her eyes' icy depths. "You don't know the half of what is really going on here."

"Then tell me, my lady." Desineus folded his hands across his heart. "Please. Because clearly, we are missing something."

"Lorelei, would you like to chime in here?" Maya turned to the stoic Moldaarin exile, whose compressed lips spoke volumes about her preference for remaining silent. "You know we are bound by intergalactic law to intervene when directly asked to do so."

"Interference is perilous," Lorelei warned.

"The Galactic Government's directive is clear –"

"And so is mine," Lorelei hissed. "Meddling is futile."

"If I may be so bold, my lady," Desineus pleaded with the Dark Heart queen. "It's not meddling when a sincere desire for assistance is put forth. I'm stating that desire fervently on behalf of Poseidia's ruling body. Please," he urged, bowing his head. "Help me understand. Help me see what we do not."

"And so, what if I do enlighten you?" Lorelei turned glowing amber eyes upon Desineus' sober countenance. "What if I open the hell realms right here and now and take you on a guided tour? What then? I know you're aware of some of the horrors hidden behind this island's pretty face." She cleared her throat and leaned toward him. "But Light damn it, you are blind to most of the Underworld's workings here. Of most of the star races' experiments. Of what free will and egoic desire and an endless thirst for more has wrought."

"Lorelei, I –" Maya began.

"Shut up," she snapped. As she rose from her seat, the chamber's air vibrated and the chandelier blinked. "Neither of you see how you blindly serve fools who think they are in charge here. But they are not. Nor have they ever been."

"I bow to *no one*!" Maya screeched, as Desineus shifted in his seat.

"You're always on your knees before the Time Lord. Take that in every way I meant it," Lorelei sneered, and Maya scrambled to her feet. The Crystal Keeper lit up like molten silver as she conjured glowing orbs in her palms. Desineus stepped between her and Lorelei, whose aura had flamed scarlet.

"Ladies, please," he urged, as three bold knocks hammered the door. The pounding seemed to shake the women to their senses. Desineus looked befuddled as their auras faded. They sighed in unison. His jaw dropped when Lorelei laughed.

"Lords with swords," she swore, her lunatic grin fading. "Might as well let her in."

"My lady –"

"She's right, Desineus," Maya muttered. "It would be best to open the door."

"All right." Deepening his breath, Desineus regained his composure and strode to the entranceway. He unlatched the chamber door, squinting at the golden being towering above him.

"Hello, Desineus," a lyrical female voice said. "May I come in?"

"Yes." He gestured for her to enter and stepped back. Desineus struggled to take in her glowing form, even as he wrestled with this most unexpected turn of events. Wondering what could possibly summon such an otherworldly being to their secret meeting filled him with equal parts curiosity and dread.

"Thank you." As she approached the polished table, her aura dimmed. She pulled the hood from a white and lapis silk tunic to reveal hip-length ginger ringlets. Turning wisteria eyes upon each somber face staring up at her, she glided into a chair beside Desineus.

"Hello, Vartayanah." Maya's voice cracked, and she cleared her throat. "It's been eons since you appeared on these shores."

"Yes."

"And so, what dire message are you here to share?" Maya's syrupy tone hinged on sarcasm. "Highest Light must feel the need to tell us something."

"Greetings to you all," Vartayanah replied in her soothing voice. "You know that words don't teach. A messenger won't be heard if the audience is not ready to hear."

"Are we not ready, my lady?" Desineus asked. "Or not worthy?"

"My dear Desineus." Vartayanah's smile revealed snowy teeth. "Energy and awareness alone govern this realm. The idea of worthiness – or its perceived lack – is pure fiction. Yet the powers that be here believe they are well-served by perpetuating this illusion ... this lie that Highest Light bestows blessings based upon merit."

"I grew up being trained in sacred studies," Desineus whispered. "The temple served as my second home. And it remains my sanctuary, yet –"

"Yet you doubt all you've been indoctrinated to believe," Vartayanah observed.

"Yes," he croaked. To his horror, as he gawked at Vartayanah, tears flooded his face. Violet and gold pulsed from her aura, and in her gentleness, he felt compelled to nestle and speak what he had sworn to secrecy. "My oath of fealty binds me to the king. I've made a promise to my childhood friend. To uphold his reign. To ensure his doctrines are carried out. And let the ages and not myself judge him."

"The ages judge no one. Nor does Highest Light."

"We really don't have time for these philosophical musings, Muse," Maya fumed. "Desineus, please. Take a moment and a deep breath, and gather yourself."

"I'm here with you now because there's less time than you know." Vartayanah's luminious gaze turned to Lorelei. "You've focused your energy and awareness exclusively upon Lesser Light. Although you understand how Lesser and Highest are forever dancing in duality on this plane of existence."

"Don't lecture me," Lorelei spat venomously as her eyes flared orange. "What could you possibly understand about me or my intentions or my understanding of energetic forces way beyond this puny realm?"

"The scales have tipped." Vartayanah's radiant calm never flickered. "Waves ripple and surge, as the dedicated scramble for sea legs. And while you lead an abuse of power, the likes of which are so egregious as to attract the Galactic Federation's attention."

"How *dare* you blame me for taking control of Poseidia's political meltdown!" Lorelei shrieked. "I'm cleaning up a Light-damned *mess* here! Can't you *see* that?"

"*Cura te ipsum*," Vartayanah murmured. "Creating a mess and then positioning yourself as the only one capable of cleaning it is an abuse of power the Universal Council of Light cannot allow."

"No one speaks to me like that and gets away with it!" Lorelei slapped the table and launched herself from her seat. She paced and flailed her arms about as Desineus and Maya gaped in horror. "I do *not* suffer fools or foolhardy star seeds or pompous ass-kissing councils lording some feigned superiority over me or my mission!"

"You *will* suffer me." Vartayanah's form flared gold and purple, and she arose to her full eight-foot stature. Instinctively, Desineus and Maya cowered in their chairs. "Hear this. All of you."

"*I will not!*" Lorelei raged on, her tantrum fueling flames in her eyes and palms.

"By the grace of Arcturus' Supreme Galactic Leaders and her Sacred Light Seer –"

"*NOOO!*" Lorelei rushed at the messenger, cherry-colored fireballs bursting from outstretched palms.

"*Aad guray nameh*," Vartayanah sang in her sweet voice, calling in Highest Light protection in the Old Tongue. Lightning bolts struck in a circle around the messenger, followed by a thunderous boom that knocked Lorelei to the ground. Maya and Desineus screamed and stumbled from their chairs. Desineus rushed to the Dark Heart queen's side, and Maya turned frosty eyes upon Vartayanah.

"Really? Was that *really* necessary?" She lunged forward, seizing a leather bag from beneath the table.

"Let the stones be, Crystal Keeper," Vartayanah commanded in a voice that left Maya backing away from the table. "Lorelei is unharmed. She is being subdued until I give you the warning the Supreme Galactic Leaders have dispatched me to deliver."

"What warning?" Desineus' cobalt eyes locked with Vartayanah's as he gained his feet beside Lorelei's motionless body.

"Ah, Desineus," she replied. "Remember that the most difficult times often teach us more about who we are and what we're capable of than privileged life in an island paradise ever could."

"My lady –"

"Upon my arrival, I told you how words don't teach. And they do not," she continued as Maya sank back into her chair. "It's one of the most humbling lessons every messenger must learn."

"And every Crystal Keeper," Maya sighed.

"Yes." Vartayanah's violet and gold aura rippled. "You know the Divine truth I am about to utter, Maya."

"I do," she whispered.

"Feel into me – into the whole of my energy system," Vartayanah replied. "Accept and allow the frequencies I offer to resonate within you to that deep knowing place words can't reach."

"Shall I do the same, my lady?" Desineus asked.

"Please."

"All right." Desineus glanced at Maya, and she nodded.

"By the grace of Arcturus' Supreme Galactic Leaders and her Sacred Light Seer, know that I appear before you to reveal Divine truth. A revelation of a coming catastrophe." She paused, letting the sacred sound of her voice sink in. "A cataclysmic unfolding that promises profound loss and upheaval across this island and extending far and wide across the planet. Betrayal at every level will precede the fall." Again, she waited, her psychedelic glow ebbing and flowing, before Maya and Desineus slowly nodded for her to continue. "If we were standing in your shoes, we would remember to think of ourselves as Divine expressions of Highest *and* Lesser, as each incarnated soul is. Made up of opposite yet interconnected energies within an indivisible whole. Like the sacred yin-yang symbol we have given you as a reminder of this dynamic, you are Highest and Lesser, forever interdependent and intertwined, for one energy cannot exist in your realm outside of relationship to the other. And so," she continued. "The task falls to you to use Lesser Light as a grounding rod for Highest Light to expand within your body and then throughout your physical world. To use your tiny seed of Lesser to anchor in a large swirl of Highest. By allowing your attention and awareness to thus serve as antennae for intergalactic good to flood the planet – and by influencing as many of your kind as you can to join in this endeavor – you serve as a beacon of hope that may yet divert the heartache that will otherwise come to pass."

"*Tathastu*," Desineus murmured in the Old Tongue after a long silence.

"Yes. So be it," Maya echoed, turning a softened gaze upon the messenger. "And so now what?"

"Ground yourselves. And then hold the line for Highest Light to flow through." As Maya was opening her mouth to ask another question, Vartayanah disappeared in a golden flash. For several moments, the Crystal Keeper and Desineus sat in stunned amazement. Then Lorelei mumbled something and stirred. Desineus saw that the Dark Heart queen needed some time to regroup, so he reached for Maya's hand. She squeezed hard as tears streaked both their faces.

"Now what, my lady?" he whispered. "What do you think we should do?"

"I don't know about you." She gave a short, sad laugh and swiped at her eyes. "But I don't get paid to think. I get paid for furthering Poseidia's apparently ill-fated agendas."

"Meaning?"

"Just a little advice, my friend," she cautioned. "There exist just as many Highest Light shysters as Lesser. So, I believe we keep on keeping on as we have been." She released his hand and patted his shoulder. "I want you to come with me to the coders' room, where we can take a look at the programming frequencies. And see if anything is amiss that you can report back to Gadeirus. Wouldn't that make you feel a little better after all of this drama?"

"Sure." He shrugged and smiled and started up a line of small talk that long years of political practice made as easy as breathing. Desineus was giving every outward sign of agreement. Yet inside he was thanking Source for the guidance he'd long been praying to receive.

THIRTY-ONE

Avalon raced along the horseshoe-shaped shoreline. Willowy grasses flattened as he thundered by. From a lone gnarled cypress in the dunes, Elysia's hawk friend shrieked in his wake. Rising from the sugary sand like attentive quartz soldiers, a round gypsum structure spiked with selenite points glowed red as the sun faded into the horizon. Night was fast approaching, and with it a growing urgency among Poseidia's silent sages. As the gelding's hooves pounded the pristine beach, one long accustomed to quelling crises emerged from the selenite structure's arched doorway. Andolphicus stood tall with outstretched arms, his waist-length white hair whipping the breeze, as Avalon neared. Soft hands that resembled a younger man's at last caressed Avalon's legs and forehead. The magician-priest's sable eyes missed nothing, never blinking as he observed the physical while communicating with the indomitable spirit before him.

"You're witnessing the Atlantean downfall, my friend," he murmured. "Come. We've much to do this night." Avalon nickered and followed Andolphicus into the crystalline sanctuary, which stretched 30 feet high and around. Inside, hay bales lined a far wall, where Dara stood munching. She whinnied at her friend, and they rubbed noses before Avalon's lips began sifting the dried timothy beside her.

As the horses ate, other hooves could be heard echoing in the distance. Andolphicus returned to the entrance to witness a luminous white hybrid horse galloping closer. In a flurry of graceful power, she sprayed sand and swished a snowy mane and tail threaded with auburn. The unicorn then bowed her head, touching Andolphicus' outstretched palms with her single spiraling horn.

"Hello, Eka," the wizard laughed, as the unicorn snorted and blowed upon his hands in affectionate greeting. "I knew you would come, as we have a Divine task at hand." He patted her silky face once more, gazing into loving amethyst eyes before retreating into the shelter. Eka stepped after him, nickering to the horses, and then she pranced toward them. Andolphicus watched the equine beings all touch noses, and not for the first time, he wondered why the Atlantean people seemed incapable of such loving harmony.

"It is what it is," he sighed, clasping a jade staff he'd leaned against the gypsum's curving interior. He prayed and moved to the structure's center. Sinking the staff into the sand, he sat cross-legged beside it and gazed into the clear quartz sphere nestled before him. Smoke whirled and filled the large globe, and as he breathed himself into Oneness, the crystal cleared, revealing Khrestes' red-tressed loveliness.

"Hello, Andolphicus," the gold-scaled mermaid said telepathically. A fiery ruby pulsed her third eye, as she smiled at him from beneath the sea. "What news have you from the surface?"

"I know not what your oracle eyes have seen, Khrestes," he replied in a mind-message coded for concealment. "But the playing and betraying continue. Arianna is the latest to fall under Shadow's spell."

"Yes." Her voice held a fine chime's resonant tone in his mind's ear. "I saw what happened. And I know Elysia's other friends and helpmates are similarly sleeping."

"They are," he nodded. "Many others who've long been grounding in Highest Light here have had their anchor lines – or their lives – severed."

"I know." She tuned fine lapis eyes to a psychic frequency. "Even our beloved dragons – once thought to be invincible – have felt Lesser Light's taint." With delicate porcelain fingers, she pointed to a gilt-scaled dragon to her left. "Ryujin still guards these waters. He lives here with us, his red and white coral castle shielding much sea life not lost to Lesser Light infiltration. Yet," she sighed. "His brother Longwang, the ancient Dragon King, was betrayed. Answering only to the Jade Emperor, Longwang's loyalty led him to eat pearls from his sovereign's own hand. Pearls poisoned by Lesser Light frequencies. And so, the same fate that befell the Ahlaielian Elders has overcome Longwang." She shook her head. "We had counted on our Dragon King, as supreme commander of storms and seas, to shield us from the Dark Heart. But here we are."

"Ah, these are turbulent times, Khrestes," Andolphicus replied. "Our numbers grow thin. The shadows lengthen. But our choice is clear, nonetheless. We will hold the line."

"Nothing dampens your spirits, my friend." A grin dimpled her heart-shaped face. "I appreciate you holding the line for me specifically by reflecting a Highest Light mirror. One that shines forth calm and centered surrendering upon all that is. And serves as a reminder that all is unfolding perfectly – in Divine timing – and not a moment sooner."

"Indeed, my dear," the wizard laughed. "Let me share the affirmation that guides me."

"Please."

"When it's not in Source's time, we cannot force it," he murmured. "When it is Source's time, we cannot stop it."

"Yes," she whispered. "In the name of Oneness, you speak the truth."

"We also cannot change this hand we've been dealt." His countenance bore a gentle certainty that comforted the merbeing to her core. "The energies that have shaped this chaotic card game are long gone."

"I see that."

"Luck with cards is just like fortune to be found anywhere in this realm," he added. "The next move is guided by now-moment alignment. And nothing more."

"*Yes.*"

"More than ever, we must keep feeling good in each moment. We must turn our attention toward anything that inspires love. Joy. Appreciation. Freedom. These feelings are sacred guidance. They are what we must keep choosing. They are how we find alignment."

"And they are how we save or shelter what falls within our spheres of influence," she replied.

"Absolutely." Andolphicus pressed his palms together across his heart. "We must accept that we can't be mad enough or sad enough or scared enough or sick enough or poor enough or hungry enough or miserable enough to empathize anyone out of suffering. Highest Light can't extend a helping hand low enough to reach Lesser depths of despair. Because you can't get there from here. You cannot receive a desired frequency if you are broadcasting an unwanted one. Just as you cannot hop on a sad vibration hovercraft and expect it to take you on a joy ride. You know this, as do I."

"I do, Wizard."

"And you also know one of our greatest blessings is our awareness. Our knowing of these truths the power brokers have long kept hidden from humans and hybrids alike."

"Controlled opposition is indeed everywhere," she nodded.

"Attempting to keep sacred knowings and Divine truth to themselves so they alone may rule from their ivory towers is the very pulsebeat of the Dark Heart elite." He gazed off at a memory that curved his lips. "Do you remember when a sphere and not a pyramid ruled as this realm's supreme sacred symbol?"

"Yes, of course." Her sweet smile turned sad. "From our Lemurian ancestors and comrades, who were this planet's first star seed explorers and Highest Light advocates. A race as incorruptible as ruby lavender."

"A race that lives on in fiery-haired family like yourself, sweet lady." His loving countenance radiated warmth. "They retreated so they could keep holding the line, you know."

"I do." In his mind's ear, her voice croaked with tears. "Although the abyss they left behind often feels like a black hole, blocking me from their loving frequencies that I dare hope still surround us."

"That abyss is just a Lesser Light illusion, Khrestes. Nothing more." He straightened his spine and studied her grieving face. "I will remind you that the void is where all possibilities dwell. Where they wait for us to align with them."

"Of course, you are correct." She covered her tearful face with porcelain hands.

"Highest Light living is very simple, but not always easy, dear one."

"I can't help but think about the masses, Andolphicus," she sighed. "For all of my awareness and tools and practiced vibration holding and disciplined focus, I'm at a loss at this juncture. What about them?"

"What about them, my lady?"

"How can I possibly ignore their suffering, when their cries grow louder by the hour?"

"Have any of them heard your offers to aid and assist?"

"Well –"

"They have not, Khrestes. Because they cannot." He shook his head. "Offering a loving frequency to someone dialed in to despair is like you pouring water into the sieve they carry. Pour all you like. Pour until you yourself are drained, and then all you've accomplished is joining them in their emptiness."

"Yes, but –"

"Jump in the hole with them, and then you're all in the hole – and you can't lead them out when you're stuck within like they are."

"You say nothing I don't know, Wizard. And, yet this lesson is the hardest for me. This acknowledging of how Highest and Lesser frequencies are split from one another – and how they seem mutually exclusive."

"Yet that's the tricky part, is it not?" Andolphicus' merry laughter slowed the merbeing's runaway heartbeat. "The truth is that even defining Highest and Lesser as such represent our stepping away from Oneness, from Source, into duality – which is necessary to having a life on this earthly plane in the first place." He paused, watching her mirrored pupils pulse as she digested his message. "Entering duality, as you know, is the only way we can manifest from Source into these physical bodies and experience all the blessings they offer."

"I do understand what you're saying. Just as I know we're all unique mixtures of Highest and Lesser, of good intentions and evil deeds. Of joy and fear and love and hate and everything in between."

"Yes, we are!" he chortled. "So, it's helpful to remember how Highest and Lesser are never mutually exclusive. They are, in fact, forever interconnected. We can't even define them except in relation to each other. How can one even see shadow except in light?"

"Indeed," she replied. "This reminder is most welcome, Andolphicus."

"But of course." He bowed his head before gazing once more into her large lapis eyes. "Which brings us to the mission at hand."

"I'm all ears, Wizard."

"As we both know, our numbers here in the earthly realm have dwindled."

"Yes."

"So, we must move away from trying to push boulders up mountains to effect positive changes. We must work smarter, not harder."

"Go on."

"All those with awareness must anchor Oneness more deeply and securely. More deeply and securely than we've yet been able to do here."

"*How?*"

"Let me first say this – we do that *not* by retreating into isolating and polarizing camps of Highest to judge Lesser. We must remember always that we cannot feel love and judgment simultaneously. And love is key to our mission." He leaned closer to the crystal ball. "We do it instead by following the wisdom inherent in sacred symbols the ancients left for us long ago."

"Do you mean the Circle of Emotion? Which is depicted in Elysia's and Alaric's wedding rings?"

"Yes. That's half of our task."

"And the other half?"

"We must ground and center ourselves, which is the most efficient way to channel energy," he explained. "And the best visual reminder of that step is the yin-yang symbol."

"I am familiar with the yin-yang concept." Her ginger locks swirled about as she nodded. "A circle split into equal but opposite swooshes, each of which has a small circular eye."

"Yes," he affirmed. "One swoosh represents Highest, the other Lesser. Each with a small round eye that opens metaphorically to the other, showing how a little bit of Lesser exists in mostly Highest Light. And equally, a little bit of Highest is present in mostly Lesser Light."

"I do understand what you're saying, except how it relates to us grounding and centering our energies."

"Highest Light is so ethereal, so high of a vibration, that it cannot be anchored in this 3D world," he replied. "But we can use Lesser Light as a grounding rod. That is its Divine purpose. Lesser's highest calling, if you will." Again, he laughed. "We who consider ourselves Highest Light workers must always remember this truth. And be careful of thinking we are somehow superior to Lesser energies. That's why we can't snuff out or subdue or remove Lesser from ourselves and hope to be more virtuous or noble – or effective, for that matter. We need Lesser to be able to access and fully use our Highest Light natures. Because if we aren't grounded, our efforts escape into the ethers. And that does little to help this realm."

"Oh, Andolphicus," she murmured in his mind's ear after long moments of reflection. "I must have been ready to receive this message. Because I feel I was really able to hear you." She beamed at him through the crystal ball. "That was the clearest explanation I've yet been able to comprehend about how – and why – Lesser Light is essential to our work here."

"My dear, you were just needing a little support, as we navigate these turbulent times." He shifted his crossed legs in the cool sand. "So, the rest of our task, if you will – after centering and grounding ourselves – is to heed the Circle of Emotion's guidance. And remember that any sense of separation or isolation or disconnection or despair is just an illusion. We must instead keep remembering how each of us is simply meant to feel good here. We must keep reaching for any feel-good feelings, and by doing so, we are automatically offering ourselves as Highest Light grounding rods."

"You make it sound so simple," she mused.

"Simple? Yes. But as I said earlier, it's not always easy. Not when it's so tempting to give attention to current events and circumstances everyone is screaming about not wanting. And as we know about this attraction-based universe, all those things we shout 'no' at come flying at us every bit as fast as our desires that have us yelling 'yes.'"

"Indeed, they do." She tinkled musical laughter. "Truly, I must focus, and stop fueling Poseidia's doom-and-gloom dramas. Which I've been doing by paying attention to them."

"You do so much more good in this world than you realize." He gestured to the masses of merfolk, dolphins, dragons, and various ocean life forms surrounding her. "You lead legions of Light Bringers. So many sea friends are helping to hold the line."

"Thank you, Wizard." A small, satisfied smile split her lips. "Water beings have long understood our Divine mission. For millennia, we've been doing our very best to help this planet from below the waterline."

"And you *have*." He chortled a deep resonant sound that chimed the selenite walls. "There's no better example than our sea friends, who embrace the ancient teachings and keep uplifting this realm vibrationally. And who understand it's only by doing our work here below the radar, so to speak, that we can be of any real help at all."

"Indeed," she replied. "And as you've so lovingly reminded me just now, we must remember that those with eyes to see, ears to hear, and hearts to feel, *will* receive the message. And heed the call."

"Look about you, Oracle," Andolphicus said, as Dara, Avalon, and Eka came to his side. "So many have been heeding the call. And that kind of pure positive focus is what will see us through."

"Absolutely."

"I have a favor to ask, Khrestes."

"Anything."

"New sound frequencies are needed to support our efforts in Poseidia."

"We've been weaving healing tones to keep Elysia and her friends alive, but –"

"But I can see in your eyes that you already know what I am about to say."

"Yes," she whispered. "They're no longer helping."

"The sound waves cannot reach the Underworld, which is where Elysia's friends are trapped. And as for our Moldaarin queen –"

"Ah, I know," she sighed. "She's with child. A joyous unfolding under normal circumstances. Yet with her severed essence, she's leaking life force even more rapidly, as the baby grows within."

"Would you be able adjust the frequencies to support her as she moves in Shadow?"

"Yes. Earlier, we made adjustments to support her friends. But we realize our vibrations are no longer in range. Still, we intuit and we sing. And thus continue our songs for her and the baby."

"Things are rapidly shifting, Khrestes. And we need to keep a positive outlook while also moving with the flow."

"I agree."

"Frequencies to balance misplaced ambitions are in order."

"Agreed," she whispered.

"This night, may we hold a sacred ceremony, in support of Elysia as well as all of Poseidia. May we merge the voices of earth and ocean. May we ground Highest through Lesser. May we simply be pure positive energy. And may we know – from breath to bones – how that's enough."

"And so it is!" She raised her arms above her head, a glorious grin lighting her face.

"And so it is." Andolphicus mirrored her movements before bowing his head. With closed eyes, he breathed into *advaita*, as she began to sing. Bell-like vibrations rang from her lips. The magician-priest allowed himself to sway, while he and his equine companions – along with every sea being encircling Khrestes – added their voices to hers. Harmonious waves rippled forth, hypnotizing all in their wake. Moments stretched to minutes and beyond. Before long, their collective awareness only perceived the singing. And within that sacred symphony, time stopped. Space opened and poured over and through itself. Alternate realities and potentials dipped and rose and flowed with each measure's melody. A mind-bending meditation ensued that stretched Andolphicus' soul from where it was tethered to his body all the way up to the Highest Light realms. In his mind's eye, he could see how his essence was serving as a guide. Thousands of souls long trapped in Lesser Light after transitioning in fear in Poseidia's dark tunnels had been released. Source warned the wizard to offer only the love vibration. As he breathed Oneness, he observed most flowed past him like fish in a fast-moving current. They neither saw nor heard him, offering proof he did not need that doing the work sacredly, secretly, silently does not draw Lesser Light attention.

Some that were curious or confused did linger. Andolphicus understood they could see a representation of his physical body and were unaware he was serving as a soul streamer. He knew they were looking to him to explain what was happening. He only conveyed in answering their questions that he loved them. And he witnessed how, in the moment when each soul was face to face with love, a choice was made. Either ascend with it to a Highest Light reality. Or drop into the hell realms. A few burst from the stream, disappearing in dazzling light. Most chose to continue along their downward-spiraling path. Highest Light cautioned him not to judge their choices, lest he himself fall out of love's shielding cloak and expose their plan. And so, deeper and deeper he dropped. Beneath his breath and beyond all consciousness. So securely was he anchored in Lesser – so fully was he surrendered in Highest – that he opened into pure positivity. As his beacon illuminated a final choice point for those departing, he came to one last knowing. He saw his own soul release. And as he dropped the body, he understood he could help Poseidia more powerfully now in spirit than would ever have been possible in the flesh.

THIRTY-TWO

Alaric awoke, blinking gold-green eyes at the chakra lights hovering overhead. Their luminescence streamed across his body in fluid patterns, yielding as he surrendered to their healing frequencies. In the pre-dawn stillness, he sank deeper into soft sheets and observed the display. Yesterday, he'd been keenly aware the light waves kept returning to his heart. Yet as he lay watching, he realized a new rhythm had emerged. The focus had shifted from his heart to the chakra just above it. The high heart – as he knew all too well – manifests Divine purpose. He'd long understood a balanced high heart blends throat with heart energies to fuel how a being creates its own reality. Alaric also realized that this chakra, nestled between the heart's passion and the throat's expressiveness, had only thawed and opened within himself as a result of the tea ceremony.

Whispering appreciative prayers, Alaric dropped into No-Mind, letting go of any preconceived notions he'd been holding about what he must do. In *advaita*, he could feel his high heart merging vocal clarity with unconditional love. This melding voiced with absolute certainty how he'd relentlessly picked at the wound of Moldaaris' destruction and kept it bleeding over his perceptions, staining them all. From love to life in general to duty to desires, every aspect of his existence for eons had been tainted. And these perceptions had even colored his notion of a happily ever after with Elysia. He breathed deeply, allowing Divine truth to continue mending the cuts he'd at best kept poorly bandaged. In his mind's eye, he saw pink skin surrounding the scabs – the promise of healing underway – thanks to the art of tea. The sheer simplicity of what his high heart was now revealing as his Highest Light path moving forward brought a surprised laugh.

"In the name of Oneness," he whispered and sat up. "For all of these centuries of striving. Of pushing boulders up mountains. Of running while shackled. To think I've had it all wrong." Alaric smiled and shook his head, the gold in his sable locks glistening beneath the chakra lights. "Life is supposed to be easy, not arduous. Flowing, not forceful. Fun and not fretful. And so, when I think about the intensity and duration of my existence paddling upstream – in fact, my adamant insistence upon it – I'm beyond words." A chuckle that held more growl than gaiety escaped his lips. He swore in the Old Tongue and slipped from the sheets. "Ah, to recommit myself to a life lacking resistance. To allow it all to fall away except what lights me up. And so it is."

Alaric showered, letting lather and steam continue his releasing. In his mind's ear, alongside the soothing waterfall sounds, he heard *tabula rasa*. The words meant "clean slate" in the Old Tongue. And though he felt he'd forever be triggered by the word "clean" in relation to himself, he was astonished to find that now, in this new way of perceiving everything, he was actually welcoming *tabula rasa* into his experience. "What miracle is afoot here?" he asked, turning his gaze to the heavenly realms. A genuine lightheartedness he hadn't known in forever flooded his senses. Unexpected giggles echoed off the stone walls in a pleasing way that begged him to sing. "*Dhanayavad ananda*," he began, an ancient Old Tongue ode to grateful bliss. Water dripped from his tipped-back head as he belted lyrics to the ceiling. Minutes of musical joy left him exhilarated when he stepped from the cascading water and donned a plush robe. Perusing the garment selection hanging by the bed, he traded the robe for an aquamarine tunic and gold belt before igniting the nightstand's heating element. As the kettle water warmed, Alaric hummed to himself while mixing dandelion, rose, and lotus petals within a strainer. Once he'd poured and steeped and sipped the tea, he settled himself into a lotus position to pray.

A soft knock soon roused him from quietude – and brought a grin. In one graceful movement, he gained his feet and glided to the entrance. Opening the door to Jon's serene face, he clutched him close.

"Good morning, Father," Jon murmured. "I trust you rested well."

"It's the deepest sleep I've had in a thousand years." He kissed Jon's ivory cheek and then held his son away from him. "Would you like tea?"

"Please."

"I'll heat more water." He refilled the kettle and prepared a tray of herbal offerings, as Jon dropped cross-legged onto the floor. When the water steamed, he placed a trivet on the tray and nestled the kettle on top. Setting the fragrant bounty before Jon, he beamed into his son's beryl blue eyes and lowered himself once more into a lotus position. "I'm so grateful for this moment. So happy to spend time together."

"As am I." His curved lips lit up the room. "Peace becomes you."

"Does it now?" They laughed, a sound that lifted Alaric to an even higher level of appreciation. "Do you remember me this way? It's been ages."

"I've only ever seen you this way." Jon's cherub face radiated love as tears misted his father's eyes. "I only see your essence. And it is *sa-*

madhi."

"Yes. I've been reminded."

"A reminder you were ready to receive."

"*Yes.*"

"And a Divine receiving that blesses our mission."

"Agreed. It's time for us all to remember we are one, Alpha to Omega, through our joined hearts." He twisted the carved ruby and emerald wedding ring around his finger, feeling its symbolic wisdom fueling his words. "Oneness is who and what we are. And it is the way forward."

"Indeed."

"In the short time I've been here, I've awakened to Divine truth." He faltered, and Jon sat stone still, a committed listener. "I came to Rohati for a reason. A purpose. I was so clear, so sure of my agenda, but – I have a deeper awareness now around my own motivations." Several moments passed in silence. "It wasn't about Oneness. It was about saving her." Alaric swallowed hard, his gold-green eyes ablaze. "For a thousand years, I've done anything – and I mean *anything* – to keep her safe. To ensure her happiness. Though until now, I've never been able to see just how much that choice has cost not only me. But our Highest Light mission."

"I understand what you're saying – and why you would feel that way."

"Yet do you see the full ironic absurdity of my position?"

"Father, I –"

"The ancients teach how we're unable to see past any choice we're unwilling to make. And I've never been willing to choose my own well-being – or the Divine's, for that matter – over hers." Alaric shook his head. "Yet that choice has not only kept me in chains for centuries, in this attraction-based universe. It's also compromised all I can offer in our endeavors to restore Source to its rightful place – as sole ruler of cosmic forces."

"Nothing has been compromised from a Highest Light perspective." Jon clasped Alaric's hand. "Everything is unfolding perfectly, in Divine timing. We're on track, I assure you."

"Intellectually speaking, I understand and agree," Alaric sighed. "Yet personally speaking – if I'm honest – I've yet to overcome my devout doubt."

"You have me and all of Rohati to help you remember to look the other way. Toward Alpha and Omega. Toward Oneness – and peace," Jon whispered.

"Feeling peaceful is the only way to have lasting harmony. And not eternal anguish, since like attracts like. Although," Alaric croaked, his voice breaking. "I feel I must affirm to you that I love her still, with all that I am. Yet to feel tranquility – and fulfill my duty to this realm – I must find a way not to think about her. Because I can't yet feel anything but despair and loss when I hold her in my thoughts."

"I know." Jon moved to his father's side and cradled him even after Alaric's sobs subsided.

"May I ask a favor?" Alaric rasped raw vulnerability against Jon's shoulder.

"Of course. Anything."

"I don't know how to do this, really. This ... turning my attention from Elysia."

"I hear you, Father. And I understand."

"I need you to keep this for me. Just for a little while." He pulled back far enough to slide off his wedding band before cupping it into Jon's hands. "Please."

"It will be my honor."

"Thank you." Alaric hugged his son and sighed once more. "I love you so much."

"And I love you," he whispered.

"I feel lighter now."

"A great weight has lifted."

"Yes. Rohati holds a vibration that facilitates relief," Alaric observed.

"She does."

"I've never cried so much, Jon."

"And I've never witnessed a transformation so beautiful." He touched his palms together in front of his chest. Alaric straightened his spine, mirroring the prayerful hand position, and then they breathed themselves into No-Mind. Minutes passed in meditative bliss, until a bluebird landed on the windowsill near the bed. Its testy *tu-a-wee* split the silence and brought soft chuckles.

"I needed that," Alaric offered at last, as the bluebird flapped away. "An auspicious omen! Bluebirds bring good news."

"Birds are always bearing Highest Light messages. We just need to be open to receive them."

"We do." He patted Jon's knee. "And now, we need tea."

"Yes!" Jon tipped warmed water into a porcelain vessel and added jasmine and rose petals. For several moments, he sat staring at the brewing alchemical elixir, as Alaric sipped his steeped beverage. "Prayer in a cup."

"*Tathastu*," Alaric said in the Old Tongue. He smiled into Jon's calm countenance. "Let it be done," he translated.

"There is much for us to see as already done." Jon met his father's unblinking eyes while sampling the decoction. "Tyrius is preparing his ship to return home. Where he will recruit as many as possible to join us in holding the love vibration."

"Good."

"Lochana has called for an ongoing celebration. Day and night, downtown Heera will sing and dance and give thanks – even as word spreads across the planet for all Rohatians to join in. As a people, as one, holding the love vibration."

"Holding the line."

"Yes."

"One who is aligned in Highest Light is many times more powerful than millions who are not." Alaric refilled his cup, watching the tea steep anew. "There is hope."

"Where there's love, there's always hope." Jon smiled and sipped, and once more reached for his father's hand. "And there's great love here to be shared. So, I'm not just hopeful. I'm certain. The love vibration will win."

"Nothing ever dampens your enthusiasm. Or shakes your faith." Alaric squeezed Jon's fingers, then arose in one elegant motion, still clasping his cup. "A new day is dawning. And though I'm late to this party, I'm most excited to revel in Heera's revelry."

"You're just fashionably late," Jon quipped.

"Deciding on the gold or silver belt trips me up every time."

"And I thought it was the coiffe." Together, they chuckled once more, as Jon stood. "Shall we go for breakfast? One needs proper nourishment before dancing. Or so you've always taught me."

"Indeed. Not to mention, it will be an honor to see Tyrius before he departs. That is, if we can persuade him to share a meal."

"Somehow, I think that can be arranged."

"Somehow, I think you're right." As Alaric reached for the lever, a rapid knocking trembled the entryway – a heavy sound that dragged his heart down. Glancing at Jon's suddenly serious expression, he opened the door to Reena's worried eyes.

"Gentlemen, good morning," she said without smiling. "I do apologize for my unannounced visit."

"Not at all, Reena." Alaric bowed his head in respect. "Please come in."

"Thank you. Yet I'm afraid there's no time for that." Tears threatened to spill from her long lashes, and Alaric placed a steadying hand upon her shoulder.

"What is it?" His gold-green eyes searched her face.

"I'm here on behalf of Lochana. She's requested your presence at a High Council meeting."

"All right," Alaric replied. "When?"

"I'm – oh dear – I'm just so sorry, Alaric," she stammered. "I'm sure you and Jon haven't made your way to breakfast yet, but ... it's urgent."

"We will come at once."

"Thank you." She turned toward Jon. "I know this is unexpected, since you were with Lochana earlier. But –"

"I understand, Reena. A dove yet guards the gateway, though the sacred hall has been breached." He glanced at his father. "You must enter alone. Highest Light splits us now not to divide, but to rise up." Alaric nodded, locking forearms with Jon before embracing him.

"Wait, Jon –" Reena began, but she quieted as father and son exchanged Old Tongue whispers. Before she could collect her thoughts, Jon slipped through the doorway, disappearing into ruby lavender shadows. "In the name of Oneness, Alaric! What just –"

"It's all unfolding in Divine perfection," he interrupted in his silky, soothing tone. "Please take me to see the High Council. And to greet Poseidia's high priest."

"But how did you –"

"*Samadhi* bears no secrets. In Oneness, all is revealed. And we must abide the revelation."

"Alaric, please! You're speaking cryptically, just as Lochana has been. Ever since the scribe and his delegation arrived unannounced."

"Walk with me." Offering his arm, Alaric pivoted with a dancer's grace and led Reena toward the stairs. "And I will explain how the end of Atlantis has just begun."

THIRTY-THREE

In timeless shadows that could just as easily belong to midnight as morning, Elysia sat shivering against a linden tree. Its hollowed height teemed with honey, a much-needed nourishment the hive's queen had readily offered her fellow royal. And while Elysia's spirit soared with appreciation for the honeybee and in fact all her animal companions on this island, her trembling legs weren't ready to rise.

"Get up," she whispered. "Get up, El, please. Just get up." Shaking her head to clear fatigue's thick fog and breathing through vertigo, she imagined deep roots anchoring her feet to the earth. Once she felt more stable, she pressed her back into the trunk, using hands newly bloodied from the continually opening balcony wounds to guide an awkward ascent. At last, she managed to straighten her legs, but the attempt drained her. "And you call yourself a queen?" She wasn't sure if she was smiling or snarling, though it felt like both, as she pushed herself away from the furrowed gray bark. She twisted and hugged the tree's roughness with quaking arms, gazing up into star-shaped petals dangling above. Their moonbeam color delighted her. Yet pregnancy had altered her senses such that the blossoms' sweet lime and honeysuckle perfume brought up bitter bile, her stomach's only contents. "Lords with swords!" she swore under her breath moments later, swiping a sleeve across her mouth, as she heard a horse's low nicker. Half stumbling, she whirled to see Gadeirus leading a black horse and eyeing her carefully. With deft fingers, he tied the horse's reins to a tree before kneeling beside her.

"I apologize, my lady. I know you're unwell, yet I must be certain," he whispered in her ear. "Have you scrambled the airwaves so we may speak and not be heard by the legions of psychics supposedly serving me?"

"Yes," she croaked.

"Then please sit down."

"Oh, no. Not after the effort it took to gain my feet." She grimaced into his oddly sober face. "I'm fine."

"Do you think I don't know what 'fine' really means in this realm?"

He chuckled, a sound that was tender and comforting. "Do you think I don't know you're with child?"

"*What*?! How –"

"Do you think, my dear Elysia, there's anything I wouldn't know about you?" With a seriousness she found equally startling and reassuring, he brushed tangled hair from her eyes. "I realize I'm not your beloved. But that makes me no less doting or devoted, given an opportunity. Especially the one at hand."

"I don't know what to say –"

"It's simple. Say 'yes,'" he whispered. "Let me minister to you. I've some skill with the healing arts."

"What skill? In my condition, I can't –"

"No wafers. No elixirs. No mind-altering substances of any kind." He reached for her hands. "The ancients used touch, in terms of sending signals along the body's electrical grid. That's what I'd like to offer you."

"Do you mean *shiatsu*?"

"Yes."

"But how would you know finger pressure points?" Her emerald eyes pierced his, and he caught his breath, thinking how despite her dishevelment, she'd never looked more lovely. "I've had such therapy before. Here, actually, in Poseidia. Ages ago. And from what I recall, it's a precise art."

"Precisely," he quipped. "And as such, it's an art best taught by those who are the absolute best. Who practice with the most precision."

"I don't follow –"

"Ah, you see, my wickedness serves me well. In many ways," he began. "My vile nature brought before me the island's best *shiatsu* practitioners. And the best are blind. Did you know that?"

"Really?"

"Yes."

"Okay, and your point is – what exactly?"

"Without the eyes, one must feel for the points," he replied. "Please. Sit down. Let me show you."

"But how do you know such things?" Her voice remained wary, yet she sank to the forest floor beside him. "And what does such knowledge have to do with wickedness?"

"Apprentices study for years to learn nuances and point combinations not readily known in even the best training academies." He clasped her wrist with care, being mindful of her abrasions, and began pressing spots that made her flinch. Yet in seconds, relief flooded her, and she found the nausea had disappeared. "I've been tutored by the island's best therapists."

"So how is that wicked?"

"Because I made it my business to find the most gifted. And charm them into my service. At various, shall we say, houses of ill-repute."

"Oh," she sighed. "That is wicked."

"That's not even the bad part."

"No?"

"No, my lady."

"What's worse than making them your whores?"

"Blinding them so they have no choice but to serve." Elysia dropped her eyes to his hands, his fingers that were so expertly kneading her forearm, before meeting his raven's gaze once more. "I allowed the labs to continue experiments initially sanctioned by my predecessor. Experiments to prove a theory that taking away one of the senses only sharpens the others. Which makes the subject even more useful. Not just for pleasure purposes, but for military ones."

"You can't be serious."

"Oh, but I am."

"Why are you telling me this?"

"Because even though I'll burn in hell, the truth is you bring out the best of whatever is left of my soul. I always feel compelled to tell you the truth." His quiet cackling sounded like crying to her ears. "The absolute, you-bet-yer-sweet-Betsy truth. Or, as the Civic Security Committee has made me swear before them on multiple occasions. The whole truth. And nothing but the truth."

"You speak of truth as facts, Gadeirus," she observed after a long silence. "My definition of truth is integrity."

"But what's integrity if not congruency? And alignment with what feels right." He chortled again, although what she heard was more like sobbing. "I'm completely congruent. I feel something so right doing the wrong things."

"Yet do you see how you're doing the *right* thing? The *Highest Light* right thing? Perhaps at the expense of the crown. Or even your life itself."

"If the crown or my life be forfeit, then so be it." As if cradling a baby bird back onto its nest, he settled her arm by her side before grasping her other hand. "Once, I cared too much about what everyone thought of me and my actions. Now, I don't give a Light damn what anyone thinks. Except," he sighed. "I do still care for Arianna's opinion. And yours."

"Mine?

"Yes, yours."

"Why would you care what I think?"

"Because I –" he paused, closing his eyes as he continued to work on her arm. "Because I love you. Even if I cannot have you, it matters not. I love you just the same."

"You barely know me," she whispered. "Perhaps it's an image you love. An idea. A painted fantasy."

"You make a most extraordinary painted fantasy, my lady. No doubt about it. But," he said, pressing tapered fingertips into her shoulder. "The way you are right now. Messy hair. Makeup free. Bantering with me in clothing that looks like you just crawled from Poseidia's bowels." Again, he laughed. "Oh, wait. You *did* just crawl from Poseidia's bowels. But no matter. You're more amazing this way than in your courting at court perfection."

"For all your wickedness, you can be kind." She smiled, and she noticed the hard lines of his face had softened. "Thank you. Not just for your kindness. But your courage. I'm most grateful for your aid."

"Make no mistake, Elysia. I'm a scoundrel through and through." He sighed a deep and slow exhale. "Yet I swear upon whatever is left of my soul, and all of my swarthy heart. I will have your back. In any fox hole or hell realm that presents itself. You have my word."

"I believe you." She studied his greenish pallor, the skunk stripe that seemed to widen by the hour. And an overwhelming compassion filled her. "There is honor in you. A king's honor."

"I'm afraid that ship sailed long ago."

"No, that's not true." She twisted so she could see his sad countenance and held his hands within her own. "The ancients have always said, 'Adversity makes strange bedfellows.' Yet when it came right down to it – even when you dragged me to your bed – you didn't violate me in that deepest way that you so easily could have."

"How *could* I?" Tears flowed from his black-circled eyes. "You're an angel, Elysia. I've told you before, and I mean it. And for all of my devilry, I respect you. In a way I haven't ever respected a woman."

"Your words prove my point," she murmured. "Respect and loyalty are key to a king's honor. Truly, you carry a regal presence within. And it's important you realize I see and feel and know that dignity so clearly."

"What's important right now is that you get some nourishment." He squeezed and released her hands and gained his feet. "I brought some snacks to tide you and the little one over until I can get you a proper meal." He took a small pouch from the horse's saddlebags and crouched beside her. She noticed his ebony attire matched a horse the color of midnight, as he offered her a velvet bag. "I stole these treats from the stable's kitchen. So much for honor."

"To hell with honor. I'm starving!" They snickered like schoolchildren, and Elysia's heart swelled with appreciation for Highest Light's help that once again had come from the unlikeliest place. His *shiatsu* offering had brought not only relief from her nausea and body aches; for the first time in such a long time, she felt warm head to toe. As her tingly fingers split a berry tart to share with him, she heard her logical mind screaming at her to be careful, to abstain from eating anything that came from Lesser Light's table. But her gut, her intuitive voice, the still, small whisper within, spoke from the depths of her being – and urged her to eat.

"There's bread and nuts and some sliced ginger root, too," he said between bites. "For whenever the nausea may rear its ugly head again."

"You know a lot about a woman in my condition," she said, finishing the tart's last bite. Groping the bag, she pulled out a freshly baked bread slice and offered him half.

"I like to think I've learned a lot about women over the years. Difficult women most of all, since they seem to be my specialty." Softly, he laughed. "Pregnant women are perhaps the most difficult of all."

"So –"

"We need to get a move on," he interrupted, closing the pouch and arising once more. "I apologize, my lady. But we need to be out of the woods and among those I still believe will offer allegiance to the crown. Just as soon as we possibly can."

"All right," she answered, even as she yearned to ask about his experiences with women – and why they'd proven so challenging. She wondered to herself if perhaps he'd fathered a child out of wedlock. But before she could think any more about it, he was hoisting her to her feet.

"Easy does it," he whispered, his arm firmly wrapped about her waist. "Lean on me."

"Okay."

"That's it." As he was helping her toward the horse, suddenly the mare's head flew up in rapt attention. Elysia first felt and then heard hooves fast approaching. In one graceful movement, Gadeirus swept her into his arms and stepped behind the tree. "Hush!" he hissed into her ear. "That could be anyone."

"Not just anyone," she replied, her eyes wide as she scanned the trees' deep darkness. "I'd know that gait anywhere!"

"What do you mean –" he began, as Avalon trotted from the shadows to stand before them.

"Avalon!" She was mindful to keep her voice down, yet in her elation, she wriggled free of Gadeirus and ran to the gelding.

"You *know* this crazy horse?" Gadeirus stood shaking his head, while she hugged and petted Avalon.

"Yes! Oh my, yes. He's a trusted friend."

"Trusted?"

"Absolutely." She giggled, while the gelding affectionately snorted and blew upon her hands. "Do you know Avalon?"

"Everybody who rides on this island knows Avalon." Tears stung her eyes as she remembered how Kevonious had said something so similar during her last magical evening with Alaric – an evening that now seemed forever ago. Avalon placed his forehead against hers and nickered softly. "My lady, local lore says that this horse is as mad as I am. And that he cannot be ridden."

"Local lore couldn't be further from the truth."

"Be that as it may, we don't have time to debate it."

"No need. Let's ride the wind."

"Let me help you onto Stevarasa."

"Her name is ... Stevarasa?" Elysia gawked at the king. "Is that a joke? In the Old Tongue, Stevarasa means –"

"Stolen essence," Gadeirus replied. "Yes, I know. I bought her and named her. On the day I ordered your essence to be split and ... stolen."

"Of course you did." She laughed in spite of herself. "I suppose we could debate that as well, when we have a moment. But time grows short."

"Indeed."

"We'll follow you."

"We?"

"I'll ride Avalon."

"You'll *what*?"

"You heard me." In her mind, she'd barely asked Avalon to kneel before he'd lowered himself to the ground. She climbed onto his marble gray back, smiling down at a gaping Gadeirus as Avalon arose.

"What in the bloody hell –"

"Are you coming?"

"Light damn it, woman." He swung a leg over the mare in one lithe movement.

"Where are we headed?"

"You know where," he muttered. "You're well-versed in island lore. And any royal realizes it's the Borderlands and not the board rooms where deals really go down."

"Yes." Elysia straightened her spine. "Poseidia's Borderlands are her extremities. Your old stomping grounds. The Pillars of Hercules."

"Most assuredly." He patted Stevarasa's neck. "Are you ready to storm the gates of hell?"

"Whatever it takes," she replied, and the horses galloped as one into obsidian darkness.

Highest Light Series Character Index – alphabetized and by A2 Chapter

(AW=specific to *Atlantis Writhing*, Book One; A2=specific to *Atlantis Splitting*, Book Two)

Abhasa (Abb-HOSS-uh=A2): Heera's lead source reflector and High Council member.

Abigor (ABB-uh-gore=A2): the hell realms' grand duke and best-known psychic who is infatuated with Lorelei and oversees Poseidia's seers.

Alaric (AL-uh-rick): snake-human hybrid and former Moldaarin king; he ruled with his dolphin-hybrid queen Elysia until Moldaaris' destruction 1,000 years before the story unfolds in 11,000 BCE.

Anahata (Ann-uh-HOT-uh=A2): shape-shifting star messenger who overtakes Kevonious' body and then Arianna's.

Andolphicus (Ann-DOLL-fick-us): wizard and high priest who married Alaric and Elysia in AW.

Arianna (Air-ee-AH-nuh): King Gadeirus' sister and Elysia's friend/ally.

Atlas (AT-lus=A2): King Gadeirus' brother.

Ava (AY-vuh): Ahlaielian missionary featured in AW and partnered to fellow Silver Ray Will; she possesses extraordinary communication and diplomatic skills.

Avalon (AV-uh-lawn): Elysia's horse friend with a difficult reputation and feisty attitude, yet he is loyal and obedient to her.

Basileia (Bass-uh-LAY-uh=A2): King Gadeirus' red-haired middle sister who committed suicide as a teen by drinking hemlock and honey.

Beeja (BEE-juh=A2): Reena's younger sister and another one of Lochana's assistants.

Berdaches (Burr-DAH-cheese=A2): divine healers on the Alpha Centauri planet Rohati.

Carinnia (Kuh-RINN-ee-uh): Linasia's daughter; Alaric was forced to marry and sleep with Carinnia in a bargain to save Elysia from reincarnating into Atlantis 1,000 years before AW takes place.

Charlaeus – (Shar-LAY-us): Poseidian politician and Alaric's former lover who becomes Elysia's friend/ally.

Chela (CHAY-luh=A2): Heeran High Council member.

Cleito (CLEE-toe=A2): King Gadeirus' mother with addiction issues.

Daayan (Die-YANN=A2): most powerful netherworld/hell realms witch found "beyond", a soul-exchange area past the tunnels.

Dara (DAH-ruh aka "Sanadara"): Avalon's companion horse from Dehk's barn and Alaric's favorite mount. Charlaeus rides her in A2.

Dehk (DEEK): Poseidian stable owner, underground political power-house, and longtime Alaric friend; he mysteriously disappeared at the end of AW.

Desineus (Duh-SINN-ee-us): King Gadeirus' chief aide and close friend.

Eka (EE-kuh=A2): a unicorn.

Elysia (Uh-LEE-see-uh): dolphin-human hybrid and former Moldaarin queen; after dying when Moldaaris was destroyed, she was reborn as a Purple Ray Highest Light missionary on Ahlaiele.

Evestus (Ev-ESS-tus=A2): a morgue security guard Elysia mesmerizes into helping them go "beyond" to a supernatural, soul-exchanging realm.

Gadeirus (Guh-DARE-us): Poseidia's current king with addiction issues and an obsessive love for Elysia; son of Poseidon and Cleito.

Gwenesia (gwenn-EE-zee-uh): King Gadeirus' sister.

Helionel (Huh-LIE-uh-nell): deceased former Poseidian king who pro-posed to Lorelei and was rejected; he had been infatuated with Elysia, and jealousy led him to mastermind a plan 1,000 years ago to prostitute Alaric as the price for saving Elysia's soul after she died when Moldaaris exploded (a plan also hatched by Helionel).

Hunter (standard pronunciation): Ahlaielian missionary and Elysia's Purple Ray partner who possesses extraordinary healing abilities.

Ixchel (EE-shell=A2): Alaric's old mentor from the Pleiadian planet Jan-gala; she helps him heal from a Cerberus bite.

Jack (standard pronunciation=A2): messenger for hire that King Gadei-rus sends to look after Elysia.

Jonastus (Jo-NASS-tus aka "Jon"): Alaric and Elysia's adopted son with a special gift for maintaining spiritual alignment.

Kenaseus (Ken-A-zee-us): featured as a Poseidian Diplomatic Relations Committee member with Jon.

Kevonious (Kev-O-nee-us aka "Kev"): Dehk's right-hand stable manager.

Khrestes (CREST-eez aka "The Ocean's Oracle"): underwater oracle and leader of merbeings and all sea life.

Leucippe (Loo-SEPP-ee aka "Leuci" with standard "Lucy" pronunci-ation=A2): King Gadeirus' youngest sister, who ran off with Lusatia's King Lech.

Linasia (Linn-AY-see-uh): Great Central Sun gatekeeper who controls soul access to the afterlife realms; she is infatuated with Alaric and works backdoor deals with all of Poseidia's power players. In AW, it was re-vealed she agreed to rebirth Elysia on Ahlaeile in exchange for Alaric marrying her daughter Carrinnia while also bedding him herself.

Lochana (Low-KHAHN-uh=A2): Heera's queen and Jon's love interest.

Longwang (LONG-wong=A2): ancient dragon king and Ryujin's brother who was poisoned by eating Lesser Light-tainted pearls.

Lorelei (LORE-uh-lie aka "The Dark Heart Queen"=A2): Moldaarin snake-human hybrid exile whose jealousy over Elysia winning Alaric's heart caused her to misuse her powers, so her gifts were surgically severed, leading her to develop Dark Heart energetic manipulation techniques.

Maya (MY-uh=A2): Crystal Keeper in charge of seers and Tuaoi Stone crystalline frequency programming.

Nayaka (Nye-AH-kuh=A2): lead Berdache healer.

Nearly Dead (standard pronunciation aka Gray Ones, Shadow Spawn=A2): Low-vibration ghouls found "beyond" Poseidia's tunnels.

Nehabkau (NEH-habb-cow=A2): Moldaarin serpent healer and Elysia's longtime friend/ally.

Poseidon (Po-SIDE-un=A2): sea god and King Gadeirus' father.

Reena – (REE-nuh=A2): Lochana's chief assistant.

Ryujin (Rye-YOO-jinn=A2): a golden dragon and Longwang's brother.

Sammaseus (Sam-MAZE-ee-us=A2): Civic Security Council chairman and King Gadeirus' cabinet member.

Selenius (Sell-ENN-ee-us=A2): false name Elysia uses in underground labs and tunnels.

Shanta (SHAN-tuh=A2): Moldaarin teacher who caught Lorelei channeling to hurt Elysia and recommended Lorelei be transferred to an Atlantean school after psychic surgery muted her dangerous shape-shifting gifts.

Sneha (SNAY-uh=A2): Rohatian High Priestess and tea ceremony facilitator.

Stevarasa (Stevv-uh-ROSS-uh=A2): King Gadeirus' black horse named in the Old Tongue for "stolen essence".

Vartayanah (varr-tie-YAH-nah = A2): Highest Light messenger sent to deliver Supreme Galactic Leaders' warning over Lorelei's abuse of power and a coming catastrophe.

"Old Tongue" Dictionary

Aad guray nameh (ahd goo-RAY nah-MAY) – I bow to Divine wisdom; provides Highest Light protection

Adhyapaka (add-ee-uh-PAHK-uh) – sacred wisdom teacher

Advaita (uhd-VAY-tuh) – non-duality or state of No-Mind

Agatah (ah-GAH-tuh) – come

Aham prema (AH-hahm PRAY-muh) - I am Divine love

Anahata – (ann-uh-HAH-tuh) – high heart

Atisakhi (at-ah-SAH-kee) – sage

Ativa sadhu (at-EE-vuh SAHD-yoo) – very good

Audentes fortuna iuvat (ow-DENT-ez for-TOO-nuh you-WATT) – fortune favors the bold

Capala (kuh-PAUL-uh=found in AW) – whore

Cura te ipsum (CORE-uh TAY IPP-sum) – heal oneself before turning attention to others

Devanagari (duh-van-uh-GAHR-ee) – mentor of all that is Divine

Dhanayavad (DAN-ah-yah-vahd) – gratitude; thank you

Dhanayavad ananda (DAN-ah-yah-vahd Ah-NAHN-duh) – grateful bliss

Durga (DUR-guh) – unattainable

Jijivisha (gee-gee-VEESH-ah) – passionate desire to live

Kavi (KAAH-vee=found in AW) – seer of the sun, direct perceiver of truth, and name of Elysia's dolphin friend who reunites her with the Ocean's Oracle

Khandayati (kahn-die-YAH-tee) – bite down

Kritajna hum, karuna hum, ananda hum (kree-TAHJ-nah WHOM, kuh-ROO-nah WHOM, ah-NAHN-duh WHOM) – I am gratitude, I am compassion, I am bliss

Lokah samastah sukhino bhavantu (low-KAH sah-moss-TAH soo-kee-NO buh-vahn-TOO) - may all beings everywhere be happy and free

Maneesh (muh-NEESH) – one who has mastered one's mind

Mira asirvada (MEER-uh as-your-VAH-duh) – my blessings

Mitra (MEE-truh) – trusted friend

Murkhas (murr-CAUSE) – fools

Namaste (NAH-must-ay) – greetings; I see the Divine in you

Namna (NAHM-nuh) – lie down

Om (OHM) - love, eternity, purity, grace

Om tare tuttare ture soha (OHM TAH-ree too-TAH-ree TURR-ay SAH-hah) – liberation from fear and suffering; letting go of what no longer serves

Priya (PREE-yah) – beloved

Rishi (ruh-SHEE=found in AW) – one who speaks Highest Light truth

Saanjh (SAHNJ) – evening or latter part of the day

Samadhi (suh-MAH-dee): the highest achievable mental union possible with the Divine while embodied

Sanadara (Sah-nah-DAH-rah=found in AW) – magnificent

Sevaka (SAY-vuh-kuh) – feces

Stevarasa (stay-vah-RAH-sah) – stolen essence

Suswagatam (SO-ah-gett) – welcome

Tabula rasa (TAB-you-lah RAH-zuh) – clean slate

Tathastu (tah-TAHS-too) – so be it

Tryasti (tree-AH-stee) – healer

Wu wei (WOO-way=found in AW) – the act of non-action, of flowing naturally with what is

Highest Light Series Key Concepts

(AW=specific to *Atlantis Writhing*, Book One; A2=specific to *Atlantis Splitting*, Book Two)

Advaita (uhd-VAY-tuh): non-duality or state of No-Mind.

Ahlaiele (uh-LAY-ull): Great Central Sun region planet and home to Kendrick, Quenna, Ava, Will, and Hunter.

Amur (uh-MOOR=A2): Atlantean boomerang-shaped fighter spaceships that tail Tyrius and Jon as they leave Zactronymus.

Borderlands (A2): Atlantean lands far from Poseidia known as the Pillars of Hercules, where Gadeirus reigned prior to becoming Poseidia's king. Lesser Light strongholds here keep vice and corruption flourishing.

Cave of the *Nilakantha* (nill-uh-CAN-thuh): Poseidian healing mushroom temple; its colorful strains include *blue entolomas* for fostering truth and *rainbow amanita muscaria* for anchoring the love vibration.

Cerberus (SER-ber-us=A2): three-headed hell realms hybrid watchdogs.

Circle of Emotion: a symbol made of a circle with a gap along its perimeter; it serves as a reminder to look away from life's perceived lack and toward love.

Color Rays (AW): Each Ahlaielian is from a ray with unique gifts. For example, golds channel money and abundance, silvers are ambassadors and warriors, and purples are psychics and healers.

Cosmic Controllers (A2): Lesser Light "reality architects" that deceive and manipulate to perpetuate misery and suffering.

Dark Heart (A2): unique Lesser Light energy manipulation technique Lorelei developed after her shape-shifting abilities were surgically muted; she is also known as the Dark Heart queen.

Gui (GWAY): Lesser Light collective consciousness that feeds off fear and the attention given to it, creating misery across the universe.

Heera (HEAR-uh=A2): the planet Rohati's capital city.

Highest Light: Divine Source or heavenly realms associated only with high-vibration emotional states, such as love, joy, and peace.

Jangala (jann-GAH-lah=A2): Pleiadian planet where Alaric goes to ask former mentor Ixchel to help heal a deadly Cerberus bite.

Lesser Light: evil or hell realms associated only with low-vibration emotional states, such as fear and anger.

Lower Dantian (LO-wur DON-tee-ahn=A2): "field of elixir" in Asian philosophy and the body's seat of life force, situated below the navel.

Moldaaris (mold-AH-rus): legendary Highest Light planet last ruled by Alaric and Elysia until Atlantis destroyed it.

Moldavite (MOLD-uh-vite=A2): a magical and transformative dark green Moldaarin bedrock stone that Atlantis reprogrammed for Lesser Light purposes after destroying Moldaaris.

No-Mind: meditative state that allows access to non-duality's magic and healing capabilities and Highest Light frequencies, such as love and joy; also known as *advaita* in the Old Tongue.

Orichalcum (orr-uh-COWL-kum=A2): Atlantis' most conductive metal, used to construct key components of the Tuaoi Stone.

Poseidia: Atlantis' capital city.

Rohati (A2): Highest Light-observing planet in Alpha Centauri's star system, within the constellation Centaurus.

Ruby lavender (A2): Atlantean lab-created crystal that proved to be incorruptible and unable to be programmed to carry out any Lesser Light plans; ultimately, it was gifted to Rohati for infrastructure repairs, and pillars of it were also created for Heera's royal palace.

Tuaoi Stone (too-WAY stone): Atlantis' chief power, communication, and healing crystal that Lesser Light forces have hijacked and corrupted.

Tunnels (A2): Excavated from obsidian bedrock, the "tunnels" refer to an underground location and are also a nickname for Poseidia's under-city experimental laboratory network.

Zacktronymus (Zack-TRON-uh-mus): cherry-mooned planet where Alaric reigned during his arranged marriage to Carinnia.

Jean Brannon was only eleven when her cautious and careful mother died, but Jean's loving dad stepped up in ways he never dreamed in order to raise two daughters on his own. Jean learned from her father that being willing to try new things – and being willing to laugh if it all went sideways – was a lot more fun than moving safely toward death. The "give it a whirl" attitude she developed toward life led her from a West Virginia country home to a New York corporate career, where mastering Belt Parkway lane changes taught her she really could do anything. That spirit of adventure, along with a love of ancient ways, has inspired her to study acupuncture, rehab old homes, and collect vintage typewriters. She's writing the first draft of the Highest Light Series' final novel on her grandmother's 1930 Smith Corona. Visit her at jeanbrannon.com.

On behalf of Absolute Love
Publishing, we hope you enjoyed

We'd love to see your online review
anywhere books are sold!

Please continue reading to browse additional
Absolute Love Publishing books. And, as always,
visit us at absolutelovepublishing.com, where
you can find free goodies, website exclusives, and
more info on all of our books and products.

Absolute Love Publishing is an independent book publisher devoted
to creating and publishing books that promote goodness in the world.

Metaphysical Fiction

Atlantis Writhing
by Jean Brannon

Bronze winner of the COVR Visionary Awards
A civilization trembling toward collapse—
and the unbreakable love that may bring
Atlantis back from the brink.

Atlantis is writhing. Chaos and greed have granted an obsessive new monarch
enough power to destroy the world—and beyond. The only thing standing
between King Gadeirus and intergalactic annihilation is Elysia and her fellow
Light Ray missionaries. As time grows short, the missionaries work to overcome the evil Lesser Light forces. When all options have been stripped away,
a symbol long lost to antiquity surfaces just in time to inspire them to con-
coct one last desperate scheme. Forbidden longings must be dealt with, too.
Cravings Elysia must confront in the presence of hypnotic Alaric, a visiting
dignitary with a scandalous past. But behind his seductive ways is a shocking
secret—an unexpected key that may help Elysia unlock her potent power and
wield it in the fight for the Highest Light.

Dead End Date
by Caroline A. Shearer

Dead End Date is the first book in a metaphysical series about a woman's crusade to teach
the world about love, one mystery and personal
hang-up at a time.

In a Bridget Jones meets New Age-style, *Dead End Date* introduces readers
to Faith, a young woman whose dating disasters and personal angst have separated her from the reason she's on Earth. When she receives the shocking
news that she is a lightworker and has one year to fulfill her life purpose, Faith
embarks on her mission with zeal, tackling problems big and small—including
the death of her blind date. Working with angels and psychic abilities and even
the murder victim himself, Faith dives headfirst into a personal journey that
will transform all those around her and, eventually, all those around the world.

Raise Your Vibration Min-e-book™ Series
by Caroline A. Shearer

Raise Your Vibration: Tips and Tools for a High-Frequency Life
Presenting mind-opening concepts and tips, *Raise Your Vibration* opens the doorway to your highest and greatest good! This min-e-book™ demonstrates how every thought and every action affect our level of attraction, enabling us to attain what we truly want in life. As beings of energy that give off and respond to vibration, it's important we understand the clarity, fullness, and happiness that come from living at a higher frequency. Divided into categories of mind, body, and spirit/soul, readers will learn practical steps they immediately can put into practice to resonate at a higher vibration and to further evolve their souls. A must-read primer for a higher existence! Are you ready for a high-frequency life?

Raise Your Financial Vibration: Tips and Tools to Embrace Your Infinite Spiritual Abundance
Are you ready to release the mind dramas that hold you back from your infinite spiritual abundance? Are you ready for a high-frequency financial life? Allow, embrace, and enjoy your infinite spiritual abundance and financial wealth today! Absolute Love Publishing Creator Caroline A. Shearer explores simple steps and shifts in mindset that will help you receive the abundance you desire in *Raise Your Financial Vibration*. Learn how to release blocks to financial abundance, create thought patterns that will help you achieve a more desirable financial reality, and fully step into an abundant lifestyle by discovering the art of being abundant.

Raise Your Verbal Vibration: Create the Life You Want with Law of Attraction Language
Are the words you speak bringing you closer to the life you want? Or are your word choices inadvertently creating more difficulties? Discover words and phrases that are part of the Language of Light in Caroline A. Shearer's latest in the Raise Your Vibration min-e-book™ series: *Raise Your Verbal Vibration.* Learn what common phrases and words may be holding you back, and utilize a list of high-vibration words that you can begin to incorporate into your vocabulary. Increase your verbal vibration today with this compelling addition to the Raise Your Vibration series!

ALOVEDLIFE

Consciously create a life you love with ALOVEDLIFE.

This bookazine by Absolute Love Publishing features stories on Intentional Living, Elevated Action, Conscious Connection, and Sacred Self Care. And because it's timeless (meaning, you can read each volume at any time,) jump in or catch up any way you'd like! Collect them all to read again and again. Find all available editions and formats at www.absolutelovepublishing.com/shop.

Mom Humor

Mom Life: Perfection Pending
by Meredith Ethington

Out-parented at PTA? Out-liked on social media? Wondering how your best friend from high school's kids are always color-coordinated, angelic, and beaming from every photo, while your kids look more like feral monkeys?

It's okay. Imperfection is the new perfection! Join Meredith Ethington, "one of the funniest parents on Facebook," according to Today.com, as she relates encouraging stories of real-mom life in her debut parenting humor book, *Mom Life: Perfection Pending*.

Whether you're buried in piles of laundry, packing your 50th sack lunch for the week, or almost making it out the door in time for school, you'll laugh along with stories of what real-mom life is like—and realize that sometimes simply making it through the day is good enough. An uplifting yet real look at all that is expected of moms in the 21st century, *Mom Life* is so relatable you'll find yourself saying, "I guess I'm doing okay after all."

───────── How-to ─────────

Preparing to Fly: Financial Freedom from Domestic Abuse
by Sarah Hackley

Are financial worries keeping you stuck in an abusive or unhealthy relationship? Do you want to break free but don't know how to make it work financially? Take charge with *Preparing to Fly*, a personal finance book for women who want to escape the relationships that are holding them back.

Drawing on personal experiences and nearly a decade of financial expertise, Sarah Hackley walks readers step-by-step through empowering plans and tools: Learn how much money it will take to leave and how much you'll need to live on your own. Change the way you think about money to promote your independence. Bring control of your life back to where it belongs—with you. Break free and live in your own power, with *Preparing to Fly*.

Self-Help & Min-e-books™

Have Your Cake and Be Happy, Too:
A Joyful Approach to Weight Loss
by Michelle Hastie

Have you tried every weight loss trick and diet out there only to still feel stuck with unwanted body fat? Are you ready to live joyfully and fully, in a body that stores only the amount of fat it needs? Then this book is for you. In *Have Your Cake and Eat It, Too: A Joyful Approach to Weight Loss*, author Michelle Hastie uses her own research into nutrition and the psychology of weight loss to help you uncover the mindset you need to transition from fat storing to fat burning, without overly fancy or external tactics.

The Weight Loss Shift: Be More,
Weigh Less
by Michelle Hastie

The Weight Loss Shift: Be More, Weigh Less by Michelle Hastie helps those searching for their ideal bodies shift into a higher way of being, inviting the lasting weight they want—along with the life of their dreams! Skip the diets and the gimmicks, *The Weight Loss Shift* is a permanent weight loss solution. Based on science, psychology, and spirituality, Hastie helps readers discover their ideal way of being through detailed instructions and exercises, and then helps readers transform to living a life free from worry about weight—forever!

The Chakra Secret: What Your Body Is
Telling You
by Michelle Hastie

Do you believe there may be more to the body than meets the eye? Have you wondered why you run into the same physical issues over and over again? Maybe you are dealing with dis-eases or ailments and are ready to treat more than just the symptoms. Or perhaps you've simply wondered why you gain weight in your midsection while your friend gains weight in her hips? Get ready to understand how powerful energy centers in your body communicate messages from beyond the physical in *The Chakra Secret*.

Finding Happiness with Migraines: a Do It Yourself Guide
by Sarah Hackley

Do you have monthly, weekly, or even daily migraines? Do you feel lonely or isolated, or like you are constantly worrying about the next impending migraine attack? Is the weight of living with migraine disease dampening your enjoyment of the "now"? Experience the happiness you crave with *Finding Happiness with Migraines*. Discover how you can take charge of your body, your mind, your emotions, and your health by practicing simple, achievable steps that create a daily life filled with more joy, appreciation, and confidence.

Pants Down: How the Trousers-to Toes Chakras Can Keep You Turned on, Tuned in, And Toned up
by Jean Brannon

Licensed acupuncturist Jean Brannon explores the fascinating connection between little-known lower body chakras and our self-limiting beliefs in *Pants Down*. In this min-e-book™, dive deeper than the well-known seven chakras to discover how these powerful energy centers can help you live in a turned on, tuned in, and toned up kind of way. Using ancient tools from Buddhism and Hinduism, as well as modern brain science, Brannon shares the tips and tools she has developed during more than 20 years of clinical practice to help you break through these constricted beliefs and live a more expansive life.

Where Is the Gift? Discovering the Blessing in Every Situation
by Caroline A. Shearer

Inside every challenge is a beautiful blessing waiting for us to unwrap it. All it takes is our choice to learn the lesson of the challenge! Are you in a situation that is challenging you? Are you struggling with finding the perfect blessing the universe is holding for you? This min-e-book™ will help you unwrap your blessings with more ease and grace, trust in the perfect manifestation of your life's challenges, and move through life with the smooth path your higher self intended. Make the choice: unwrap your gift today!

Anthologies & Guides

Love Like God: Embracing Unconditional Love

In this groundbreaking compilation, well-known individuals from across the globe share stories of how they learned to release the conditions that block absolute love.

Along with the insights of bestselling author Caroline A. Shearer, readers will be reminded of their natural state of love and will begin to envision a world without fear or judgement or pain. Along with Shearer's reflections and affirmations, experts, musicians, authors, professional athletes, and others shed light on the universal experiences of journeying the path of unconditional love.

Love Like God Companion Book

You've read the love-expanding essays from the luminaries of *Love Like God*. Now, take your love steps further with the *Love Like God Companion Book*. The Companion provides a positive, actionable pathway into a state of absolute love, enabling readers to further open their hearts at a pace that matches their experiences. This book features an expanded introduction, the Thoughts and Affirmations from *Love Like God*, plus all new "Love in Action Steps."

Women Will Save the World

Leading women across the nation celebrate the feminine nature through stories of collaboration, creativity, intuition, nurturing, strength, trailblazing, and wisdom in *Women Will Save the World*.

Inspired by a quote from the Dalai Lama, bestselling author and Absolute Love Publishing Founder Caroline A. Shearer brings these inherent feminine qualities to the forefront, inviting a discussion of the impact women have on humanity and initiating the question: Will women save the world?

Animal Prints on My Soul
by Candace Gish

Animals can be our heroes, our confidantes, our coaches, and our best examples of unconditional love. In *Animal Prints on My Soul*, we explore the human-animal bond through the experiences and stories of women. Featuring horses, dogs, cats, birds, and more, animal lovers will connect with these ordinary – yet extraordinary – stories of how animals impact our lives.

Our Mothers, Our Daughters
by Candace Gish

The mother-daughter relationship defines who we are, how we view ourselves, and what we want for our lives. Much like this multi-faceted relationship, the lessons in *Our Mothers, Our Daughters* are strong, yet soft. Through a collection of curated stories, readers journey alongside moms and daughters as they share poignant moments and messages of an everlasting bond.

Podcast Journal
by Candace Gish

Never forget your favorite podcasts again! These journal pages for podcast listeners will help you keep track of your favorite episodes, hosts, and topics. Most importantly, *Podcast Journal* will help you remember the important takeaways for your own life. With an easy-to-follow format, you'll bring the best of the podcast world into your own in no time!

Middle Grade and Young Adult Books

Different
by Janet McLaughlin

An Amelia Island Book Festival selection

Twelve-year-old Izzy wants to be like everyone else, but she has a secret. She isn't weird or angry, like some of the kids at school think. Izzy has Tourette syndrome.

The Soul Sight Mysteries by Janet McLaughlin

Haunted Echo
Sun, fun, toes in the sand, and daydreams about her boyfriend back home. That's what teen psychic Zoey Christopher expects for her spring break on an exotic island. But from the moment she steps foot onto her best friend Becca's property, Zoey realizes the island has other plans.

Fireworks
Dreams aren't real. Psychic teen Zoey Christopher knows the difference between dreams and visions better than anyone, but ever since she and her best friend returned from spring vacation, Zoey's dreams have been warning her that Becca is in danger. But a dream isn't a vision—right?

The Adima Chronicles by Steve Schatz

Adima Rising
For millennia, the evil Kroledutz have fed on the essence of humans and clashed in secret with the Adima, the light weavers of the universe. Now, with the balance of power shifting toward darkness, time is running out.

Adima Returning
The Sacred Cliff is crumbling and with it the Adima way of life. Weakened by the absence of their beloved friend James, Rory, Tima, and Billy must battle time and unseen forces to unite the greatest powers of all dimensions.

Serafina Loves Science! by Cara Bartek

Cosmic Conundrum
Sixth grader Serafina Sterling finds herself accepted into the Ivy League of space adventures for commercial astronauts, where she'll study with Jeronimo Musgrave, a famous and flamboyant scientist who brought jet-engine mini-vans to the suburbs.

Quantum Quagmire
Serafina suspects something is wrong when her best friend, Tori Copper, loses interest in their most cherished hobbies: bug hunting and pizza nights. When she learns Tori's parents are getting a divorce and that Tori's mom is moving away, Serafina vows to discover a scientific solution to a very personal problem so that Tori can be happy again.